SOUTH LANARKSHIRE
Leisure & Culture
www.library.southlanarkshire.gov.uk

South Lanarkshire Libraries

This book is to be returned on or before the last date stamped below or may be renewed by telephone or online.

Delivering services for South Lanarkshire

09. 12. 14.

2 9 DEC 2017

1 0 MAY 2019

0 7 JUN 2019

1 8 SEP 2013

23. 12. 14.

06. 01. 16.

2 3 SEP 2019

~CL

1 2 NOV 2013

2 NOV 2019

CL - BL

28. 01. 16.

0 4 JAN 2020

08. 10. 14.

22. 11. 14.

- 2 NOV 2016

2 2 NOV 2016

- 2 JUL 2021

0 2 DEC 2022

G

2 8 FEB 2017

05 APR 2023
1a CLYDEVIEW
SHOPPING CENTRE
BLANTYRE
G72 0QD
01698 823808

FLYNN, KATIE
A CHRISTMAS TO
REMEMBER

£12.99

2 3 FEB 2023

1 3 JAN

Katie Flynn

A Christmas to Remember

CENTURY

Published by Century 2013

2 4 6 8 10 9 7 5 3 1

First published in Great Britain in 2013 by
Century
The Random House Group Limited
20 Vauxhall Bridge Road, London, SW1V 2SA

www.rbooks.co.uk

Addresses for companies within The Random House Group Limited can be found at:
www.randomhouse.co.uk/offices.htm

The Random House Group Limited Reg. No. 954009

A CIP catalogue record for this book
is available from the British Library

ISBN 9781780890463

The Random House Group Limited supports The Forest Stewardship Council® (FSC®),
the leading international forest certification organisation. Our books carrying the FSC®
label are printed on FSC®-certified paper. FSC® is the only forest certification scheme
supported by the leading environmental organisations, including Greenpeace. Our
paper procurement policy can be found at www.randomhouse.co.uk/environment

Typeset in Palatino by Palimpsest Book Production Limited,
Falkirk, Stirlingshire

Printed and bound in Great Britain by
CPI Group (UK) Ltd, Croydon, CR0 4YY

For Graham and Deb – not before time!

Letter to the reader

Dear Reader,

Ideas! People often ask me where my ideas for a story come from, which is not always easy to answer. They come from various sources, but when I'm asked I can usually reel off two or three. *The Girl from Seaforth Sands* came as a result of driving down a road in Seaforth and seeing a young girl emerging from a doorway like a bullet from a gun and rushing away up the road. I had recently interviewed a lady aged 104 about her life, and it was when she told me that her father was a shrimp fisherman and expected his children to prepare his catch for potting that I remembered how she had also said that she left the house at a run whenever she heard his shrimp-laden hand-cart come rumbling up the street.

Well, that was the start of one story, and of course there have been many others. The idea for *The Liverpool Rose* came after visiting the Boat Museum in Ellesmere Port. It's a fascinating place and touring the canal boats was a first for me. Then my friend Eileen and her husband Jim took Brian and me for a day out in their narrow boat and I couldn't wait to put it all into a book.

But when I started *A Christmas to Remember*, it was because of a parrot. I was interviewing people for *A Village with a View*, which is a non-fiction book all about Everton, and I went to the home of a charming couple who owned an extremely intelligent parrot. Whilst I listened to his owners telling me about life in wartime Liverpool, the parrot stood on his perch, fixing me with a bright, compelling eye, and very slowly lifted his right wing as high as it would go. Then, making sure I was still watching, he lifted his right leg, also as high as it would go, and fell sideways off his perch, uttering a shriek of amusement as he did so. He repeated the trick over and over and by the time his owner shut him up by throwing a cloth over his cage I was completely sold on the idea of putting him in a book. He should have been in *A Christmas to Remember*, but somehow he didn't fit. I was waiting for him to appear in the story and do his party trick, but he never did; instead Crippen, the pig, took centre stage, so the intelligent parrot will have to stay in my memory, awaiting his chance for stardom.

Hope you enjoy Crippen the pig, and *A Christmas to Remember*, of course.

All best wishes,
Katie Flynn

Chapter One

It was almost five o'clock on a dreary December day. Occasional snowflakes floated down and the puddles were rimmed with ice. Albert Payne stood behind the counter of his tobacconist shop and surveyed the almost empty shelves with a jaundiced eye, for his stock-in-trade was still hard to come by. He had sold all his cheap cigarettes earlier in the day, and although the sign over his window read *Albert Payne, Purveyor of Fine Tobaccos* he had had few customers for his more expensive products. The trouble was that money was short and what cash was available, he knew, would be spent on food for the festivities and toys for the children. Yet he could not help envying the hurrying crowds he could see through his window, with their shopping baskets bulging and their faces wreathed in anticipatory smiles. He thought, without bitterness, that they would be looking forward to a family Christmas, the first since the end of the war, which had been over for four months.

The holiday was fast approaching, however, and Albert would spend it alone. Furthermore, the shop four doors down from his own had been empty for weeks, and when it first came on the market he had promised himself that he would enquire about rent, rates and so on. He had planned to turn it into a nice little café, or a tea room, because even before the war it had saddened him that his customers were almost always male, save for the odd woman coming shyly into the shop to buy a present for her husband, and he longed for some pleasant female company. If he had opened a tea room he had intended his daughter Janine to be manageress. But he, who had been so active during the hostilities, had left it too late; Janine, ungrateful girl, had spurned his offer of a little business of her own – albeit one her father had every intention of visiting regularly – and had gone off to the States, chasing after some Yank who had promised marriage.

Albert wondered whether he would do any good by remaining open, since only two people had come in all afternoon and neither of them had actually bought anything. He could change the *Open* sign to *Sorry, we're closed*, lock the door and go up to his flat, a cold and cheerless place since he had not yet put a match to the fire, nor turned on the gas beneath the kettle. But if he did this it would seem as though he were giving up, admitting that no last-minute customer would come hopefully in to buy the polished meerschaum pipe, or even better the beautiful leather tobacco pouch which any smoker of good sense must long to possess.

Albert sighed and told himself that when he closed at six o'clock he would go round to the landlord of the empty shop and find out what rent was being asked. Then he remembered that Mrs Clarke, who was married to his occasional assistant, and came in a couple of times a week to clean the flat and do some cooking, had made a batch of scones the previous day. Albert licked his lips; Mrs Clarke's scones were delicious, even if you only had margarine to spread on them, but as it happened he had some strawberry jam . . .

He turned towards the door, intending to put up the *Sorry, we're closed* sign, but before he could do so it burst open and a small person hurtled in, nearly knocking him over and ignoring his faint protest. Swerving round the counter, she sat down behind it, saying urgently as she did so: 'Don't tell 'em I'm here! Oh, please shut the door; and if they come asking, say you've not seen me!'

Albert stared at his uninvited guest. She was a small girl, shabbily dressed, with mousy hair straggling to her shoulders and large brown eyes, which were now fixed appealingly on his face. 'Don't let 'em get me!' she hissed. 'Oh, please, close the perishing door.'

Albert found himself obeying, but scarcely had his hand touched the latch when the door was thrust open from the outside and two boys, red-faced and panting, tried to push past him until the second of them, the taller of the two, grabbed his companion's arm. 'She ain't here, Fred,' he said, staring round the empty shop. 'She must ha' gone next door.' He turned to Albert. 'Sorry, mister; it were a mistake. We're tryin' to catch a young thief what stole fruit off me uncle's stall.'

Albert opened his mouth to say that the girl who had shot into his shop hadn't been carrying anything, then realised that to do so would give the game away. Instead he scowled at the lads. 'I don't believe a word of it; I reckon you hoped to nick a few fags off my display,' he said coldly. 'Gerrout, the pair of you, and don't come back.'

The elder of the two boys began to protest but Albert

3

pushed them both out, shut and locked the door and hung up his *Sorry, we're closed* sign. Then he walked over to the counter and looked down at the girl still crouching on the floor. 'What's up?' he said bluntly. 'Don't try telling me you're playing Relievio, because it won't wash. Those young fellers meant business.'

The girl stared anxiously up at him. 'Have they gone, or are they still hanging about outside?' she asked. 'Suppose they're hiding somewhere, just waiting for me to come out? Oh, dear, whatever shall I do?'

Albert saw that the girl's big brown eyes were full of tears, and went over to the door to check that the lads were not hanging about outside. As far as he could see the pair had disappeared, so he locked up again and turned to the fugitive. 'They're not outside; the crowds are thinning and if they had been hanging around I'd have seen them,' he said. 'I'm going to make a cuppa in my flat. You can come up and tell me what's been goin' on while you drink it.'

The girl got to her feet with an anxious glance at the door, then followed Albert up the stairs and into his small, chilly kitchen, where he lit the gas and got out the scones. Then he raised his brows at his visitor. 'Well? Fire ahead,' he said.

The girl knuckled her eyes. 'Well, to start at the very beginning, I was evacuated to a farm in Norfolk during the war and Mrs Bell, the farmer's wife, sent me a whole ten-shilling note through the post as a Christmas box. She said I was to spend it on whatever I liked, so I thought I'd spend it all on Gran, because she's so good to me. I'd seen a little Christmas tree which only cost a bob, and then I saw, further along the same

4

stall, a beautiful glass angel. I picked it up and held it out towards the stallholder, along with the ten-shilling note.' She sighed tremulously. 'Only the boys must have seen the money and tried to grab it and in the struggle the angel got broken, so then the stallholder tried to grab the note saying I'd have to pay for the angel anyway, and the boys were still trying to get it away from me so I hit out and ran like a rabbit.' She sniffed, then smiled. 'I'm very sorry about the angel, and the little tree, because I reckon Gran would have loved them. And I'm truly sorry I led the boys to your shop, mister. I didn't mean to bring 'em down on anyone else.'

Albert laughed. 'I've dealt with worse in my time,' he assured her. 'The first place looters used to head for when there had been a bad bombing raid was a tobacconist. I used to keep a cudgel under the counter – still do – so I'm not frightened of those lads. They won't come back, and they won't attack you a second time, not unless you go waving a purse full of money under their noses again.'

The girl murmured a protest, but then grinned. 'It was just the ten-bob note,' she said. 'Well, that's one mistake I shan't make again.'

'Did you know either of the boys?' Albert asked. 'Do they go to your school, or live in the same neighbourhood? If so, mebbe you ought to talk to the scuffers. It's bad enough having spivs hangin' round on every corner without thieves like that attacking young girls. But weren't you shopping with a pal? Kids these days tend to go round in pairs; it's safer, what with pickpockets and handbag snatchers taking advantage of the Christmas crowds.' As he spoke he had been making the tea, and now he poured two mugs, one of which he handed to his guest. The girl perched on Albert's kitchen stool, whilst he sat himself down in the creaky basket chair and waited for her answer.

'Well, no, I was alone. I only came back to Liverpool at the beginning of the autumn term, so I don't know many people. In fact the girls in my class . . . well, they don't seem to like me very much.' She gave a watery smile. 'You know what kids are like, or perhaps you don't, but I can tell you they tend to follow the lead of anyone who's pretty or popular, and for some reason Marilyn Thomas, who's both, seems to dislike me a lot.' Albert saw her forehead wrinkle into a frown. 'I can't understand why. She manages to keep her head above water in class and her mam runs a corner shop, so she always seems to have sweets and stuff. She's generous too, handing out liquorice sticks and penny dabs to her friends, and she always has nice clothes and lots of pocket money.' Having begun to unburden herself, the girl continued. 'Miss Cracknell, my teacher – the kids call her Clackem because she's pretty free with slaps and nips – was all right at first, only then I realised she'd made a mistake in the maths question she had given us and I said so, and – and when she disagreed I got out my old exercise book from the Norfolk school and showed her where her working was wrong. Ever since then she's hated me. And that makes it easier for Marilyn to pick on me, because Miss Cracknell turns a blind eye.'

Albert dropped a saccharin tablet into his tea, stirred it vigorously and took a big swallow. 'Have you thought

6

of asking Marilyn outright? Why she hates you, I mean?' he said mildly. 'I know Mrs Thomas; I know most of the retailers on Heyworth Street, and she seems a decent enough woman.' He stared very hard at his visitor. 'Come to think, Mrs Thomas isn't the only one I know. I've seen you marketing round here, haven't I? With an old lady?'

'That's right. The old lady's my gran, Mrs Williams,' the girl said eagerly. 'We live above the milliner's shop. And I'm a Williams too, Theresa Williams, only most folk call me Tess.'

'And I'm Albert Payne, as you'll guess since it's written on my door and above my shop window,' Albert said. He held out a hand. 'How do you do, Miss Williams . . . or may I call you Tess?'

They both laughed and Albert spread jam on two of the scones and gave one to the girl. 'Mrs Clarke cleans for me and does a bake once or twice a week to keep me going – she's done so ever since Mrs Payne died – and I can tell you she's a very good cook. Her scones melt in the mouth. By the time you've eaten yours and drunk your tea you can be certain those lads will have given up ages ago.'

Tess said that this seemed an excellent notion since she was sure that her attackers would not continue to hang around in the dark, and Albert warned her again against shopping alone. The girl nodded. 'But I don't mean to do any more shopping today,' she said. 'For one thing it isn't only the boys I'm scared of, it's the stall-holder whose angel they broke. I mean to buy Gran something really nice for Christmas, and I plan to get myself a job in the next few days so I'll have a bit more spare money. I'd love to get a bird for Christmas dinner; just a small one, you know.'

Albert grinned. 'A sparrow?' he suggested. 'That's what I'll be having, a nice little roast sparrow, along with potatoes and Brussels sprouts, of course. That'll make a grand Christmas dinner.'

They both laughed, though Tess sobered up immediately, saying that she did not mean to let Gran's first peacetime Christmas dinner be blind scouse. Then she cast a hopeful glance at Albert. 'I suppose you don't need a delivery person, Mr Payne? Or someone to serve the customers on the run up to Christmas?'

Albert shook his head regretfully. 'Sorry, queen. I'm not exactly rushed off my feet, even at this time of year,' he said. 'Were you job hunting this afternoon?'

Tess nodded vigorously. 'Yes, but no luck. Well, I'd only tried a couple of shops – Deering the bakers and Gaulton the greengrocer – but they were fixed up, so—'

'If you were looking for counter work you've got to be tidy and neat as a new pin,' Albert interrupted. 'And if you were looking for delivery work you'd need a bicycle. But didn't you say your gran lived over Miss Foulks's shop? Hats and such would be light enough for a kid like you to deliver, only you'd have to smarten yourself up a bit before applying for the job.'

Tess nodded. 'I'd have to smarten myself up a lot, not a bit,' she said. 'But I do have a Sunday dress, and though my coat is thin it's still quite respectable, even if one or two of the buttons are missing.'

'Buttons are cheap; go to Miss Roberts who runs the haberdashery stall in Paddy's Market,' Albert advised. He glanced out of the kitchen window and got to his feet. 'Time you were off, young Theresa,' he said, 'but just in case, we'll go out the back way and I'll walk you up to your gran's flat.' He smiled at her. 'I'm sure there's no need, but I dare say we'll both be happier once you're safe indoors once more!'

Tess was grateful for Mr Payne's company, for though it was only a short walk to the milliner's shop she found that she was still nervous, fancying every shadow hid a vengeful money snatcher. However, they reached the door of the flat without incident, but when she invited her new friend in to meet her gran Mr Payne told her that he had to get back. 'You go up and tell her all about your adventures, and face that Marilyn out; you may be surprised at the result,' he said. 'And pop in from time to time to let me know how you're going on.'

Tess agreed to do so, and bade him goodnight. Pulling out her key, she unlocked the door and hurried up the stairs which led straight into the flat's small, square hall. The smell of something good cooking came to her nostrils and she burst in upon Gran, who was stirring a large saucepan in the kitchen, eager to tell of her exciting, if perilous, day.

Gran turned to greet her, her eyebrows rising. 'Where have you been, chuck? It's so late I was about to send out a search party. It doesn't do to be on the streets after dark, let me tell you, or not by yourself at any rate.' Her eyes brightened. 'Don't tell me you found yourself a job? I do my best, but things aren't cheap and there's no denying I'm a poor manager . . .'

'Oh, Gran, you aren't a poor manager, you work

miracles with the money we've got,' Tess said warmly. 'And you're a grand cook, so you are. Tomorrow I'll try for a job again, only this time I'll dress up a bit, do you credit.'

'You're a grand kid, young Tess, and I mean to make a few extra pennies towards our Christmas dinner myself,' Gran said mysteriously. 'But food isn't important, queen, not really.' She trotted across to Tess and enveloped her in a huge cuddly hug. 'We've got each other, a roof over our heads and food in our stomachs, even if it isn't turkey and plum pudding. That's enough for me. But you still haven't told me where you've been all day.'

'Well, I didn't get a job, but like St Paul on the road to Damascus, I fell among thieves,' Tess admitted, and began to tell Gran the whole story, only leaving out that she had been proffering the ten-shilling note as payment for a glass angel, since she still hoped to be able to buy something similar before Christmas Day dawned. The stallholders on Paddy's Market were famous for their bargains; maybe she would find an angel as pretty as the first.

Gran listened and was a most appreciative audience, gasping, laughing and exclaiming, though she told Tess severely that she really must remember that what one might do in a Norfolk village was best avoided in a big city. 'I know you told me Mrs Bell said she never locked her doors, and that the young lads left their bicycles on the village green or leaning against their houses, but if you did that in Liverpool you'd soon regret it,' she said. 'I dare say there's pickpockets and thieves in most big cities, but it just ain't worth their while to try it on in villages and such. Haven't I told you to push your purse well down in your pocket or keep it up your knicker leg at this time of year? If I'd known about that ten-bob note I'd have come with you.' She had heaved a deep sigh, looking at Tess with anxious blue eyes. 'There must be someone in your class who would go around with you. You say that Marilyn doesn't like you and the rest of them follow her lead, but there must be someone who's got a bit more sense.'

'I'll find someone, only it seems it's going to take time,' Tess said regretfully. 'Oh, when I think of the farm and the village kids . . . well, I had plenty of friends there, so why should I find it so difficult now?'

Gran began to speak, then seemed to change her mind, but after a pause she began again. 'The truth is, you're different, chuck,' she said gently. 'I know you try to imitate the others, but you don't speak with a Scouse accent, so they think you're posh. And the village school brought you on a treat so you're streets ahead of the local kids, which is why you're in a class with girls who are mostly two years older than you. And you've done yourself no favours by telling the teacher she was wrong.' She chuckled. 'If there's one thing a know-all dislikes it's another know-all; you've got to learn tact, young lady, else you'll get nowhere in this life.'

Tess smiled. It was not the first time that Gran had warned her against being too clever, and she had truly tried, several times having to bite her lip when she saw the teacher making an obvious mistake in the problems she was writing up on the blackboard. So she said humbly: 'I know you're right, Gran, and I don't say

11

anything when she makes a mistake anymore, but honest to God, her spelling! If you could only see it . . .'

While they spoke Gran had been stirring her pan of scouse and now she seemed to realise that it had reached perfection, for she pulled the pan off the flame and began to dish up. 'Tell you what, queen, that Miss Cracknell is bound to live somewhere near the school; I dare say you could find her address if you asked around a bit. Suppose you take her a Christmas present? A little box of chocolates, or I could make a batch of those crunchy oat biscuits you're so fond of. Being as how she's working she may not have time to bake for herself. That isn't a bad idea.'

Tess felt a smile spread across her face. 'The biscuits would be best because I'm pretty sure Marilyn gives her chocolates from time to time,' she said. 'Only last week I heard one of the girls saying she'd seen Marilyn slipping a little box of sugared almonds, whatever they may be, into Clackem's desk and getting ever such a sweet smile from that miserable old woman.'

Gran tutted. 'Don't be like that. If you're going to make any headway you've got to be sincere,' she said. 'I'll bake the biscuits this very evening and you can take them round to Miss Cracknell's place tomorrow, all wrapped up in fancy paper. You can tell her you made them yourself, if you like.'

'No, no, she'd think I was being a cooking know-all,' Tess said, giggling. 'I'll let her think I bought them.' She looked appreciatively at the plate of stew Gran was handing her. 'Gosh, that looks good and smells better! If I could take a plateful of that round to old Clackem I'd guess I'd be her favourite pupil for the whole of next term. Oh, Gran, you're a princess so you are!'

Albert Payne returned to his shop with the comfortable feeling of one who has helped someone else and been properly appreciated. He decided that Tess Williams was a nice little girl and hoped, since she lived so near, that she would pop into the shop from time to time, as he had suggested. She could tell him how she was getting on at school and whether she had managed to get a job to help with her grandmother's shaky finances. He wished he could have given her work himself, but his slender profits would not allow him to employ anyone besides Mr Clarke in the tobacconist's shop, though if he did start another business in the empty premises up the road that would be a different story. Although he had not entirely abandoned the idea of opening a tea room, lately he had been reading in an American magazine, which the local newsagent had acquired for him, how ice cream parlours were sweeping the States. He knew – none better – that no one in his area had even considered such a new and foreign idea, but he truly thought that such a place would go down well with local youngsters. Liverpool was being rebuilt as fast as the authorities could afford it, and by the time his ice cream parlour was up and running – if he did start one – he would be sure of a great many customers, for it would be summer, a time when ice creams and fizzy drinks were eagerly sought and sales of tea and coffee, he imagined, slumped.

Albert reached his shop and unlocked the door, slipping inside and making sure the Yale lock clicked home when he pulled it closed behind him. He checked that all was well, then made for the stockroom and the flight of stairs which led up to his flat. As he crossed the small square hall and entered the kitchen, he was suddenly aware of a feeling he thought he had conquered. It was loneliness. His wife Louisa had died before the outbreak of war, and though he had grieved deeply Janine had been a schoolgirl, living at home, so he had been far too busy to be lonely. When war had broken out Janine was fifteen, pretty and lively, and eager to help in the war effort, taking a job making parachutes at a local factory. She and Albert had muddled along all right. They had both adored Louisa and missed her dreadfully, but the dangers and hard work which the war brought meant that every minute of every day seemed to be filled to capacity. In fact, when America entered the war and her soldiers and air force personnel began to flood into Britain, Albert was the last person to realise that Janine, who spent her spare time working in the American PX club, was dating Staff Sergeant Da Silva and was serious about him. She had brought him into the shop a couple of times, had invited him to share their Sunday dinner on at least one occasion, and now Albert thought ruefully that in his secret heart he must have known that sooner or later his pretty daughter would marry and move out of the flat.

But to go to the United States of America! Never in his wildest nightmares had he thought of such a thing. Mario came from a small town in Nevada called Silverpeak – daft name – and his family owned a grocery store and a 'soda fountain', no doubt similar to the establishment he dreamed of owning. Janine intended to work until the babies came along so that she and Mario might save up enough money to buy a small farm – though

14

they called it a ranch – in the beautiful countryside surrounding Silverpeak, and to do her credit she had invited her father to go with her across the Pond, as her boyfriend called the Atlantic, and stay for as long as he could be spared from the shop.

Albert walked across the kitchen, aware that he was shivering though he had not removed his coat, and bent to light the fire he had laid earlier, aware not only of loneliness but also of a strong desire not to have to eat the meal he had planned, a piece of cold meat pie, a packet of Smiths crisps and a couple of rounds of bread and margarine: cold comfort on such an icy day. He supposed he could light the oven and heat up the meat pie, but it seemed pretty pointless really. After all, what was food? It was just fuel which one devoured so that one could keep going.

Albert went into the pantry and extracted the slice of meat pie; it was smaller than he remembered and the crust looked grey rather than golden brown. He carried it across the kitchen and then, on impulse, chucked it on to the fire which was just beginning to take hold. He decided he fancied fish and chips. His favourite shop, Pownall's, would be frying already; if he hurried, he might get a nice piece of haddock. He was halfway to the kitchen door when a nasty smell of burning caused him to stop in his tracks. He had feared that the slice of pie might put out the fire, but instead it had caught and was causing a most horrible smell, and clouds of smoke. Sighing, he retraced his steps, poked the flaming pie through the bars of the grate, then added a couple more pieces of kindling. It was far too cold to sit in the kitchen all evening without a fire; best get this one going properly before he went out for fish and chips.

Half an hour later, with haddock and chips wrapped in a copy of the *Daily Mirror*, Albert returned to the flat. The fire was now burning brightly and the fish and chips smelled good, but the minute he closed the door behind him the loneliness swept back. It was all the fault of that skinny little kid who had bolted into his shop and hidden behind the counter. He could picture her in his mind, getting slowly and reluctantly to her feet, casting terrified glances towards the shop door. She was a scrawny kid, he reflected now, with fine untidy hair, ragged clothing and plimsolls whose soles flapped as she walked. Yet she spoke nicely, without a trace of the Scouse accent, and had seemed bright enough, though she had not had the sense to dress decently when searching for a job. Perhaps she wasn't as bright as all that. But then he remembered she was living with an old grandmother, and had made no secret of the fact that money was short. She would be very conscious that her Sunday clothes were meant for special occasions; he remembered how Janine had cherished her green pleated skirt, pale yellow blouse and green cardigan, to say nothing of her shiny black shoes. Thinking back, he realised he could not blame Tess for not wanting to wear her best clothes in the rough and scuff of the market.

He unwrapped the fish and chips and put them out on a plate, reflecting as he did so how nice it would have been to share them with someone. That girl, that Tess, who had so many problems, but who had trusted him;

it would have been nice to share his supper with someone like Tess.

He had already fetched vinegar and salt from the cupboard where he kept such things, and now he sat down and pulled his plate towards him. He began to eat, telling himself as he did so that having saved Tess from the louts who had been pursuing her, he would like to keep up the acquaintance. It would be interesting to hear Marilyn Thomas's reaction when she was asked straight out why she didn't like Tess. And that teacher, that Miss Cracknell: if Tess had been his daughter he would have been up to that school before you could say Jack Robinson, demanding an explanation for her unfriendly behaviour. If it had been Janine . . . but then he scolded himself; interfering between pupil and teacher wouldn't help matters. The old lady – what was her name now? He was sure the girl had mentioned it – oh, yes, Mrs Williams. Well, he supposed she could have said something, but from what Tess had said she had not tried to do so. Probably she knew best, knew that poking her nose in would only make things worse.

Albert reached for a slice of bread and margarine and wiped it round his now empty plate. Then he took a swig of tea and gave a deep, satisfied sigh. 'That was grand,' he said aloud. 'And tomorrow I'll go round to the landlord of the empty shop and find out what sort of rent he's asking. God knows I've been saying I'll do it long enough.'

It had not been difficult for Tess to discover Clackem's address, nor had it been hard to wrap the delicious crumbly biscuits in bright Christmas paper, to put the little parcel carefully in Gran's wicker shopping basket,

17

and to set out on foot for her house. It was not far from the school, which was probably why she'd chosen to live there, Tess thought. What was hard was forcing herself to walk up the short path to the front door, pick up the knocker, which was made of brass and in the shape of a lion's head, and rap. In fact, Tess walked up and down the short street several times before she worked up enough courage to seize the knocker. It seemed a long time before anybody came, and she was just beginning to think, hopefully, that Miss Cracknell must be out when she heard footsteps approaching the front door. They sounded like the footsteps of someone wearing sensible, low-heeled brogues, the very shoes that her teacher favoured.

The door opened abruptly, fortunately swinging inwards so that Tess was not knocked off her feet, and Miss Cracknell stood there, thin arched eyebrows rising, mouth snapping 'Yes?' and then adding 'Oh, it's you!' so that sweat popped out all over Tess's brow and she had to fight an urge to turn and run. But then she remembered that she was wearing a thick grey overcoat and a matching grey skirt with two big patch pockets, and that Gran had plaited her hair and tied it with a short length of red ribbon. In other words she had taken the advice both of Albert Payne and of Gran; she was neat as a new pin and should be feeling confident as a result.

But the teacher's abrupt remark had knocked her temporarily off balance. She grabbed the beautiful parcel in its bright scarlet and green Christmas paper and thrust it into the teacher's hands. And then she said something so sensible that afterwards she wondered what had put it into her head. 'Good morning, Miss Cracknell. I've brought you a Christmas gift from my grandmother, because she's an awful good cook and she said teachers were busy people and didn't get much chance to do fancy cooking. And we both hope you enjoy them . . . so happy Christmas, Miss!'

Miss Cracknell's mouth opened and closed but no words came out. Tess waited for perhaps ten seconds, then turned on her heel. She had taken two steps away from the front door when Miss Cracknell croaked one word: 'Wait!'

Tess turned back in time to see her teacher's brown-clad figure disappearing into the darkness of a short hallway. What on earth was the woman about to do? But she was back within seconds, her face rather flushed. She held out a small screw of paper which, in her turn, she thrust at Tess. 'Seasons greetings,' she said stiffly. Then she shut the door firmly, leaving Tess staring at its green-painted panels. She was turning away, wondering what was in the screw of paper, when another voice spoke.

'What the devil are you doin' here, Tess Williams?' it said disagreeably. The speaker stopped beside her and peered into her face, and Tess recognised a girl in her class at school. 'Hopin' to curry favour wi' old Clackem? I seen you walkin' up and down the road, pluckin' up the courage to go creepin' up to her front door. What did she give you then?' She laughed hoarsely. 'A saccharin tablet?'

'Oh, shut your gob!' Tess said. She couldn't bear Matilda, who was fat and spiteful as well as being the stupidest girl in the class and one of Marilyn's chief

19

hangers-on. 'What makes you think she gave me anything? I was only delivering something for my gran.' She turned and began to hurry down the street, determined not to get into an argument with a girl she thoroughly disliked, and though Matilda followed her for a few yards she soon gave up when Tess broke into a run. Tess had pushed the screw of paper into her pocket as soon as she heard Matilda's voice and decided to leave it there until she reached the flat once more, reasoning that it was too small to contain anything really interesting. As she unlocked the door and began to climb the stairs, she fingered the little packet, thinking wistfully how nice it would be if her teacher had pressed a couple of bob into her hand, but whatever was inside the tissue the most cursory exploration with her fingers told her that it wasn't coins. In fact, it felt like nothing so much as a couple of pebbles. But even as she pulled the packet out of her pocket she realised that Clackem was unlikely to play a practical joke on her. You only did that to your friends.

As she entered the kitchen, Gran, who was baking, looked up from the sheet of pastry she was rolling out and smiled encouragingly. 'Well?' She peered into the basket. 'Ah, I see you've delivered the biscuits. Was she pleased with them? Or did you simply hand them over and run?'

Tess giggled. 'That's more or less what I did,' she acknowledged. 'But she called me back and gave me this. Then she went back into the house and slammed the door.'

Tess held out the small packet, then carefully began to unwrap the screw of paper whilst Gran watched with her nose only six inches from Tess's outstretched hand. And when the tissue was peeled back, there, in Tess's palm, were what appeared to be two smooth white pebbles, of the sort Tess vaguely remembered collecting at the seaside when Mrs Bell had taken her and Jonty down to the nearest beach before it had been closed to the public. Tess knew she would never forget her very first visit to the seashore, and in her little room at the farm she had treasured the pebbles, shells and seaweed she had found there.

But now she said 'Stones!' in a disgusted voice and was about to chuck the pebbles down on the table when Gran began to laugh. 'They're not stones, you silly girl,' she said. 'They're sugared almonds; haven't you seen sugared almonds before?'

Tess snorted, then began to giggle helplessly. 'Oh, Gran, didn't I tell you that I'd heard one of the girls saying that Marilyn had given Clackem a box of sugared almonds? Oh, wouldn't Marilyn be furious if she knew Clackem had passed part of her present on to me!'

Gran laughed too, but when Tess offered her one of the sweets she shook her head. 'I love them, but Miss Cracknell meant you to have them,' she observed. 'You eat them up, chuck; I reckon you deserve them.'

'I'll leave them for later,' Tess decided. 'Is there anything you want me to do around the flat, Gran? Only if not there's still a chance I might get delivery work of some sort. If I had a pal who wanted work as well we could deliver carpets for old Abraham's, but I couldn't manage that on my own. Still, there's a heap of shops which might employ me just for the last couple of days

21

before Christmas. So if you don't mind, I'll go off and see what I can find.'

Gran beamed at her. 'Don't worry too much, queen, because I've got myself some work which will pay quite nicely,' she said. She indicated the large sheet of pastry which, now she looked at it closely, Tess realised almost covered the top of the kitchen table. 'I'm making luxury mince pies for the baker down the road, and they're paying me pretty well because it's a rush job, a party for a couple of dozen people. The baker's asked me to make sausage rolls and some fancy cakes as well, so we'll be able to afford a small chicken even if we can't run to a turkey, and after all, who wants a turkey? But I'm afraid you won't be getting a cooked dinner until Christmas Day, queen, because I'll be too busy baking to start making meals.'

'In that case if I get work as well we'll be rolling in cash,' Tess said gaily. She was delighted with the news, because since Gran would be earning, and would undoubtedly spend such earnings on special food, her own money could be saved for Gran's present, which must be a good one. Accordingly, she set off for the market, and, having earmarked a pair of pale blue mittens and a matching hat which she knew Gran would love, she hung around by the stall until the owner began to pack up. Then she bargained briskly and got both for ten bob, and on her way back to the flat was asked by a fat little woman who lived in one of the courts off the Scotland Road to carry her bulging canvas bag home for her, being promised a sixpence if she would take it right into the kitchen. As though this job had brought her to the attention of other shoppers, Tess carried bags, parcels

22

and boxes from six in the evening until past ten o' clock, when she returned to the flat well pleased with herself and able to contemplate the great day ahead with excitement and pleasure.

As Gran had foreseen, by Christmas Eve they had not had a cooked meal for three days and had worked like slaves to make sure that their Christmas would be a good one. When Tess had finished hanging up the paper chains she had made in school she was very tired and knew Gran must feel the same, but she knew also that this did not matter. What mattered was having a Christmas to remember – a grand peacetime Christmas – which they could enjoy talking about during the long, cold days of winter.

They had a frugal supper of Spam sandwiches, made themselves hot water bottles and took to their beds, and as she cuddled beneath the blankets Tess realised that she had scarcely thought about the farm all day. Startled, she sat bolt upright in bed, then lay down slowly, realising for the first time that she no longer felt that her home was the farm. Her home was here now, with Gran, and the two of them were a proper family. The Bells had been kind to her, had made her welcome – she remembered how good Jonty had been about sharing – but they were not her own family; that was just her and Gran.

The realisation gave her a warm glow, for though she would continue to miss her friends from the village as much as ever, it was perfectly natural to do so. What had not been natural was the sore, uncomfortable feeling in the back of her mind that she had been rejected by the Bells. She had wondered whether Gran, being a relative, had been forced to take her in . . . perhaps would not have done so had the Bells wanted to keep her. But now she knew she was in her right place, and she snuggled down, already sure that the following day would be a good one.

Chapter Two

Christmas Day dawned, icy but clear, and Tess got up early to take Gran a cup of tea in bed and wish her a happy Christmas, handing over the neatly wrapped parcel and watching as she opened it to reveal the hat and mittens. Gran was clearly delighted with the gift and promptly fished under her pillow for an even smaller parcel which she gave to Tess. 'I didn't buy it, but I don't wear it any longer so I thought you'd like it,' she said, as Tess unfolded the paper to reveal a tiny silver locket in the shape of a heart.

Tess gasped. 'It's the best Christmas present in the world, but how can you bear to part with it?'

'I've had it for years and thought it was about time you took it on instead of me,' Gran said. 'My husband – only he wasn't my husband then – gave it to me instead of an engagement ring. Now mind you take care of it, because it's what you might call irreplaceable. If you wear it under your clothes it'll be safe enough. Only you'd best take it off at night because the chain's a very fine one and could easily snap if you turned over quickly, or had a bad dream and tugged at it.'

'I'll be very careful,' Tess promised, fastening the chain round her neck. 'Oh, Gran, I wish I had something as good to give to you.'

Gran's eyebrows rose. 'You couldn't have given me

anything I'd like more than these,' she said, promptly putting on the mittens. 'After we've had our dinner we'll take a walk, and judging by the frost on the window pane these will keep me a lot warmer than even the prettiest locket.'

'Right. Now, while you drink your tea I'm going into the kitchen to light the stove and start the porridge,' Tess said gaily. 'It's too early to put the chicken on and I prepared the sprouts and peeled the potatoes last night, so if you like we can have our walk after breakfast.' She beamed at her companion. 'If you want the truth, Gran, I reckon we shan't feel much like moving after our Christmas dinner. At the farm we always stayed in and played games, and listened to the king's speech.'

'Oh dear,' Gran said, looking stricken. 'I knew you'd miss the Bell family and all your friends from the village on Christmas Day. I'm afraid I'm not much company for a girl of your age.'

Tess could have kicked herself. Here was Gran, straining every nerve to make their first peacetime Christmas a memorable one, and she had scuppered her efforts by thoughtlessly talking of the farm. She went back to the bed and took Gran's hands, still mittened, in her own, shaking them gently up and down. 'Listen, Gran, you and me are all the family I want, and though I was happy at the farm I always knew I was never really part of the Bell family, though they were very nice to me, and Jonty was a real pal. But I wasn't even a villager, though I kidded myself that I was. You could blame the government, because they plonked children down anywhere they chose and no one could do anything about it. I admit it's taken me a while to get used to living in a city, and being in a small family, but if you want the truth I wouldn't go back to the Bells even if they asked me to, which they won't.' She looked at Gran's face and was pleased to see that the anxious look had faded. 'Now no more grumbling or regretting times past; let's get on with being our own proper little family!'

After Christmas things seemed rather flat, for the weather remained extremely cold, and though Tess tried to offer her services to anyone who wanted a delivery person or counter hand she had no luck. She and Gran, having splashed out for the festive season, now had to tighten their belts, and when a letter came from Jonty Bell suggesting that they might like to visit the farm there was no possibility of their going, even if they'd wanted to. The train fare was out of the question, and anyway they were just beginning to settle down in Heyworth Street and Tess did not want to spoil things. Of course she would have loved to see Jonty and her other friends, but she knew instinctively that it was not the right thing to do. Norfolk was full of airfields and the Bells entertained members of the air force from time to time, and one of the things the young airmen had said was that during initial training no leave was allowed. At the time Tess had thought this was rather mean, but now she felt she understood the reasoning behind it. If she went back to the farm whilst still not completely at home in Liverpool the visit might merely increase her discontent. If, however, she and Gran saved their visit for the summer, when of course there would be much more to do on the farm, they would both enjoy the holiday but would return to the city without too many regrets.

Jonty's letter was a long and interesting one and it must be confessed that Tess felt a pang when she imagined her old friend sitting at the kitchen table, one hand pushing his sandy hair into a tuft on top of his head whilst the other gripped the pen and held it poised over the pad of paper. It was the second letter he had dispatched from Norfolk and Tess did her very best to reply as entertainingly, but it was difficult. For a start, she knew all the people Jonty was writing about: the teachers at the village school, the other pupils, and of course the entire Bell clan. On the other hand, the only people Jonty had heard of in Liverpool were Gran and herself. She could scarcely describe all the members of her class to him, and it would not do to admit she had no school friends, so her own letters had tended to be about the odd trip to the cinema, or shopping expeditions with Gran.

Now, having penned a polite refusal to Jonty's invitation, she looked up from addressing the envelope and glanced across at Gran, who was sitting in the creaking old basket chair near the fire, knitting industriously. She and Tess had gone to Paddy's Market a couple of days earlier in search of an old jumper or cardigan which they could unpick in order to use the wool to make Gran a scarf the same shade as her Christmas present. Tess waved the letter between Gran's spectacles and her flying needles. 'Gran, is there anything you want from the shops? Only I've written back to Jonty asking him to thank his mother for her invitation and saying that we'd like to come in the summer if that's all right with them. Have you got a stamp? I'd like to send it off straight away, just in case Mrs Bell would like to ask someone else instead of us.'

Gran put her knitting down and picked up the big black handbag at her feet. Tess often teased her by saying that the bag contained everything but the kitchen sink, and now it disgorged some pennies which Gran handed to Tess. 'You'll have to buy a stamp, chuck; I've used up all the ones I got for Christmas cards,' she explained. She shivered, glancing towards the kitchen window, where the frost flowers were still in evidence in the corners of the pane. 'Tell you what, if you pop into the corner shop and buy some margarine – I've got some coupons in here – we'll have hot buttered toast when you get home.'

She held out her purse and Tess went to take it, then hesitated. 'But that means visiting Mrs Thomas's shop, and Marilyn helps in there sometimes,' she pointed out. 'You've never sent me in there before, Gran. Suppose she just grabs the book and rips out all the coupons? What'll I do then, eh?'

Gran giggled. 'Don't be so daft, queen. If she did such a mad thing I'd have the scuffers on her tail before you could say Sir Stafford Cripps,' she said, twinkling at Tess, and for the first time it occurred to Tess that Gran looked awfully young to be anyone's grandmother. To be sure she had a thick thatch of curly snow-white hair but her skin was soft and young-looking and her sparkling blue eyes could have belonged to someone half her age. Taking the purse, Tess asked the question which hovered on her lips. 'How old are you, Gran? I've never thought to ask, but apart from your white hair you could be almost any age.'

'I'm the same age as me tongue and a few years older than me teeth,' Gran said, chuckling, then sobered up. 'Why do you want to know? You've never asked before.'

Tess shrugged. 'I don't know. Go on, Gran, how old *are* you?'

'Old enough to know better,' Gran said smartly, picking up her knitting once more and pushing her spectacles, which had slid down her straight little nose, back into position. 'Satisfied?'

'Mm-hm,' Tess said. 'Oh well, you're jolly young to be a grandmother anyhow. Is there anything else you want from Mrs Thomas's shop?'

Gran put down her knitting, got to her feet and crossed the kitchen to her store cupboard. 'Tell her you'll have anything she's got off ration. I'm rare fond of bloater paste. But of course she doesn't know you, so she's unlikely to hand out any little extras.' She returned to her chair, sat down and picked up her knitting once more, then glanced up at Tess over the tops of her spectacles. 'Good Lord, girl, are you still here? Get off if you're going, or the shops will all be closed. And that means the post office as well, so if you want that letter to go tonight . . .'

'I'm going, I'm going,' Tess said hastily, pushing Gran's purse deeply into her coat pocket. 'See you later, Gran. Margarine and bloater paste, and I just hope Marilyn isn't in charge.'

She gave Gran a cheery wave, shot out through the

kitchen doorway, slammed the door behind her and hurtled down the steps, narrowly avoiding a nasty fall, for each stair was rimmed with ice. Despite the fact that it was mid-afternoon there were few people about. Tess made her way to the post office, bought a stamp, stuck it to her letter and popped it into the yawning mouth of the big red post box, then set off for the corner shop. Opening the door, she found a short queue waiting to be served and to her dismay realised that today must be the day Marilyn earned her pocket money, for the older girl was behind the counter wearing a smart pink overall and taking down an order from the customer at the front of the queue. She did not notice Tess, who when her turn came went straight to Mrs Thomas and asked for margarine and bloater paste. After receiving a small piece of margarine wrapped in greaseproof paper and a little pot of bloater paste, she paid the sum required, took the goods and set off for the door, just as Marilyn muttered something to her mother and grabbed her coat. Struggling into it, she slipped round from behind the counter. To Tess's dismay, the older girl followed her out of the shop.

Outside, dusk was already falling and when Tess turned to face her she saw that Marilyn was scowling. 'What were you doing in my mother's shop?' she demanded angrily. 'We don't want the likes of you in there. No doubt you were looking for a few sweets or some biscuits to nick. Well, my mam knows how to treat people like you.'

'Our ration books are with your mam so we've got no option but to shop there,' Tess said, and even as she spoke she remembered the advice that both Gran and

Albert Payne, the tobacconist, had given her. Clutching the paper bag in which reposed the tiny block of margarine and the jar of bloater paste, she took a deep breath and looked Marilyn in the eye. 'Why do you hate me?' she asked baldly, and even as she spoke she saw several members of her class, all hangers-on of Marilyn, congregating near the shop doorway. They were obviously meeting Marilyn out of work, and had she noticed them before Tess would not have acted quite so boldly. It was one thing to confront Marilyn alone and quite another to take on a whole gang, particularly on their own doorstep. But Tess knew that to show how she felt would be fatal, so she continued to stare straight up into Marilyn's face and repeated her question. 'Why do you hate me, Marilyn?'

For a moment the older girl stared at Tess with her mouth dropping open, but then she pulled herself together. 'Hate you? I don't hate you, I despise you,' she said scornfully. 'And I'm not the only one; all me pals think the same. You come bargin' into our class, showin' off, pretendin' to know better than the teacher . . .'

Marilyn's friends were drawing closer. Most of them were reputed to be bullies and Tess wished she was taller and stronger – in fact less of a victim, she supposed unhappily. She glanced at the horrible Matilda, who was edging closer, and saw that the fat girl was balling her hands into fists and obviously longing to hit someone, preferably Tess herself.

Tess took a deep breath and pushed her mousy pigtails back over her shoulders. 'That's no reason to hate anybody, and I only queried Clackem's figures once, even

32

though . . . but it was only once. Go on, Marilyn; *why* do you hate me? There must be a better reason than you've given me so far.'

Marilyn sighed. 'I don't have to have a reason, and I don't have to tell you what it is,' she said loftily. 'But everyone else what lives around here has been here for ages. We all know each other, and each other's mams and dads, and we've all heard tales about *your* mam, so we don't want to get to know you. Understand?'

Tess stared at the older girl in complete bewilderment. 'What do you know about my mother?' she enquired. 'Whatever it is, I don't know it, so you'd best enlighten me.'

Marilyn's admittedly pretty face was promptly pulled into a most horrible sneer. 'Your mam was no better'n she should be, an' your perishin' gran must know what her daughter was like . . .' she began, but that was all she managed to say before she found herself being attacked by a furious Tess, who had dropped her bag and launched herself at Marilyn with such force that she knocked her to the ground. The margarine went one way, the bloater paste another, but Tess neither noticed nor cared. She just wanted to make the older girl eat her words.

In less than a minute there was a melee on the pavement outside Mrs Thomas's corner shop, for all Marilyn's friends, seeing their leader punched in the stomach and unable, for a moment, to free herself from her attacker, attacked in their turn. Tess was definitely getting the worst of it, for though Marilyn had disengaged herself and got shakily to her feet her friends continued to thump and kick at any part of Tess which came within range.

33

As her rage cooled, Tess began to realise that she had best escape before any serious damage was done, but just as she delivered a parting thump on her nearest aggressor, someone seized her collar and she was dragged upright.

'What the devil's goin' on here?' said a reproving voice. 'Anyone 'ud think the third world war had started. What's goin' on?'

Tess looked up. Her captor, or perhaps rescuer would be a better word, was a tall, fair-haired boy she vaguely recognised as someone she had seen on the way to his school whilst she was heading for hers. She did not know his name, but he was looking from her to Cynthia, the girl she had been fighting, as if waiting for a reply from one of them. Tess took a deep breath and rubbed her left eye, which was watering and felt suspiciously tender, then opened her mouth to tell him that it was nothing much, but before she could speak he had turned to Marilyn. 'I know you wouldn't start a street fight, Marilyn, so what's it all about?'

Marilyn shrugged. 'No idea, except that one started it,' she said, indicating Tess. 'She's a rare troublemaker, Snowy. But I weren't involved. If you want to know more, you'd better ask her.'

The boy stared at Marilyn for a long moment, then scrutinised Tess and raised a brow. 'Well? That puts the ball in your court, chuck. So what's your version?'

Tess took a deep breath and looked across at Marilyn, and for the first time saw a look of pleading in her enemy's eyes. For a moment she was tempted to give the other girl away, to say that though she herself had indeed struck the first blow, it had been Marilyn's cruel

34

and totally unjustified taunt which had got under her skin. She thought quickly. If she told, she would probably be disbelieved, and life at school would become even more difficult. If she did not tell, then even if Marilyn never became her friend she might stop being her enemy. But how to invent a reason for the fight? She took a deep breath. 'It was my fault. I'd been into Mrs Thomas's shop to get some rations and as I came out I collided with Cynthia here. We're in the same class at school. She – she doesn't like me much, and next thing I knew we were fighting.'

The boy released his hold on the two girls and turned to Marilyn, standing cool and composed as though she had never so much as thought a bad word, let alone used one. 'Oh, well. I reckon girls is just like us fellers sometimes!' He ran a hand through his crisp fair hair and grinned at Marilyn.

Cynthia picked up her shoulder bag from where it lay on the icy pavement and began to peer at it. 'If me handbag's ruined you can bleedin' well pay for a new one, Tess Williams,' she said viciously, glaring at Tess. 'It were all your fault. Marilyn were right when she telled us in school to steer clear of you.'

The boy called Snowy looked questioningly at Tess. 'I'm gettin' confused,' he announced. 'If it were an accident, like what you said, then how come it's your fault if the bag's busted?' His glance went from Tess to Cynthia and then to Marilyn. 'Come on, Marilyn, you weren't involved. Whose fault is it if the bag's busted?'

Marilyn was about to reply when Tess gave a squeak of dismay. 'Oh my God, my shopping!' she wailed. The bloater paste was still whole and appeared undamaged, but she pointed a trembling finger at the tiny packet of margarine, or rather what had once been the packet of margarine. In the melee someone had trodden on it and it was smeared right across the pavement. 'My gran will be that upset . . . oh, whatever shall I do?'

No one spoke for a moment, then Snowy addressed Marilyn. 'Tell you what, why don't you get your mam to give Tess here a little pot of homemade jam? You can't do nothin' about the margarine 'cos that's on ration, but I know your mam makes jam sometimes. Wouldn't that do?'

Tess looked at her enemy and saw that Marilyn was nodding, though she also saw that there was a strange glitter in the older girl's eyes. Still, it was a generous offer and she accepted it immediately. 'Gosh, thanks ever so much, Marilyn,' she said gratefully. 'Are you sure your mam won't mind?'

Marilyn shrugged. 'Your gran's a good customer; I don't think she'll mind at all. But come with me into the shop so that I can explain what happened to the margarine.' She turned to the boy. 'Were you goin' to call for me, Snowy? Or were you just passin'?'

'Just passin',' the boy said; he grinned lopsidedly at Marilyn. 'School starts in a couple of days and there's a perishin' great hole in my satchel, caused, no doubt, by the weight of books. Go on, you two. Mrs Thomas will understand that accidents happen.'

Tess wished she could suggest that Snowy came into the shop as well, but knew this would be a real giveaway, revealing the fact that she feared Marilyn's attitude might change as soon as they were out of Snowy's sight.

36

However, Tess reasoned, it was up to her to make the most of the present situation, so as they entered the corner shop she touched Marilyn lightly on the arm and whispered: 'I'm sorry I hit you, Marilyn. I won't do so again. Only you did say . . . well, you did say . . .'

Marilyn gave her a wide smile. 'Shut your mouth,' she said very slowly and distinctly. 'And be thankful Snowy White came along. He's me feller, if you hadn't already guessed. And I won't have you tellin' my mam a pack of lies, so just shurrup and let me do the talkin'.'

They had joined the end of the queue, and when they reached the head of it Mrs Thomas smiled at her daughter. 'Back already, dear?' she said. 'Have you changed your mind about takin' a break?'

'No-o, not exactly,' Marilyn said. 'Mam, this is Mrs Williams's granddaughter. When she come out of the shop just now with her margarine, she slipped on the ice and landed on her shoppin'. I know you can't give her no more margarine, 'cos it's on ration, but if you could spare a bit of jam in an old jar she'd be ever so grateful.'

Mrs Thomas, who was a tall, somewhat stringy woman, with grey hair pulled into a hard little bun on the nape of her neck, a large and commanding nose and a pair of very shrewd brown eyes, nodded briskly. 'I'll fill an old honey jar,' she said. She smiled at Tess. 'You wait here, queen, while I fetch it through; me daughter will serve the customers whilst I'm gone.'

'Thank you, Mrs Thomas,' Tess murmured. It was a pity that Marilyn did not mean to make peace, but it seemed that Mrs Thomas, at any rate, did not share her daughter's view of the Williams family. I don't believe

Marilyn had any reason to say what she did about my mother, Tess thought, as she stood to one side of the shop and watched Marilyn dealing with the customers. She had to admire Marilyn's efficiency, and found herself wishing that she too was a tall, slender blonde who could take on the task of serving a line of customers with such apparent good humour. Of course Tess knew that the good humour was an act, or at least she supposed it was, but in any event by the time Mrs Thomas returned with several spoonfuls of jam in an old honey jar the queue had disappeared.

Outside again, Tess turned hopefully to the older girl. 'Can we call it pax?' she asked. 'I'll try to forget what you said about my mother.'

Marilyn stared very hard at Tess. 'You're goin' to have a black eye, and serve you bloody well right,' she said nastily. 'As for cryin' pax, I don't do that with the likes of you. And don't think just because . . . Oh, hi, Snowy. So you did wait after all!'

Snowy gave Marilyn a long, considering look. 'If I heard what you said right, I've still not got to the bottom of that perishin' fight,' he said crossly. He looked from one girl to the other, then jerked a thumb at Tess. 'You! Didn't you say you was in Marilyn's class? You're a bit small, ain't you? Don't try and tell me you're the same age, 'cos I shan't believe you. And what'll your mam say when she sees you've gorra black eye? 'Cos it's turnin' kind of purple already.'

Marilyn broke into hasty speech. 'Tess doesn't have no parents. She lives with her gran above one of the shops on Heyworth Street. She were at a village school in the war, so she's way ahead of her year.'

The boy nodded. 'Got you. Well, I'm off. Your pals are comin' back, Marilyn, so I'll be on my way. See you some time.' He strode away from them and Marilyn only waited until he was out of hearing before addressing Tess in a low, hissing whisper.

'Just remember what I told you. Snowy White's my feller and don't you go tryin' to make trouble for me, else I'll make you regret it. Comprenny?'

Tess had been about to thank Marilyn again for the little jar of jam but this was too much. 'And don't *you* forget that there was nothin' wrong with my mam, and she's dead now so she can't defend herself,' she said. 'I've tried to be friendly – I never told that feller you'd called me names, and all the thanks I get is more nastiness from you. Well, be like that, Marilyn Thomas; see if I care! People who are nasty for no reason have a way of bein' paid out. And I'm sure you're no exception.'

Marilyn opened her mouth to reply but Tess did not intend to hang around. Snowy White had said Marilyn's friends were coming back, and her eye was beginning to sting. She did not feel capable of defending herself again and fairly flew along the road. In fact she was so busy looking over her shoulder to make sure that Marilyn and her gang were not following that she didn't see the tall fair-haired boy barring her path until he seized her and gave her a playful shake. 'What's up wi' you and them other girls? Let's have the truth now.'

Tess sighed. 'It wasn't anything important. It wouldn't have happened, the fight I mean, if I'd been looking where I was going.' She looked up at the boy's face and realised for the first time how extremely good-looking he was. No wonder Marilyn was so keen not to give him a bad impression, but to Tess his looks were immaterial. All she wanted right now was to return to Gran with the bloater paste and the jar of jam. But the boy was gripping her arm and she realised she would have to produce a more satisfactory reason for the fight than she had done so far, so she took a deep breath and prepared to lie convincingly. 'All right, all right. If you're determined to know the truth, they accused me of trying to get into Clackem's good graces by taking her a Christmas present,' she said. She looked hopefully up at him. 'Now can I go home? Only my gran is waiting for the shopping and she'll worry if I'm long away.'

But the boy continued to hold on to her arm, looking down into her face with a puzzled expression. 'But that's no reason for fighting,' he said slowly. 'Look, I'll walk along with you, so you won't be late, and you can tell me just exactly what happened.'

Tess shook her head firmly. 'I won't,' she said. 'It's none of your business, you know. Don't boys fight occasionally for stupid reasons? I'm sure they do. When I was at the village school someone was always fighting and it was nearly always boys. So if you'll please let go of my arm we can both go on our way.'

The boy laughed, but let go of her arm. 'Awright, but just how are you going to explain that black eye to your gran? And there's a scratch runnin' from the corner of your left eye right down into the neck of your blouse. You look as though you've been shut in a cage with a wild cat . . . and I'm just hoping the wild cat wasn't Marilyn, because damn it, queen, you're half her size.'

40

Tess chuckled. 'I don't know who it was,' she admitted frankly. 'Honest to God, Snowy, it could have been anyone. Only not Marilyn.'

The boy looked relieved. 'That's all right then. But why are they so agin you? No, don't tell me, let me guess. You ain't a local girl – no accent – and you're bright, which is why you're in Marilyn's class. So really it's you bein' different which is the trouble. Am I right?'

Tess nodded, feeling considerable relief, and knowing that he wasn't so far out at that. Had she been in a class with girls her own age she was pretty sure she would have been accepted. She remembered an incident on the Bells' farm when Mr Bell had come home, triumphant, one market day, bringing with him a pony fourteen hands high to replace the little cob that his son rode. He had let it loose in the meadow where four or five other horses, all known to one another, were grazing, and within ten minutes the new pony was being bullied by its companions. Tess and Jonty, leaning on the gate and watching the goings-on, were worried that the newcomer might be injured, but Mr Bell said that if the bullying persisted he would move the new pony and Rufus, the little cob, into a pasture by themselves. 'Horses is just like people and rarely take to a newcomer first go off,' the farmer had observed. 'But they'll all settle down in time, just see if they don't.'

He had been right, and now Tess, much amused, told the remembered story to Snowy White and was rewarded by his spontaneous laughter. 'I've never thought of gals bein' like ponies, but I reckon you've hit the nail on the head,' he said, grinning down at her. 'Tell you what,

41

littl'un, you need someone to give you lessons in the Scouse dialect. Want me to take you on? I'll only charge you tenpence an hour!'

He laughed again and Tess laughed too. 'I wouldn't mind at that, only I'd have hard work to find your fee,' she admitted. 'To tell you the truth, my gran's job hunting for full time work now that Christmas is over and not having much luck, so if you hear of anyone needing a helping hand, tell 'em Mrs Edith Williams would be happy to oblige.'

By now they had reached the milliner's shop and Tess produced the key which hung round her neck. 'Thanks very much for your company, Snowy. What's your real name, by the way?'

'Oh, I'm really Desmond – ghastly name – but of course everyone named White gets called Snowy.' And then, as Tess turned the key in the lock and swung the door wide, he added: 'Want me to come up with you and explain how you got your black eye?'

Tess shook her head firmly. 'Thanks, but no thanks. Me and Gran are going to have bloater paste on toast for our tea and I'm afraid it won't stretch to three,' she said. 'Cheerio, Snowy. I expect I'll see you around.' And with that she gave him a little wave, closed the door firmly and ran up the stairs.

Desmond, alias Snowy White, stood staring at the closed door for a moment, aware of a feeling of pique, for he had confidently expected to be invited up to Mrs Williams's flat, and to find himself with the door virtually banged in his face was a salutary lesson. After a few moments, however, he turned away, telling himself that she had not meant to snub him. Had she been a couple of years older he was sure she would have jumped at the chance to invite him to meet her grandmother, but she was only a kid, after all. Still, she had said herself that she would see him around, and having made up his mind she meant no harm he strolled down Heyworth Street, then turned and retraced his steps, pretending to examine shop windows as he went, though heaven knew there was little enough to examine. Blast had seen off most of the glass and several of them were boarded up, save for a small square perhaps two foot by four, just enough to let some light in, for glass was strictly rationed and even private houses came under the same rules.

Reaching the milliner's shop once more, Snowy stood staring at the window, or what had once been the window, contemplating his own future. He had no desire to become a part of the building industry, nor did he intend to work in a factory, or even in an office. An only child, he dreamed of going to university and becoming a member of the medical profession, either a doctor or a dentist for choice. All through the war his parents had put away any money they could spare in a savings account which they referred to as the 'education account', and Snowy knew that he owed it to them, as well as to himself, to do sufficiently well at school to gain a university place. He also knew that this would be hard, because many of those who had joined the forces would now be eligible to take the places at university that they had turned down in order to fight for their country, which might mean he would need first-rate exam results to get in. But Snowy was ambitious and hard-working and was quite prepared to fight for his future.

There was talk of National Service coming in for young men aged eighteen, who would serve in one of the forces, so that the experience built up during the war would not be lost. But that was for the future, not yet settled, and Snowy thought there would probably be some sort of exemption, otherwise the colleges would be empty and medical men would have to be brought in from abroad, which would never do.

As he continued to gaze at the milliner's window a woman came and stood beside him, staring at the window as he was doing, then turned to face him. 'Wotcher lookin' at, chuck?' she enquired genially. 'Don't say she's gorra new hat or two to sell? If so, I reckon I'll be her first customer, 'specially if she's gorra blue one.' She gazed up into Snowy's face, her little dark eyes blinking rapidly. 'I's a trifle short-sighted. Can you see a blue hat in there?'

'There's nothin' on display so far as I can see,' Snowy said, peering through the small square of glass. 'But the shop's open; why don't you go inside?'

The little woman sighed. 'I reckon she's sick of the sight of me,' she said, lowering her voice. 'I've been in and out of there ever since Christmas, 'cos me niece is gettin' married in March. I gorra coat and skirt – real smart, they are – off of Mrs Hatchett's stall in the market, but d'you think I can find a hat what matches? Norra chance! Still, I keep on tryin'.'

'A wedding in March!' Snowy said. 'Still, by March some of the shops may actually be rebuilt, so I'm sure you'll find something suitable.' He gave her his most winning smile. 'Good luck wi' your search, missus.'

'Ta,' the old woman said, and entered Miss Foulks's premises, shutting the door carefully behind her. Snowy stood for a moment, smiling to himself. His father always vowed that Liverpool people were the friendliest in the world, and wasn't it true? That little woman had questioned him as openly as though they had known one another for years, and he had answered in the same vein. And now he knew why little Tess whatsername had refused to invite him up to her flat to meet her gran. It was because she'd been away from Liverpool for six years and still had the stiff and starchy manners learned in some other part of the country. Satisfied that his charm had not let him down, Snowy turned away from the milliner's shop and set off down Heyworth Street once more. I'll keep a lookout for that young Tess, he told himself. She's a nice kid, bright as a button by the sound of it, and she needs someone to keep an eye if those little cats have got it in for her. God, who'd ha' thought girls could be such young horrors! But it's like she said when she were tellin' me about the horses; they may start off pickin' on the new one, but it won't last. For a start I'll have a word with Marilyn, tell her she's to keep the other girls off of young Tess.

Satisfied that he would be doing the right thing, Snowy continued on his way down Heyworth Street.

Chapter Three

By the time summer came, Albert Payne and young Tess were good friends. At first she had only popped into his shop for a quick exchange of news once a week or so, and these visits had been ruled by customers; if he was serving someone she would wait quietly by the counter until the customer had gone, and then tell him how her life was going, but would make her farewells as soon as another customer loomed.

The more Albert saw of her the more he liked her. And when she came into the shop at the start of the summer holidays he was delighted. 'Good morning, young lady. How can I help you?' he asked jokingly. 'Now that you're out of school for six or eight weeks I suppose you'll be desperate to find some work so that you'll have a bit of money to spend.'

'That's right,' Tess said, hurrying round the counter and beginning to help him set out his recent delivery of cigarettes. 'But not straight away – I shan't be seeing you for a while, Mr Payne, and I shan't be getting a job either. Mrs Bell has written asking would I like to go to Norfolk for a few weeks this summer.'

Albert felt a sharp stab of disappointment, but he did his best to hide it in the face of her sparkling eyes and obvious pleasure. 'Well, that's fine, I'm sure,' he said slowly. 'Before the war I used to close the shop for a week and take Louisa and Janine off down to Rhyl or Prestatyn or Llandudno, somewhere on the coast anyway. We always had a grand time – I don't suppose the sun really shone every day, but that's how I remember it – and this year I mean to close the shop and go on day trips by coach. Some of them go all the way to Aberystwyth – that's a town I really like – so I thought mebbe I'd do that, because it's cheaper than getting lodgings and I could space the days out, like.'

'Well, so you can; there's nothing stopping you,' Tess said enthusiastically. 'That would be really nice, Mr Payne, and when we got back we could exchange holiday stories. That would be grand, wouldn't it?'

'Yes, grand,' Albert Payne said faintly. It would not do to admit that he had intended to invite Tess along. Going in a coach by oneself, he thought, would be much less enjoyable than going with a lively, chatty young person like Tess. But of course he could not spoil his little friend's pleasure by telling her so, so he smiled and changed the subject quickly, asking whether Mrs Williams would go with her to the Bells' farm.

Tess shook her head. 'No, not this time, because as you know she's got a really good job in the bakery and daren't risk losing it,' she told him. 'She's been there about six months so she could take a few days off, but the journey to Norfolk is very long and tiring and not worth doing just for a couple of days at the farm. So she's to see me off on the train next Monday and Jonty Bell will meet me at Norwich Thorpe. Oh, I can hardly wait!' She had been beaming up into Albert's face but suddenly the happy look disappeared. 'Oh, Mr Payne, I shall miss you, and I expect you'll miss me, but I've had an idea. Why don't you ask Gran if she'd like to go with you on the coach, for one of the trips at least? I'm sure you'd get on like a house on fire and I wouldn't feel so mean about leaving Gran on her own.'

Albert laughed but shook his head. 'Don't use me to salve your conscience, young lady,' he said with mock severity. 'I expect your gran has her own ideas on what she would like to do whilst you're away, and it won't include a coach trip with a stranger.' He did not say so, but he thought that the last thing he wanted was the company of an old lady who probably needed a stick to help her to get from one end of Heyworth Street to the other. Albert was a great walker, and one of the trips he had intended to take was a visit to Snowdonia, where he could be dropped off at ten in the morning and picked up again at six in the evening having walked for most of the eight hours, apart from a stop at a convenient hostelry for a pint of beer and a sandwich. Even more leisurely walks such as going up the Great Orme by tram and down on foot, he thought, would be beyond an old lady. But Tess was looking at him so hopefully that his heart smote him. She was a kind little thing, trying to find him a suitable companion for a coach trip whilst getting her grandmother a nice little holiday as well.

'Oh, do consider it, Mr Payne! I'm sure you'd enjoy my gran's company. I know you've never met her, but . . .'

'No, I've not met her, but I've seen her passing my window and I knew it was her because you were carrying her basket,' Albert said. He remembered the tiny, plump little woman who had hung on to Tess's arm and thought that, delightful though she might be, she would hold him up at every turn. No, he really must discourage Tess from plotting. Why, the child's grandmother must be old enough to be his mother, or if not his mother, at least an aunt.

When Tess took her leave, saying she was on her way to Lime Street to buy a third class ticket to Norwich Thorpe, Albert saw her off with mixed feelings. He knew he would miss her, knew also that his coach trips would not be such fun now that he had no one to go with. He had hoped that his ice cream parlour would widen his circle of friends, bring him into contact with others whose company he could enjoy, but his plan had come to nothing. He had visited the landlord of the empty shop down the road, but when he was shown over the premises he had realised that the shop was far too small for even the tiniest tea room. Furthermore, it had no water supply, which would have meant toiling up the stairs to the flat above every time one wanted to fill a kettle, so he had regretfully abandoned his scheme.

He was still mentally scanning his acquaintance for someone who might enjoy a coach trip when the bell above the door tinged as it was pushed open by a customer. Albert finished arranging his packets of Players and turned to smile at old Mr Grundy, a long-time customer. 'Mornin', Fred,' he said jovially. 'I've just had a delivery. Want some Gold Leaf?'

On Monday morning Gran was up betimes and so was Tess, for excitement would not let her remain in bed on such a day. She had packed her case days earlier and repacked it practically every morning since. Gran had made her a delicious carryout the night before, but the

49

sandwiches would be made at the last minute, since there was nothing worse than opening a packet of sandwiches only to find the bread curling up and going dry. Accordingly, despite knowing that the train she was to catch did not leave Lime Street until eight forty-five, Tess was in the kitchen fully dressed by seven o'clock and informing Gran that she was too excited to eat.

Gran, placidly cutting bread and sandwiching Spam in some and tomatoes in others, looked disapprovingly at Tess over the top of her spectacles. 'You've been like a fly in a tar box for the best part of a week, thinking that something would come up to prevent your going,' she said severely. 'In fact I've taken offence. Anyone would think I was an evil prison warder, intent upon keeping you in Heyworth Street when your whole heart and mind was set on escaping back to Bell Farm. How you'll tear yourself away when your holiday's over, I can't imagine. Perhaps you'll decide to stay, so if that's in your mind . . .'

Giggling, Tess bounced across the kitchen and flung both arms round Gran, squeezing her tightly and plonking a kiss upon the older woman's smooth pink cheek. 'Oh, Gran, you are daft,' she said affectionately. 'When I first came back to Liverpool I admit I was pretty unhappy. It was mostly because the other girls at school hated me. But now I wouldn't go back to the farm full time even if they paid me. I've several friends in my class now, and ever since Snowy White took me up, so to speak, no one's tried to bully me. But best of all is you and me. We're a little family and we look out for each other. I just wish you could come to the farm as well, but I know it's not on, not this year at any rate. The Bells

50

are nice, but if I'm honest I know they've only invited me to keep Jonty quiet and because I can be useful. It's not that they're hard, exactly . . . well, I suppose it is really. Farming isn't a nine-to-five job, Mrs Bell used to say, it's twenty-four hours, and it makes farmers despise anyone not working all out.'

Gran returned the hug and, in her turn, kissed Tess's cheek. 'I was only teasing, queen,' she said remorsefully. 'I know you wouldn't desert me, although one of these days, when you're older, you'll want a place of your own and a husband too. And now sit down and eat your porridge. I shall come to the station with you, because it's always nice to be waved off, and I shall expect a nice newsy letter telling me all about the farm as soon as you've time to pen one.'

'I will write, I promise,' Tess said sitting down at the table and pulling her bowl of porridge towards her. 'But don't expect a letter straight away . . .' She giggled, spooning porridge. 'Remember the postcards, Gran, when all us kids were first evacuated? Our teachers had already written our home address on one side and we were to fill them in and send them off as soon as we were told what our new address was going to be. Gosh, when I look back and remember what a frightened little kid I was, I'm astonished that I managed to send that postcard at all. And of course I didn't go to the Bells at first, but to that nasty old lady who begrudged every mouthful of food I ate, and then the ones who nagged me about wetting the bed, until I was so scared I tried to run away. Only then Mrs Bell took me in and everything was different.'

Gran nodded, sitting down opposite Tess and beginning

to eat her own porridge. 'That's all best forgotten,' she said between mouthfuls. 'Just you concentrate on the list of stations we made out. Don't forget, porters are there to help people when they have to change trains. Oh, dear. In a way I wish I was going with you, but I suspect that it would probably be you leading me and not vice versa.' She smiled as Tess jumped to her feet and took her empty bowl over to the sink. 'It's a brilliant day already. Are you sure you want to wear your mackintosh? You'll be awfully hot by the time you reach Norwich Thorpe. Only I dare say it wouldn't fit into your suitcase, so perhaps you had better wear it.'

'I might as well,' Tess said. 'Have you finished your porridge, Gran? 'Cos if you're ready we might as well leave. I know trains are always late, but you never know, this one might be the exception.'

Gran laughed but got to her feet. 'All right, all right, I knew how it would be,' she said resignedly. 'Just give me time to visit the lavvy and I'll be with you.'

Twenty minutes later Gran and Tess, Tess carrying a suitcase and listing heavily to port, arrived at Lime Street station. Gran suggested they might go to the refreshment room and have a cup of tea, since it was quarter of an hour before their train was due, but Tess pointed out that if she drank too much and the train was very crowded she might have to get out when it stopped to find a Ladies and then the train might go off without her, so she and Gran perched on one of the benches until their train was announced. Gran bought a platform ticket and carried Tess's mac over her arm whilst Tess teetered along in her wake. They got aboard and bagged the corner seat by the simple expedient of putting Tess's mac down on it and the suitcase on top of that; then Tess shooed Gran back on to the platform, worried that the train might suddenly start and carry the older woman off too. Instead she let down the leather strap to open the window and leaned out so that they could say goodbye. For once the train was on time and they could hear the engine getting up steam even as the porter came along, waving his flag and slamming doors.

Tess tilted out at a perilous angle, waving violently as the train's speed increased and Gran's figure got smaller and smaller, and presently, as she turned away from the window and returned to her seat, she was aware of a tight feeling in her throat, and tears beginning to gather in her eyes. Gran was such a lovely person! She had been as good as a mother to her granddaughter, possibly even better, sharing all Tess's hopes and fears, and getting the job in the bakery so that they could manage financially. Tess intended to begin earning as soon as she could find someone willing to employ her, but this had not yet happened, and partly, she knew, it was her own fault. Gran had talked to Clackem, telling her that at the Norfolk school they had expected Tess to get a scholarship to one of the fee-paying schools in the area and go on to further education. Gran had pointed out that a scholarship girl would be a feather in the cap of her council school and most particularly of her teacher, and ever since that meeting life had been a lot easier for Tess. With the teacher on her side, actually setting her homework which would help rather than hinder her, Tess saw that if she worked all out she might eventually go to university and herself be a teacher, which as far as Clackem was concerned was what every bright girl should aspire to.

But now, sitting in her corner seat and watching Liverpool's houses and factories gradually disappearing and rolling countryside appearing in their place, scholarships, examinations and university were the last things on Tess's mind. In her imagination she was sliding a hand into the nesting box at the farm and taking the warm brown eggs which lay there. Then she was holding the bucket of sweet milk and dipping her fingers into it so that the leggy little calf, born only a few weeks previously, might suck the milk off them. There were so many tasks which, the previous year, had seemed more like fun than work. Tess hugged herself and looked around the compartment, which was only half full. A woman was immersed in a copy of the *Echo* while her son was staring out of the window and asking every five minutes: 'Are we nearly there yet, Mam?' They sat opposite Tess, and beside her, further up the seat, was a middle-aged couple who had already told Tess that they were going to visit their daughter who worked in Rugby, and her fiancé, whom they had never met.

When asked where she herself was bound, Tess had just replied she was to stay with relatives, for though this was not precisely true she had no desire to fall into conversation. She much preferred her own thoughts, and time to anticipate the visit to come.

The train drew to a halt at Norwich Thorpe and the young man who had been chatting to Tess on the last leg of her journey swung her case down from the rack and followed her along the corridor and down on to the platform. He stood the suitcase at his feet, then looked around him. 'You said you were being met—' he began, but he was interrupted.

'Tess, you idiot, over here!'

Tess looked around wildly but could see no one she recognised, then spotted someone pushing his way towards her. She stared. When she had last seen Jonty he had been about her own height and wearing short trousers and a stained shirt. But the person who approached was a good deal taller than her and broad shouldered, and wearing patched jeans, a leather jacket and stout working boots. He reached her side and grinned and then Tess knew him immediately. Oh, he might be taller and broader, his hair lightened by the hot summer sun and his clothing that of a young man rather than a boy, but he was still undoubtedly her old pal.

'Jonty!' she gasped, and grabbed his hands in both of hers. 'Oh, Jonty, I'm so sorry I didn't recognise you. You've changed so much!' She turned to the young man who had carried her case for her. 'This is my pal, the one I told you would be meeting me. Jonty, this is Mr Potter, who's come here to take up a job with the Norwich Union Insurance Company. He was kind enough to help with my case, but now he can go along to the guard's van and fetch his trunk.' She smiled gratefully at the young man. 'Thank you for your help, Mr Potter. I'll be all right now.'

She bent to pick up her suitcase, but Jonty was ahead of her. He grabbed it, grinned at young Mr Potter and began to stride towards the barrier, where he surrendered his platform ticket and Tess showed her own ticket. Then they were out on the concourse. 'We're going to have to catch a bus to the village,' Jonty said, glancing at the large watch on his wrist, 'but the next one won't be along for half an hour. Want to grab tea and a wad in the refreshment room? You look as though you could do with feeding up.'

'You look as though you've been doing too much feeding altogether,' Tess said frankly. 'You're *huge*, Jonty. How on earth have you managed to get so tall and broad in such a short time? And your hair always did get lighter in summer, but I swear you didn't have so many freckles before.'

'Don't be so bloody rude,' Jonty said as they entered the refreshment room. 'Didn't anyone ever tell you not to make personal remarks? And anyway, if I've changed, so have you. If you want the truth, if I hadn't recognised the suitcase – and that tatty old mac – I'd have walked right past you.' He grinned down at her. 'I'd have said *What a pretty girl; pity I don't know her from Adam*, and gone on looking for you.'

Tess felt a warm blush creep up her cheeks and sent a silent *thank you* winging from her mind to Gran's, for she knew very well who was responsible for her improved looks. As soon as the invitation to revisit the farm had arrived, Gran had taken her to Lillian's Hairdressing Salon, and begged Miss Lillian herself to see what she could do with Tess's fawn-coloured mop. Tess had expressed her own preference for a short style, and after staring at her new customer from every angle, Miss Lillian had done them proud. Tess's hair had not been cut for many months and resembled nothing so much as a tangled gorse bush, so Miss Lillian had washed and combed and sprayed and cut, and an hour later, when Tess had peeped into the mirror, she had seen a different person, one with a cap of shining hair the colour of light oak which fitted her head neatly and somehow managed to draw attention to her large brown eyes and small pointy-chinned face.

Then there had been her clothes. During school holidays Tess always wore her oldest and shabbiest skirts and blouses, but Gran had shaken her head. 'You'll not get a job looking like a ragbag,' she had commented. 'Furthermore, when you go to visit the Bells I want to be proud of you. I agree you can take old clothes and boots to wear when you're working on the farm, but when you go to meet old friends, and when you arrive at the farm itself, you must look your best.' She had bought Tess a navy blue cotton dress, which she said was suitable for a train journey since navy was less likely than paler colours to show the smuts which were an inevitable part of rail travel, and a pair of navy court shoes. So now she felt self-confident and grinned cheekily at her companion. 'Why? What's different about me? I'm sure I'm no taller or fatter than I was when we said goodbye last September.'

Jonty shrugged. 'I dunno. Maybe it's the clothes.' He chuckled. 'Wait till Ma sees you, gal. She's already planning how best you can help out; did she tell you when she wrote that our land girl has been demobbed? And Maggie doesn't want to work on the farm – my sister has got herself a job with the Milk Marketing Board, if you please – so if you intend to swan around looking beautiful you've got no chance. It'll be up at six, in the milking parlour, mucking out the cows, feeding the pigs and doing all sorts. You'll be all right for clothing, because Ma hung on to Patty's overalls. She said she wouldn't be needing them, her being a city girl.' He jerked his head at an empty table for two against the wall. 'Go and bag that table whilst I go to the counter, 'cos it's not waitress service. What do you fancy?'

'The biggest cup of tea they've got on offer, a cheese sandwich, if they've got one, and a currant bun,' Tess said at once. 'I'm perishin' well starving. I suppose they don't do chips?'

Jonty gave a derisive snort. 'Chips? At three in the afternoon? Course not. But are you sure you want a sandwich *and* a bun? Ma's made a grand sausage meat pie and she'll do mashed spuds to go with it, and a feed of runner beans. Will your appetite be up to it?'

'Yes,' Tess said baldly. 'But if you can't afford it . . .'

Jonty had been about to head for the counter but turned back to give her a friendly punch on the shoulder. 'Course I can afford it; I'm a rich young farmer, aren't I? Or I shall be once all this austerity business is behind us. I'm tellin' you, I'm bloody glad I live on a farm! I reckon folk in towns and cities are hard pressed to feed themselves, unless they've got good gardens, that is.'

Tess murmured something appropriate and watched as he joined the queue at the counter and came back balancing their order on a small tray. She thought he had taken a great leap away from her, but then remembered the difference in their ages, which hadn't been so noticeable when she lived here since thanks to the shortage of teachers, most of whom had joined the forces, she and Jonty had been in the same class at school. In her last year in the village it had included children from the ages of nine to fourteen. She and Jonty had both managed the work easily, though Jonty had been blatantly uninterested and had very little self-confidence where school work was concerned. Indeed he had sometimes copied Tess's answers, saying that schoolwork was boring and of little use if one intended to work on the land. He seldom read a book, though she recalled he was hot stuff at mathematics. When she left the farm he had been about to start at the grammar school to work for his School Certificate and this, she imagined, had given him the self-confidence which he was now showing.

Jonty put the tray carefully down on the table. 'Now let's catch up on what's been happening to us both,' he said. 'I like your hair, by the way; it's really smart.'

'I like yours too,' Tess said politely, only realising she was speaking the truth after she had done so. When she had been at the farm Mrs Bell had occasionally attacked her son's hair with the kitchen scissors, reducing an untidy thatch to something resembling a mouse-nibbled hay crop, but he was obviously getting proper haircuts now he was at the grammar school. 'I say, this bun's not half bad. How long have we got before the bus leaves? I take it there's still a bus stop on the opposite side of the Yarmouth Road, just outside the station? Only I don't fancy having to lug my suitcase all the way up to Surrey Street!'

Tess and Jonty caught the bus with plenty of time to spare and presently got off about half a mile from the farm, because the bus took the main road through the village. Despite the fact that it was now late afternoon, the sun was still very hot and both she and, she suspected, Jonty were downright relieved when they reached the short drive. Tess paused to look at the house which had been her home for so long. At first glance she could see no changes; there it stood, a tall, red-brick house with the attic windows catching the brilliant rays of the sun. Then she saw that the ivy on the right-hand side of the house, which had begun to creep halfway up the rosy bricks, had been hacked down, and the trees which crowded close on the other side had been pruned so that they no longer cast a comforting area of shade over Mrs Bell's herb garden.

Tess turned to look doubtfully up into Jonty's face. 'It hasn't changed much, except that the ivy's gone and the trees ought to look bigger but they look smaller,' she said. 'And – and Jonty, something's just occurred to me. I don't mean to be horrid, but looking at the house I can't help remembering how hot my room was in summer . . .'

'Don't worry.' Jonty grinned. 'Ma didn't like having to put you and Patty up in the attic: too hot in summer and too cold in winter. You'll be all right this time – she'll tell you what's been happening when we get indoors. Come on, don't stand there like a donkey. Ma will have the tea on the go and be waiting for us.'

'Sorry,' Tess said. They crossed the farmyard and let themselves into the kitchen, a huge room which was, as far as Tess could make out with one rapid glance, unaltered. Mrs Bell came over and gave Tess a peck on the cheek, telling her that she was very welcome. She was a large woman, her thick golden hair streaked with white and held back from her round and rosy face with a number of hair grips.

'How are you, my woman?' she said, but Tess had

seen the hastily stifled look of dismay on her hostess's face when she took in the navy dress and shoes, and hastened to reassure her.

'These are just my best clothes for travelling in and for going to church on Sundays,' she said quickly. 'I've got my old stuff in the suitcase, and Jonty says I can wear Patty's overalls while I'm doing mucky jobs.'

'What nonsense, Tess; as if I'd expect you to work when you've come on a visit,' Mrs Bell said, but Tess saw a blush creep up her hostess's cheeks and when Jonty gave a rude crow of disbelief his mother shot him a darkling look which boded ill for her son when she got him alone.

However, he was bidden to take their guest upstairs to her room so that she might change. 'Because we don't want you to go a-messin' up of your nice new clothes,' Mrs Bell said tactfully. 'I expect Jonty's told you that Maggie's got a job in Norwich. She come home weekends from time to time but mostly she stays with her Aunty Daff up on Unthank Road, 'cos she can walk to her office from there. So you won't need to go up to the attic, my dear; I've given you Maggie's room.'

'Oh, but what about weekends . . . ?' Tess was beginning, but Jonty ushered her away before she could say any more. As they climbed the stairs, he explained.

'Maggie's got a boyfriend,' he hissed, grinning. 'Can you imagine, my sister has actually managed to find herself a boyfriend! She came home one weekend but she was just miserable. She wouldn't help on the farm or in the house, kept talking about this Philip Broster, telling us how wonderful he was. She says they mean to marry as soon as they've saved enough to take on the

61

rent of a flat or a cottage. So you needn't worry that you're taking her room. Dad told her she'd have to sleep in the attic whilst you were with us, so I doubt you'll see her before you go home.'

'Oh. That's all right then,' Tess said faintly. 'But I don't know why you're surprised that Maggie's got a boyfriend. She's really pretty.'

Jonty shrugged. 'Do you think so?' he said, with brotherly incredulity. 'Anyway, the room's yours whilst you're here, so you needn't worry that Maggie will try to oust you. How long will it take you to change?'

'Ten minutes,' Tess said rather rashly, with thoughts of sausage meat pie in the forefront of her mind, and when Jonty had thundered down the stairs she was forced to hurry, tearing off her beautiful dress and shoes, having a quick splash at the washstand and then donning her old grey skirt and blue blouse, both of which were a trifle small, which just went to prove, she thought as she left the room, that Jonty was not the only one to have gained some weight after all.

Downstairs in the kitchen Tess greeted Mr Bell, scrubbing his hands at the sink. He was a tall, spare man, with a long, rather lugubrious face, though appearances were deceptive, for he had a keen sense of humour and enjoyed a joke. He was not demonstrative, so Tess was surprised when he patted her on the head before taking his place at the table. At his wife's command he removed his greasy tweed cap and threw it at the hook on the back door. Tess smiled. 'You ought to go on the fair, Mr Bell,' she said. 'If there was a cap throwing contest you'd win hands down. Wish I could throw anything as accurately as that!'

62

Jonty laughed. 'That's a thought, Dad,' he said approvingly. 'You have come out of your shell, Tess Williams!'

'Never you mind our Jonty,' Mrs Bell interrupted. 'Just you sit down so's I can start dishin' up. And don't encourage Mr Bell to go hurlin' his cap at the door; if I've told him once I've told him a hundred times that my kitchen int a fairground.'

Tess settled in her place and began to eat. The food was lovely but it was eaten more or less in silence, apart from such requests as 'pass the salt' or 'can I have another piece of bread please?' and Tess remembered that it had always been the way, in order to finish eating and return to farm work as quickly as possible. She smiled to herself, thinking how different life was with Gran. They chatted away at mealtimes, telling each other any interesting news they had gleaned during the day, interrupting, laughing and generally enjoying the talk as much as the food. But now she had to wait until the meal was finished and Mr Bell had returned to the farmyard before the farmer's wife spoke up. She was clattering dishes into the sink whilst Tess dried them and Jonty put them away.

'You'll not know that Mr Bell is using the pastures beyond the cut to fatten beef cattle,' her hostess began. 'He go into Norwich every two or three weeks and buy poor stock which he can see will make up, given the right grub. Of course we're still mainly arable – sugar beet and wheat as well as the orchards – but beef cattle are worth a tidy sum, and there's talk of getting more pigs . . .'

'Oh, you do go on, Ma,' Jonty cut in, no doubt seeing that Tess was struggling to find an appropriate comment. 'She'll find out for herself how things have changed as time goes on.'

Mrs Bell looked reproachful. 'She don't know we've bought Larkin's, so things have changed a lot,' she pointed out. She turned to Tess. 'I didn't tell you we'd bought Willow Farm, did I? Old man Larkin retired and neither of his sons wanted to work the land. The farmhouse is terribly rackety and run down, but one of these days when we've time to spare we'll do it up and either sell it or pass it to young Jonty here when he's got hisself a wife and needs a place of his own.'

Tess stared at her old friend. He had changed, to be sure, but he was still a boy and the thought of him marrying and taking on the Larkins' ramshackle old farmhouse was hard to swallow. Jonty saw her staring and gave her a reassuring grin.

'Ma reckons a farmer wants a wife . . .' he began, but this was too much for Tess's gravity and she burst into song.

'*The farmer wants a wife, the farmer wants a wife, ee-aye-endio, the farmer wants a wife.*' At this reminder of their old school game, Jonty began to laugh, and Mrs Bell looked from one to the other, a frown creasing her brow.

'What's so funny?' she asked. 'A farmer do want a wife. That's not like other jobs. That take two to run a successful farm.'

'Yes, I know, Ma, it was just that the words I used are the same in one of the games we played at school,' Jonty said soothingly. He glanced at the draining board and saw that nothing remained to be done, and jerked his head at Tess. 'Come on, Tess. I've got to shut the hens up before it gets dark – in case of foxes, remember? Going to come with me?'

'Of course,' Tess said quickly and was suddenly aware

that she did not want to be left in the farmhouse with Mrs Bell. She realised she had never known the older woman very well, because what with school and the multitude of tasks on the farm she'd spent very little time actually talking to her, so she followed Jonty quickly.

Outside in the cool air of evening Jonty led her straight across to the stable where the two big carthorses Solomon and Sheba and the two ponies Rufus and Biddy lived. 'Actually, Dad and I saw to the stock earlier, knowing you were coming,' he said. 'But Tibbs has had kittens in Sheba's manger, and I thought you'd like to see them. We'll keep one or two, because they'll be good mousers like their mother, but the rest will go to neighbours. Want to take a look?'

Albert had a rush of customers after his latest delivery of cigarettes and tobacco, so he did not call on Mr Clarke to stand in for him until four days after Tess had left. He might not have done so then, but he had received a card from his young friend which had cheered him considerably. She said that she had reached Bell Farm safely and was enjoying both the work and meeting old friends, but had *only been into the village once, because there's so much to do here. Mr Bell has bought the farm next door, Willow Farm. The land is rather neglected, but not nearly as bad as the house. The family moved out six months ago and no one's touched it since, but doubling the acreage has meant double the work. The Bells' land girl has left as well which means Jonty and I are busy from dawn to dusk. Coming home will be a positive rest cure! Hope you are enjoying your coach trips. Wish you were here. With best wishes, Tess.*

Reading between the lines, Albert suspected that Tess

was missing Heyworth Street. She had been happy on the farm in wartime, had made many friends at the village school, but from what she said it seemed her hosts did not regard her as a guest but as an unpaid farm hand. He thought Tess was far too bright not to realise it, and although the last thing he wanted was that she should not enjoy her holiday, he couldn't help hoping, at the same time, that it meant that at the end of her three-week stay she would be happy to come back to Liverpool, her gran and the pals she had made here, including himself. So he tucked the card away in his wallet, closed the shop early and went along to the offices of the coach company he favoured. A coach was going to Rhyl the very next day – in fact a coach went to Rhyl every day – so he bought a ticket and returned to the flat above the tobacconist's shop feeling happier than he had done since Tess had left.

Next morning he awoke to find sunshine streaming through a gap in his bedroom curtains. He jumped out of bed, a pleasant feeling of anticipation causing him to choose his favourite short-sleeved shirt and his best lightweight trousers. He washed hastily, then went through to the kitchen for a substantial breakfast of porridge and toast. When he and his dear Louisa had gone on coach trips she had packed a great many sandwiches, a fruit cake and a flask of tea, but Albert did not intend to eat a solitary picnic on Rhyl beach; no indeed! He meant to go to the best restaurant in town and have a light luncheon of ham salad, followed by a fish and chip supper before the coach set off for Liverpool once more. He pictured himself with his trouser legs rolled up, paddling in the sea, and wished he could have bathed – he was a strong swimmer – but did not think he could do so on a coach trip, where there would be no facilities for drying wet and salty bathing trunks. Paddling would have to do, therefore; he just hoped no one he knew from Heyworth Street would see him indulging in what was generally regarded as a childish pastime.

Albert reached the coach station and found that he was amongst the first of the would-be passengers to arrive, which had been his intention. He looked at the half-dozen women standing uncertainly beside the steps which led into the scarlet-upholstered interior, and suggested that they might as well get aboard and choose their seats before other passengers arrived. The women agreed that this was a good idea so long as the coach driver did not take exception to such forward behaviour, and presently Albert had taken his favourite place, the window seat right at the front of the bus on the passenger side, and was making himself comfortable.

He was glad he had done so when the vehicle began to fill up and the driver stood at the top of the steps with his checklist of passengers in one hand, ticking people off as they boarded. Albert was relieved to see that there was a good sprinkling of men amongst the trippers, and though most people seemed to be accompanied, there were one or two lonely souls like himself. At the last minute a handsome white-haired woman hurried up the steps just as the driver slid into his seat, and when she had given her name and been ticked off the checklist she smiled at Albert. 'Do you mind if I sit here?' she said, indicating the empty seat beside him. 'I'm afraid I'm sometimes travel-sick, so I don't want to sit at the back – it's always worse there, don't you think?'

Reluctantly, Albert agreed that the motion of the coach could be unpleasant if one were occupying a rear seat, and the woman sat down with a word of thanks. 'Isn't it marvellous weather for the seaside?' she said happily. 'I've been looking forward to this for days. I wondered how I would get on, being by myself, and I did mean to arrive at the coach station earlier so that I could choose my seat. But I managed to oversleep and then I had to run most of the way, a thing I haven't done for years. I expect you were early, since you got the best place in the whole coach!'

'I was,' Albert admitted. He had intended to smile briefly at his fellow passenger and then to turn his shoulder on her, putting a stop to any attempt at conversation. But this woman, he was suddenly sure, was not the type to force her unwanted attention on anyone. In fact, chatting now and then would shorten the coach journey, make the fifty miles or so pleasanter than they might have been, so he smiled at his companion and held out a hand. 'Since we're fellow passengers, I think we ought to introduce ourselves,' he said. 'My name's Payne . . . and you are . . . ?'

'I'm Mrs Williams,' the woman said. She chuckled. 'I'd take a bet that half the people on this coach are either Williams, Evans or Jones. And when we get to Rhyl we'll find even more Williamses, Evanses and Joneses. Have you ever been to Rhyl before? This is my first visit.'

By now the coach was bumping down towards the tunnel which would take them up on to the Wirral. Albert nodded. 'Oh yes, I've been to Rhyl a great many times, though this is my first visit since the war. When my wife was alive we had a holiday somewhere on the Welsh

68

coast every summer. After she died my daughter and I used to have days out, visiting Chester or Wrexham or one of the little Welsh villages where you could get a meal and a drink, but of course the beaches were all closed during the war so we couldn't go there. My wife and I were great walkers, but Janine didn't take after us, I'm afraid. After the war I fancied starting an ice cream parlour and putting Janine in charge, though of course the financial side of it would have been my concern, but she upped and offed to America to marry a GI. She's got a good job in the family business, earns a far better salary than I did at her age and keeps trying to persuade me to have a holiday over there.' He chuckled. 'Wish I could, but money's pretty tight and I'm still hoping to have my own ice cream parlour one of these days, even if I have to employ someone else to run it.'

His companion heaved a sigh. 'I'd really love to run an ice cream parlour, but I expect jobs like that go to the young, and very right and proper too,' she added. 'Still, I can't help wishing.' She looked hard at him. 'It's a good idea, you know – you'd be the first in Liverpool. Have you investigated any likely premises?'

'One or two,' Albert said truthfully. 'But I've found nothing suitable so far. I can't afford a large rent, but cheaper places either don't have a water supply or aren't connected to the electric. With ice creams you need efficient refrigeration, so I suppose I shall have to abandon my dream.' That made him sound a much more interesting person than he really was, Albert thought, but why not? He and this Mrs Williams were, after all, ships that pass in the night. He could tell her anything, any number of lies – not that he would, of course – and she would think him one hell of a fellow, as his daughter would have said. But the time had come to ask some questions on his own account. 'But how about you?' he asked. 'Do you have a job?'

At this point the bus emerged from the tunnel and the bus driver began to address his passengers, telling them that they would stop in about forty minutes at a café with a big car park, where they might make use of the facilities and have a cup of coffee or tea if they wished. Mr Payne and Mrs Williams smiled at one another. 'I shall invite you to share a pot of tea with me, Mrs Williams,' Albert said grandly. 'I might even run to a scone . . . but you've not answered my question. Are you a working woman?'

His companion pulled a face. 'I certainly am. I was widowed in the early thirties and worked until the war began as an accounts clerk, but now I work at Deering's.'

She obviously thought that Albert would know Deering's, but on the spur of the moment he could not call it to mind so merely remarked that no doubt she would enjoy the coach trip all the more because she was not free every day. Mrs Williams nodded her agreement and they began to talk of other things.

The rest of the journey passed very pleasantly. Mrs Williams told Albert that she had intended to bring a packed lunch, but because she had overslept she had not made herself so much as one sandwich and would have to buy a meal at one of the many cafes in town.

'I'm the same,' Albert admitted ruefully. 'Louisa and I always made sandwiches and brought a flask of tea, and during the war Janine and I did the same, but today I made up my mind to treat myself. I know several cafés – or I used to know them before the war – and there's one on the front called the Seagull. They used to do an excellent ham salad, and charge half a crown for three courses, bread and butter and a cup of tea. Will you join me?'

Mrs Williams said she would be delighted but insisted that each should pay for their own meal. 'Just because I sat myself down next to you doesn't give me the right to expect you to pay for my lunch,' she said. 'But I do hate eating alone in a café, so if you're sure you don't mind I'll come with you to the Seagull. Only – do you mean to go on the beach during the course of the afternoon? If so, we might take a walk along the sands together. I'd enjoy it far more with a companion and I dare say you might feel the same.' Albert agreed that he would and presently the pair found themselves descending from the bus on the crowded promenade and promising the driver that they would congregate beside the clock tower on the prom by six o'clock at the latest.

''Cos I'm warnin' you, I'll leave this here resort at a minute past six and if you're left behind that'll be your blame,' the driver said jovially. 'Have a good time, ladies and gents, and don't forget to bring me back a stick of rock wi' Rhyl written right the way through it.'

The passengers began to move away, eager to explore the delights of the seaside town, and Albert offered his arm to Mrs Williams. He found, as they walked along the prom, that he felt proud to be with such an attractive and well-dressed woman. Mrs Williams was only an inch or two shorter than Albert and had, besides a great deal of curling white hair, a pair of big blue eyes, a straight little nose and a soft pink mouth. She wore

71

a blue cotton dress which exactly matched her eyes and a pair of comfortable white sandals, because, as she had already told him, she too was a keen walker and knew that fashionable shoes would soon ruin her day. Despite the earliness of the hour the beach was already crowded and Albert pointed this out, saying that, had she indeed brought sandwiches, she would have been hard pressed to find a secluded spot to eat them.

Mrs Williams agreed, and presently suggested that they might walk along the beach now, since the tide was going out and people were starting to leave in search of lunch. Albert agreed and courteously turned his back whilst his companion hitched up her skirt, removed her sandals and trotted joyfully into the little white-topped waves.

'It's a good thing my granddaughter can't see me now; she'd say I was entering my second childhood,' Mrs Williams said. She gave a squeak and pointed at the water through which she was wading. 'Look at that shell! Can you reach it without getting too wet?'

'I can if you'll hold my jacket,' Albert said. He had shed his jacket along with all his formality, and felt he had known Mrs Williams for years. But it wasn't until they were seated opposite one another in the Seagull café, having been lucky enough to find a table for two, that Albert discovered he had met Tess's grandmother at long last.

The waitress had arrived to give them each a buttered roll, whereupon Mrs Williams had remarked that these were very similar to the ones she made at Deering's when she was on the baking shift.

Albert stopped with a buttered roll halfway to his

72

mouth. 'Do you mean Deering's on Heyworth Street? If so you must walk past my shop every time you go to work: *Albert Payne, Purveyor of Fine Tobaccos*. Do you know it?'

His companion nodded, a dimple peeping beside her mouth. 'Course I do! And you know me, though we've never actually met. I'm Tess Williams's gran, and you're the man who rescued her when some lads chased her into your shop.'

Albert stared for a moment, quite bereft of speech, but then he too began to smile. 'Well, of all the odd coincidences . . .' he said. 'And what a happy one! I've often wanted to meet you, because of course I've heard a great deal about you, but somehow it's never happened. How Tess will laugh when we tell her how we met! Forgive me, but you don't look old enough to be anyone's grandmother, let alone a great girl like Tess's.'

'Oh, dear,' Mrs Williams said. 'If I tell you, will you promise not to say anything to Tess?'

Albert frowned, 'I don't understand,' he said slowly. 'I don't wish to deceive Tess . . . do you not want me to say we've met?'

Mrs Williams shook her head impatiently. 'No, no, nothing like that. But the truth is, I'm not anyone's gran. During the war I got friendly with an elderly lady who was actually Tess's grandmother. But she died just before the end of the war and when the authorities were looking for someone to take care of Tess I'm afraid I misled them. My name was Williams too, you see, Edith as well, so when they asked about an Edith Williams I stepped forward. I couldn't bear the thought of my friend's grand-daughter being put in a children's home, which would have happened, because she had no other relatives willing to take her on. And once I started the deception, and Tess never queried our relationship – she was only six when she was evacuated, and since Edith and her daughter didn't get on she hardly remembered her grandmother at all – I couldn't get out of it; didn't want to, in fact. Tess is a grand girl, marvellous company and bright as a button. At first we had a struggle to manage but she never complained even when food was scarce, and she's got a healthy appetite. Only then I got the job at Deering's – at first it was just for special Christmas orders, but when they realised I was a good worker they took me on full time.'

'And you still never told Tess that you're no relation?' Albert asked incredulously. He grinned. 'You say she's bright as a button, so why on earth hasn't she done her sums? There's just no way you could have a granddaughter her age. When are you going to tell her? You'll have to do so some time!'

But his companion shook her head. 'I shan't, because Tess herself has found a way round it, though she hasn't realised it yet. She has a friend called Lucy who lives on Mere Lane. They walk to and from school together, and one day Lucy came in early, whilst I was still making Tess's butties. They went into the front room because I had the wireless playing and they wanted to check their French homework, and I heard them talking. They were laughing about how women hate to reveal their age and Tess told Lucy that even her gran kept her age a secret though she simply had to be in her mid-forties at least. I heard Lucy say, "Your gran's ever so young-looking. In fact, apart from her white hair, you'd be surprised to find that she was forty, let alone fifty-five." So now Tess has got it fixed in her head that I'm fifty-five, and I'm not saying anything!'

Albert made a dignified little bow. 'Lucy was right,' he said. 'Ah, here comes the waitress. Shall I say tomato soup, ham salad and ice cream for two?'

On the way home in the coach Albert reflected that he felt as though he had known Mrs Williams for years. They planned to book a coach trip to Llandudno for the following week and would meet up beforehand to be sure of sitting together. By now Albert felt it was only sensible to suggest they should use each other's Christian names, though his companion said that she would prefer it if he called her Edie.

'And don't forget I'm fifty-five and need a hand going up and down steps,' she said, gaily, as they stood on the pavement outside Albert's shop. 'I suppose you're right and one of these days I may have to tell Tess the truth, but that day hasn't come yet. She's a dear girl and sets enormous store by the fact that we are a family. Her mother – well, let's say she wasn't the maternal type, and I suspect she was often made to feel like an outsider on the farm too, though I'm sure the Bells didn't mean to do so. To tell you the truth I think the invitation to visit them again has been a revelation to Tess. I know she's only been there a week but she's working all out and having to visit friends in the village at the end of a very hard day. I'm certain she's valued, but perhaps not in quite the way she would like, so I'm sure she'll come back to us very well content with her life here. Though of course she'll never quite forget her happy days on the farm and her friend-ship with this boy Jonty, and I wouldn't want her to.'

'Good, good,' Albert said absently. He was thinking how nice it was to spend time with an intelligent woman who shared many of his own interests. They had discussed the possibility of his setting up an ice cream parlour in various locations, but had decided in the end that he had been right to aim for a property on Heyworth Street. There was little bomb damage here, and because of her work in Deering's Edie Williams knew a great deal about catering. She agreed with him that water and electricity supplies were essential and pointed out that premises which had been used for food preparation were the sort he should be looking for.

'The shop right next door to Deering's will come on the market within the next six months, I believe,' she told him. 'But there will be others, as places run by elderly folk become too much for them to cope with, what with rationing and rules and so on. Become a burden, in fact. So I'll keep my eyes open and you must do the same.'

Albert agreed to do so, immensely heartened by the fact that this new and delightful friend had actually suggested a partnership, for though she enjoyed her work at Deering's she was ambitious and saw a part share in an ice cream parlour as a definite step up. She quite agreed with Albert that Tess should continue her education, but knew that she could do so by taking evening classes, which would leave her free to earn money in the prospective ice cream parlour. So now he let himself into the shop, sniffing the familiar scent of tobacco and Ronuk floor polish, and wishing that he had had the courage to suggest that Edie Williams might accompany him up to his flat for a cup of cocoa before they parted. But had she refused, on no matter what grounds, he would have felt deeply humiliated. Best, therefore, not to push things, not to try to run before he could walk.

Satisfied that he had done the right thing, Albert locked the door and shot the bolts across, then crossed the stockroom and ascended the stairs, feeling the weariness of a long day, but also a sense of achievement, because he had made a friend.

He pushed open the kitchen door and lit the gas under the kettle; a cup of tea would be welcome and he wondered whether he should put a soothing lotion on his arms, which were turning pink and stinging. He went through to his bedroom and, in what he still thought of as 'Louisa's half', found a bottle of something called moisturiser, which he knew his wife had spread on burnt skin in days gone by. He unstoppered the lotion, and by the time he had spread it on his forearms the kettle was boiling.

He got into bed that night knowing that he would fall asleep almost at once, for the day, though infinitely pleasurable, had been a long one. During the drive home, the driver had started a sing-song. Albert, naturally shy, would not have joined in, but Edie would not allow him to remain silent. 'You must know the words, so sing up,' she urged him. 'Tell you what, if you give it a go I'll pay for your glass of beer when we stop at that café place.'

Albert did not feel he sang well, but he joined in with such verve and vigour that Edie Williams told him he had a grand voice and insisted on buying him half a pint of Worthington's, though she herself stuck to coffee.

'You ought to join a choir; it would get you out a bit and you'd enjoy it,' she had told him. 'There's lots of choirs around in Liverpool, the city being so near Wales.

77

Well, they used to call it the capital of Wales at one time, because Cardiff's such a long way off. What d'you say?'

Albert had laughed. 'I'll think about it,' he had promised, and now, as sleep claimed him, he saw himself dressed in Tyrolean shorts and a perky hat with a feather, dancing up Heyworth Street, singing and playing a musical instrument. Even in his dream he laughed at the absurdity of it, but then he was on Rhyl beach once more, paddling at the water's edge and shouting out to Mrs Edie Williams that she was the prettiest woman on the coach and he was a lucky fellow to have her company.

Chapter Four

By the time Tess had been at the farm for ten days she had slipped thoroughly into the way of things. Because the only other worker was an old man of seventy-five, who prefaced most of his remarks with a grumble about the lack of proper assistance, Jonty and Tess found they were supposed to be in several places at once, and had almost no time to themselves. Tess was thankful that the majority of the fruit in the orchard close to the house would not be ripe until after she had left, but even so there was a deal of work to be done. The field known as the hazel pasture, because it was hedged on one side with well-grown hazels, now contained a number of pigs and small shelters into which the sows could just about cram themselves along with their squealing, fighting progeny. The only boar, Crippen, was now the sole occupant of the big brick-built pigsty up against the house, and since he had an uncertain temper Jonty and Tess steered well clear of the enormous creature, leaving Mr and Mrs Bell and old Adam to deal with him. The original plan had been to take Crippen to the sows when they were ready for mating, but because of his evil temper they now took the sows to Crippen, and though an unpopular beast he fathered huge litters of piglets and so was unlikely to be sold on, though Jonty frequently suggested it.

Despite the fact that it was August, the weather was uncertain. The days were hot and sunny but at night as one slept – or tried to sleep – upstairs the heat was unbearable, and when on one particular night Tess heard the thunder rumbling ever nearer she was conscious of a strong desire that the storm would break, preferably overhead, so that cooling rain might fall.

Lying there in the dark, her nightie long since cast off, she heard Jonty getting up and padding across to his window in the room next door. Hastily she pulled on her skimpy nightgown and went to her own window, for by leaning out of the casements they could converse comfortably, which, when it was too hot to sleep, they frequently did. Now, as she poked head and shoulders out into the night, she saw Jonty doing the same and drew his attention with a little whistle. He turned to face her and grinned, his face shiny with sweat, his hair dark with it. 'Hiya, Tess,' he whispered. 'Bloody hot, isn't it?' His mother disapproved of night-time conversations, seeming to think that because both parties were in their nightclothes it might be considered improper. She had tried to forbid what she clearly considered to be an indelicate practice, so now Jonty and Tess kept their voices down while they enjoyed their midnight chats.

'Yes. I think it's the worst so far,' Tess said. 'But I wouldn't be surprised if that storm you can just hear rumbling away came in our direction. If it brings really heavy rain . . . but perhaps it won't.'

'Well, I can't sleep, so I'm going to get up,' Jonty muttered. 'The horses don't like a really bad storm. Rufus and Biddy tend to go right up to the trees at the far end of their pasture. They probably think they'll be safer up

80

there, but of course they're wrong. If you come with me we can get them down to the stable before the thunder panics them into rushing right up the hill and into the fringe of the wood. Are you on?'

Tess looked wistfully at her bed; it had been a hard day, what with bringing all the new stock into the yard so that the Ministry vet could inject them, on top of all their other work, and they had been on the go until nine o'clock or so. She was extremely tired, but she knew she wouldn't sleep whilst the stifling heat remained, so she agreed that she would dress and give him a hand. Since she did not have to wash or brush her hair she was downstairs in the kitchen in ten minutes, finding both Jonty and his father ahead of her, and the thunder growing closer every minute. She had not noticed the wind when she had stuck her head out of the bedroom window, but when she and the two men stepped into the yard a gust almost knocked her down. Jonty linked his arm in hers and began to pull her towards the five acre, but Mr Bell grabbed his son's arm. 'Look at that,' he shouted disbelievingly. 'That's what they call a tornado – a twister, some say . . . my God, look at my wheat!'

The youngsters stared, and Tess at any rate was appalled. The wheat looked as though someone had driven an enormous tractor round and round, flattening three-quarters of the crop and leaving the rest bent and broken, and the wind had not done with them yet, for it seized the poultry house and dashed it against a stand of trees. Terrified hens found their home in splinters and themselves in unwanted flight, until the wind dropped them as casually as a man might discard a cigarette butt. Then the noise began in earnest. The thunder was directly overhead now and rain was coming down in huge drops, straight as arrows, and nearly as dangerous. From the clouds overhead lightning forks jabbed to earth whilst every now and again sheet lightning arced from cloud to cloud, illuminating the scene as brightly as day, every flash accompanied by a clap of thunder so loud that Tess put her hands over her ears, trying to shut out the appalling din.

'Come to the ponies,' Jonty bawled, but his father shook his head violently.

'No, don't go near 'em. They'll be mad with fear,' he bellowed. 'They'll run you down without even knowing it. If you leave 'em they'll quiet when the storm passes.' He laughed suddenly and pointed. 'If they see that they'll run a mile without stopping, same as I would.'

'That' was one of his wife's voluminous cotton nightgowns. It had been pegged to the line but had fought like a mad thing to get free and was now flapping away across the meadows like some gigantic ghost. Had the ponies not already been panicked by the storm they would most certainly have taken against what must have appeared to them to be a living nightmare. 'If we can't quiet the ponies then what should we do?' Tess shouted against the wind. 'I don't think we can collect the hens, they really are at the mercy of the wind. Once it drops we can shut them in the stables, but until then we'll have to rely on their common sense.'

Jonty was beginning to say that everyone knew hens didn't have any common sense when, in the way of such things, the rain changed from vicious spears to a more normal downpour and that in turn stopped suddenly and allowed cooler air to take its place. Mr Bell sighed and Jonty put his arm round Tess's waist. 'We'd best get back to the house, 'cos there's nothing we can do here in the dark,' he said resignedly. 'With a bit of luck we'll get some sleep before Ma comes rattling on our doors, reminding us that breakfast will be ready in twenty minutes.'

The three of them crossed the yard and re-entered the kitchen, only to find Mrs Bell setting out a large plate of bacon sandwiches and a jug of cocoa on the big scrubbed table. 'You'll need to be up betimes judging from what I've seen through the window,' she said gruffly. 'You'll want to get some sleep, though, and most folks sleep better on a full stomach than on an empty one, so get this lot down you or it'll be breakfast time before you know it.'

As Tess finished her sandwich and drained her cocoa, she wondered what on earth they would do about the wheat. She supposed that some of the crop might be saved but guessed that a good deal of it would have to be ploughed in, since it would be too muddy and broken for cutting. It was an awful shame and would make the Bells' life, which was a hard one at the best of times, even harder, but though they grumbled and called down curses on the weather farmers were used to catastrophic conditions, and she supposed that they had savings against such happenings. As she made her weary way back to bed, she reflected, not for the first time, that the Bells had done pretty well out of her. She had worked as hard as she could at every task she'd been given and though Jonty, she knew, had implored his mother to pay her at least some of the wage which would have gone to Patty, the land girl, Mrs Bell had been resolute in her refusal. Tess, in the scullery cleaning vegetables for market, had heard her reply to Jonty's plea. 'She's not here to work, she's here to have a bit of a holiday,' she assured her son. 'Many a gal would be grateful for our hospitality. And she eats hearty; almost licked her plate when we had that stew the other night. Oh aye, young Tess should have no complaints about the way she's treated. And it's not as though she was a woman grown and capable of doing a woman's work—'

But at this point Jonty had broken in. 'She works just as hard as Patty did, and a good deal harder than Adam,' he had said angrily. 'And in your heart you know it. If she were to leave tomorrow we'd be in dead trouble and so I'm telling you.'

But his mother refused to be convinced. 'She do very well out of us,' she repeated obstinately. 'And now let's hear no more, Jonty. No one's ever accused me of acting unfair or bein' mean, and I won't have you sayin' such things.'

Tess, shaking caterpillars out of the cabbage, had grinned to herself. She knew a great many girls who would have been horrified had someone asked them to work as hard as she had been doing without a wage, but she was not one of them. It would have been nice had Mrs Bell handed over a few bob at the end of the week, but because they had bought the farm next door she appreciated that money was tight, or tighter than usual at any rate. So when she went downstairs on the day after the storm she expected to be given a great many jobs, but hoped she and Jonty might have the evening free to see the cinema show in the village hall.

Mr Bell was working with Adam, milking the cows,

so it was only her, Mrs Bell and Jonty who sat down to the usual farm breakfast of homemade sausages, eggs and fried bread. Tess thought Mrs Bell seemed somewhat uneasy, and presently realised why, when her hostess cleared her throat and began to speak.

'Well, Tess my dear, you couldn't have come to stay at a worse time, what with storms, and that there twister thing a-ruinin' of the wheat crop. You and Jonty will be busy today, because the poultry will have to be rounded up and a great deal of repair work put in hand. Father and I took a look round, what he called "assessing the damage", and it's plain he and Adam will be busy remakin' the poultry run, mendin' fences an' seein' to any injured stock. That means you and Jonty here will have to fetch in the hens and recapture any pigs what have broke out of their field last night, to say nothin' of makin' sure all the cattle are properly fenced in and not runnin' wild across the marshes.' She smiled ingratiatingly at Tess. 'But once that's done you can have the rest of the day to yourselves to go into the village and meet your old friends.'

Jonty snorted. 'Some time we'll have free after doin' that little lot,' he said bitterly. 'Mebbe the poultry will come back when we take their food out to them, but pigs can be that contrary I reckon it'll be a week before we've got them all back in the hazel pasture. Tell you what, Ma, have you forgotten the cinema show is due to come to the village hall today? If you give us our ticket money and a bit extra for cushies – it's nice to have somethin' to suck when you're watching a fillum, and I've got some coupons over – we can have at least one afternoon off.'

Mrs Bell looked rather startled, then nodded reluctantly.

85

'All right, I'll give you the money, though it'll be a miracle if they're still able to come to the village after that storm. But you'll have to round up the stock first, else them pigs will be fields away or floatin' in the cut dead as bacon. Come to think, if they get as far as the Broad and try to swim across it they'll cut their own throats; 'tis a well-known fact that pigs cut their throats when they try to swim, and how'll you feel then? So you be a good lad, Jonty, and start bringin' the beasts home as soon as you've ate your grub.'

Jonty began to protest, but Tess broke in.

'We'll do whatever we can and talk about going to the pictures later,' she said tactfully. 'Come on, Jonty; let's start by getting the poultry back. We can put them in the tack room tonight because I don't reckon Mr Bell will have found a new poultry shed. Just remember that the storm hit everyone alike; I bet there's not an unwanted poultry house in the whole of the county of Norfolk.'

So presently she and Jonty, each carrying a bucket full of a mixture of meal, water and cooked vegetable peelings, emerged into the yard and began making the familiar clucking cry which the hens knew well. Almost immediately, and giving loud, delighted squawks, both hens and ducks came from every quarter of the compass, homing in on the farmyard and beginning to gobble the food which Tess and Jonty dispensed with a prodigal hand. 'There's too many to count, so I've no idea whether they're all here,' Jonty said, emptying the last of the food on to the cobbles. 'No use in shutting them into the tack room in broad daylight, but we'd best get a couple of straw bales from the stack and spread them out over the floor ready for tonight. I know hens prefer to perch and

86

perhaps Dad'll put some poles across the far end, but if he doesn't have time they'll have to roost on the floor, and to be honest, I reckon they'll be safer there than perching in the trees. I say, did you notice the grass in the orchard? There's more windfalls down than you'd believe possible.'

Tess had noticed. 'I expect when we've got all the pigs back into the hazel pasture, checked the cattle and made a note of all the broken fencing, uprooted hedges and stuff blown into the canal – I mean the cut – we'll be sent to collect them, so that your mam can bottle or preserve any which aren't too badly damaged,' she said rather wearily. 'Thank God Crippen wasn't out with his numerous wives last night, but shut securely in his sty. I wouldn't fancy arguing with him if he decided he didn't want to go back into captivity.'

'Nor me,' Jonty said with feeling. They reached the hazel pasture and saw, with considerable relief, that the pigs were all present, though almost every one of the little wigwam-like shelters of which the Bells had been so proud was no longer usable. They went into the field to check, and having provided themselves with buckets of pigs' swill were able to count the animals as they came greedily to the troughs. These were undamaged, but as they left the field once more Tess was dismayed to find a number of day-old chicks trodden into the mud, and very dead indeed. She began to pick up the little corpses, unable to prevent a trembling lip, a most unfarmerly approach, and when Jonty told her to put the chicks down so that the pigs could eat them she turned on him, telling him he was heartless and that some life might be left in one or two of the little balls of yellow fluff.

'Don't be daft. They're dead as doornails – deader, in fact,' Jonty said. 'And so are those kittens. Do leave them, Tess, it'll only upset you . . .'

'Oh, but surely the pigs won't eat dead kittens?' Tess said, horrified, gazing pitifully at two little corpses she had overlooked before. 'Where's their mother? And why on earth did she let them leave the stable? They're too young to wander off by themselves . . . Oh, look, that white one isn't dead at all! I saw its little head move!' She knelt down in the mud and managed, not without difficulty, to extract the white kitten and then the tabby, but Jonty shook his head at her.

'If Tibbs is dead then they'd be better off dead too,' he observed. 'Their eyes aren't properly open yet and they need their mother's milk. Oh, Tess, don't go scratchin' round for the rest of the litter. God knows how they got all the way from the stable, but I'm sure the other six will still be in Sheba's manger, and safe as houses. Probably Tibbs took fright at the storm and imagined she was carryin' these two to safety. She wouldn't have known better; she's only a young cat, mebbe no more than two or three years old, and I'm sure she's never seen a storm like the one last night.' He peered hopefully at Tess as they let themselves out through the gate and headed for the stable. 'Look, if you're determined to try and save those kittens you'd best wash the mud off them before you put them back in the manger.'

Tess stared at him. 'Wash the mud off them?' she squeaked. 'How can you be so stupid, Jonty Bell? After all they've suffered, cold water would be the final straw. I'm taking them into the kitchen. I'm sure your mother will find up a nice dry piece of blanket and an old shoe

88

box for them. They can lie in front of the fire until the mud has dried. Then it can be brushed off and they can go back to their nest in the manger.'

Jonty heaved a sigh. 'At least you're learning that farming isn't all picking apples, riding ponies and collecting eggs under beautiful blue skies,' he said resignedly. 'Poor old Tess! Look, you go into the kitchen and I'll check that Tibbs and the other kittens are all okay.'

But this Tess refused to do, saying that she would accompany him to the stable first to make sure that the kittens had a mother to go to. She could imagine that Mrs Bell would not be at all pleased if she found her son and her temporary helper spending all their time spoon-feeding two tiny kittens, who might not survive their ghastly ordeal no matter how zealously they were nursed. They entered the stable to find it unusually light, because tiles had blown off the roof. And once they were in Sheba's stall Tess realised at once why Tibbs had fled. Two of the big heavy tiles had plunged straight into the manger in which she and her kittens had lain. It had killed two of the little things outright, but four still remained, and as Tess bent over the manager Tibbs looked up hopefully, uttering a plaintive little meow which said as clearly as any words: 'Oh, I'm so glad to see you. Please take care of me and my babies!'

Without a word Jonty seized Tibbs and two of the kittens and Tess took the other two in her free hand. Then they marched across to the farmhouse. Mr and Mrs Bell were both in the kitchen, and Tess waited for an explosion of wrath from one or other when they realised that she and Jonty were bringing them more work and not less. But she wronged them. Mrs Bell grabbed a basket and lined it with a piece of dry towelling, then took the cat and her kittens and placed them in it. Then she shook her head over the state of the little creatures Tess had been holding. 'They're in a poor way, the little rats,' she murmured. 'What ha' come to them?'

'We don't know; these two were in the mud in the hazel pasture, quite near the gate,' Tess said tremulously. 'We thought they were dead at first, but then the white one seemed to be trying to move his head and the tabby opened one eye.'

Mrs Bell looked up from her contemplation of the basket of kittens. 'Where's the other two?' she demanded. 'I'd be ready to swear Tibbs had eight, and there's only six here.'

Tess explained sadly that the other two had been killed by falling roof tiles.

Mr Bell came over and examined the kittens curiously, and even as he did so the warmth seemed to have its effect and the white kitten gave an enormous yawn and then began the weaving motion of the head which indi-cated that it was hungry and searching for Tibbs's nipple. The farmer laughed. 'They'll do,' he said. 'You've done well. Tibbs have good kittens and they'll go to good homes. But what news of the in-pig gilts? Any of 'em aborted? It do happen if a storm terrifies a critter.'

'We didn't see any dead piglets, and we had a good look round,' Jonty said at once. 'What about the horses and the cattle, Dad? And I'm afraid the day-old chicks took a battering. There's a deal of dead ones, trod into the mud by the hazel pasture. And none of the hens brought chicks with them when they came running for the food.'

His mother shook her head chidingly at him. 'And you a farmer's son!' she said reprovingly. 'A broody hen won't leave her nest no matter if the world were come to an end, and one with chicks is the same. Nor they won't come for food; you have to go to them. So out wi' you, young Jonty, and look in ditches, haystacks, any outbuildings what are still standin', and listen, because a happy hen make a croodlin' noise.' She turned to Tess and her rather dour face softened into a smile. 'I reckon you've had enough for one day, my dear. Jonty's quite capable of finding the broodies if you'd like to stay in the kitchen and have a nice cup of tea and a fresh baked scone.'

'Oh, no thanks, Mrs Bell. I know very well what to do with broodies, and if Jonty and I search separately then we can be through in half the time,' Tess said. 'Is there anything else we ought to do whilst we're outside? Only I think we ought to hurry, because I believe it's starting to rain again.'

They were halfway to the door when Jonty was suddenly struck by a recollection. 'Ma, if we spend hours searching for the broodies we'll never get to the cinema show,' he wailed. 'And it's only here for one day, you know it is, and they're showin' *Jungle Woman*, which I missed first time round. If we're not finished in time for the matinée performance, we may not get in for the evening show because that's always very popular. We don't mind missing our dinner, do we, Tess? Can't you and Dad find the broodies? Or Adam, if he's not busy?'

Mrs Bell did not reply, but Mr Bell spoke up. 'Tell you what, if you find the broodies and finish off the yard work say by five o'clock, I'll get the car out and run you into the village in good time for the evening performance. How'll that suit you?'

Tess stared. Not only was petrol still both rationed and in short supply, but Mr Bell treated the car like a much-loved elderly relative and seldom took it out of its shed, save once a week to fetch supplies. But she and Jonty rushed to the back door, delighted at the prospect of a lift into the village, and were soon combing likely hiding places, finding not only broodies but mother hens with a dozen or so chicks cuddled safely beneath their wings.

By five o'clock the yard work was finished and the cattle and horses had been checked to make sure that none had strayed. Jonty and Tess returned to the house, where they changed into clean clothing, gulped down a cup of tea and were given money for the cinema show. Then they hurried out to the car, bickered briefly over who was to have the front seat – Tess won – and were soon agreeing to meet Mr Bell outside the village hall when the picture show was over.

On their arrival Tess and Jonty were immediately surrounded by friends, eager to discuss the dreadful results of the storm, but as soon as the doors opened and Miss Fletcher, who ran the committee in charge of the hall, began to take the money the storm was forgotten in a wild rush to get into the hall so that the youngsters might sit with their friends and not get 'hemmed in' by the older members of the audience.

Tessa knew the mobile cinema was highly prized by all the villages upon which it called. The films were usually old but no less popular for that, and were on two large reels, so that when the first reel came to an end there was an interval whilst the second reel was fitted into position, during which entertainment was provided. Tess would have preferred to chat, for she and Jonty had managed to occupy seats amongst most of their old friends, but then Mr Lyons, the projectionist, who also chose the films, called for silence and his sister, a very large lady indeed, came on to the stage and stood leaning against the piano which another member of the Lyons family played. The talk faded to quiet whispers and Miss Lyons announced that she would sing an old favourite. The pianist struck up, Miss Lyons opened a cavernous mouth and one of the village boys commented to his neighbour that they'd be lucky if Miss Lyons's weight did not cause the piano to career across the stage and crash into the audience. For some reason this remark caught the fancy of those who heard it, some of whom began to snigger. As is the way of such things the sniggerers' neighbours began to laugh, quietly at first but then more and more loudly, until the whole hall was helpless with mirth. In vain did the pianist jump to his feet and demand silence, in vain did Mr Lyons threaten that they should never see the second reel. Had it not been for old Mr Larkin clambering on to the stage to call everyone to order as Miss Lyons fled from it in tears, it is doubtful whether the Lyons Mobile Cinema would ever have visited the village hall again. As it was, practically every member of the audience apologised, begged pardon and explained that the laughter had not been caused by Miss Lyons's singing and was simply a sort of mass hysteria in which one person's mirth – prompted by something completely unrelated to what was going on on the stage, naturally – had set the entire audience giggling. The adult members of the audience put their

93

heads together and had a whip-round and old Mrs Bailey, who ran the village shop, produced from some hidden corner a box of chocolates which, judging from the picture on the lid, was probably pre-war stock, but, as Jonty pointed out, it was the gesture which counted. Miss Fletcher presented the chocolates to Miss Lyons, along with many apologies, and the audience settled back to enjoy the second reel of *Jungle Woman*.

At the end of the film the audience got to their feet, and Jonty grabbed Tess's hand. 'The last bus has gone, and Dad won't realise that the interval was about three times as long as usual,' he reminded her. 'I don't much fancy a five-mile walk; what'll we do if he's gone home without us?'

Tess stared at him, eyes rounding with dismay. They had had little sleep the night before, followed by an exhausting day, and the thought of having to walk five miles, possibly in the rain if the weather had not improved, was not a pleasant one. But Jonty, seeing her dismay, gave a crow of triumph. 'Gotcha!' he said. 'You can't believe my dad would let us down! He'd soon realise that the picture was taking longer than it should have done and he'd wait, even if we were an hour over our time.'

Tess laughed as they emerged from the stuffy interior of the village hall into the roadway and saw the old bull-nose Morris, with Mr Bell at the wheel, waiting for them. 'I didn't really think he'd leave us in the lurch,' she protested. 'But you know him much better than I do.' She punched Jonty hard in the ribs and smiled as the air woofed out of his lungs. 'Serve you right, Jonty Bell, for trying to scare me!'

The ride home in the car was enlivened by an exact recital of everything that had happened during the interval, even the memory of it setting both Tess and Jonty off giggling once more. Mr Bell smiled but said he just hoped Mr Lyons would not punish the entire village by taking them off his list of visits. Then, as they drove along the country lanes towards Bell Farm, he told them how he had passed the extra time. 'Bob Tillett and Sam Hornigold were waiting for their kids to come out of the village hall too,' he said. 'We had a good old mardle about that there storm and what it had done to the land. We were lucky, you know. Bob lost two fields of barley as well as a couple of cows. His skiff on the Broad sank too, but he reckon he'll bring it up when he and his farmhands have got the time. Sam, on the other hand, is still searching for two of his store cattle what got through a hole the storm had torn in his hedge and made off the Lord know where. Still, as we told each other, it was a freak storm and unlikely to occur again.'

The rest of the drive was filled by Jonty telling his father the story of *Jungle Woman*, so that by the time they reached the farm Tess was quite startled to drive into the yard and see a gap where the henhouse had been, and the stable door swinging loose, for Mr Bell had decreed that the horses were safer out in the field than shut into a stable which had had a large section of its roof blown away.

As they ate their biscuits and drank their cocoa before going up to bed, Mrs Bell took Tess to one side and thanked her for all the hard work she had done that day. 'You're a grand little worker; I just wish the gal Maggie was more like you,' she said. 'But there you are, Maggie's

95

always been ambitious and she know the farm will go to our Jonty when Father and I pass on, so it's up to her to make a life for herself.' She smiled down at Tess with more kindness than she had ever shown before. 'Goodnight, gal. I'll let you lie in a bit tomorrer. I reckon you deserve it.'

A week after the storm had passed over Tess awoke feeling a mixture of pleasure that she would soon be going home and sadness at leaving Bell Farm. But today was to be a holiday. Because they had managed to put right most of the storm damage, Mr Bell had announced that they would take a picnic and go down to the coast so that Jonty and Tess might have an outing before Tess left them. 'A day away from the farm will do us all good,' he told her firmly. 'Adam's coming in early and Jonty's Uncle Keith is drivin' over to keep an eye on things while we're away.' He had turned to his wife, for they had been in the kitchen, about to sit down to their evening meal. 'Will that suit you, my woman? I'm sure you deserve a bit of a holiday same as these youngsters do.'

Mrs Bell had smiled. 'That will do us all good,' she declared. 'I'll pack a basket with good things and we'll spend the whole day on the beach.' She had looked at Tess. 'How do that appeal to you, my dear? I remember checking you could swim when you first came, because being so near the Broad we couldn't have taken you else.'

'Oh, I can swim all right,' Tess had said excitedly. 'But I don't have a swimming costume . . .'

Mrs Bell had looked smug. 'I've two or three of Maggie's old ones upstairs; one of 'em's bound to fit

96

you,' she had assured Tess. 'I'll look them out and you can try them for size. Let's hope the weather stay fair.'

That had been several days earlier, for a whole day away from the farm had taken some planning, and now at last the day itself had arrived. Tess got out of bed and went over to the window to pull back the curtains. It was another brilliant day, but there was a sultriness in the air even at this early hour and Tess thought uneasily that that sort of heaviness presaged thunder. How unfortunate it would be if their one and only day out was ruined by bad weather! But she washed hastily, dressed in her coolest cotton frock and clattered down the stairs, narrowly beating Jonty. The kitchen was very hot, despite Mrs Bell's having flung all the windows wide, but it was clear that the farmer's wife intended the day to be a good one for there were two baskets set out on the table already well supplied with quantities of Mrs Bell's delicious cooking, as well as two mammoth flasks of tea and a paper bag fairly bursting with ripe plums.

Breakfast was a jolly meal, with old Adam and Uncle Keith promising that everything would be done as though the Bells were actually present. Keith was Mrs Bell's elder brother, a grey-haired middle-aged man who ran the local auction and lived with his wife Mabel in a neat little house in a nearby town. He had farmed before the war, but had sold up during the Depression, and was always willing to help out when his sister needed assistance.

Everyone ate as fast as they could in order that the family might get away, and the minute they had finished Mr Bell began to hustle them out to the car, not allowing

Tess to start on the washing up when she tried to do so. 'When I say a holiday, I mean a whole day,' he assured her. 'So hop into the car, young woman, and no argufying.' Tess was happy to do so, and as the car left the farm behind Mrs Bell announced that they should have a tune. Tess had never heard her hostess sing before and was astonished by the power and sweetness of her voice, but soon the men and Tess herself were joining in as loudly as they could. By the time they reached the shore they had run through a repertoire of most of the popular songs of the day, ending up with 'Five Minutes More' by Frank Sinatra. They were still singing it, or perhaps belting it out would be more truthful, when Mr Bell drew the car to a halt alongside the beach of his choice. This particular part of the shore had never been mined because it was deemed impossible for an invasion force to come ashore here, but it was, as usual, deserted, so the group settled themselves in the shade of a dune, only a few feet from the little waves, and Mr Bell produced a couple of big stripy umbrellas. He then revealed that he was wearing his swimming costume under his clothes, which astonished Tess. He had told her he had learned to swim as a boy, but she could not imagine him doing so and was quite relieved when Mrs Bell said, primly, that she herself must be content with a paddle, for the only costume she had ever owned had been outgrown years since.

Tess was amused when Mr Bell began to manoeuvre the umbrellas into an odd sort of changing room, for since he was already wearing his costume there seemed little need for such modesty, but as she and Jonty ran down to the sea to test the water Jonty told her that his father was very shy. 'And wait till you see his costume; Ma knitted it for him the first time they took Maggie and me to the seaside. Before the war, it was,' he explained. 'Do you know what wool does when it gets wet?'

'Dunno; my costume isn't made of wool,' Tess said, as they splashed into the shallows. 'Tell me!'

Jonty chuckled. 'It gets long and droopy. Dad wears a belt so his trunks won't fall off, but they look pretty horrible, I can tell you. I suggested he might buy a proper pair but he says it'd be a waste of money 'cos we only go to the seaside a couple of times a year and no one sees him when he goes for a dip in the Broad.'

Mrs Bell had decreed that they should eat their picnic as soon as she had set it out, and would not allow bathing until an hour after the food was eaten. Tess assured her that she had never heard of anyone drowning from cramp, but her hostess was firm, so as soon as Mrs Bell's preparations were complete Tess and Jonty charged back up the beach and flopped on to the sand to devour their lunch. The heat was such that they quite pitied Mrs Bell, the only one who would not be able to bathe, but once the remains of the picnic were tidied away she accompanied them down to the shore and wandered along it, tucking her skirt into her bloomers so that she could go in up to her knees. Jonty and Tess were both strong swimmers, but Tess was astonished at Mr Bell's prowess. She could manage a creditable side stroke but her attempts at a crawl were pretty poor, so when they began to compete, swimming between the breakwaters, Mr Bell was usually the victor, though Jonty was never more than a couple of feet behind him. After frolicking in the waves for well over an hour, they returned to their encampment among the dunes and lay down, meaning to have a little rest, but to Tess's astonishment she fell instantly asleep. When she awoke it was to find that the farmer's wife had moved the umbrellas as the sun moved round. 'Otherwise you'd find yourself with a nasty case of sunburn,' she told her young guest. 'Now, I brought a couple of bottles of my homemade lemonade and some of them scones you and Jonty are so fond of. Want them now? If so you can't bathe again for another hour.'

By the time the last of the picnic food was eaten and packed away it was four o'clock, and the heat did not seem to have lessened. In fact, when they piled into the car, hot, salty and well content with their day out, it actually seemed to be hotter than ever. The very air burned, and as they drove through the countryside Tess drew Jonty's attention to a heavy black bank of cloud approaching them quite rapidly, and turning the blue of the sea to as forbidding a grey as that of the clouds themselves. Mr Bell heard the uneasy murmurs in the back of the car and glanced in his mirror. He had put the hood down before they set out so that they might enjoy the breeze of their going, but now he slowed the car and drew in to the side of the road. 'That look like rain,' he said prosaically. 'Best get the hood up.' The words were hardly out of his mouth before the wind, which had been non-existent, suddenly began to toss the tree under which they had parked. Jonty, Mr Bell and Tess all got out of the car, and though it had not seemed necessary at first it soon became clear that the combined strength of the whole party might be needed to get the hood into position. Indeed, they had just fastened the last stay when the gale arrived, ripping part of the canvas and causing Mr Bell to shout to Jonty to hold it on.

Too late. Mr Bell had engaged first gear and begun to pull out into the road again when, with a shriek and a howl, the gale seized the hood and ripped it from its moorings. Like some gigantic bat it flapped away, first taking the line of least resistance along the road but then seeming to decide that it preferred the open fields. It leapt the hedge and was momentarily lost to view behind a stand of trees. Mr Bell jammed on the brake and drew on to the verge once more whilst his wife wailed that they would never see the hood again and might as well go home before the wind did more damage. But Mr Bell ignored her. 'Come on, you two,' he shouted. 'I can't afford to lose that there hood. Jonty, you and Tess go to the right of them trees and I'll go to the left. First one to spot it give a holler.'

Tess obeyed, though she thought they had little hope of recovering the hood, but fortunately she had not allowed for the effect of the trees and she and Jonty cheered simultaneously as they entered the little wood and saw a gigantic, bat-like creature lying at the foot of a pine tree, looking so pathetic, as though its bid for freedom had been cruelly curtailed, that Tess found herself murmuring words of comfort as she and Jonty, having shouted the news of the capture to Mr Bell, began to pick up the great dusty object. Then they returned to the car, taking their places on the back seat and laying the hood across their laps. Mr Bell was last back, and as he came he had a hand pressed to his forehead and was looking pale and shaken. 'Ran into a low branch,' he mumbled. 'Gave my head one hell of a whack.' He wrenched the

101

door open and almost collapsed into the driver's seat, then turned to his wife. 'You've always wanted to have a go at driving,' he said in a slurred voice. 'Now's your chance. I'm seein' double . . .'

'Oh, Dad, hadn't I better do it? I've driven a tractor—' Jonty began, only to be firmly overruled by his mother.

'Nonsense!' she said briskly. 'When we was first wed I took the wheel from time to time; reckon I can still remember how. Now get you out of that seat, bor! Jonty and Tess will give you a hand round t'other side. But let's have a look at your head first. Then I'll know whether to make for the farm or the hospital.'

As she spoke she leaned over and took her husband's hand away from his forehead, revealing a lump the size of a hen's egg with a deepish cut running across it.

Tess gasped, but Jonty shook a reproving head at her. 'Dad's pretty tough; I don't reckon he'll need the hospital. If Ma washes the blood off and puts some iodine on it he'll be fine,' he said cheerfully. 'Come on, Tess, let's get Dad into the passenger seat and see how Ma manages.'

Tess was doubtful, for in all the time she had known the family Mrs Bell had seldom, if ever, taken the lead in any project. She was sure that her hostess had no idea how to work the gears, for instance, but in the event she was proved wrong. To be sure, for the first half-mile or so the Morris hopped along more like a kangaroo than a car, with its engine roaring one minute and faltering the next, but presently Mrs Bell managed to get into second and then third gear, and despite the gale they reached the lane which led to Bell Farm just as hail began to fall so fiercely that Mr Bell told his wife to stop the car. 'You can't drive in this,' he told her as huge pieces of ice the size of tennis balls continued to rain down on them. 'You've done well, my woman, but 'tis time I took over.'

Tess expected Mrs Bell to object, to point out that since she had got so far she might as well carry on, but as more and more of the huge lumps of ice descended from the ominous black clouds it became clear that the farmer's wife was no keener to continue to drive than her husband was to let her. Instead she left the driving seat just as her husband reached the door, and the two changed places. The engine was still running, so Mr Bell only had to wait until his wife had slammed the passenger door before he put the car in gear and it moved gingerly forward. Tess and Jonty had reacted to the hail in the only sensible way they could: they had dived under the heavy canvas hood, raising it so that they could see ahead of them without leaving its shelter. 'Well, folks say it's been a queer old summer, but I've never seen hailstones this size before,' Jonty murmured as one bounced on his head. 'Any crop left standing will be flattened by this little lot.' He jerked upright suddenly, and Tess saw his eyes widen with dismay. 'The horses! They'll be half mad with terror!' He leaned forward and addressed his father. 'Dad, the horses! It ain't only Rufus and Biddy – the carthorses is out as well. Can you drive straight to the five acre so's we can make sure they're all right?' By now, however, Mr Bell was swinging the car off the lane and into the farmyard, and he shook his head decisively.

'No point,' he said briefly. 'Knowing Solomon and Sheba they'll have backed up against the big haystack, which will shelter them from the worst. I'm more concerned with getting the car into its shed before—'

He stopped speaking as a hailstone even larger than the rest made a huge dent in the car's bonnet, and Tess was not surprised when the engine died. Mrs Bell jumped out of her seat, moving more quickly than Tess had ever seen her, and by the time Tess herself and Jonty had emerged from under the hood and got themselves out of the car Mr Bell, head lowered against the onslaught of those unbelievable hailstones, was ushering Mrs Bell towards the kitchen door. Over his shoulder he shouted at his son. 'Don't open the tack room door, or the poultry will likely rush out and get themselves killed. There int much we can do about the beasts till the storm's over, so get you into the kitchen.'

Tess was only too glad to obey, for it was almost impossible to see through the hail, and judging from the noise it was doing more damage than she would have believed possible. She could imagine the terror of animals out in the pastures in such a storm, but realised that there was very little anyone could do to help them. They would have to take their chance, and only when the storm had eased would the Bells be able to assess the damage. Accordingly all four of them bolted for the kitchen, where they found Adam and Uncle Keith staring out through the window, almost unable to believe their eyes as the ground grew white with ice.

'You're back, master,' Adam said, grinning at his employer. 'I never sin anythin' like it in all me born days. I doubt there'll be a beast left livin' if this hail continue.'

'Nonsense,' Mr Bell said bracingly. He had clearly recovered from the blow on the head.

'I reckon it's arable farmers what'll suffer the most. Oh, I don't deny you'll mebbe lose one or two of the store cattle, but if the pigs took shelter . . .' Keith said, but Mrs Bell had other things on her mind.

'I reckon the car's had it,' she announced. 'One of them big hailstones – only they's more like bullets – bashed into the bonnet as though it was made of cardboard. And the hood had already gone, torn near in two by the wind. As for the pigs, I doubt the makeshift shelters we knocked up will save them from a battering. Still, we'll do what we can to put things right, as soon as the storm's over. Can you stay on, Keith?'

Her brother pulled a face, but nodded. 'Aye, I'll do what I can,' he promised. 'But while we wait for the weather to ease we might as well have the pie you left for us. Good thing the wind hasn't affected the Aga; the pie's warming in the oven, and the spuds must be nicely cooked by now.' He turned to his nephew. 'You're soaked to the skin, bor. Go you up to your room and change into somethin' dry, and the same goes for the rest of you,' he added. 'No point in courtin' pneumonia.'

By the time they had changed and eaten the meal which Mrs Bell had prepared, the hailstorm had stopped and an uneasy silence seemed to hang over the country-side. Mr Bell had insisted that everyone should eat before even beginning to see to the stock, but as soon as the last mouthful was eaten he pushed back his chair and jerked his head at Adam. 'We'd best see what damage has been done,' he said gruffly. 'Though I dare say we'll find it quicker to make a note of what's unharmed.' He gave a grim little chuckle. 'If we've got away without the new stores stampeding, like they do in cowboy

105

fillums, I reckon we'll be luckier than we deserve.' He shook his head sorrowfully, then winced and put a hand over the neat dressing his wife had applied to his forehead. 'Darn it! How that iodine do sting!' He turned to his wife. 'You stay here, Mother; the rest of us will check the beasts.' He turned to Tess, his smile kindly. 'You stay here if you've a mind, my dear. The four of us should be quite enough . . .'

Adam had already left the kitchen and was crunching over the ice in his big rubber boots when Tess heard him give a startled exclamation. The next moment he burst back into the room, his weathered face paler than usual. 'Crippen's gone!' he shouted. 'He's bust clean out of his sty and there int no sign of him! Oh, master, he'll be in the devil's own temper. Gawd help anyone what crosses his path!'

Everyone except Mrs Bell immediately left the kitchen to examine the sty, not because they did not trust Adam's word, but because the sty was so solid that they could not imagine how the great boar had escaped from it. But escape he had. The door to his pen had been torn clean off its hinges, and of Crippen himself there was no sign. Tess had intended to stay with Mrs Bell, but at the thought of an exciting pig hunt she went back to the kitchen, got her oilskins and returned to the yard. She was amused to see Adam stirring the straw of Crippen's pen as though he suspected that the great beast might have burrowed into it to hide from the storm, but as soon as Mr Bell issued his orders Adam expressed his willingness to join in the search. 'Not that he'll be difficult to find, 'cos he's that big we're scarce likely to overlook him,' he said. 'And knowin' Crippen he'll be in a rare bad mood. In fact it's likelier he'll be huntin' we than we huntin' him.'

Mr Bell turned and glared at the elderly farm worker. 'Go and get a couple of mangel-wurzels down from the loft,' he commanded. 'Crippen's rare fond of 'em, so if we can't persuade him by other means mebbe bribery will do it.' He turned to his brother-in-law. 'I reckon he'll ha' gone to the sows in the hazel pasture. 'Tis only natural to seek the company of your own kind when things go wrong.' He turned to Jonty and Tess. 'You two check on the horses and the cattle down by the cut. Let's hope they're all safe and sound, but cattle panic easy.'

'Right away, Dad,' Jonty said quickly, and Tess, who knew him very well, guessed that he would check the horses first, for of all the farm animals the horses were his favourites. But Mr Bell was still talking.

'And if you catch so much as a glimpse of Crippen make a note of where he is and come and tell Keith, Adam or myself. Likely he'd make mincemeat of you.'

'Oh aye, you're right there, master,' Adam said lugubriously. 'Likely he'll make mincemeat out of us an' all, 'cos that there boar ain't a lover of folk. Once, when I were cleanin' his pen, thinkin' he were shut in the other half of it, mind, he come rushin' out and tried to crush me agin the wall. If I hadn't had a couple of turnips in a bucket for to bribe him, I reckon I'd ha' been a dead man.'

'Yes, yes,' Mr Bell said impatiently, for they had all heard the story of Adam's escape from death by Crippen many times. Indeed, it was the reason why the boar had been christened Crippen, for even as a young pig he had shown definite signs of hostility towards humans.

The search party set out. The two big carthorses came eagerly over from where they had taken shelter in the lee of a small wood, but Rufus and Biddy, wild-eyed and trembling, kept their distance, so Jonty rushed back to the barn to find a couple of turnips and returned waving the food enticingly. The ponies delicately approached, tiptoeing across the field, and Tess saw, with relief, that the hailstones were actually melting quite fast, and guessed that by the following day they would all have gone.

But in the meantime she and Jonty had work to do, and it proved to be hard work, too. One of the store cattle lay dead in the cut, or at least Tess assumed it was dead, until she slithered down the bank and saw that its eyes were open and blinking. Horrified, she and Jonty tried to get it to its feet, but the poor beast expired whilst they were still struggling, so they left the carcass and returned to the farm, where Mr Bell told them that his guess was wrong, or at any rate if Crippen had gone to his sows he was there no longer. Tess guessed that, having won his freedom, Crippen had taken off for pastures new. Unfortunately they could not follow his trail as they would have done normally because the fast-melting ice had left the lane little better than a muddy morass. However, there were two sizeable holes in the hazel hedge which even Tess guessed must be Crippen's entry and exit holes, so it was fairly safe to assume that the great boar would have followed the lane and might not be very far ahead of them. Mr Bell and Adam, who knew the animal best, warned Tess and Jonty to get well out of the way and not to try to intercept Crippen if he decided to return to the familiar farmyard. Adam, nervously clutching a mangel, said that he would try to tempt the creature with the food he most enjoyed, and Mr Bell waved the walking stick which he had seized as they left the farm kitchen and said grimly that he would not hesitate to defend himself should the need arise.

But for half a mile it seemed as though the pig hunt had got off on the wrong foot, for there was no sign of Crippen and they were getting closer to the Broad with every step they took. 'If he get among the bulrushes, he'll likely drown,' Adam said, and Tess could not help noticing that he sounded hopeful. 'It'd mebbe be for the best, master.'

Mr Bell turned a fulminating glare on the old man. 'That boar's worth a deal of money,' he pointed out. 'I don't deny he's got a nasty temper, but we can't afford to lose him. Look at the size of him.'

'I am looking,' Adam said, licking his lips, probably at the memory of Crippen's enormous haunches, Tess supposed. 'He'd cut up real good, would Crippen; there'd be enough bacon on him to last for a year.'

Mr Bell had begun to say that Crippen was worth a lot more alive than dead when they came within sight of the Broad, and Adam gave a triumphant yell. 'There he be, master,' he shouted, pointing ahead of them. 'Look at him, look at him, happy as a pig in muck! But how are we to coax him out of there is more'n I can say.'

Tess, following Adam's pointing finger, could only agree with this sentiment. The boar had made himself a wonderful wallow by crushing down the reeds and bulrushes until he was half submerged in muddy water, and was obviously quite happy to champ on the grass and sedge which came within his reach. In a cowboy film, Tess thought, someone

109

would have produced a lasso, though she pitied anyone holding the business end of such a thing with Crippen at the other. But as it was, Mr Bell began to give his orders. 'Keith, stay well back but prepare to guide him towards the farm if he comes out of that there mud of his own accord. Adam, here's my walkin' stick; you stand guard so he can't go no further up the lane, and give the mangel to Jonty. If the worst come to the worst mebbe a bribe will bring him back to the farm. I'm goin' to fetch the pig net.'

'Oh aye?' Adam said, taking the proffered stick and handing the mangel to Jonty. 'If'n you fetch the pig net you'd best bring the trailer as well, 'cos I don't fancy tryin' to persuade Crippen to walk home all tangled up in the nettin'.'

His employer snorted. 'I'm a-goin' to bring as many turnips, swedes and mangels as I can carry. Once we've netted him out of his wallow we'll bribe him back to his pen. I dare not leave him loose in case he decide to go further into the Broad, but he's a greedy blighter so I reckon temptation may work.' He strode purposefully off up the lane, and the remaining four kept their eyes uneasily on the great animal, who was clearly enjoying himself more than he had done for many long years.

'Does he know we're here?' Tess murmured after twenty minutes. 'If so, he's clearly not in the least worried. And I think he does know, because every now and then I see his wicked little eye peering at me as though to say *Come nearer if you dare*. And he's quite right, because I wouldn't dare. Nothing would make me get any nearer.'

Presently, however, Mr Bell reappeared and began marshalling his troops. Jonty handed the mangel to Tess

110

whilst he, Keith, Adam and Mr Bell took a corner of the pig net each. Adam managed to keep hold of the walking stick and the pig net, while Tess did as she was bidden and kept well back. She watched with considerable apprehension as the four of them crept towards the mud-splattered pig, net at the ready, but they had not got far when Crippen appeared to realise that his freedom was in jeopardy. He lurched to his feet with a horrible squelching sound and began to back out of the mud, his little eyes glinting malevolently and his mouth gaping open to show his excellent tusks.

'Let the net down, boys,' Mr Bell shouted. 'Keep clear of them tusks, Adam. Ah, he's comin' your way. He don't fancy goin' back to his sty now he's got his leg loose! We'll use the net to guide him in the right direction, but keep clear! He'll have us down like ninepins given half a chance.'

For a moment, all was confusion. Crippen's gigantic hindquarters were in the pig net and his massive head was pointing at last in the direction required. But just when Tess thought they were about to win, Crippen turned more quickly than one would have thought possible for an animal his size, and charged straight for poor Adam, dragging the net and the three other men with him. Adam gave a roar of mingled fear and rage. 'This way, master! This way, everyone,' Adam bawled, but even as the words left his lips Crippen, head down and trotters twinkling, shot between Adam's legs and galloped off, carrying the old man with him and heading in the direction of the village.

Tess had heard Adam described as 'a fellow who couldn't stop a pig in a passage', but had never appreciated

111

the truth of it until now. For Adam was bowlegged and Crippen had not only charged between those legs but actually carried Adam for several yards, the old man wielding the walking stick like a lance before sliding over the animal's massive rump to land with a bone-jarring thump on the ground, all tangled up in the pig net and in no very pleasant humour.

Tess, trying to stop laughing, heard him muttering dire threats of what he would do to Crippen when he caught up with him, and admired his courage when he set off in pursuit, grimly dragging the pig net behind him. Jonty was laughing too, and so was Uncle Keith, but Mr Bell had clearly seen no humour in the situation. 'After them!' he shouted, very much in the manner of one of the cinematic heroes Jonty so admired. 'If we let him reach the village . . .'

Everyone immediately sobered, for the amount of damage an outraged boar could do was considerable, and the pig's owner would be responsible.

Tess, seeing the farmer's speed begin to slacken, thought Crippen had beaten them. 'Only I reckon he'll be too tired to wreak havoc as he would have done had he been fresh,' Tess panted, as she and Jonty entered the village. 'Besides, I dare say everyone will be out checking on the damage the hailstones have done and no doubt they'll give a hand to get Crippen back where he belongs.'

This was true, and in fact the only person injured by Crippen's escapade was Tess herself. Unwisely, once he was back in his own pen, she felt quite sorry for him and leaned into the sty to give him the last of the mangels. Far from showing appreciation of her kind act, however, Crippen grabbed it so quickly and wrenched it from her fingers so rudely that within five minutes her wrist was swollen to twice its normal size and was plum-coloured as well. Tess wailed and turned to Jonty for sympathy, but got none. 'I *told* you not to go near him, because he's that ratty he'd bite his best friend if he had one,' Jonty said. 'Oh, Tess, I planned to do all sorts over the next couple of days, because you've worked so hard . . . It hasn't put you off us, has it? You'll still come back next year, won't you?'

This conversation took place after Tess had visited the doctor in the village and been told to wear a sling and to put cold water compresses on her wrist two or three times a day. 'You'll be fine, but don't let Mrs Bell tease you into using that arm,' the doctor had said, clearly well aware of Mrs Bell's propensity to see that everyone around her was doing their bit.

So now Tess pulled a face at her old friend. 'Of course it won't put me off coming again, if I'm invited,' she said. 'But you're to write me long interesting letters, Jonty, and I'll write to you, and we'll telephone each other every two or three months; we'll arrange when by letter.'

Later that day Mrs Bell approached Tess and suggested that she might like to stay on, since they were sadly in need of extra help to undo the damage caused by the hailstorm. 'That's been a terrible summer, first the awful heat and the drought, then the gale, and lastly that there hailstorm,' she said. 'If you'd care to stay on for the last two or three weeks of the school holidays, me and Mr Bell – and Jonty too – would be rare grateful.'

For the first time, Tess thanked providence for her injured wrist. 'It's awfully kind of you, Mrs Bell,' she said meekly. 'But the doctor told me not to use my arm for at least three weeks, maybe longer. So I wouldn't be very much use, even if my grandmother would allow me to extend my – my, er, holiday.'

Mrs Bell sighed. 'Mebbe you're right,' she said resignedly. 'Mind you, if you wanted to stay on for longer and go back to the village school I'd not deny you'd be a grand addition to the workforce—'

But here Tess felt she had to interrupt. 'So you see, it's impossible,' she said, as though the other woman had not spoken. 'But if you still need somebody next summer, I'd be glad to come over for two or three weeks. And now I promised Jonty that I'd see if I can milk with one hand. See you at suppertime, Mrs Bell.'

Leaving the kitchen she went across to where Jonty was working in the milking parlour, half amused and half annoyed by Mrs Bell's assumption that she would be prepared to leave her grandmother in order to work for nothing at a job which was both hard and taxing. But though a part of her was outraged at Mrs Bell's assumption, another part admired the older woman's singleness of purpose. Mrs Bell put the farm before everything else, apart from her family. Had Maggie been as keen to work at Bell Farm as Jonty was, she would have been roped in to do all the jobs that Tess had been coping with and, Tess suspected, would probably have never received a penny. Even during the war when things had been difficult, with labour short and extra paperwork on every side, Tess had been aware that farmers' children were expected to pull their weight on the farm and were rarely paid for their trouble. However, Jonty was receiving a good education because his parents thought it important, and he would never want for anything that the farm profits could provide. School uniform, sports equipment and dinner money would be forthcoming as a matter of course. If he wanted a new record for his Dansette gramophone player – a new possession – he only had to tell his mother how much money he needed and it would be given ungrudgingly, and every Saturday he received sufficient pocket money to pay for his sweet ration.

Tess picked up a milking stool which stood against the cowshed door and went and squatted by Violet, a placid creature who would not object if Tess fumbled to milk her with one wrist bandaged. She saw Jonty turn his head to grin at her, and when he raised his eyebrows and said 'Well?' in an amused voice she realised that he had guessed what his mother wanted to say. She was tempted to admit that she was rather hurt by Mrs Bell's assumption that she would be willing to stay on at Bell Farm, though she had made it plain from the start that she meant to go home to her grandmother as soon as her three weeks were up. But that would only hurt Jonty, for though he might laugh at his mother's tight hold on the purse strings Tess knew he loved her and his father and could never bring himself to criticise them to others.

So she just said: 'Mrs Bell suggested I might stay on for a little longer, but I told her I couldn't. I'm so sorry, Jonty, but I promised Gran . . .'

Jonty stood up, lifted his galvanised bucket of milk clear of Cowslip's rear end – she tended to kick out – and came over to Tess. 'I'm sure she understands that you can't let your gran down,' he said tactfully. 'And I expect she told you you'd be very welcome to come back next year.' He gave her a wicked little grin, raising one eyebrow as he did so, a trick he had been practising in his bedroom mirror ever since seeing Perry Como doing it on Pathé News. 'Especially if you were sensible enough not to sprain your wrist in the meantime.'

Chapter Five

Tess arrived at Lime Street station lugging her suitcase and a large canvas holdall full of good things which Mrs Bell had packed up for her to take home for Gran. 'We never paid you no wage, my woman, money being a bit on the tight side,' she had said as she handed over the bulging bag, 'but I thought as how your gran might be glad of a few eggs and that.' Tess, scrambling into the front seat of the Morris – the damage had not proved as severe as the Bells had feared – had thanked her hostess whole-heartedly, though she thought that the extra luggage would probably prove a great nuisance.

When they reached the station Tess shook hands with Mr Bell and had prepared to do the same with Jonty, but he shook his head. 'Dad's goin' to the feed merchant and I'm stayin' with you until you're aboard your train,' he said, grinning. 'You'll need all the help you can get with carryin' your bags.' He lowered his voice. 'Ma meant it for the best, but by the time you reach Liverpool you'll be cussin' the extra weight. And you'll have to be rare careful 'cos of the eggs.'

'Oh, Jonty, you needn't wait,' Tess protested. 'How are you going to get home? Or is Mr Bell going to come back for you?' she added as the farmer drove off.

Jonty raised his brows and seized the holdall. 'Never

heard of buses?' he asked. 'I can catch the ten o'clock to the village from here. Or I can have a mooch around the city and get the one that leaves at noon. Whichever I get I'll have plenty of time to see the last of you.'

And so it had proved and now Tess, struggling with the suitcase and the canvas holdall, looked round hopefully when she heard a voice hail her as she crossed the concourse.

'Hey, Tess Williams, isn't it? Where are you off to?'

Tess dumped her suitcase and smiled at the fair-haired boy who had addressed her. 'Snowy! What do you mean, where am I going? Home, of course.' She looked hopefully up at him. 'Going to give me a hand with my luggage? To tell you the truth it's a perishin' miracle I've managed to get this far without dropping something.'

Snowy seized her suitcase, smiling broadly. 'All right, all right, so it was the wrong question; I should have said where have you been. Come to think, I've not seen you around since the school holidays started.' He peered at her. 'Go on, where have you been?'

'To Norfolk, to the farm I lived on during the war.' Tess picked up the holdall. 'Are you going in my direction? If so, I'd be grateful if you'd give me a hand.'

Snowy frowned, pretending to consider. 'Well, last time I got you out of trouble you didn't even ask me up to your place for a drink of water,' he pointed out. 'So I'll carry your case, ma'am, if you'll ask me in when we reach Heyworth Street.'

Tess also pretended to consider, then nodded, and they set off. On Lime Street, Snowy jerked a thumb at the queue for taxis and the even longer queue for a tram. 'Which?' he asked. 'Are you goin' to ride like a lady or join the scrum aboard a number thirty-one?'

Tess had not even considered the question since she had spent many hours wedged into stuffy compartments simply longing for a breath of fresh air, so she shook her head. 'Neither. Will you think I'm taking advantage if I say I'd rather walk? Only I've been shut up in frowsty trains since early this morning . . .'

'Suits me,' Snowy said briefly. 'Come on, then, best foot forward. Can you manage that holdall or shall I take that as well as the suitcase?'

Tess shook her head as they set off at a brisk pace. 'No, I can manage it easily,' she assured him. 'Incidentally, what were you doing on the station? It's pretty plain you weren't meeting me because I wasn't able to tell anyone what time my train would arrive. It depended on when Mr Bell's car managed to get us to Norwich Thorpe. Did you have a fearful hailstorm about three days ago? We did, and the Bells' car took a rare beating. One of the hailstones made a huge dent in the bonnet.'

Snowy gave a disbelieving snort. 'Dented the bonnet?' he said incredulously. 'They must have cars made of paper in Norfolk. Pull the other one, kid; it's got bells on.'

'Aha, then it was just a freak hailstorm, and not countrywide,' Tess said wisely. 'But I can prove that I'm speaking the truth when we get back to the flat because I cut out a piece about it from the *Eastern Evening News*. Not that I care whether you believe me or not,' she finished.

Snowy flung up his free hand in a gesture of submission. 'Sorry, sorry,' he said. 'But I've not told you what

I was doing on the station. I was seeing off a cousin of mine who came to stay for a couple of days. She's a rare clever girl and has got a scholarship to a private school somewhere in North Wales. She came over here to get her school uniform . . .'

Tess interrupted. 'Oh, Snowy, I'm so sorry! You must have had your exam results. Did you get good marks?'

'Fancy you remembering,' Snowy said, his tone sarcastic. 'And you not even bothering to say goodbye to me when you went off to Norfolk! But yes, you're quite right, I've got my results and if I do as well in my School Cert next year I'll be taking up a place in the sixth form. What about you? I remember Marilyn saying you were bright.'

Tess stopped short so abruptly that the woman walking behind her cannoned into her. Apologies were exchanged before Tess turned an incredulous face to her companion. 'Marilyn Thomas said I was bright?' she squeaked. 'But she doesn't like me! Oh, I know I haven't been bullied since you started keeping an eye on me, but I can't imagine her ever throwing me a nice word.'

'Well, she did then, if you count her saying that you might get a scholarship,' Snowy said definitely. 'She's all right is Marilyn, but I guess she was jealous of you at first, you being so young and still managing to get to the head of the class. Still, she left school at the end of the summer term and she's working already, so you won't need to worry about her when term starts.'

Tess began to walk once more, looking up at Snowy as they went. 'I bet she's got a super job, with a decent salary,' she said wistfully. 'When I leave school I'll go straight into a job too, because Gran works terribly hard and it's about time I contributed something to our little household. Gran would like me to try for a scholarship but I mean to tell her it's not on. Why, if I got a place at a private school it might be years before I began to earn.'

Snowy nodded. 'I know what you mean,' he admitted. 'I'm an only child and my parents can well afford for me to go on to further education. But for you it's different, and it's different for Marilyn too. Her dad went off in the early days of the war with some young floozy, leaving Mrs Thomas to bring Marilyn up by herself. That's why she took over the corner shop. And it's probably why Marilyn's jealous of you.'

'Jealous? Of me?' Tess said incredulously. 'Why on earth would she be jealous of me? I don't have a mother, though Gran's as good or better than any mother could possibly be. So how can Marilyn be jealous?'

Snowy smiled knowingly. 'Can't you guess? Marilyn would have given a great deal to be able to get a scholarship. She's got a job behind the haberdashery counter at one of the big stores – I'm not sure which – but I believe she despises shop work, or at least shop work on the haberdashery counter. And the salary's nothing to write home about, believe me.'

Tess shrugged. 'Well, I think she's mad,' she said. 'Jobs aren't easy to find and she's so pretty she'll soon be moved from haberdashery into something more interesting. Why, she could be a mannequin and show off beautiful dresses and smart suits. Don't tell me she wouldn't like that!'

Snowy laughed. 'So could you – show off dresses and

suits, I mean – and you've got brains as well,' he pointed out. 'What made you have your hair cut short, when everyone else is wearing it long?'

Tess giggled. 'I don't suppose you've ever read *Anne of Green Gables*,' she said. 'It's a grand story. I read it for the first time before I was evacuated, and because it was my favourite book I took it down to Norfolk with me. It's all about this girl, Anne, who's an orphan and goes to live on a farm run by an elderly couple who had asked for a boy and were very disappointed to get a girl. But Anne is a real little devil, red-haired and freckly, and she decides to dye her hair black. Only something goes wrong and her hair comes out green. So she has to have her head shaved and it regrows a sort of reddy-gold colour and is like a curly cap on her head. So when the hairdresser asked me how I wanted my hair done I said short and crisp, hoping that mine might curl too, only as you can see it didn't work. But I like it and I don't care if it's not fashionable. It's easy to keep tidy and provided I have a trim every four or five weeks it's no trouble at all. Gran likes it too,' she added defiantly.

'So do I,' Snowy said, just as they reached the milliner's shop and the green-painted door which led to Gran's apartment. 'Look, are you sure it'll be all right for me to come up? Only if you'd rather I visited you another day, when you've had a chance to warn your gran . . .'

'Nonsense; we reached an agreement and I know Gran wouldn't want me to break my word,' Tess said. 'Besides, she's at work. But she'll have left me a snack and knowing Gran there'll be plenty for two, so you're very welcome to come up. You can take a look round the flat and if you're very good you can have a read of my copy of *Anne of Green Gables*, though I dare say it'll seem a bit babyish for someone who's recently entered her teens.'

It was not far from Deering's to the flat and Gran set off up Heyworth Street aware of a tingle of excitement. Tess was coming home – in fact she should be home by now – and Gran couldn't wait to hear from her own lips how her holiday had gone. She had written home several times but hadn't said much about how she was enjoying herself, if indeed she was. She had explained that the weather had made everything difficult, but hadn't gone into detail, saying that she would tell Gran all about it upon her return home. Gran guessed that the letters were written not in the privacy of her own room but in the kitchen, on the long wooden table she had described, with Jonty sitting opposite and Mr and Mrs Bell glancing curiously at their guest's writing paper as she kept Gran abreast of events.

It had been different for Gran, of course. She was able to write about all that had happened at Deering's and in the flat, but now that she thought about it she realised that she too had not been entirely frank. To be sure, she had said that she and Albert Payne had gone on a few coach trips together, but had let it appear that when they reached their destination they had gone their separate ways. She was not sure why she had not admitted that she and Albert shared a very pleasant friendship, but knew that once Tess was home all would be revealed.

Reaching the green front door she unlocked it,

hoping, as she hurried up the stairs, that Tess would have pulled the pan of potatoes over the flame and found the two tiny chops which she had managed to acquire from the butcher down the road. A can of Batchelors Peas, round and fat, awaited the tin opener and in Gran's bag nestled a small sponge cake. She intended to make a custard to pour over the cake, which would do for a pudding.

Already smiling at the thought of the news-filled evening to come, she opened the door, and even as she did so she heard a voice. She guessed that Tess would be chatting away to herself as she made a nice cup of tea and Gran smiled as she crossed the hallway and opened the door into the kitchen. 'How you do run on, you daft girl,' she said, her tone half teasing, half affectionate. 'I'm not sure whether you're talking to the pan of potatoes or the teapot, but—'

At this point she entered the kitchen and saw both Tess and Snowy. She stopped short, a hand flying to her heart. 'My goodness, aren't I a silly old woman! Who's your friend, Tess? You must introduce us.'

Tess rushed across the room and enveloped Gran in a huge hug, knocking her hat askew and causing her to drop her shopping bag. Laughing and exclaiming, she said excitedly: 'It's Snowy White, Gran – I'm sure I've told you about him. He's the one who kept an eye on me so I wouldn't be bullied, and he very kindly offered to carry my suitcase from the station, which was just as well because Mrs Bell packed a canvas holdall full of nice things and I couldn't have managed both bags by myself.'

Gran smiled at the boy. She guessed him to be a couple

of years older than Tess and remembered how frightened Tess had been about going to and from school until some young feller had taken her part. Obviously this was the young feller in question, so she gave him a big smile. 'How do you do, Mr White,' she said cheerfully. 'I believe I have reason to be grateful to you, since Tess likes school now that she's not being bullied. In fact I keep telling her she ought to sit for the School Certificate, but she's that obstinate . . .'

'It's not that I'm obstinate; in a way I'd like to take the exam, and the Higher too, but I'd like to work and earn money as well,' Tess explained. 'If I could do both that would be grand, but I can't see someone paying me *not* to work for them, can you?'

Snowy laughed. Apart from murmuring how do you do, he had said nothing, embarrassed to be found making himself at home in the flat when its owner was not present, but now he smiled. 'If you keep on coming top of the class you may yet end up going in for further education, like me,' he said. 'But right now I'd best be off. You'll have a lot you want to discuss, and I'll only be in the way.'

Gran assured him he was wrong, and said she would whip up some Welsh cakes to go with the tea they were about to drink, but Snowy still shook his head. 'Another time,' he said. 'I must be going home or my mother will wonder what's kept me.' He smiled at the two women and Tess accompanied him downstairs, returning almost at once to give Gran another hug.

'You don't know how marvellous it is to be home,' she told the older woman. 'Our kitchen is only small, but when there are only two of you in the family what

125

do you need with a huge kitchen? And it'll be nice to go to bed tonight with my own things around me: my books, my clothes, my raggedy doll and the pictures I cut out of old geographic magazines. And right next door I'll have you, my very own gran.'

Her smile was so wide and delighted that any thought of revealing the secret of her friendship with Albert disappeared from Gran's mind. Bide your time and the right moment will come, she told herself. Instead, she went over to the stove and prodded the potatoes; yes, they were cooked right through. She should start the chops now. But Tess was still chattering. 'And it will be lovely to talk at mealtimes again,' she said contentedly. 'The Bells don't, you know – talk at meals, I mean. I don't believe they think it's rude, they just want to finish as quickly as possible so they can get back to work.' She twinkled at Gran. 'But you and I can tell each other what we've been doing over the past three weeks,' she said contentedly. 'I've got masses and masses of news. Norfolk's had really weird weather and life's been truly hard for farmers.'

The story lost nothing in the telling, and long before the chops were cooked Gran knew all about the hail which was the size of tennis balls, the gale which had carried off the Morris's hood and the twister which had wrecked a whole field of wheat. Naturally, she oohed and aahed in all the appropriate places, expressing her sympathy for the Bells and laughing heartily when Tess related the story of Crippen's escape and recapture.

When Tess finished her tale with the invitation to stay on at the farm Gran felt a moment of panic, but it was short-lived. Tess assured her that though the hard work and long hours had not put her off the farming life, she was pretty sure it would never be for her. 'I'm a city girl, even though I love animals and growing things,' she assured Gran. 'So you needn't worry that when I'm older I'll look round for a job on a farm. There are all sorts of careers I might take up, but right now I've got another year in school – maybe two if the government decides to make education compulsory for a further year – so it isn't a decision I have to make in a hurry.' She looked quizzically across the table at the older woman. 'And now it's your turn, Gran. You mentioned in your letters that you'd met Mr Payne at last. Did you get on? You didn't say much apart from the fact that you'd been on the same trips a few times. Go on; I've told you everything that happened to me, now you can jolly well do the same.'

Tess listened to Gran's story with interest and, it must be confessed, a little anxiety. She had been so happy to return to the flat, to Gran and to her old life, but now it looked as though that 'old life' was going to be rather different from her imaginings. Gran made no secret of the fact that she and Albert Payne had talked of going into partnership in order to start an ice cream parlour, or a soda fountain, as Albert apparently thought it should be called, quoting his daughter Janine, who worked in one in America.

'Of course, such an enterprise would need capital – that means money to set it up – and neither Albert nor I can lay our hands on that sort of cash,' she explained. 'But banks will lend on security, and Albert owns his shop and the flat above it. So perhaps, if we can find the right premises—'

At this point Tess felt she must interrupt. 'You and Mr Payne are daydreaming,' she said accusingly. 'Just like I do when I talk about getting my School Certificate, then my Higher, then going to university . . . You'll never persuade a bank to lend you money for a daydream, any more than it would help me to take my School Certificate, let alone to sit for a scholarship.'

'You aren't daydreaming,' Gran said. 'And neither are Albert and I. Oh, we may not find premises and get a loan this year, mebbe not even next, but one of these fine days we'll do it, you'll see. And in the meantime we'll both save up and go without, and—'

'Gran, I don't like to be selfish, but what about me?' Tess said plaintively. 'I don't fancy saving up and going without for years and years just to get an ice cream parlour I don't believe in! And if I'm not daydreaming, what about the scholarship? You've always said that if I did get into the grammar school you'd see me right, because scholarships don't pay for everything, though they're a big help.'

She was laying the table for supper, and Gran was mashing the potatoes. Tess plonked the salt cellar and the pepper pot down on the table, glancing across at Gran as she did so, and was immediately swamped by guilt, for the pink had drained from the older woman's cheeks and she looked both unhappy and remorseful. Gran began to apologise, saying she had got carried away, that of course Tess's education must come first and if she managed to get a scholarship she, Gran, would be the proudest person in the world and

128

would cast all thoughts of ice cream parlours – or soda fountains – out of her mind and concentrate on seeing that Tess had everything a grammar school girl would need.

Tess had just sat down, but at these words she threw herself at Gran and gave her a hard hug, tears of shame filling her eyes. 'I'm sorry, I'm sorry. I'm the biggest pig in the world, even bigger and piggier than Crippen,' she said, her voice breaking. 'Oh, Gran, you and Mr Payne must go ahead with your ice cream parlour and not give me a thought. After all, I don't know that I *want* to go on to further education; after another year of being bossed about and shouted at I might well be glad to leave school and get a job. And if I was earning money I could do lots of nice things, including helping to set up the ice cream parlour . . . Wouldn't you like that? I'd be a first-class waitress and you and I would be working to-gether . . . Mr Payne too, perhaps . . . and earning lots and lots of lovely lolly!'

Gran laughed but shook her head. 'Dear Tess, don't you listen when I'm talking? Your education must come first. And now let's eat our supper before it goes cold.' She hesitated, then met Tess's eyes squarely. 'You – you do like Albert, don't you? I know he was your friend before he and I had exchanged a word, but . . .'

'Oh, Gran, of course I like him,' Tess said quickly, feeling her own colour rise hotly to her cheeks. 'But – oh dear, I suppose I must be honest; I do feel just the tiniest bit jealous. You see, at the farm there are the Bells, and Adam, and lots of cousins who come over from time to time, and – and me, who is no one in particular. But

129

here . . .' she gestured round her at the small, well-appointed kitchen, 'here it's just our family, which is you and me, and now we're going to add Mr Payne . . .'

'And Snowy White,' Gran said quickly. 'He's a new friend of yours so far as I'm concerned. Or doesn't he count?'

Tess began to giggle. 'I'm not planning to start a business partnership with Snowy!'

'Oh, go on with you,' Gran said, laughing. 'And now let's take a leaf out of the Bells' book and stop nattering and start eating!'

Despite the best of intentions Tess overslept the next morning, which meant she was in a rush to get into the kitchen before Gran left for work. Gran had apologised the previous evening for not taking Tess's first whole day home off, but Saturday was Deering's busiest day and Gran did not want to let them down. So when Tess entered the kitchen she had already spooned porridge into two dishes and was about to sit down at the table. She looked up and smiled as Tess burst in, then gestured to her marketing bag which she had stood ready by the door.

'I'm sorry to send you out with a list of messages a mile long on your first day home, love,' she said apologetically. 'I meant to do some shopping in my break, but we were so busy yesterday that I only got ten minutes off. Still, you can call for Lucy – or Snowy, for that matter – and I've put a bit extra in the housekeeping purse so you can treat yourself and your pal to a bun and lemonade once you've got everything on the list.' Tess slid into her seat, saying, as she spooned golden syrup, that it would be a lovely change to go into proper shops again after three whole weeks of only visiting Mrs Bailey's Post Office and Grocery.

Gran pulled her cup of tea towards her and took a sip. 'Well, I'm glad you feel like that, because I've not got our rations this week which means you'll have to visit Mrs Thomas,' she said. 'But you seem to be getting on better with Marilyn, from what you've told me, so there should be no difficulty there.' She ducked her head, then looked at Tess from under her eyelashes. 'I wonder if you might pop in and tell Albert – Mr Payne, you know – that you're back. And – and ask him if he'd like to come over for supper this evening.'

Tess had been looking forward to renewing her friendship with various people in the shops Gran frequented and seeing friends from school who would also be doing their household messages, but now, strangely, she felt like a cat whose fur is stroked the wrong way, or like a child whose treat has been removed. It was odd, because she really did like Mr Payne; it was just that having him over for a meal on her first day home felt like an intrusion.

But Gran was looking at her, her eyebrows rising, and Tess broke into hasty speech. 'What time shall I say?'

Gran, looking relieved, gave Tess a beaming smile. 'Well, he closes his shop about six, so if he could be here for half past we can eat then, and you can tell him all about the Bells and the farm.'

'Haven't you done that already?' Tess said, and could have kicked herself. Her tone had been too sharp.

But if Gran had noticed, she did not let it show. 'No, queen, I've not said anything. Did you want me to?

131

Albert and I don't discuss other people's business, and anyway you will tell it all much better than I should.' She pushed her porridge plate away from her and got to her feet. 'I hate to impose on you the moment you get home, love, but can you do the washing up and tidy stuff away? You can make yourself a meat paste sandwich at midday, but don't worry about supper. I've the makings of a salad, some Spam and a couple of pounds of new potatoes, so if you wouldn't mind scrubbing them I'll put them on the stove at about quarter past six.'

'Right. I'll do that at lunchtime,' Tess said briefly, having already decided that she would come back before six o'clock, do any small jobs that were needed and then go off out again, pretending that a friend had asked her for a meal. She still felt miffed and asked herself why she should share her supper with Mr Payne on her very first full day home, though she knew she was being unreasonable. However, she would have gone off without a word had Gran not stopped her in her tracks. 'Hold on a minute, Tess,' she said as the girl began to descend the stair ahead of her. 'Why don't you ask Snowy or Lucy if they'd like to come for supper? Then we might have a hand or two of cards when the meal's over, a foursome being easier than a threesome.'

'Well, I don't know . . .' Tess began uneasily. She felt that the wind had been taken out of her sails and suddenly suspected that Gran had guessed she meant to invent another invitation. She felt quite ashamed of herself, because it was a mean thing to do.

'Of course, you can't know whether your friends have already made other plans,' Gran said when Tess did not finish her sentence. 'But if you'd like to pop into the bakery at around twelve-thirty you can tell me what you've arranged. Mr Deering's very good, so if either Snowy or Lucy will be coming for supper I'll buy a couple of Cornish pasties – staff rates, you know – and you can scrub a few more potatoes and we can have quite a little party.'

By now they had reached the end of the stair and were standing on the pavement, and Gran slipped an arm through Tess's and gave it a little shake. 'Don't worry yourself over me and Albert Payne,' she said gently. 'You and I are family, but even family have pals that they like to spend time with.' She let go of Tess's arm as a large man with startling ginger hair standing up in spikes all over his round head crossed the road and grinned at the two women.

'Well, if it ain't Mrs Williams! And this must be the granddaughter we've heard so much about.' He held out a huge hand, the fingers like sausages. 'How-de-do, young lady? I'm Jacob Jones, chief baker at Deering's, and your gran's me best worker.' They shook hands and then Jacob Jones and Gran crossed the road and disappeared into the baker's shop, Gran looking over her shoulder as she did so.

'Cheeribye, Tess,' she shouted. 'Don't forget the washing up!'

Tess stood where she was for a moment, staring at the closing door of the bakery. Should she return to the flat and do the washing up right away? But no, that would be a waste of energy, since she would be returning to the flat for her sandwich lunch. She had pushed the list of messages into her jacket pocket, but now she got it out and scrutinised it, giving a rueful little smile as she did so. Gran mustn't have done any shopping at all during her three-week absence, she thought, because judging from the shopping list it seemed the pantry at home must be pretty well empty. It would certainly take Tess most of the morning, and since she had no idea where Snowy lived she had best call on Lucy and see if her friend was free, first to accompany Tess round the shops, and second to come to supper at the flat.

Accordingly, Tess hurried along to Mere Lane, only stopping once en route to buy a cabbage and some more potatoes from Mr Gaulton. But when she reached Lucy's house a disappointment awaited her. No one answered her knock, but a woman in a wrap-around overall with her hair in curlers and her teeth obviously still reposing in a glass by her bed popped out of her front door and gave Tess a gummy grin. 'Hello, ducks. Is you after young Lucy?' she asked brightly. ''Cos if so you're out of luck. Her dad's ship come in a couple of days ago and he's took the whole fambly off down to the coast for a seaside holiday. Seems Lucy's mam has a brother what works on the fairground in Rhyl, so they moves into his caravan and the whole lot of 'em has two whole weeks of fun almost for free, they say.'

'Oh! Well, that's nice for Lucy and her brothers and sisters,' Tess said vaguely. She knew that Lucy had brothers and sisters, all younger, but had never actually met them. 'Do you know when they'll be coming home? Only I've been away myself and only got back yesterday.'

The woman shrugged. 'Work it out for yourself, queen,' she advised. 'They left this mornin' so they'll be back two weeks today . . .'

The screech of a whistling kettle split the air and the woman flapped a hand and turned back into her own house. 'Sorry, ducks, that's me kettle; I gorra turn it off or else . . .' The rest of the sentence was lost behind the slammed front door.

Tess waited a moment but the woman did not reappear so she turned her footsteps in the direction of St Domingo Road, feeling suddenly lonely. Doing the messages with someone else was fun; you could chatter as you walked, go to St John's Market and buy a bag of little red apples for sixpence; they could have sat down at one of the outdoor tables attached to Dorothy's Tearooms in Church Street and had lemonade and a bun with the money Gran had given her whilst enjoying the sunshine, for it was a beautiful day. But alone none of this was possible; oh, you could do it all right, but you'd feel self-conscious lacking a friend to share it with. So it was rather glumly that Tess retraced her steps and headed for Mrs Thomas's corner shop.

Despite the earliness of the hour there was the usual queue of hopeful housewives waiting to be served, but instead of Mrs Thomas behind the counter Tess recognised the woman known locally as Fat Betty. She was a cheerful soul who helped out at small shops when illness or holidays made her services necessary. Tess had seen her in the Thomases' shop before, enjoying a gossip as much as the work, laughing raucously and cracking jokes, though it was well known that Betty would not handle money. That was left to her son Willie, who was slow but reliable, and cut out points and crossed out coupons with meticulous care. Tess knew that Mrs Thomas's sister Freda would be somewhere on the premises, popping in now and then to see that all was as it should be, although she thought herself far too superior to actually work in a corner shop.

'That Freda!' Tess had heard Fat Betty comment, when the other woman was out of hearing. 'I dunno why she thinks she's so bleedin' important, just because her hubby's a steward on the Irish ferry. Still an' all, she checks Willie's sums and atwixt the pair of 'em they're never so much as a ha'penny out.'

The queue began to edge forward and Tess was edging with them when she felt a hand clutch her arm. She turned, and saw it was Snowy. 'So this is where you are. I suppose you thought it were the last place I'd look, knowing how you and Marilyn feel about each other,' he said, scowling at her. 'Well, I'm not waiting here among a lot of perishin' women. I'll meet you outside.'

'Please yourself,' Tess said indifferently, feeling cross. What right had Snowy to be annoyed to find her in the Thomases' shop? Come to that, why should he expect her to be anywhere in particular? So she stayed in the queue and when at last she reached the counter she made no attempt to hurry fat Betty or Willie, but stood waiting patiently whilst the small amounts of butter, sugar, bacon and other rationed commodities were carefully weighed, wrapped and tenderly placed in her basket. Then she left the shop and looked around for Snowy, but despite his promise to wait she could see no sign of him. Shrugging, Tess turned her steps towards the next shop on her list, but no sooner had she set off than she saw Snowy leaning against the wall, clearly waiting for someone. As she reached his side he gave a pretended start – she thought it was pretended – and smiled down at her.

'Good girl! Ain't it a glorious day, though? Where's your list of messages? If it's not too long I thought we might get a tram out to Princes Park so you and I could go on the lake. Can you row? Ever tried? And then there's the café; we could have a bite of lunch. My mam was in a generous mood this morning, so I can afford to splash my lolly about a bit.' Tess handed him the list and he examined it then gave it back to her, patting her head and taking her marketing bag from her. 'I'll carry this,' he said briskly. 'Are you on? To go out to Princes Park, I mean, as soon as this lot is finished?'

Tess pretended to consider, though her heart gave a joyful leap at the thought of a trip to Princes Park and a row on the lake, as well as what Snowy had described as 'a bite of lunch'. And what was even nicer, she had an invitation of her own to offer. But some womanly instinct she had not known she possessed told her not to jump at the chance of Snowy's company like a fish at a fly. Instead, as they walked towards the market, she pretended to consider.

'I like Princes Park, and though I can't row I'm sure I could easily learn,' she said cautiously. 'Gran sent me to call on Lucy, who's in my class at school, to see if she'd like to come back to the flat for supper this evening . . .'

'Lucy? Do you mean that scruffy kid what lives on Mere Lane, the one with all the younger brothers and sisters? Well, of all the perishin' nerve,' Snowy said. 'What's wrong with me, eh? Ain't I your pal?'

'Oh, she said I could ask either you or Lucy, whichever was free,' Tess said airily. She still thought Snowy had a

137

cheek to expect her to hang around waiting for him, but he was easily the best-looking boy in the neighbourhood and she supposed it had made him conceited. Well, no, not exactly conceited, but he definitely thought that any girl seen in his company was to be envied. Before she could comment on the fact, however, they were diving into Mr Charles' fishmonger shop because Gran's list had included potted shrimps, and Tess thought that if Mr Charles had two jars she would buy them both and eat one in a sandwich instead of the paste Gran had suggested. It would cost a bit more, but Tess adored potted shrimps.

As they came out of the shop, she turned to Snowy. 'Are you going to come to supper then? Gran's invited Mr Payne so's we can have a hand of cards when supper's over. What do you say?'

Snowy was in the middle of saying that he'd definitely come to supper and to thank her gran very much, only he would have to return home to warn his mother that he had been invited out, when Tess suddenly clapped a hand to her mouth. 'Oh, Geronimo, I completely forgot! I was supposed to go round to Mr Payne's shop to pass on Gran's invitation. Not that I imagine he's likely to turn it down because I think he's got his beady eye on my gran.' She saw Snowy's brows rise. 'Oh, I know she's old, but there's talk of the two of them . . . but never mind that, I'm sure he's a very nice fellow. Well, I know he is, but we'd better go there next, just in case Gran isn't his only friend. She'd be cross if I had to tell her that Mr Payne was already spoken for this evening.'

'Let's gerron the tram then,' Snowy shouted as one drew up beside them. 'This'll take us up Heyworth Street in five minutes flat.' He swung himself on to the platform and thumped the heavy marketing bag down before heaving Tess aboard, and very soon they were pushing the tobacconist's door open and Tess was doing her best to give the man behind the counter a friendly smile.

'Hello, Mr Payne. I've got an invitation from my gran; she wants you to come to supper after you close. We'll eat at half past six,' she gabbled. 'Snowy here is invited as well, and after supper she thought we might have a hand of cards. If you're willing, that is.'

Mr Payne had been piling packets of cigarettes up into small pyramids on the shelf behind the counter, but now he stopped work and swung round to greet her. 'Hello, young Tess!' he said cheerfully. 'We've missed you, your gran and me, so it's grand to see your bright young face again. As for supper, I'd be delighted, and if we're playing cards I'll bring my loose change, though your gran and I usually play for matches.'

Tess had been feeling much more relaxed about Mr Payne's friendship with her gran, but she began to bristle inwardly again when he mentioned that they had played cards together before. However, she knew she was being silly. Why should Mr Payne not visit her gran, who would have been lonely while Tess was in the country? So she made no comment, merely saying that they would look forward to seeing him not a moment later than six-thirty. Then she and Snowy left, closing the door carefully behind them, and made for the flat above the milliner's to unload the marketing bag before heading back to the shops.

*

139

'Well, I've had a grand evening. I don't know when I've laughed so much, or enjoyed a game of cards more, and I hate to be the first to break up the party, but if I don't get my beauty sleep I'll not be able to do my stock-take, which I like to do on a Sunday because there are no interruptions from customers.' Albert Payne turned to his hostess. 'So thank you very much, both for a delicious supper and for a grand evening.'

Tess saw that Snowy was nodding vigorously and thought with satisfaction that she too had enjoyed herself. In fact, she reflected that her first day back in Liverpool had been a great success. There had been the trip to Princes Park; Snowy had been a delightful companion, rowing her round the lake whilst they chatted. Then he had let her take the oars, and when she had made a mess of her first attempt had only laughed and praised her as her efforts grew more successful. They had eaten a sandwich at the café and drunk lemonade, and Tess had not failed to notice the envious glances cast upon her by other girls when they saw her tall, fair-haired companion. There was no doubt about it, Snowy was a handsome bloke, and she was lucky that for some reason – she was still not sure what that reason was – he had decided to befriend her. She supposed it was partly due to the fact that he had taken her side and prevented other pupils from bullying her, so that now he felt a bit possessive towards her, but whatever the reason, she was happy with the outcome.

Then there was Gran's little party. By the time she and Snowy returned to the flat above the milliner's shop Tess realised they were both feeling somewhat apprehensive, but once they were seated round the kitchen table

140

enjoying an excellent meal, the initial stiffness which even Gran must have felt gradually melted as conversation became general. Indeed, by the time they had settled round the card table, and were discussing which game they should play, they might have been lifelong friends, and Tess's niggling feeling that Mr Payne and her gran were becoming too close had completely disappeared. She realised that this was due largely to Snowy, who laughed and joked and told amusing stories, and she was grateful to him.

They rounded off the evening with a cup of cocoa and some of Gran's shortbread biscuits, and then Tess accompanied the two men down the stairs so that she might bolt the green door, whilst Gran tidied up and set the table for breakfast.

Once outside on the pavement, Albert shouted a last goodnight and headed for his shop, but Snowy lingered. He had already thanked Gran for a delightful evening and a delicious meal, and now that he and Tess were alone she half expected him to make some plan for the morrow, but instead he pinched her chin, said 'See you around, kid', and loped off. Tess stood for a moment, staring after him, then shrugged, a puzzled frown on her brow. But Snowy was quite a bit older than she, and unlikely, in the normal way, to pay much attention to someone of her age. However, she was sure he had enjoyed himself, as she had, and would very likely suggest another outing some time.

Tess turned back to the flat, shot the bolt across and climbed the stairs, letting herself into the hall and re-joining Gran in the kitchen. Gran, laying two places at the table, smiled at her. 'Tired?' she queried.

141

'Thank the Lord tomorrow's Sunday, so we can both have a lie-in . . . unless you and Snowy have planned another outing, of course.'

There was a distinct question in her tone, and Tess felt obliged to be honest. 'No, but I expect Snowy's got plans of his own,' she admitted. 'The thing is, Gran, he's a good deal older than me and he's got a girlfriend. I couldn't understand why he wanted to go around with me today, but it's just occurred to me that maybe Marilyn's on holiday, so he's at a loose end. When I went for our rations Fat Betty was behind the counter, which usually means Mrs Thomas is off somewhere.'

Gran frowned. 'Well, that's a bit off,' she said. 'But of course he stopped you being bullied, so perhaps he thinks of you more as a younger sister, someone his girlfriend wouldn't see as competition.'

Tess bristled. 'If he thinks of me as a younger sister . . .' she began, then deflated. Now that she thought about it she could quite see Gran's point. In fact she supposed that his attitude, when teaching her to row, had been almost that of an indulgent uncle. Never once had he behaved as a boy behaves to his girlfriend. She looked across at Gran.

'I didn't mean . . .' Gran began, but Tess cut across her.

'Sorry, Gran. I didn't mean to snap,' she said remorsefully. 'I didn't much like the younger sister bit, I'd rather think of Snowy and me as just pals. After all, he's only ever walked me home twice, and he met me on Lime Street station yesterday by accident, so I mustn't start reading too much into it.'

Gran looked relieved. 'You're a sensible girl,' she said approvingly. 'And whilst we're on the subject of friendship, may I remind you that Albert and myself are just like you and Snowy: good friends. So no need to worry that you'll suddenly find yourself with a step-grandfather.'

Tess felt the hot blood rush up her neck and into her cheeks. What a fool she had been! She had clearly let her feelings show despite her good intentions. 'I am sorry, Gran, truly I am,' she said humbly. 'It's just that at the farm I often felt out of things, and once I got home I knew that you and I were a family once more and that's how I want it to be. For always.'

Gran had been turning away to go to her room but now she turned back, her expression quizzical. 'Oh yeah, pull the other one, honey,' she said in a mock American accent. 'So you don't intend to get married one of these fine days? And you've given up your secret urge to continue your education and go to university? And if you were offered a really well paid job in foreign parts, you'd turn it down? Let's have a little honesty here, young lady.'

Tess began to protest, then stopped short. 'All right, all right, I give in. We've both got a right to our private lives; our dreams, if you like. Isn't that what you're trying to say? One of these fine days I expect I shall want to marry some fellow, and the same goes for you. No, don't shake your head, it's the truth and it's about time I realised it. And now let's go to bed, or else Mr Payne won't be the only one unable to get out of bed tomorrow morning.'

She thought that the subject was exhausted, but Gran caught her arm as she was about to go into her own room. 'Dear Tess, would it make you very unhappy if I asked you to call Mr Payne Albert – or even Uncle Albert if you'd prefer?' she asked. 'Only he and I have been using first names for a while now so it sounds rather odd when you are so formal.'

'All right; I'll call him Albert if it'll make you happy,' Tess said rather gloomily. 'Goodnight, Gran. Sweet dreams.'

'I don't why it is, but the holidays seem to whizz past in no time at all, and school terms last for ever,' Tess said. She was making up her carryout whilst Gran washed up the breakfast things.

'It's because you enjoy the freedom of the holidays,' Gran said. 'But I thought you enjoyed school as well. And most of the girls who took pleasure in being unkind to you will have left, so less of the long face if you please! Don't forget, your schooldays are supposed to be the happiest days of your life.'

Tess snorted. 'I wonder who said that? I bet it was some old twerp in his forties, but I'd better get a move on since I want to call for Lucy. She will still be in my class, thank the Lord.' As she spoke she pushed her lunch tin into her satchel, slipped on her jacket, for the hot August had given way to a cool September, and set off down the stairs, closely followed by Gran. They said their goodbyes on the pavement and Gran disappeared into the bakery whilst Tess hurried towards Mere Lane, but before she had gone more than a few yards she saw Snowy coming along the pavement towards her.

'Aren't you going to school?' he asked rather breathlessly as he reached her. 'I thought we'd walk at least a part of the way together. Or are you going to drop me like a hot potato now I've scared off all your enemies?' he added with a grin.

Tess stopped and stared up at him. Ever since what she now thought of as Gran's little party in the flat above the milliner's shop, she had seen hardly anything of Snowy. She had glimpsed him once or twice in the distance, sometimes with a group of boys his own age, sometimes alone, but he had never done more than grin and wave, had not invited her out or even strolled alongside her, chatting. Once, when she had gone up to Mrs Thomas's shop in the late afternoon, she had found the place empty but for Snowy and Mrs Thomas herself. Snowy had been talking urgently, with many gestures, but as soon as he heard the shop bell ting and became aware of Tess's presence he had stopped speaking abruptly. 'We'll talk later,' he had said rather grimly, and had brushed passed Tess without a word, as though he had never met her. Tess had bought the items on her list and left the shop expecting to find Snowy waiting for her. If he was going home too they might just as well walk together as not. But though she kept a weather eye open she saw no sign of him, and was forced to conclude that he had no desire to be seen in her company. So now, on this crisp September morning, she felt justified in giving him a very cool nod before continuing on her way.

'I'm going to call for my friend Lucy, not that it's any business of yours,' she said. 'Cheerio.'

As she spoke she turned into Mere Lane, expecting Snowy to continue down St Domingo Road, but he stayed beside her, actually plucked at her jacket, and, when this did not stop her, grabbed her arm. 'Listen, Tess Williams, you owe me something, because it's your fault that Marilyn won't speak to me. And now she's been and gone and took up with some feller she met on holiday, and I'm out in the cold, thanks to you.'

'To *me*?' Tess's voice rose to a squeak. 'How can it possibly have anything to do with me? I've not spoken to Marilyn since I came back from the country, though I did take a peep at her on her haberdashery counter. So what's your gripe, Mr Desmond White?'

At her use of his real name, Snowy grinned, but the grin was fleeting. A frown descended once more. 'Remember the day you came home from that farm in Norfolk? Well, it seems that one of Marilyn's aunties was meeting a train at the same time. The stupid old bag saw me giving you a lift with your suitcase and followed us. She told her daughter that I'd found myself a new girlfriend.' He gave a contemptuous snort. 'Some girlfriend! You're just a kid, just someone to waste time with when your real girlfriend's got other fish to fry. So anyway, the old bag told Marilyn I were two-timing her, and Marilyn met this feller—'

'Someone to waste time with?' Tess's voice rose once more. 'How *dare* you, *Desmond*, and now would you kindly let go of my arm?'

This time Snowy flushed, and reading retribution in his glittering eyes Tess tore herself free and began to hurry along Mere Lane, but Snowy caught her up and grabbed her arm once more. 'Don't try to pretend you weren't jealous of Marilyn and me,' he said between clenched teeth. 'I saw you taking notice of the way girls looked at me when we were in Princes Park. Why did you invite me up to your gran's place, if not to make it look as though we were more than just pals? I dare say you boasted about having a feller at last, which is how it got to Marilyn's ears.'

Tess was so indignant that for a moment she could not speak, but then she found her voice. 'You *asked* if you could come up after you'd carried my suitcase home,' she reminded him. 'And it was *Gran* who invited you for supper and a game of cards. As for boasting about it, I never did any such thing! Indeed, now that you've shown yourself in your true colours I shall regret that I ever let you into our flat. I'm sure if Gran could hear you she'd tell me never to bring you home again, and now if you don't stop hanging on to my arm I'll . . . I'll . . .'

Snowy gave a sneering laugh and continued to hold her arm. 'Don't think you can just walk away and leave me looking a fool,' he said angrily. 'I want you to go to Marilyn and explain that it was all a mistake; that we met on the station by accident and your beloved gran asked me back for a meal because I'd been kind to her dear little girl.'

It was too much. Tess drew back her foot and kicked Snowy in the shins, and, when he doubled up, smashed her fist into that part of him to which she had never given a name. Snowy gave a howl of pain and let go of her arm, clutching himself and beginning to wheeze threats. But Tess, freed from his grasp, shot along Mere Lane just as Lucy emerged from her front door.

Lucy was smiling. 'Why's you runnin'? We've got plenty of time; even if we walk slow as slow, we'll still be in school before half past eight,' she said. 'You're sweatin' like a pig, Tess. Don't say someone's after you!'

147

Tess began to giggle. 'You could say that. I've made Snowy extremely angry, and when he wouldn't let go of my arm I kicked him and then punched him in the unmentionables, and left him threatening all sorts. Do we have to go back down Mere Lane, Lu? Isn't there another way to school?'

Lucy gave her friend an indulgent glance. 'You can't go around beatin' up the best-lookin' guy in Everton, even if he does annoy you,' she said reprovingly. 'An' I guess we can go through the back streets; we've got time. But I don't suppose he'll hang around waitin' for a second helping, let alone he must know he were in the wrong because you say he didn't let go when you asked him to.' She cocked an eye at her friend. 'So what'll it be? Face the feller now, or later? You can't go through life avoidin' everyone what you've disagreed with.'

'You're right. We'll go down Mere Lane and take our usual route,' Tess said, though not without a qualm. She had always thought Snowy kind, easy-going and sweet-tempered, but today she had seen a side to him she had never even suspected. She knew he thought quite a lot of himself but had not realised that, when crossed, he could be downright vicious. She was glad she had hit first and then run like a rabbit, though she did not suppose that he would have done more than give her a clip round the ear and a mouthful of abuse. But as Lucy said, she would have to meet him on other occasions. So the two girls took their usual route to school, and though there had been no sign of him Tess entered the classroom feeling a trifle apprehensive in case one of her school-mates had seen the fracas. But apparently no one had observed Snowy's humiliation, and when Tess left school

148

at the end of the day, casting panicky glances around as she emerged through the gates, there was no sign of him.

'Come back to the flat with me; I'm scared he'll be lying in wait,' Tess urged Lucy. 'If you do I'll tell you the whole story and we'll have lemonade and Gran's shortbread. In a way it's fairer to Snowy if I do, because I suppose he did have a reason to feel rather cross with me. But there's no point in asking for trouble and I simply don't want to have to listen to his woes all over again.'

Lucy agreed, and the two girls got safely to the flat over the milliner's shop without so much as a glimpse of a tall, fair-haired figure. Once there, they took the shortbread and a bottle of Corona and went and sat in the parlour window, where they could watch for anyone approaching the flat. But they saw nothing of Snowy, and by the time Gran arrived home, full of the day's doings at the bakery and wanting to hear how Tess had got on in her new class, Tess had managed to convince herself that Snowy's rage would cool and that even if they could never be friends, at least they need not be enemies.

She had to admit to Gran that there had been what she described as 'a bit of a falling out', but did not say that they had actually come to blows. And anyway, she told herself with an inward grin as she got ready for bed that night, it had scarcely been an exchange of blows, since she had been the one doing all the blowing. She just trusted that Snowy would leave her alone in future. After all, if he thought about it logically and coolly, instead of when he was hot with disappointment and temper, he would surely realise that losing his girlfriend had had nothing to do with Tess, and that handsome as he was he would soon find a queue of girls anxious to replace Marilyn Thomas. And once he got himself a new girlfriend, surely he would not continue to be angry with Tess?

But two days later, as Gran was placidly preparing their evening meal, the kitchen door was flung open and Tess burst in. She was red in the face and clearly very annoyed about something. Gran raised her brows. 'What's bitten you, my love?' she asked. 'Don't say you and Snowy have had another falling out!'

Tess ground her teeth. 'Gran, you know you said you didn't mind continuing to work at the bakery if I wanted to try for the scholarship?' she asked. 'If you really meant it then I mean to study like crazy and come top, and that'll show him.'

'Show who?' Gran asked placidly. 'Never make important decisions when you're in a rage, queen. Tell me what's bitten you.'

'It's that bloody Snowy White; he's been talking about me, Gran, saying I'm just a jumped up little nobody without a brain in my head. Saying the school won't put me in for the scholarship because they know I'm not bright enough to get it. So will you, Gran? Go on working at the bakery, I mean.'

Gran had been buttering slices of the loaf, but she put her knife down and crossed the room to give Tess, half in and half out of her jacket, a hug. 'Of course I will, silly,' she said warmly. 'I've told you over and over that your education is the most important thing, so if I've got Snowy to thank for your decision to sit for the scholarship I'm downright grateful to him. And I'll tell anyone who wants to listen that I'm backing you to win!'

Chapter Six

'Something smells good, Ma. Grub ready yet?' Jonty Bell came into the kitchen in his stockinged feet, wellingtons in one hand. 'I got up early so I could finish all my chores and have time to clean up before I go down to the station to meet Tess. She's really looking forward to seeing all the changes which have taken place over the past three years. Can you believe it, Ma? It's three whole years since Crippen escaped, and three whole years since Tess has set foot on Bell Farm.' He stood his boots down by the back door, shrugged himself out of his waterproof and looked appreciatively at the large pan in which his mother was frying sliced potatoes. 'I bet Tess doesn't have lunches like the ones *you* make, Ma. Oh, I can't wait to see her funny old face again! Of course I've tried to tell her about all the changes that have taken place . . .'

Mrs Bell clicked her tongue reprovingly. 'My dear boy, you're about as fond of writing letters as your pa, which means not fond at all. How often have you written over the past three years?' She smiled as Jonty felt his cheeks begin to grow hot. 'Well, never mind. You're seeing the gal in a couple of hours, so you can catch up with each other's news then.'

Jonty came across the kitchen and examined the cold beef joint and the jar of horseradish which would accompany it. 'I love a cold beef dinner, but what are we having

152

for supper?' he asked as Mrs Bell began to dish up. 'I hope it's something special, being as how it's Tess's first day back.' He looked searchingly at his parent. 'You know what we agreed, Ma? That now we've got our farmhands back she won't need to work. Only she's here for just a couple of weeks, though when I spoke to her on the phone last night I tried to persuade her to stay longer. I don't see why she won't,' hc added in an aggrieved tone. 'When you consider how she's slogged at her books, first to get that dratted scholarship and then to get her School Certificate, you'd think she'd be glad of a break. Isn't it odd?' he continued. 'She found the maths paper really difficult but thought the other subjects – English, history and so on – a doddle, whereas I was the exact opposite. I waltzed through maths and physics, but I had hard work with what you might call the arts subjects. So I suppose you could say Tess and I were like Jack Sprat and his wife.' He put on a childish lisp and quoted the old nursery rhyme. '*Jack Sprat would eat no fat, his wife would eat no lean, and so betwixt the two of them they licked the platter clean.*'

Mrs Bell was laughing and exclaiming that both he and Tess were grand trenchermen when it came to their grub when the back door opened again and Mr Bell came in with Adam and the other two farm workers, Harry and Daniel, all in their stockinged feet. They slung their wellingtons under the coat rack and hung up their oilskins, for the day had begun wet, though Daniel, coming in last, commented that 'the rain be clearing nicely; 'twill be a sunny afternoon, I reckon, so young Jonty can wear his best to meet his girlfriend.'

Mr Bell nodded placidly but his wife gave Daniel a

reproving frown. 'She int his girlfriend, she's just a friend,' she said. 'Why, you fool, Dan'l, they hant met for three years; if she were his girlfriend I reckon she'd ha' come a-visitin' every time I invited her.'

'Oh, Ma, you know very well why she's not come until now,' Jonty said. 'She's been taking exams, and when she wasn't actually in school she's been working, so the expense of her education didn't fall just on her gran. But the exams are over for a bit, which is why she's agreed to spend two weeks with us now.'

'Ah well, if she int your sweetheart, she int,' Daniel said peaceably. He took his place at the table as Mrs Bell began to heap golden fried potatoes on a plate already generously spread with thick slices of cold beef, and licked his lips. 'Gor, missus, that don't only smell good, that look good, and I reckon that'll taste good,' he said. 'Pass the ketchup, young Jonty.'

An hour later Jonty viewed his reflection in the long mirror which graced his bedroom with some satisfaction. He was wearing his Sunday clothes – well-pressed grey flannels, a white shirt, old school tie and tweed jacket – and thought he looked just as he ought. The rain had stopped, though the puddles still glittered when he glanced into the farmyard below his window, and he had slicked his hair down with water and meant to wear the new cap his mother had bought him last time she had visited Norwich. It was a heather mixture tweed, almost the same as his hacking jacket, and he thought his mother had done well to get such a close match.

Having satisfied himself that he looked all right, Jonty glanced at the heavy watch adorning his wrist. If he left right away he could catch the two-thirty bus, which would get him to Thorpe station about five minutes before Tess's train came in, but he did not intend doing so. He meant to linger in his bedroom until he had managed to miss the bus so that he might ask his father if he could borrow the Ford. Jonty had passed his test the previous year and often drove into the village or the city. He was hopeful that in time his father might agree to his having the Prefect whilst Mr Bell himself continued to use the Morris. In truth, Jonty had begun to wince inwardly every time Mr Bell took the wheel of the Ford, for the older man was not a good driver. Self-taught, he seemed to think changing gear unnecessary, never depressed the clutch when braking suddenly and would demand in a hurt tone: 'Why do the perishin' engine cut out whenever I stop? That don't do it when you're behind the wheel.'

Jonty had tried to explain but his father had only sniffed. 'Nonsense, bor,' he had said robustly, and next time he wanted to turn left had set the windscreen wipers going. Jonty still cringed when he remembered what had happened next. His father had let go of the wheel and leaned forward until his nose almost touched the windscreen. 'What's them things a-doin', when I told 'em to turn left?' he said in an aggrieved tone. 'Oh, I don't like these new-fangled things. *And* the roof won't fold back, it's made of some hard stuff, I dunno what you call it, and the windows is glass not Perspex; what'll happen if a stone fly up and hit the windscreen? Answer me that.'

Naturally enough, Jonty had decided not to try to explain, save to say that the Morris was on its last legs, only really fit for short runs into the village, whereas the Ford, a far younger vehicle, would still be in excellent

155

trim in twenty years. 'You bought the Ford to replace the Morris,' he had reminded his father on several occasions. 'I learned to drive in it, because you didn't think the Morris was reliable. But now all you do is moan, and drive the Ford as if it were a tractor. It won't do, Pa! Why not let me take over the Ford and you stick to the Morris, since you clearly prefer it?'

They had been in the old cart shed at the time, for both cars were now garaged there, and Jonty had looked hopefully at his father across the cracked and much dented bonnet of the bull-nose. 'Well, Pa? Wouldn't that be the best solution? Only I worry that your style of driving is more suited to the Morris, and if you go on refusing to depress the clutch . . .'

'That there Ford Prefect cost me a deal of money and I int ready to hand it over to a young greenhorn,' his father had said obstinately. 'When you've got the money to pay off the instalments, then we'll mebbe discuss it again.'

So now Jonty checked that the bus would have roared into the village and roared out again without him before he descended the stairs and emerged in the kitchen. His father was sitting at the table drinking a large mug of tea. He looked up as his son entered the room. 'You've been prettyin' yourself too long; you've missed the perishin' bus,' Mr Bell said. 'And don't think I can't see through you, because I can. You'll be wantin' to drive me lovely new car so you can show off to young Tess. Am I right?'

Jonty grinned. 'Got it in one, Pa,' he said breezily. 'But of course I'll borrow the Morris if you'd rather.'

Arthur Bell gave a contemptuous snort. 'Have you

drivin' my poor old Morris as if you was Juan Fandango or whatever his name is. No siree!'

'Fangio. Juan Fangio,' Jonty murmured. 'And if I could drive like him I might even get the Morris to go at more than thirty miles an hour. As it is, however, I'd be happy to take the Ford off your hands full time; you can take the payments out of my wages.'

This was a nasty one, because like all farmers' sons Jonty was unpaid, but his father, grinning, raised a hand, acknowledging a hit. 'All right, all right, you can meet your young lady in the new car,' he said. His eyes raked his son from head to toe. 'If she reckernise you, that'll be a miracle! Fine as bloody fivepence you are. The last time she seen you, you were in gumboots and school uniform. Ah, well, times change and young men with 'em.'

So it was with his father's blessing that Jonty jumped into the Ford, put it into reverse, backed out of the shed and then slammed it into first. The car, though the family always referred to it as 'new', was in fact a couple of years old, having been bought second-hand at a car auction the previous year. It was blue with red leather seats and Jonty had wanted to name it Priscilla, after his favourite cow, but his mother preferred Bluebell, and in general the family just referred to her as 'the Ford'. Jonty wound down his window and drove carefully along the ruts and puddles of the lane, keeping to a steady fifteen miles an hour until he reached the tarmac road whereupon he put his foot down and sped towards Norwich, only slowing and stopping when he reached the traffic lights where Thorpe Road and Riverside Road met.

Outside the station he parked the car and glanced at the clock above the entrance to the concourse. Tess's train was not due for another half-hour, so Jonty went to the Gents where a glance in the mirror above the handbasins confirmed his worst fears: the pleasant summery wind had dried out his carefully smoothed hair, which now stood on end as though he had suffered a bad shock. Jonty wet his hands under the tap and applied both palms to his sandy mop until it agreed to lie down once more. Then he went to the refreshment room, bought a cup of coffee and sat down to wait.

Tess sat in the corner seat which she had managed to acquire after her last change and glanced out at the passing scene, reflecting that Norfolk looked the same as ever. Who had said *Very flat, Norfolk*? She rather suspected it was Noël Coward, and though as a lover of the county she naturally resented the remark, she was forced to admit that there was some truth in it. Later on, when they were nearing Norwich and were crossing the Halvergate marshes, one could see miles and miles of level, watery countryside, the view only broken here and there by a farm or cottage.

Because telephone calls were expensive and had to be carefully planned, she and Jonty had mainly kept in touch by letter and Tess had to admit that because of the pressure of schoolwork and her various jobs – she had cleaned offices, served in small shops, become a Saturday waitress at a big Lyons restaurant and worked as a holiday relief on the Irish ferry – her letters to her friend had been scrappy affairs. As for his to her, 'few and far between' would be putting it mildly. But none of that mattered now; she was on her way to see Jonty and the Bells, the four horses and Crippen the boar, and would spend two whole weeks in their company.

Mrs Bell had invited her before, but Tess had been firm, assuring her would-be hostess that she dared not leave her studies until the exams were over. But now she was the possessor of her School Certificate and would start studying for her Higher when school reopened in September. When Jonty had passed his School Certificate two years before she had suggested that he might take his Higher and then go on to university, which was what she intended to do, but in his reply to her letter he had not attempted to hide his horror. *I've had enough of being taught*, he had written in his round, rather childish handwriting. *I've told you before, Tess, that since I'm going to farm there's no point in all this education stuff. Ma and Pa insisted that I should take my School Cert, and now that I've got it I'm glad I did, but that doesn't mean I intend to shut myself up in a classroom for another two years. Besides, most universities want Latin and I never did it. So though I'm longing to see you and talk over old times, just don't you mention education, or I'll punch you on the nose.*

She had laughed and replied in kind, but understood his views. Striding his father's acres, one day to be his, in a howling gale, with the rain driving into his face and the mud trying to suck his boots off with every step, he was happy and fulfilled. His maths would come in handy when ordering up foodstuffs for the beasts, or checking accounts, but history, geography and English would have been forgotten and unregretted as soon as he left the hallowed premises of the grammar school. For her part, Tess knew her feelings about the farm were ambivalent.

159

She loved it in the summer, but she remembered from her days as an evacuee how she had hated the cold winters. It was all very fine when the ponds and lakes froze, when even the Broad became a solid block of ice, because then you wrapped up well and skated or sledged or snowballed to your heart's content. But she remembered being told all about the winter of '47 when the poor little birds had frozen on the trees, and Jonty had seen a water vole frozen into the ice, his little legs stretched in a desperate attempt to swim through water which was becoming more solid with every second that passed. He had told her how they had driven the pigs into the big barn, having to carry some of the piglets because the snow was so deep, and Mrs Bell had sent her cuttings from the *Eastern Evening News* about the devastating floods which had followed the freeze when warmer weather had melted twelve-foot drifts, as well as the foot-thick ice. It had sounded terrible yet exciting and Tess thought the children had probably enjoyed the whole experience, but she was no longer a child and knew that she would have hated the cold, worried when food ran short, and wept over the devastation of so much that the Bells had worked for with increasing despair.

But they had weathered it – excuse the pun, she told herself – in their usual sturdy fashion. The orchards had borne fruit that summer of '47 but it was a poor crop compared with previous years, and the sprouts in the five acre had emerged smashed into the mud and stinking of rotting leaves as the flood receded. But the Bells had gritted their teeth, given their workers a raise in wages and continued to spend their money cautiously, for mechanisation was beginning to make itself felt, and

Jonty was pushing his father to buy modern machinery, to restock one orchard whose trees had been particularly badly affected, and to sell off stock, which would cost more to feed than they would bring in as full-grown cattle.

Tess sighed and looked up at the string rack above her head, upon which rested her small rucksack. She had packed a pair of slacks, a couple of shirts, some underwear and her pyjamas, but hoped she would be able to borrow wellington boots and oilskins if the weather turned nasty, which, remembering her last visit to the farm, she knew was all too possible, even in summertime.

The train jerked and Tess recognised that they were drawing near the end of their journey. She glanced around the compartment: a couple of soldiers, a woman with three children who had begun the journey noisily but had fallen asleep as the day wore on and an airman, who had irritated Tess earlier by constantly twirling his moustache. But now, as the train jerked to a halt and a porter shouted 'All change! Norwich Thorpe; all change!' the airman stood up and reached her rucksack down, handing it to her with a little grin. Then he picked up his own attaché case and gestured to her to go before him into the corridor and join the queue to leave the train.

'Thanks very much,' Tess said, smiling at him. 'I don't suppose you could help me to put it on my back, could you? Only I may be catching the bus . . .'

'No sooner said than done,' the officer said gallantly, taking the rucksack back and arranging it between Tess's shoulder blades. 'Comfy? Good girl. Now, if you were in the services during the war . . .'

161

Tess laughed. 'I was in nappies during the war,' she said. 'Well, perhaps that's a slight exaggeration, but I truly wasn't old enough to join any of the services, though if I had it would have been the WAAF.'

'Aye, you're right there, the Waafs were a grand bunch,' the airman agreed. He jumped down on to the platform and held out his hands, taking hers and swinging her down from the train. 'If you are going in the same direction as myself we might share a taxi—' he began, but Tess interrupted.

'Thanks, but I think I'm being met,' she said just as a tall young man, his sandy hair slicked to his head, approached them. 'Ah, here comes my friend now.'

'Ah, so I see; then I'd best be off,' the airman said, sketching a salute; not that Tess noticed: she was staring too hard at Jonty.

'Whatever have you done to yourself?' she asked. 'Is it Brylcreem on your hair? Because if so it makes you look like a lounge lizard, and I don't like it.' She spoke with all her usual frankness, then clapped a hand to her mouth and said through her fingers, 'Oh, dear, if Gran heard me making personal remarks she'd give me what for.'

'What for?' Jonty said, grinning. 'And it's water, not Brylcreem.' Tess thought the flash of his white teeth in his tanned face made him look even more attractive, but of course it would never do to say so; instead she jerked a thumb at the railway official waiting to clip tickets.

'Shall we go? We've timed it quite nicely; if I remember rightly there's a number seven leaving in twenty minutes, which will give us plenty of time to reach the stop and join the queue.'

Jonty took her hand and pulled her towards him, planting a chaste kiss on the side of her face and knocking her neat little hat to one side. Tess righted it as they queued for the barrier and scowled at her companion. 'Less of that soppy stuff!' she said sternly. 'Else I shan't sit next to you when we get aboard the bus.' As she spoke she tucked her clipped ticket back into her handbag.

'Who said anything about catching a bus?' Jonty said as they headed towards the row of parked cars. When he reached the Ford he unlocked the passenger door and swung it open, turning to Tess. 'Your carriage awaits, madam,' he said rather grandly, though he spoiled the impression he was trying to make by adding: 'and take that perishin' rucksack off and chuck it on the back seat, otherwise you'll likely go through the windscreen the first time I put the brakes on.'

Tess complied, then slid into the front passenger seat as Jonty walked round the car and unlocked the driver's door to get behind the wheel. 'Well? What do you think of the Bells' new addition? I wanted to call her Priscilla, after the very first cow I milked, but Ma insisted it should be Bluebell because of the colour, so we don't bother much with names: it's either the Morris or the Ford.'

'Oh, you've still got the Morris then?' Tess remarked as they emerged on to the main road and Jonty turned the car's nose in the direction of home. 'I half expected Mr Bell to pop out and get into the driving seat when you opened the door. I know he used to get very ratty with you when you drove the old bull-nose up to the harvest field, with the harvest tea in your mam's big basket.'

'Oh, that's all a thing of the past,' Jonty said airily, although Tess was amused to see that he crossed his fingers as he spoke. 'Dad's on the verge of agreeing that if I take on the repayments for the Ford, I can consider it more or less mine. The truth is, Tess, that fond though I am of my old man I have to admit – just between ourselves, mind – that he's a lousy driver. In fact, I believe he's a good deal happier driving the Morris than he is behind the wheel of the Ford. And since he seldom gets out of second gear, hardly ever depresses the clutch and considers the windscreen wipers an invention of the devil, put on the windscreen merely to confuse him when he indicates right or left, I feel he's better sticking to the old car which is much less complex.' As he spoke they reached the derestriction sign and Jonty began to increase his speed, until they were spinning along the turnpike at fifty miles an hour.

Tess took the opportunity, because he was concentrating on his driving, to steal a look at his profile. He was not handsome, she decided regretfully, but he had a very nice sort of face, and now that his hair had begun to dry it was springing back into its usual clumpy, sandy locks. Taking stock, she noted the freckles, which ran in a band across his nose and cheeks, his determined cleft chin and the greenish-hazel eyes now fixed steadily on the road ahead. She let her glance slip to the strong column of his neck, tanned by the summer sun, and his broad shoulders and chest, which tapered to a narrow waist and long legs. She was just thinking that he had not only grown a lot but had greatly improved when he shot her an amused sideways glance.

'Know me again?' he asked. He pulled a face. 'That's

164

not fair; the driver has to keep his eyes on the road no matter how much he'd rather take a good look at his passenger.'

Tess laughed. 'Well, judging by the speed you're doing we'll be back at Bell Farm in no time, and then you can stare at me all you like. Only I don't believe I've changed at all.'

Jonty slowed the car as they approached a sugar beet lorry, then indicated and pulled out, speeding up again. As he pulled in front of the lorry, Tess chuckled. 'Oh, Jonty, doesn't it remind you of days gone by? When your dad was driving, for instance, we would have stayed behind that lorry in the hope that it would lose a couple of beet as it turned off to head for the Cantley factory, because every pig born adores sugar beet. But now we're responsible citizens, I reckon, and wouldn't dream of nicking a spilt beet when the driver hasn't netted his load.'

Jonty laughed. 'You devil, Tess! You saw me looking in the rear-view mirror as we passed the turning. But the driver took it slow, so I guess if you want to give the pigs a treat you'll have to pick up windfalls in the orchard; they're mortal fond of Beauty of Bath, which are the earliest variety we grow. Now, what do you want to do for the next few weeks?'

'*Two* weeks, you mean,' Tess said quickly. 'I did tell you I'd have to go back after two weeks. I'm sure I told you in one of my letters that as soon as Miss Foulks told the landlord she was retiring and giving up the shop, he decided it would be far easier to let as one unit, shop and flat together. He's given us a month to find new accommodation, but it's going to be hard because rents are continually going up and decent housing is hard to find within our price range. If we could live on the Wirral, or even in the suburbs, it might be easier, but as it is I need to be near my school and Gran has to be close to the bakery . . .'

'Hey, what's wrong with public transport? It's what folk in the country have to use all the time, unless they're lucky enough to own a car,' Jonty pointed out. 'Why shouldn't you live in the country and catch a bus every morning? It's what us ordinary people have to do!'

'Oh, ha ha, very funny,' Tess said. 'Three days a week, and sometimes four, Gran bakes bread; her shifts start at two in the morning, and believe me, there are very few buses or trams running through the night. I admit it would be all right for me – living further away, I mean – but it wouldn't do for Gran. Once or twice, when I've seen how tired she is after a night shift, I've suggested that she ask her boss to let her do days only, but she gets paid double time, possibly more, for night work so it just isn't on.'

'Hmm, then I quite see you have a problem,' Jonty said, having given the subject some thought. 'No chance of your gran getting a job well away from the city, something not connected with the bakery, I mean? After all, there are other jobs. Which reminds me, since you say you must go home after a mere two weeks in Norfolk, I take it you've a job lined up?' As he spoke he was turning off the tarmac road and entering the rough little lane which led up to the farm, and he had to slow his speed considerably, for the hot summer had left the lane with huge iron-hard ruts and ridges which the morning's rain had turned into a skating rink.

166

'Well, not exactly, but I'm being considered for holiday relief in a factory nursery, so I need to get back for the interview,' Tess explained. 'Don't think I wouldn't rather stay on at Bell Farm, but the truth is I can't do it. Also, someone has to search for accommodation. Gran does her best when she isn't actually working and Albert – Mr Payne, the tobacconist – is a tower of strength, but so far neither of them have turned up what we need.'

Jonty nodded thoughtfully as he swung into the farmyard, coming neatly to a halt right outside the back door. 'I see. I take it you've given up all thoughts of this ice cream parlour? If not, couldn't you sell ices from the hat shop and keep the flat?'

Tess shook her head sadly. 'No can do; if we took on the hat shop we'd have to go for Change of Use, and anyway it isn't really big enough. Uncle Albert's daughter Janine runs a soda fountain in the United States and told her dad ages ago just what he'd need. The floor space would have to be twice the size of the hat shop and the equipment . . . well, it's out of the question at present. Just a dream, in fact.'

Jonty cut the engine and came round to open Tess's door and help her out on to the cobbles. 'Right, I see your problem. In you go!' he said cheerfully. 'Ma and Pa will both be in the kitchen, waiting to welcome you. I'll bring your rucksack.'

Jonty had been astonished when he had seen an elegant young lady accompanied by a member of the Royal Air Force descending from the train. In the sensible part of his mind he knew that this elegant young woman with the short cap of golden-brown hair must be his Tess – he

167

still thought of her as his Tess – but if she thought that he had changed, he told himself as he drew the car to a halt outside the back door, then she had changed every bit as much. Until she had opened her mouth and commented so rudely upon his hairstyle, he had felt quite frightened of her, so different, so sophisticated, had she seemed. But then he had realised that his old pal hadn't changed at all, merely shrugged grown-upness over the funny little Tess he knew, so all he had to do was grow accustomed to the new look. Even thinking the words *new look* made him glance at Tess's clothing as he followed her into the farmhouse. She wore a neat little navy straw hat – the one he had knocked askew when greeting her – and a blue cotton dress with a long full skirt, cinched at her narrow waist with a navy blue elasticated belt, and on her feet she wore high-heeled white sandals.

Jonty opened his mouth to tell her that she'd best go up to her room and change at once, otherwise, sure as check, she would find herself ruining her best clothes before anyone but the Bell family had seen them, but then he closed it again. His parents were exclaiming, shaking Tess's hand over and over, introducing her to Harry and Daniel, the farmhands she had never met, whilst Adam hovered, anxious to add his greetings with all the rest.

Presently the workers left and Mrs Bell poured out cups of tea and offered slices of fruit cake, and once seated round the kitchen table Mr and Mrs Bell were able to ask Tess what she thought of the Ford Prefect, and to add that she must admire the many changes which she would discover when Jonty showed her round.

'I dare say you'll guess we told the boy to let you

know all that go on here,' Mrs Bell said, giving her son a reproachful look. 'But he int no hand with a pen and likely he forgot all the important things. Still an' all, you're here yourself now, and when Jonty bring you in for your supper you can tell us what you think.'

'I'm sure you've worked marvels. Jonty did his best, but I'm afraid many of the things he mentioned didn't mean much to me,' Tess explained. 'He said you're in a group of farmers who share things like combine harvesters, and you're in a pig club, so when you slaughter one of the baconers you take it in turns to keep half the carcass and send half to the government.' She glanced round the room as though looking for spies, and added in a hushed tone: 'Only I bet you and the other members of the pig club have thought of a way to keep a good deal more than half of every fifth pig, or whatever it is.' Jonty saw that his own guilty smile was echoed on his parents' faces and reached over to dig Tess in the ribs.

'If you knew the number of forms we all have to fill in regarding a pig's life from the moment it's born until its death you wouldn't say such a cruel thing,' he said, whilst his father muttered beneath his breath what Jonty knew to be agreement.

'She've hit the mark, wouldn't you say, Mother?' Mr Bell said. 'Pigs be contrary critters, and a bottle-fed piglet ain't no wuss nor one what feeds from the old sow.' He got to his feet. 'Now if you're going to see round the farm before that grow dark you'd best get out of them fancy clothes, young Tess. Mother have left your old dungarees on your bed and I reckon you've not growed much, not like our Jonty here what have shot up like

169

Jack's beanstalk. I trust Jonty have told you that you ain't here to work – the honest truth is, my woman, we don't need you now we've got the fellers back – but we still think you'll likely want to do a few little tasks – feedin' the poultry, mebbe bringin' the horses back from the meadow – so it's best you wear the overalls when you int goin' out somewhere with your young man.'

Jonty laughed. 'Best remember we're just pals,' he told his father reprovingly, following Tess as she began to mount the stairs. 'I know you don't like people thinking that you're my girlfriend, Tess, but there's no need to worry. I've been taking Melissa Richmond to the local hops in the village hall – her pa's got a big farm over Mulbarton way, so the parents approve. By the way, what's happened about that boy, Snowy something or other? You've not mentioned him in any of your letters for ages, so far as I can recall.'

They had reached the landing at the top of the stairs and Tess turned towards him with what Jonty thought was a rather hesitant smile. 'Oh, Snowy and I are good friends,' she said airily. 'But, I've heard no word of this Miss Richmond until this very day. I take it she's your girlfriend?'

Jonty shrugged. 'One of many,' he said casually. 'You can't imagine a handsome fellow like myself would lack admirers? There's many a girl would scratch Melissa's eyes out for a chance to get near me.'

Tess giggled and opened her bedroom door, and then, as Jonty passed her on the way to his, she swung her haversack with deadly accuracy, catching him a smart blow on the bottom.

Jonty spun round, intent on revenge, only to find the

bedroom door slammed in his face while a mocking voice said: 'Too late. You've got to get up very early in the morning to catch me napping, Jonty Bell.'

'Just you wait, that's all,' Jonty said. He opened his own door, went inside and raised his voice. 'See you in the kitchen in five minutes!'

Albert Payne and Edie Williams were seated at the kitchen table of the flat above the milliner's shop when they heard the letter box on the ground floor rattle. They had been eating breakfast – porridge and toast – and drinking tea, but at the sound Albert got to his feet, wiped his mouth and set off across the kitchen. 'I'll go,' he said rather unnecessarily. 'I expect there'll be one for you from Tess; that girl's a wonder! She's written to you just about every day since she left. I'm hopeful of getting one from Janine sometime soon, because in my last letter to her I asked if anything was wrong since she'd not written for six months, but then she's an awfully poor correspondent, so I can't say I'm particularly worried.'

'Right you are,' Edie said cheerfully. 'I'll be making us both a carryout. I'm really looking forward to the trip, but for the sake of the decencies we'd best get aboard the coach separately.'

Albert, with his hand on the doorknob, turned and smiled at her, his eyes twinkling over the top of his spectacles. 'If the folk on the bus could see us sharing our breakfast they'd think the worst,' he observed. 'Come to that, so would young Tess. But whilst the cat's away the mice will play; not that we have been playing, or not in a naughty sense at any rate.'

Edie smiled back. 'You've been the perfect gentleman,

171

as always, Albert,' she assured him. 'And we'd never have thought of you coming up here for breakfast if that coach trip last week hadn't started so perishin' early. But there you are, we've established a tradition and a very nice tradition it is too. In fact, I think we'll keep it up even after Tess gets home.'

'You'll change your mind if she shows us a disapproving face,' Albert cautioned. 'Aren't we lucky that it's a brilliant day? I've packed a towel and my bathing shorts so we can have a dip in the briny. I take it you've done likewise?'

'Oh, go away with you,' Edie said, laughing. 'You'd best see if you can catch the postman and collect your own mail, then we can read our letters together.'

She began to prepare the packed lunch which they would share, for though in the past they had preferred to eat in restaurants or cafés, because they were saving hard they now usually took sandwiches for midday. She was wrapping them in greaseproof paper when Albert returned, a little breathless after pursuing the postman and climbing the narrow stairway which led to the flat. He sat down at the table. 'Three for you, all from house agents, a bill for me from my cigarette supplier, and one personal one each; yours from Tess and mine from Janine,' he said. He handed her envelopes to Edie, opened his bill and pulled a face, then opened his daughter's missive and sighed. 'No doubt her life is full of excitement, but her letters don't reflect it,' he said ruefully. 'Perhaps it's because she was always closer to her mother than to me, but sometimes I think we've grown so far apart that if we met we should scarcely recognise each other. But it's all part of being a parent – the letting go, I mean – so I mustn't grumble, but be glad that she's enjoying a wonderful life in another land. It's just a pity that she can't write it all down in a way that a distant father can understand. Want to read it? I'm sure Janine wouldn't mind.'

Edie read the letter quickly, then looked quizzically across at Albert. 'She's having fun and enjoying her life,' she pointed out. 'Some people have the gift of description and others . . .'

'Haven't,' Albert said with a reluctant grin. 'If I'm not being nosy, what has Tess got to report?'

The letter was a short one, but Albert smiled as he read. 'Your Tess knows how to write,' he said, handing the pages back. 'Janine isn't the only one having a whale of a time. But I wouldn't swap with either of 'em. I've not been to Blackpool for years!'

Edie got to her feet, scooped up the food she had prepared and put it into the rucksack which Albert found the most convenient way of carrying their picnic. Glancing at the clock on the mantelpiece, she gave a squeak of dismay. 'Oh, Albert, look at the time! I haven't been to Blackpool for ages, either, not since I was four or five, in fact, and I shall be heartbroken if we miss the coach. Do let's hurry.'

Despite the fact that it was a lovely day, with the sun streaming down out of a cloudless blue sky, they both took their mackintoshes off the hook by the kitchen door and hurried downstairs to head for the pick-up spot for the Blackpool coach. 'I'll write to Tess as soon as we get home this evening,' Edie said. 'And you must write to Janine as well. Do you include her husband in your letters?'

'No, since he's never so much as added a few words to the bottom of hers,' Albert admitted. 'And I'd love a photograph – perhaps a wedding group, if they have such things in the United States – but she's never sent one.'

'It was signed off *Love from Janine and all*, but you would think they could send a picture,' Edie said. She glanced at her watch. 'Better get a move on, or we really will miss the coach. And when you reply to Janine's letter, just you tell her that a photograph of her wedding group would take pride of place on your mantelpiece. That should fetch 'em . . . young people don't realise how we old 'uns appreciate such things.'

By now they had reached the coach stop, and even as Edie began to say that she would draft the letter for him, the vehicle for which they waited drew up alongside and they climbed aboard. They both liked to occupy the front window seat and took it in turns to do so, and now there was an amicable squabble over whose turn it was. Edie said it was Albert's turn this trip and he said it was Edie's, but in the end he settled the matter by pushing Edie ahead of him and then taking the seat next to her.

They arranged themselves comfortably and began to plan their day. First they would go on the beach, perhaps have a bit of a paddle, look for shells and pretty stones. They would eat their picnic there if it stayed fine, and then they meant to attend the tea dance held daily in the Tower. They would see the menagerie before going right to the very top of the Tower and looking down at not just Blackpool but also distant Southport and perhaps even Liverpool itself.

'Then we'll have a nice cup of tea and one of those

174

delicious iced buns which they sell in the Winter Gardens,' Albert said contentedly. 'Then we'll have lots to tell Tess and Janine when we write.'

'Well, I don't know when I've enjoyed a day more,' Edie said contentedly. The two of them were strolling along the prom as the sun began to sink in the west. 'We did just as we said we would . . .'

'And then we had fish and chips out of newspaper, and came down on the prom to say a last goodbye to the sea,' Albert said contentedly. 'You're right, Edie; it's been the best day of the summer so far.' An idea suddenly occurred to him. 'Edie, suppose we have our photographs taken? There's a booth near the Winter Gardens . . . or we could go to the funfair and poke our heads through those round holes so that when the picture is developed it will look as though we're in cowboy gear, or a mermaid and a merman . . . would that amuse Janine, do you suppose, and encourage her to follow suit?'

Edie thought this a splendid idea, but time was short so they trotted briskly along the pavement, checked that their coach was at the stop, and continued on to the fairground. They chose to be pictured as what Edie described as 'cowpersons', and having paid out their money and left their addresses felt they had done all they could to persuade Janine to send a picture, and returned to the prom, where the other passengers had already started to board the coach. Albert and Edie took their places and began to chat to the bus driver, telling him what a grand day they had had, and asking him how he had spent the long and sunny hours. 'For I remember you telling us once before that you left the

175

coach in a big car park on the outskirts of town and came in with your mates to enjoy a go on the funfair or a couple of games of bingo,' Albert said. 'My friend and I took a look at the funfair but decided we'd spend our money on fish and chips instead.' He laughed. 'Not such fun as the big wheel, but more filling.'

The bus driver agreed rather absently and began to count heads, for though a good few of the passengers knew each other there was always the chance that someone had boarded the wrong coach, or misunderstood their time of departure, so that the driver of each of the great vehicles drawn up alongside the prom had to check his passenger list carefully against the number of seats already filled.

The time for departure came and went and they were still one passenger short. Their driver walked along the line of coaches still waiting to be filled but could not find his missing charge, and when at last he returned to the coach Albert suddenly remembered something. He stood up and leaned close to the driver. 'Excuse me, Bob,' he said urgently. 'If you remember, when we were setting out this morning you said that a chap called Edwin Briars had sent one of his mates along to say he'd got one of them 'orrible bugs, and was busy throwing up, so couldn't take his place on the coach. He had paid for his ticket and I believe you told his mate that since it was illness he could get a refund from the coach office.'

Bob struck his head with the back of his hand. 'Wharra fool I am. Fancy me forgettin' that,' he said. He grinned apologetically at the seated passengers. 'I'm sorry, folks; it seems I've held us up for nothin'. But never mind, I'll put me wellie down and have us all back in the 'Pool no more'n five minutes after we're due.'

Having done his duty, Albert returned to his seat. Edie rummaged in her pocket and produced a bag of humbugs; they both took one and leaned against each other as the bus roared on through the deepening darkness. They were all but asleep, might have slept, in fact, save that someone at the back of the vehicle began to sing an old Vera Lynn favourite, 'We'll Meet Again'. Other songs followed as the coach pounded along, Bob's voice joining in the chorus with as much enthusiasm as though he had not already had a very full day and must, like most of his customers, be longing for his bed.

They were about halfway home and travelling pretty well flat out, Albert guessed, when the driver gave a gasp. 'Something's up with the steerin'!' he said hoarsely. 'The old girl won't answer to me hand on the wheel.' He slammed his foot on the brake but nothing happened and the next moment the headlights went out, the bus swerved crazily and, for Albert at least, the world turned violently upside down and darkness descended.

Chapter Seven

Albert came to to find he was lying on what seemed to be grass, at the foot of what looked like an enormous mountain. There was something pinning him down; he realised it was a coach seat, probably the very one he had been sitting on when the driver had declared that the steering had gone. Albert tried to wriggle out from under the seat, whispering Edie's name in a tiny thread of a voice as he did so, and heard a soft moan.

Edie! It must be her, trying to respond to him saying her name. He turned and felt around, found nothing except the grass upon which he lay. Nothing. Painfully, he stretched his hand out further and – oh joy! – felt a shoulder, then an arm, an elbow, then a wrist. But as his fingers felt lower he nearly recoiled in horror. The wrist was gashed open, he could not tell how deeply, the hand beneath it was sticky with blood and the blood was still welling out.

Immediately all his first aid training during the war rushed to the forefront of his mind. Panic receded. First, stop the bleeding. He pulled a clean white handkerchief out of his jacket pocket and managed to wriggle on to his side so that he had both hands free, then bound the handkerchief tightly round Edie's wrist and began to shout. His voice, which had refused to obey him earlier, came out loud and clear, and as his shouts began to echo round the bus – for it was the coach itself which loomed over him, not a mountain – he saw lights flashing, glimpsed the starry sky through a gap in the mangled metal, and demanded that someone come at once before Edie bled to death.

Things happened quickly after that. Many vehicles lit up the scene, including several ambulances, and the drivers and passengers of other buses, and those from their own vehicle who had managed to escape with minor cuts and bruises, were milling around trying to help. Firemen came also, with their heavy-lifting equipment, so that it was not too long before Albert and Edie were both freed, though Edie had not regained consciousness. She and Albert were dispatched to hospital in the same ambulance and all the way into the city Albert held Edie's hand and talked comfortingly to her. 'You'll be all right; there was a doctor waiting to give you a shot of something when we managed to get you out from under that seat,' he told her. 'They don't know quite how bad your injuries are yet, but I mean to stay with you and see you get the best of all possible attention. Thank God for the National Health Service! Hey, Edie, now the government will pay all your bills so you can concentrate on getting well again without having to worry about money. I dare say you'll be back in Deering's by next Monday, raring to go, but if you aren't you'll get sickness benefit. Oh, we'll see you right, never you fret.'

He was crouching beside the stretcher bed in the ambulance, trying to sound both cheerful and positive, but in fact he felt downright terrified, Edie was so white, so drained. The ambulance men had dressed the dreadful wrist and now it was tightly swathed in white bandages, but they had also told him that his missus, as they called her, might have other injuries: a broken shoulder, three broken ribs, an elbow which had been jerked out of joint and a broken tibia, all on her left side.

'Is your missus right-handed?' one of the ambulance men had asked.

Albert cleared his throat. 'Yes,' he said hoarsely. 'Thank God for small mercies.'

'Well, even so you'll find yourself doing all sorts of housework for a few weeks yet,' the ambulance man said. He had looked keenly at Albert and then, seeming to like what he saw, added: 'Or maybe it's more likely to be months than weeks. But I can see you're the sort of feller who's learned to cope with trouble. In the forces, were you, during the war? They teach you how to stay calm in the face of adversity.'

Albert, however, had had to shake his head. 'No, but I was an ARP warden and a member of St John's Ambulance. I had to deal with all sorts, which has stood me in good stead tonight.'

Edie Williams heard voices, though none that she recognised; they were echoing, strange, coming at her from several different angles. She tried to listen, but the words which she could catch made no sense. So she tried instead to open her eyes to see what was happening. Her eyelids, heavy as lead, refused to lift. Then a voice that she did know came to her ears. It was Albert's voice, her good friend Albert, and he was telling her that she would be all right. Edie found this immensely comforting, though she saw no reason for him to say it.

If she was in danger she could not imagine what form such danger could take. She opened her mouth to ask Albert what he was talking about, but no sound came out. For a moment more she tried to listen, and then she made another attempt to open her eyes, but as she did so a violent pain shot from her shoulder right down to her fingertips. She gave a gasp and a moan, and the voice she did not recognise spoke comfortingly. 'There you are, Mrs Williams. Just a little injection to help keep the pain at bay until you're stronger.' Edie was suddenly sure that she recognised that voice. Not to whom it belonged; she recognised it as the sort of voice a doctor uses to a patient. She tried to nod her head to show that she understood, but she was sinking into what felt like a bed of feathers, which, if she allowed them to, would float her into the darkness from which it seemed she had barely emerged. She made another effort to lift her lids, to demand to be told where she was and what had happened to her. She knew of course that she was Mrs Edie Williams . . . but other than that she was still fighting to regain her full senses when she felt her hand taken once more, and a voice both dear and familiar spoke close against her ear.

'It's all right, Edie. Our coach ran off the road and you got the worst of it. If only I'd insisted on having the window seat! Sometimes it don't do to be a gentleman, because it was you who found yourself crushed by the weight of the coach. The doctor's given you an injection and he says you'll sleep for hours, and when you wake up I'll explain more, but now all you have to do is go to sleep, because sleep's the best medicine, they say.' Edie's hand had lain motionless in Albert's, but at his words she put every ounce of her strength into giving his fingers a tiny squeeze, and then, almost thankfully, she sank into the feathery darkness.

'Hey up, someone's coming up the lane. Oh, it's the telegraph boy . . . he's coming here!'

Jonty and Tess had just left the milking parlour, each carrying a brimming galvanised bucket. A couple of days ago they had taken themselves off to Mundesley and Tess, with many squeals, had allowed Jonty to teach her to do the front crawl, and then to swim on her back, two skills which had eluded her until then. It had been a happy day, and just now they had been discussing what they should do the following day, for that too was to be a holiday. Jonty wanted to visit the Nicholas Everett Park, for he had a friend who sailed on Oulton Broad and had offered to lend Jonty his yacht for the day. The yacht, the *Merry Dancer*, was moored at the park and Jonty, who usually crewed for his friend, was looking forward to showing Tess all the delights of the Broad. In fact they had been discussing whether to take a picnic or to go to Waller's Fish Restaurant when they emerged from the milking parlour to see the telegraph boy turning into their yard.

Tess's hand flew to her heart, then she gave herself a shake. 'It's daft, I know, but ever since the war even the sight of a telegraph boy in the street gives me the shivers. Only I expect it'll be for one of the hands, or for your father and mother, not for me.'

'Yes, I'm sure you're right,' Jonty said, but Tess thought he looked uneasy. 'Still, work must go on! Let's get this milk to the cooler, and then we'll go in and see.'

The back door opened, and Mrs Bell exchanged a few

words with the telegraph boy before beckoning to Tess. 'That's for you, Tess,' she called. 'Best stand the milk down and come and read it. The feller say it's reply paid.'

Tess began to lower her bucket to the ground, but Jonty seized it and jerked his head at the kitchen door. 'Don't worry about the milk; I'll deal with that,' he said. 'Just you read your telegram, and if it's from your gran wanting you to go home early . . .'

But Tess was already taking the envelope from the boy. She opened it and swiftly scanned the contents, and felt the blood drain from her face. She turned wide eyes up to Mrs Bell. 'There's been an accident. Gran was on a coach trip with Mr Payne and he's telegraphed to say the coach went off the road and Gran's in hospital.' She had barely finished speaking before Jonty was at her side, gently taking the telegram from her.

He read it aloud. '*Gran in hospital after injuries in coach accident stop come home stop Albert Payne.*'

Tess turned to her hostess. 'Oh, Mrs Bell, I'll have to go at once. Can Jonty drive me to Thorpe station? Oh, but I've got to reply to this . . .' She clasped her head as though to still her whirling thoughts. 'What should I say? I can't tell Albert what time I'll arrive in Lime Street because I don't know . . .'

Jonty ushered her gently into the kitchen, sat her down in a chair and then addressed the telegraph boy, who was standing waiting, pencil and telegram form at the ready. 'I reckon you can't do better than to say *Coming asap stop Tess.*' Jonty glanced at his mother. 'Can you do without me for a few days, Ma? I'd like to go back with Tess because she may need someone to give a hand. I'm not suggesting that I'd be gone long, but surely a few days wouldn't hurt?'

'Oh, Jonty, if only you could . . .' Tess began, but at that moment the back door opened and Mr Bell strode into the room. The telegraph boy, clearing his throat meaningfully, indicated the reply paid form.

'If you wouldn't mind, miss, the sooner you give me your reply the sooner it'll reach the sender,' he pointed out.

Tess stared. 'Oh! Oh, I see; the telegram was sent to me so it must be I who reply to it. Only Jonty said exactly what I would have said myself.' She seized the boy's pencil and wrote swiftly: *Coming asap stop Tess*.

The boy studied the form. 'The sender paid for another eleven words,' he pointed out rather reproachfully. 'Isn't there anything else you'd like to add?'

Jonty laughed, but Tess just shook her head. 'No, I think it's better to keep it short,' she said. 'It's no use pretending that I've any idea when I'll reach Liverpool, because I haven't. We've already missed the first train, the one I would have been catching in a few days' time, and I've no idea when the next one leaves, let alone arrives. So that's it, thank you.'

The boy tucked the reply-paid form into this pocket, sketched a vague salute to the assembled company and left. Tess watched him mount his bicycle and ride off across the yard, then turned to Mrs Bell, who was explaining what had just happened to her husband. '. . . so if it's all right with you, Father, Jonty would like to go back to Liverpool with Tess, just for a couple of days,' she was saying. 'I don't say we shan't miss him, because we shall, but he deserve a day off now and again.

184

Tomorrow was going to be a holiday anyway, so he can go with my blessing, if you're of the same mind.'

Mr Bell nodded slowly. 'Good idea,' he said. 'And then if there's nowt much wrong with the old lady he can bring young Tess back to enjoy the rest of her time with us.' He looked at the telegram, laid out upon the kitchen table, then smiled at Tess. 'It don't say your gran's badly hurt, so if she can manage it she's very welcome to come back with you and Jonty. Mother'd take good care of her, feed her up so's she gets well all the quicker.'

Tess smiled back at him, but knew it was a poor effort. 'I don't think Mr Payne would have sent a telegram if Gran's injuries weren't serious,' she said. 'And she wouldn't be in hospital either, not if they were trivial.'

'True,' Mr Bell said, nodding his head. He turned to Jonty. 'If you're going to go, best get a move on. You want to pack a bag, and you'd best leave me a list of tasks you'll want one of the men to take on.' He turned to Tess. 'You'd best be packing yourself, my woman, and Mother here will put you up a few little treats for your gran . . .'

'Right,' Tess said, heading for the stairs, but Mrs Bell detained her. 'Wait you a minute. Where's Jonty goin' to lay his head? We don't want no gossip . . . some folk have evil minds.'

Tess laughed, unable to stop herself reflecting that it was Mrs Bell whose evil mind would start thinking things if she and Jonty shared the flat in Gran's absence. But on this score at least she was able to reassure her hostess. 'He'll sleep in Mr Payne's spare bedroom, I expect,' she promised. 'And thank you so much for inviting Gran; I know she'd love to come as soon as she's well enough, because she's said many a time how she regrets the fact that Bell Farm is such a long way off. If it was nearer she'd have come over long ago to thank you in person for your kindness to me.'

Mrs Bell began to ask whether there was anything else she could do to help but her son shook his head at her. 'Leave it, Ma. If I'm to go to Liverpool with Tess then Pa will have to drive us to Norwich Thorpe and you might as well come along too. Then all the way there you can be finding out how best to help the Williamses.' With that he disappeared up the stairs close on Tess's heels, and in less time than Tess could have believed possible they were packing themselves into the Ford with Mr and Mrs Bell in the front and Tess, Jonty and all their luggage in the back.

Tess had only experienced Mr Bell's driving when he was at the wheel of the Morris, and found his erratic progress in the Ford rather frightening; indeed, under normal circumstances she would have been terrified, but because she was longing to reach their destination she made no complaint as the tyres squealed on corners and the driver, instead of indicating right or left, kept turning the windscreen wipers on and off. It was Jonty who hissed in his breath between his teeth at every junction, for Mrs Bell seemed to take her husband's driving for granted, though she did suggest mildly, as they turned into the station forecourt, that they might accompany the young people on to the concourse and have a cup of tea in the refreshment room 'to calm our nerves'.

Mr Bell, parking askew so that he took up two spaces,

looked vaguely affronted, but the others were too busy sorting out their luggage to soothe hurt feelings. Instead, Tess and Jonty hurried to the ticket office where Tess produced the telegram and the station master himself spread out timetables and helped them to plan the route which would bring them to Liverpool Lime Street most rapidly.

Because they had missed the train Tess would normally have caught they had several changes, but provided the services were more or less on time they should reach their destination by early evening at the latest. Mrs Bell had packed them some sandwiches and apples but nothing to drink, because she knew that vendors of tea, coffee and lemonade lined the platforms at most country stations in order that travellers might quench their thirst.

Tess and Jonty made full use of these facilities but even so, by the time their train drew in to Liverpool Lime Street, they were hot and tired and Tess's anxiety had grown to nightmare proportions. She fairly tumbled out of the carriage, festooned with bags and baskets, and looked wildly round the platform. She did not expect to see Albert, knowing that he could have little idea of her possible time of arrival, but she thought he might have arranged for one of Gran's colleagues at the bakery to meet each train. However, there wasn't a face she recognised to be seen, so she was doubly glad of Jonty's calming presence. He helped her to collect everything – his own possessions were in the rucksack on his back – and then the two of them set off. They had reached Lime Street itself and were staring rather hopelessly at the lengthy queue for taxis when Tess's attention was caught by the headline on the fly sheet behind which a newspaper seller was offering copies of that day's *Echo*. The fly sheet said, in enormous black letters: *Coach overturns, many injured*.

Tess gasped and grabbed Jonty's arm. 'That must be when Gran was hurt. Buy a copy, Jonty,' she begged. 'No wonder Albert sent us that telegram! I pray my poor darling gran isn't badly hurt! She and I are such a happy little family . . . Oh, if anything happens to Gran . . .'

'Join the queue,' Jonty ordered. 'I'll get the paper.'

He left her, and Tess had turned to join the queue when, further up it, she saw someone she knew. He was staring straight ahead, not acknowledging her, behaving, in fact, the way he had always behaved since their falling out three years previously. But now, in her thirst for information, Tess would have questioned the Devil himself, had he been present. She abandoned her luggage and went over to the tall, fair-haired figure already halfway up the queue.

'Snowy! Oh, Snowy, I'm in the most dreadful trouble. Have you read the *Echo* this evening? Yes, of course you have, you've got a copy. I've been away, but Mr Payne sent me a telegram to say my gran was in hospital after being injured in a coach accident. I don't know which hospital she's in, so I suppose I'll have to go straight to Heyworth Street, unless . . . oh, Snowy, do you know where they took the injured?'

When she had first accosted him Snowy's eyes had been cold as ice, his mouth set in a sneer, but as she explained it was as though the ice melted and the old Snowy, the one who had been her friend, suddenly reappeared. She was clutching his arm with her right hand and now he took it in a reassuring grasp. 'They're in the Stanley Hospital, or most of them are at any rate. I've a cousin who's a nurse there and she said they'd taken most of the injured. But look, Tess, you take my place in the queue and I'll go to the back . . . or would you like me to come with you to the hospital? I'm awful sorry your gran was on the coach but of course, coming from Liverpool, most folk seem to know at least one of the passengers. I say, is all that luggage yours?'

'Yes – no – well, it's mine and my friend's,' Tess said rather wildly. 'He's gone to get a copy of the *Echo* because I thought it might mention the hospital, but now you've told me . . .'

But at this point Jonty joined them, raising his brows at Snowy. 'Who's your friend?' he asked, then stuck out a hand. 'How do you do, whoever you are! I heard you offering to give up your place in the queue to Tess. It's awfully good of you, and if you don't mind we'll accept, because we're very anxious to get to the hospital and find out just how bad Mrs Williams is.'

Once more, Tess watched as Snowy's expression changed from concern to suspicion and then, warmingly, to a sort of friendship. As Snowy turned from them to go to the back of the queue, they both called their thanks, but before they could do more the next taxi to return to the rank drew up, and others in the queue ahead who had heard the conversation stood to one side and pushed the young pair into the vehicle with an injunction to the driver to: 'Drive hell for leather to the Stanley Hospital, mate.'

*

189

In the taxi, Jonty put a comforting hand on Tess's. 'I expect Mr Payne will be with her, but of course they won't tell him an awful lot, because he's not a relative,' he said. 'In fact the doctors will be waiting for you, because if they need a signature and your gran can't give it herself, then you, as her next of kin, will be the one whose go-ahead they need.'

Tess nodded, peering out through the dusk. 'But if she needed an emergency operation I'm sure they wouldn't wait for my say-so,' she pointed out. 'When it's a matter of life or death . . .'

Jonty gave a theatrical sigh. 'That's right, look on the black side,' he said resignedly. 'I hope when your gran sits up in bed and asks why you've quit your holiday when it's got almost another week to run, you'll apologise to me for getting in such a lather.' He looked at her curiously. 'Who was that chap, by the way? The one who gave up his place in the queue to us.'

'Oh, just a fellow I used to know, but we fell out and I haven't come across him for ages,' Tess said vaguely. 'Ah, here's the hospital. Oh, I am stupid, Jonty. We've got all this luggage which we'll have to drag round the hospital with us! If I'd had a grain of sense, I'd have got the taxi to drop us at the flat and wait whilst we lugged this stuff upstairs and left it in the kitchen. Still, we're doomed to carry it with us now, so we might as well get going.'

The taxi had drawn up in front of the revolving doors of the hospital and Tess and Jonty got out, collected their baggage and approached the foyer, and as they did so Tess gave a groan of dismay. 'Look at all those people! It's visiting time, that's why it's so dreadfully busy. Still, we'll ask at reception for Gran's ward, and perhaps someone will take us to it. It's a big hospital and awfully easy to get lost in.'

They reached the reception desk and a stern-looking woman in a white coat surveyed them and their luggage through a pair of horn-rimmed spectacles, but as soon as they gave Gran's name she seemed to know it, and shook her head. 'You can go up to the ward, my dear, but I don't think you'll be allowed to visit Mrs Williams tonight,' she said kindly. 'Indeed, there would be little point in it, as I believe she's still sedated. She's in a small room on the end of one of the wards, and is only allowed one visitor at a time.'

Tess felt the blood drain from her face. 'Is she – is she very ill?' she faltered. 'I was staying with friends and received a telegram which just said she'd been injured in a coach accident. My Uncle Albert sent the telegram . . . is he here? In the hospital, I mean. Because if he is I really must see him.'

The lady behind the desk reached for a large book and scanned the names in it, then nodded, albeit a trifle reluctantly. 'Ye-es, a Mr Albert Payne has spent a great deal of time here today, either in the waiting room or at Mrs Williams's side,' she admitted. 'Are you a relative? I'm afraid if you aren't—'

'I'm her granddaughter and her next of kin; there are only the two of us so far as I know. My mother – Mrs Williams's daughter – died at the start of the war,' Tess said. 'Jonty here is an old friend who is staying in Liverpool for a few days. Do you think Gran will be well enough to see him before he has to go back?'

'I've no idea,' the woman admitted. 'You'll have to ask

191

the doctor. But of course your Uncle Albert may have already done so.'

Tess opened her mouth to say that Albert was just an honorary uncle and then closed it again. There was no harm in a little deception if it would help Gran to get better, and she was suddenly sure that Albert's friendship could only do good, so she said: 'Then we'd best go along to my gran's ward and find Uncle Albert at once. Could you direct us, please?'

Albert sat by the bed, waiting. He had seen the doctors, who had simply accepted him as someone with Mrs Williams's best interests at heart, and had told him quite enough to make him determined not to leave the hospital again until she had regained consciousness. Sister told him that they were now satisfied Mrs Williams had no internal injuries, but she had lost a good deal of blood and now she lay very still with tubes leading from various containers into her good hand. The 'bad' wrist had been stitched and rebandaged and her broken bones set, save for the ribs which Sister assured Albert would knit themselves, given time.

What worried Albert most, and he knew it worried the hospital staff too, was the fact that she had not yet recovered consciousness, though he had been immensely heartened when she had returned the pressure of his hand the previous night. But Sister was encouraging. 'She's strong and determined; I'm sure she's just using this period of complete shutdown to help her to mend,' she had said. 'So you must not worry, Mr Payne, or she may become conscious that all is not well.' She had smiled kindly at him, a fat, bustling little woman, always on the go, seldom sitting down for more than a few minutes at a time; a woman in fact very similar to the one now lying so still and silent in her hospital bed. For some reason this gave Albert the feeling that whilst Sister Bowen was on duty his dear Edie was in safe hands, though conversely, of course, it meant that when Sister Bowen went off duty and Night Sister appeared, Albert was reluctant to leave the hospital in case Edie took a turn for the worse.

So now he sat on the uncomfortable little bench, holding Edie's hand and watching the slow drip drip as the blood transfusion made its way from the bottle into the back of Edie's hand.

When he heard a soft tap on the door he was so surprised that he let go of Edie's hand, for nurses and doctors bustled in and out without so much as a by your leave, and since it was only Edie who occupied the small room no one else had any reason to tap on the door. Albert went across with a finger already to his lips, but he had barely got the door open before Tess was clutching his hands, and he saw tears rolling down her white and frightened face.

'Oh, Albert, I came as soon as I could,' she whispered. 'Poor darling Gran! Please may I see her, just to reassure myself that . . .'

But Albert had already stood aside to let her through and in seconds she was bending over the bed, her voice low but full of love. 'Darling Gran, it's your Tess; I've come home! You must get better, because we're such a little family, just the two of us, and if one goes . . .' But the figure in the bed had stirred. And even as Tess turned wildly towards Albert, Gran spoke.

'Tess, Tess,' she said in a tiny, cracked voice which Albert hardly recognised. 'I knew . . . I knew . . .'

'You knew I'd come,' Tess said tenderly. 'And you were right; as soon as I got Albert's telegram Jonty and I set out for the station. Oh, Gran, now that I'm here you've simply got to get well!'

Albert went quickly over to Tess where she stood by the side of the bed. 'Wait until we tell the staff,' he whispered. 'They've been waiting for her to speak, and now she's done it I'm sure she'll begin to improve. But we mustn't tire her. Just reassure her that you won't go far, and you'll be here for her when she wakes tomorrow.'

Tess did so, and Albert took her arm and was about to lead her from the ward when Gran spoke again. 'Dear Albert, thank you,' she said. Albert looked back eagerly, but Edie's eyes had closed once more and she turned her head into the pillow, making it plainer than words could that she just wanted to sleep.

Albert and Tess left the small room together, to find Jonty awaiting them in the corridor. He grinned sheepishly from one to the other. 'I didn't want to come in. It didn't seem fair somehow to see your gran for the first time when she's so ill,' he explained. 'But I gather from your expressions that you're pleased about something. I'm so glad.'

Albert beamed. 'She's spoken, and recognised us both,' he said joyfully. 'Sister Bowen said that once she came round getting better would just be a matter of time. She'd had a bang on the head during the coach accident, you see, and they were afraid there might be brain damage, though Sister Bowen thought it a remote possibility. But we must find someone in authority . . .' He broke off as a figure approached them, and when she got close enough Tess could see that it was a sister. She glanced at Albert and saw that he was smiling once more as he went to meet the nurse. 'Sister Bowen, Mrs Williams has come round and recognised us,' he said. 'As you know, I could hardly bear to leave her side while she was unconscious, but now we'll go home and return tomorrow morning, if that's acceptable.'

Sister said it was and accompanied them to the foyer. 'But don't come too early, because Doctor does a ward round in the mornings,' she told them. 'Just get yourself a good night's sleep.' She turned to Tess. 'I don't know whether your uncle has told you, but he didn't escape unscathed from the accident himself. He's nursing a broken collarbone and a great many contusions, but nothing that won't mend so long as he doesn't try to do too much.'

'I won't; I'm not such a fool. I've got to get fit so I can keep an eye on Edie,' Albert said. 'Good night, Sister, and thank you for everything.'

The trio pushed their way through the revolving doors to find that a light drizzle had begun to fall. Hospital visiting must have just come to an end, for as they hesitated on the pavement people began to stream out of the hospital and a long queue formed at the nearest tram stop. Tess and Jonty were still clutching their baggage and Tess would have been glad to have hailed a taxi, but the majority of the visitors were waiting for trams or buses and there was no sign of a taxi rank, so she supposed they must do likewise. When she suggested it, however, her companions disagreed. 'Judging by the length of the queue it'll be hours before you can get on the tram or bus you want, and then we'll be downright unpopular because of all our luggage,' Jonty pointed out. 'Is it too far to walk?' He grinned at Albert. 'A couple of hours away from Bell Farm and she's forgotten how to use her legs! Come on, Mr Payne, you take her left arm and I'll take her right and we'll get her moving between us.'

Tess laughed, assuring her old friend that no help would be needed, and very soon they were at the tobacconist's shop and Albert Payne was unlocking the door, leading them up the stairs and ushering them into his neat little flat. Once in the kitchen he put the kettle on the stove and asked Tess to make tea whilst he showed Jonty the room which he would occupy whilst he was in Liverpool.

'My flat and that of Mrs Williams are very similar,' he told the young man. 'I've planned for a long time to turn my spare bedroom into a proper bathroom, but I've never actually got round to doing it.' He pulled a face. 'I'm afraid I'm a great one for putting off making decisions. In fact, this horrible accident has already taught me a much-needed lesson. Mrs Williams and I have been talking about starting an ice cream parlour somewhere in this area, but we've never actually got round to doing anything about it. But now I can see that one never knows what life has in store, and in future *carpe diem* shall be my motto.' He smiled at his young companion. 'You'll find the bed is already made up, for though I had no idea that you were coming back with Tess I had an intuitive feeling that someone might need my spare room and rushed home this morning to get it ready. There's a clean towel on the rail and soap and a flannel by the basin, but the water in the ewer will be cold, I'm afraid.'

Jonty looked at his hands, then at his reflection in the small round mirror on top of the chest of drawers. 'I'd like a wash, and I don't mind the water being cold,' he said. 'I really do appreciate your kindness, Mr Payne.'

'It's a pleasure,' Albert said formally. 'I'll leave you now, but the tea will be brewed in ten minutes and I dare say you could do with a bite to eat. I'm sure young Tess would pop down to the bakery and buy a cake . . .'

Jonty laughed. 'No need,' he said cheerfully. 'My mother packed a basket with all sorts of things, amongst which was a very large fruit cake. I dare say that will stave off hunger pangs until bedtime.'

It was two days before Tess decided to allow Jonty to meet her grandmother, for Edie Williams was languid, apt to fall asleep in mid-sentence and, to put it mildly, not looking her best. But on the third day one of the nurses approached her patient with a bundle under her arm which she spread out on Edie's bed. It proved to be a very pretty bedjacket in pale pink wool with lavender-coloured ribbons, a gift from Miss Foulks, who had owned the milliner's shop. The nurse smiled encouragingly as her patient exclaimed with pleasure, and flourished a hairbrush. 'I'm going to make you beautiful, Mrs Williams,' she announced. 'Your granddaughter wants to bring her young man to visit you today, so you really must look your best.'

'Oh, but nurse, I wanted to wait until the bruising

round my right eye had gone—' Edie began, only to be swiftly interrupted.

'Now no nonsense please, Mrs Williams; the young man has come all the way from Norfolk, leaving his parents to do all the work on their farm in his absence, so naturally, now you're so much better, he is planning to go back home. He may stay on a day or two, but your granddaughter wants the pair of you to meet as soon as possible, so if you will kindly sit up straight I'll start to brush your hair out.' She suited action to words, tutting disapproval as the brush caught in the older woman's thick white locks. 'Goodness, what a lot of tangles, but what beautiful hair you have, Mrs Williams.'

She worked away with a will and presently handed her patient a mirror. 'There! See what a difference I've made! Now slip on the bedjacket and when the visitors begin to arrive they'll be bowled over. Indeed, if you let a couple of locks of your beautiful hair fall across your black eye you'll be the belle of the ward.'

Edie Williams looked in the mirror and gave a little purr of satisfaction. The nurse had done her work well, and Edie found herself looking forward to meeting Jonty instead of dreading that he would think her a hideous old hag. She just hoped that Albert would accompany the youngsters and be equally impressed by the transformation.

Jonty descended the stairs and came out into the stock-room of the tobacconist's shop. Tess had rearranged her interview for the job of nursery assistant at a factory way out in the suburbs, but when he had suggested accompanying her she had been, not exactly brusque, but perhaps a little sharp. 'There's no point in the pair of us trailing out there, and there'll be nothing for you to do because it's just factories and houses, no shops or anything,' she had said. 'You've been awfully good about helping Albert, so why not spend today exploring Liverpool? There's all sorts, you know. There's the Picton Library, the Walker Art Gallery, the museum . . . oh, no end of things to see. You'll want to go to Paddy's Market because it's easily the cheapest place to pick up little presents. And for my part I'd rather think of you enjoying yourself than trying to hurry the interview so I can get back to you.'

This conversation had taken place in Albert's kitchen and Jonty had seen Albert giving Tess a quizzical look, though he had said nothing. But Tess had been staring at him, so Jonty had said, 'All right, all right, I know when I'm not wanted. You go off, love of my life, and I'll take a look at this Liverpool of yours.'

For a moment Tess had looked stricken and, seeing that look, Jonty had hastened to reassure her. 'It's all right, you daft girl, I was only teasing. And you're right, of course; I really ought to take a good look at Liverpool before I go home. Dare I suggest we meet for a bite of lunch at Lyons Corner House? We could say we'll meet at one o'clock, but if you're still engaged I'll have a bowl of soup and a crusty roll, and that'll see me right till suppertime.'

Tess had agreed to this. She had popped into the tobacconist's at nine and come up to the flat so that Jonty might see her interview suit, which was a grey coat and skirt, a navy blue shirt and matching shoes. Jonty had approved – he had been eating his breakfast at the time – and Tess had smiled gratefully and patted his cheek. 'Thanks, chuck; wish me luck,' she had cried, and had then broken down in giggles. 'I'm a poet and didn't know it,' she announced, heading for the kitchen door. 'See you at one o'clock, unless I'm held up.'

Now Jonty crossed the stockroom and joined Albert behind the counter. 'I'm off on a voyage of exploration,' he said merrily. 'It would be too bad to go back to Bell Farm without having seen anything of Liverpool. Tess has told me I must visit the Picton Library and some art gallery or other . . .'

Albert pulled a face. 'Dull work,' he exclaimed. 'What you want to do, Jonty, is to take a ride on the overhead railway. Now that's something you won't see in any other city in Britain, I can guarantee it. What's more, it's the only way of getting to see all the shipping in the docks. There are really big liners, and tankers . . . oh, all sorts.' He sighed. 'Wish I could come with you and show you around, because though there's still the devil of a lot of bomb damage which hasn't been put right, I'm proud of my city.'

'Norwich is just the same; a lot of the bomb sites have become wild gardens, they tell me,' Jonty said. 'Well, I've seen for myself how rosebay, willowherb and meadowsweet have flourished in the heart of the city, so don't think I'll judge Liverpool harshly because they've not managed to rebuild completely yet. Any more hints? Only if I meet madam at one o'clock and can't reel off a list of the attractions I've visited she'll give me a rare old telling off.'

Albert grinned. 'I'd put money on the fact that Tess has never set foot in the Picton Library *or* the Walker Art

Gallery,' he said. 'You know how it is, Jonty; Parisians have never climbed the Eiffel Tower, Londoners look blank if you ask them about Westminster Abbey, and we're just the same. If you can find me one Scouser who's been inside Liverpool Cathedral I shall be astounded.'

'I think I'd better buy a street map, because I bet the cathedral is nowhere near the overhead railway,' Jonty said resignedly. 'I expect it's a huge cathedral, so I suppose I really ought to take a look. Is it very old?'

To his surprise Albert put a finger to his nose and winked. 'That would be telling,' he said mysteriously. 'And now off with you, young Mr Bell, or you'll never see any of the sights. By the way, I trust you were impressed upon meeting Tess's gran? She's a wonderful woman and Tess is a lucky girl!'

Jonty smiled. He had thought Tess's gran very pretty, very young-looking and very charming, and now he said so, and was rewarded by the delight on his companion's face.

'Yes, she's a grand lady,' Albert said, just as a customer pushed open the shop door. He raised his voice. 'Thank you, Mr Bell. See you this evening.'

Jonty emerged on to the pavement and looked around. It was all very well for Tess to reel off a list of attractions, but he had no desire to spend the morning searching for something to look at. He decided to go first to Paddy's Market on the Scotland Road, though the only present he intended to buy was a small gift for his mother; his father and the farmhands would get cigarettes from Albert's emporium – a packet of twenty Players for his father and packets of ten Woodbines for the farmhands – and in the meantime he would ask a passer-by how to reach the overhead railway. But of course since it ran alongside the docks he must go towards the Mersey. Halfway down the long road which led towards the river Jonty saw a figure heading in the same direction and, speeding up, touched the other's arm. 'Excuse me . . .' he began, and then frowned into the face of the young man he had stopped. 'Haven't I seen you somewhere before? I was just about to ask you how I could get on to the overhead railway . . . I'm *sure* we've met before, though I can't imagine . . .'

The other interrupted, grinning. 'You're Tess Williams's bucolic friend,' he said. 'A few days ago I gave up my place in the taxi queue to the pair of you. How's her gran? She's a nice old bird, and I know Tess is real fond of her. But what are you doing out alone?' He grinned suddenly, a flash of white teeth in an admittedly handsome face. 'I've seen you and Tess on Heyworth Street a couple of times, but here you are, all by yourself.' He grinned again, somewhat maliciously. 'Does this mean that Tess has got a job to help finance her schooling?'

'No, not exactly. She's gone for an interview, though,' Jonty said, rather stiffly. He had suddenly remembered Tess saying that she and this boy – what *was* his name? – had fallen out. Perhaps he should apologise and find out for himself how to get aboard the overhead railway, but before he could do so the other had shot out a hand to take Jonty's, his smile now of genuine friendship.

'I'm Desmond White, better known as Snowy. And you are . . . ?'

'I'm Jonathan Bell. Tess was evacuated to my parents' farm during the war.'

'Jonathan Bell? I don't know why, but I thought . . . Jonty! Of course, you're her friend Jonty; she often used to talk about you,' Snowy said easily. 'But look, I'm going on the overhead railway myself , so all you need do is follow me.'

Chapter Eight

Rather to his surprise Jonty had an enjoyable and instructive morning. Snowy had said that he knew the city like the back of his hand and he soon proved that this was true. The two boys whizzed from one place to the next, leaving the Anglican cathedral until last, since it was a standing joke amongst local people. It had been started nearly fifty years ago and was still unfinished. 'Of course, there was bomb damage in the May blitz,' Snowy told his companion. 'But you know what they say about Scousers: they'll argue about the number of angels who can dance on a pinhead just for the pleasure of disagreeing, and the cathedral's a case in point. I reckon Albert told you to go there as a joke, so we won't bother with that but go straight on to the school where I'm just finishing and Tess will be starting in the sixth form in September, since I know she got her School Cert and will be heading for her Higher.' The two boys had been walking towards the art gallery but suddenly, as though struck by his own words, Snowy halted and put out a hand to get his companion to stop too. 'I say, if her gran can't work for weeks, what'll Tess do about that? Will she be able to stay on at school?'

'I've no idea; she doesn't talk much about her academic hopes because she knows I was never any good at school-work, though I did manage to get my School Cert,' Jonty told his companion. 'But why should her gran's accident stop Tess from getting her Higher? I don't understand.'

Snowy snorted. 'It's pretty plain you're one of the landed gentry who don't need to struggle,' he said rather contemptuously. 'Don't you know that Tess delivers newspapers, sells fruit on a stall in St John's market, acts as a part-time waitress at weekends, and anything else which will pay her enough money to help her gran out? Surely *you*, a close friend, must have been told such things?'

Once more Jonty stiffened, about to tell Snowy that of course he understood, but then he realised that this was not strictly true. Tess had told him all right, but he had not yet seen for himself how hard it was for people who could not grow their own food, keep a few poultry, or have a share in a pig, so the glance that he turned on Snowy was apologetic. 'I'm afraid you're right about one thing: until I came here and saw the queues for anything off ration, and the tiny amounts of food you get in exchange for your coupons, I couldn't understand why Tess had to work . . . well, I suppose I thought it was for pocket money. But we Bells aren't landed gentry, honest to God we're not; we farm our land and we work bloody hard. In summer we do a twelve- or fourteen-hour day, longer when beasts are giving birth, or we're getting the harvest in, and the rewards aren't all that brilliant either. Incidentally, what do *you* do? You've been quick enough to criticise me and my family but you've not said a word about your own.'

They had stopped walking during this exchange, but now they started again, Snowy having changed his mind and headed instead for Paddy's Market. He raised his

205

brows. 'Me? What do I matter? But I have to admit I'm one of the lucky ones. Both my parents are teachers; Dad's a headmaster and Mother runs the English department in his school. So I don't have to deliver newspapers or help out in a corner shop in order to go to university.'

'Lucky old you,' Jonty said, but he didn't mean it; the mere thought of having a teacher in his own house was frightening. Expectations from such parents would be high, but thinking it over, as Snowy ushered him into the market, Jonty realised that he would not exchange his life on Bell Farm for anything at all. The long hours and the small rewards were worth it when you considered the freedom one enjoyed. Oh, Snowy – and Tess too for that matter – might be able to visit museums and art galleries; they might have their choice of several different pictures at the cinema whereas, by and large, Jonty only had whatever Mr Lyons's mobile picture house provided. Snowy and Tess could go round the shops and see all sorts of different goods, even if Tess, at least, was unable to buy very much. She had told him how she and her friend Lucy sometimes caught the ferry to Woodside to enjoy a whiff of country air and a walk through woods and fields. But this was an expedition which had to be planned for days in advance. The girls had to save up to buy their passage on the ferry, and the picnic – which they called a carryout – would be pretty boring when compared with the sort of thing Jonty's mother would have provided. I can stroll along the lane and pick a handful of ripe blackberries, or help myself to wild apples or hazelnuts, Jonty told himself with deep content. A city is all very well for city folk, but it wouldn't do for me.

He glanced at his companion, who was rifling through the second-hand clothing on one of the stalls, and grinned to himself. Snowy might think him an ignorant country boy but he knew the meaning of the word bucolic, knew Snowy had not meant it kindly. But what did it matter, after all? *Sticks and stones may break my bones but words will never hurt me*, Jonty quoted to himself. But I wonder why Snowy had that dig at me? Could it be that he's jealous because I've known Tess longer than he has? Well, it's not important, because I'll be going home in a couple of days and the next time I see Tess it'll be on the farm, in the country we both love, and Tess will have left Snowy and the city behind her. I just hope she'll get this Higher Certificate and then come down from the clouds, because what's the use of a university education for a farmer's wife?

He was so startled by his own thoughts that he exclaimed aloud, causing Snowy to swing round, several very pretty chiffon scarves draped across his arm. 'Would your mam like one of these?' he said, indicating the scarves. 'Or doesn't she go in for stuff like this? It's summer so you won't see much winter stuff about, but if I were buying for my mother I'd choose this pink one, because it's her favourite colour.'

'My mother likes blue,' Jonty said. 'But I tell you what, Snowy, is there a stall selling slippers? My mother's had her present pair for years; I reckon she'd be delighted to have a bit of a change.'

Snowy grinned. 'Any Liverpudlian would tell you that there's nothing you can't get on Paddy's Market,' he announced. 'Follow me!'

The two boys had a successful morning and were

getting along like old friends when, at a quarter to one, Jonty begged to be directed to Church Street, so that he might meet Tess and find out whether she now had yet another job.

'We're going to have lunch at Lyons Corner House,' he disclosed. 'That is, if the interview's over by then. If not I'll hang about for a bit; I suppose I might walk up towards Love Lane and hope to meet her, but it's a bit risky; chances are we'll miss one another.'

'Right. Then we turn left here and keep going for a bit and at the next junction turn right,' Snowy said instructively. He dug a hand into his pocket and examined his loose change. 'Tell you what, if Tess doesn't show, you and I can have a bite of lunch together. Of course, if Tess does turn up then I'll make myself scarce, two being company and three a crowd.'

'Oh, I'm sure Tess won't care if she meets two lads instead of one,' Jonty assured him. As they strode towards Church Street he glanced across at Snowy. 'I remember Tess telling me something about a falling out she'd had with you, two or three years ago. Don't say you still bear a grudge.'

'Course not!' Snowy said stoutly, but Jonty saw a betraying flush creep up his cheeks. 'It was just . . . Oh, hell! The truth is, Jonty, that I behaved bloody badly. I had this girl, you see, Marilyn Thomas . . .' He whistled softly. 'Wharra smasher, as we say in these parts . . .'

He went on to explain what had happened and at the end of the recital they had reached Lyons Corner House and stopped outside, eyeing the hurrying crowds, many of whom pushed past them to enter the restaurant. Once, customers had been served by little waitresses known

208

as Nippies, but since the war Lyons had become self-service. Jonty eyed the hurrying crowd but failed to pick Tess out until she was on top of them, flinging her arms round his neck in an exuberant hug. 'Got it!' she said exultantly. 'I start next Monday and work from seven in the morning until seven in the evening for a month. After that I'll be back at school, of course, but they'll want me then from five until seven. The money's not marvellous, but at least it will be regular.' She tugged at his arm. 'Come on, I'll pay for your lunch, since I'll soon be earning, but I'm afraid it'll just have to be soup and a crusty roll. Oh, how I love those crusty rolls . . .' She broke off, having apparently seen Snowy for the first time. 'Well, what a coincidence,' she said drily. 'Fancy seeing you, Snowy White. Are you about to get yourself a meal? Because if so—'

Jonty, feeling thoroughly embarrassed, interrupted. 'I met Snowy earlier in the day when I was searching for the overhead railway,' he said. 'He very kindly looked at my list of attractions and took me in hand. I wouldn't have seen the half if it hadn't been for him, and you should see the slippers I bought for Ma! Well, you will see them, as soon as we get back to Mr Payne's. And in the meantime the three of us might as well eat together; indeed, since I can't see a single table free, we'll be lucky if we only share with each other and not with some grumpy old fellow so eager to get his grub inside him that he's splashing gravy all over the place.'

Tess gave a reluctant smile: this had happened to her and Jonty on their previous visit to the Corner House, and she quite saw his point. '*Better the devil you know than the devil you don't*,' she quoted airily, giving Snowy a rather doubtful smile. 'Come on then, let's join the queue at the counter. Grab a tray, fellers.'

Albert was cashing up early since he and Tess wanted to be at the hospital in good time. Now that Edie was on an ordinary ward, visiting hours were restricted and they were only allowed to spend one hour with her. Today they needed every minute of that hour, because Tess would want to describe her interview and Albert, who had popped into Deering's in his lunch hour, had a great many goodwill messages from the staff to pass on. Also, he had cooked an old favourite of his wife's – Woolton pie – which he meant to serve to himself and his young friends before they set off for the hospital. He had never before attempted baking, but Tess had left him with a ball of made-up pastry and a list of instructions, and when he had put the pie in the oven he was really pleased with his efforts. As his wife's recipe had instructed, he had steamed a quantity of vegetables – carrots, broad beans, peas and turnip – for twenty minutes. Then he had thickened the vegetable water with cornflour. Rolling out the pastry had been easy, and lining the pie dish with it had pleased him. He thought of how he would surprise Edie with his cooking skills when she came out of hospital, and now, having finished cashing up, he locked the shop door and went up to the flat to check that the pie was ready.

He opened the oven door with great caution and lifted it out, standing it on the kitchen table. He was just beginning to congratulate himself on its golden perfection when there was a sharp rap on the kitchen door and Jonty and Tess came in. Tess was smiling. 'I got the job!' she said. 'Oh, and Snowy's downstairs. I told him to wait. He's been very good to Jonty, taking him round most of the places he thought he ought to see, so I wondered if you might ask him to share our supper. He's bought Gran a little present, and would like to come up to the hospital with us for evening visiting. It seemed a bit harsh to tell him he could but we were going to have supper without him first.' She stared at the pie. 'I say, you've made a good job of that, Albert. Just wait till Gran comes out of hospital; she'll be that impressed!' Albert looked rather doubtfully at the golden-crusted Woolton pie, then drew imaginary lines from top to bottom and from side to side and smiled to himself. Yes, it would do very well for four people. He had already scrubbed a panful of potatoes and put them over the flame, so he turned to Tess, nodding his head. 'How nice that you and Snowy are friends again,' he said. 'Run down and tell him he's very welcome to share our supper.'

So presently the four of them settled down to enjoy the fruits of Albert's labours, chatting merrily as they did so. 'Are you sure your parents won't worry?' Tess asked Snowy, as they began to eat. 'I know Gran always got in an awful stew if I was late back from school.'

'I don't think they'd have worried, but just in case, I telephoned from the box on the corner,' Snowy said. He grinned at Jonty. 'Yes, we are on the telephone, which no doubt makes *us* landed gentry so far as you're concerned.'

Jonty grinned too, then turned to Tess who was staring at him, clearly baffled by the remark. 'When we met this morning Snowy accused me of being landed gentry,' he

211

explained. 'But we know each other pretty well now so we don't need to swap insults.'

The meal was a great success and afterwards the four of them set off for the hospital, arriving just as visiting started, and if Snowy was taken aback by the sight of Gran looking so pale and wan he hid his surprise very well.

'Poor Mrs Williams, haven't you had a horrid time,' he said, eyeing her bandages and the injured leg in its plaster cast. 'It'll be a while before they let you out of this place.' He plunged a hand into his pocket and produced a square package which he handed to the patient. 'There you are! Lavender water and scented soap; Jonty said they were the sort of things any woman would like, so I hope he's right.' He grinned as she exclaimed with pleasure, unwrapping the brown paper to reveal his gifts. 'What's the grub like in here?'

Albert and Tess knew from experience that Gran found talking tiring, so they let her chatter away for the first ten minutes, and then, at an almost imperceptible nod from Albert, Tess began a spirited and probably apocryphal account of her interview. Gran lay back against her pillows and smiled and smiled as Jonty and Snowy told next of their own shopping experiences, and at the end of their recital Albert took over. He described every step in the creation of a Woolton pie, and Gran laughed until tears ran down her cheeks. She mopped them away merrily, however, saying that when she came out of hospital Albert should have the honour of cooking her first meal of freedom, as she called it, and she very much hoped that he would make her a Woolton pie just as beautiful as the one he had described.

Albert promised to do so and was just elaborating on the recipe which, by then, he would have learned to follow when the bell sounded and a tall, stern-looking nurse came to turn them out of the ward.

They walked home, Tess with Albert and the two boys following behind, but when they reached Albert's shop and Tess would have said goodbye and thanks to Snowy, Jonty cut across her. 'Hang on a minute,' he said urgently. 'Snowy and I have been talking and we believe there's a problem which should be discussed.' He turned to the older man. 'Can we come up to your flat, Albert, and have a parley?'

'Course you can; I was just about to suggest it,' Albert said heartily, if untruthfully. 'Tess will make us some cocoa and I bought some ginger snaps and shortbread biscuits whilst I was at Deering's.' He produced his key and ushered them all into the flat, Tess leading the way. Albert, locking up again, thought what a fortunate thing it was that he had bought those biscuits. He didn't suppose that the boys' 'problem' would be anything important, so the sooner they drank up their cocoa and ate their biscuits the sooner he would be able to get to his own bed. But once seated at the kitchen table with mugs of cocoa and a plate of biscuits before them, he realised that he had wronged the lads.

Snowy looked carefully round the table, making sure that he had everyone's attention, and then spoke sombrely. 'I'm awful sorry to put the cat amongst the pigeons, but I don't believe you've realised what it will mean to your finances, Tess, to have Mrs Williams unable to work, for months. She'll be able to walk with crutches for the three months it will take her leg to heal, but that wrist!

213

You told me yourself, Jonty, that Albert said it was very nearly severed, and unless I'm much mistaken that may mean that she can never use it properly again. And the same goes for her shoulder. It doesn't take an expert or a doctor to read the pain on her face when she has to move her left arm even a little bit. And she's a baker! I can't see her pummelling dough or rolling out pastry or even icing cakes the way she's always done. So she must either get a very different sort of job – when she's well enough to work at all, that is – or Tess will have to give up the thought of getting her Higher and going to university, and stay here at home, looking after her.'

There was an appalled silence. It had clearly never occurred to either Albert or Tess that Edie's injuries were such that she might never take up her old job again. But having been forced to realise the truth, Albert cleared his throat and reached across the table to pat Tess's hand. 'We'll find a way, queen,' he said huskily. 'All along, Edie has said that your education is the most important thing in her life. She says you'll be the first person in her family to go to university, and she's determined you should have your chance.' He smiled rather shyly round the assembled company. 'Well, this forces my hand. I shall simply have to get that ice cream parlour going, because even if she can't do much else Edie will be able to sit behind the counter, tell the girls what to do, take the money and give change.'

'But Albert, the whole point of the ice cream parlour was that you were going to set it up together,' Tess pointed out. 'You can't be in two places at once, and all the buying of equipment, finding wholesalers to sell you ice cream and fizzy pop, getting staff you can trust . . .

214

honest to God, it'll be beyond Gran's capabilities for months and months. I can't believe she'll never work again, but I *can* believe that it will be a long while before she can cope, and a new venture . . . Oh, Albert, I know you mean well, but I think it's out of the question.'

Snowy cleared his throat, then turned to Tess. 'You've got a job, albeit only for a month, this very day,' he pointed out. 'That shows you are employable, because if the factory wants you so will other people. I'm all in favour of you getting your Higher, but I don't believe you'll be able to do so for a year or two. After all, I remember you telling me that your gran had stepped into the breach when they couldn't find any other relative to take you on . . .' Albert saw Snowy's hands tighten on Tess's shoulders and realised that Jonty had noticed too, and had given a little nod.

Snowy continued, almost as though he had waited for Jonty's approval before he spoke. 'Tess, you told me once that if it hadn't been for your gran you would have had to go into a children's home, so you owe Mrs Williams a good deal. It's not everyone of her age who would offer to bring up a child, even if they were related, so now that the positions are reversed it's your chance to return the favour.'

'I'll be glad to do so,' Tess said eagerly, 'but will I be able to earn enough to rent a place and pay all our expenses? Girls of my age usually have parents . . .'

'Edie may have an insurance policy,' Albert said. 'And she'll obviously get sickness benefit. I don't know about her pension, but I won't have her worrying. Edie has no need, as yet, to face up to such problems . . .'

Tess pulled a face. 'I'll speak to my teachers about

215

deferring,' she said. 'Oh! I've had an idea. Gran keeps a folder full of such things as insurance policies in the right-hand dresser drawer.' She jumped to her feet as she spoke and hurried across Albert's kitchen. 'I'll just go and fetch the folder; then we will have a much better idea of Gran's finances.'

Albert began to nod his agreement, but then he changed his mind. None of the three young people present knew that Gran had any secrets, but he knew, and he had no idea what papers his friend's folder might contain. He started to tell Tess that there might be private documents in the dresser drawer, but Tess was already descending the stairs. Albert sank back on his chair and looked ruefully from Jonty's face to Snowy's. 'When she brings that folder back, I think we ought to tell her not to open it,' he said. 'Everyone's got a right to a private life and Edie's no exception. She might not like the three of us knowing all the intimate details of her life, even if they're mainly financial.'

Jonty looked puzzled, but nodded reluctant agreement and, catching Snowy's eye, raised his brows. 'Should Snowy and I make ourselves scarce, go for a walk round the block or something?' he suggested. 'Though I'm sure a lovely lady like Mrs Williams would just tell us to go ahead. She doesn't strike me as the secretive sort, and, after all, if there are insurance policies in that folder, Tess will have to contact the company in order to make a claim on her grandmother's behalf.'

'I know what you mean,' Snowy said slowly. 'I remember someone saying something once . . . Yes, I rather think we ought to insist that Tess waits until her gran is better and can decide for herself how to go on.

216

There's someone called an almoner – I think that's the word – in every hospital, who helps patients sort out such things. If Tess asks her to, she'll call on Mrs Williams and help her with her affairs. She may get a grant to pay the rent on the flat . . .'

'I doubt she'll do that; they're under notice to quit, because the landlord thinks he has found someone who will take on the flat as well as the hat shop,' Albert said. 'Though there are another three weeks before they actually need to leave the premises. Mrs Williams and I have toyed with the idea of taking the shop on ourselves, possibly to get Change of Use and start an ice cream parlour, but we would need a large loan from the bank and we've not even approached them with the idea yet. If we did that it would mean that Tess would have a built-in job, so to speak, though she would have to get some experience first. But as it is, I can't see a bank loaning us the setting-up money whilst Edie is so obviously incapacitated. What do you lads think? Could Tess and Edie run such a place if the bank consented to give us a loan? And how long would they give us to pay it back?'

The three of them talked over the problem at some length, finally deciding that it must be Albert's first task, as soon as he had a moment free, to approach the bank, though Snowy asked rather curtly why he had not already done so.

Albert felt heat rise to his cheeks. Honesty would be painful, but it would be best in the long run. 'I'm afraid I'm not a very brave man,' he said apologetically. 'Taking on responsibility for a new venture terrifies me. I was all right when it was just a dream, something Edie and I talked about when we went off on our coach trips, but as soon as it became a real possibility, I simply shut it out of my thoughts. I say, hasn't Tess been rather a long time? Suppose she can't find the folder? It's not like Edie to leave something as important as documentation lying around loose. I wonder if I should go round to the flat.'

'No point,' Snowy said at once. 'Sit down, Mr Payne, and let's talk seriously about Tess getting some sort of full-time job and putting off her examinations until Mrs Williams is well again.'

Tess had hurried into the kitchen of the flat above the milliner's shop and gone straight to the Welsh dresser. Gran had never made any secret of where she kept the folder and Tess pulled it out and rifled through the contents, but it proved to be no use since it held their old ration books, their identity cards, a great many wage slips and little else. Tess was turning away, disappointed, when it occurred to her that there was another drawer, into which she had never looked. She and Gran referred to it as 'the old cutlery drawer', and since the knives, forks and spoons it contained were indeed old they seldom, if ever, so much as opened it. But now Tess did so, and moving the cutlery out of the way she saw that the drawer did indeed hold something she had forgotten. It was a manila wallet with a little brass clasp, and as soon as she saw it Tess remembered having seen it once before. She had received a letter from the landlord explaining that their rent would be going up on quarter day. Gran had sniffed, nodded to herself a couple of times and opened the old cutlery drawer, beginning to move the knives and forks and then changing her mind, but not before Tess had caught a glimpse of the wallet. 'Dear me, I must be going senile,' Gran had said cheerfully. 'This should be in my document folder, not amongst a whole load of ancient knives and forks.'

I wonder why she didn't want me to know this was hidden under the cutlery, Tess asked herself, carrying the wallet over to the kitchen table and clicking the clasp open. Yes, this is the one Albert and the others want. There really are insurance documents, and lots of other papers as well. But I'll take it back to the others, and we'll look at them together. She began to pick up the wallet without first fastening the clasp and it promptly spilled a great many papers on to the kitchen table. Cursing, Tess began to shovel them back, pausing over one which had a pattern of flowers all round the top and announced itself to be the *Birth Certificate of Edith May Rogers, 15 August 1905*. Tess chuckled to herself. What a scamp her grandmother was! She had fobbed Tess off when she had asked her age, but now here was the proof in Tess's hand. She began to push the birth certificate back into the folder, then stopped short. 'Hang on a minute,' she murmured to herself, 'something's wrong here. Gran told me her maiden name was Rogers, which means this is her birth certificate all right, but then if she was born in 1905 and I'm sixteen going on seventeen, and say Mam was about eighteen when I was born, then she must have had her daughter when she was only ten years old!'

But this was absurd; she was jumping to conclusions like a trout at a fly, Jonty would have said. The birth certificate simply must be wrong; was such a thing possible? Forgetting her intention not to pry, she began

219

to go through the other papers and soon came across her own birth certificate. She had seen it before, had had to produce it in order to be accepted at the grammar school so that she might sit for her School Certificate; no mystery there then. She was registered as Theresa Jane Williams and on this form at any rate they had got her birthday right. Tess began to cram the papers back into the folder, then changed her mind and took her grandmother's birth certificate back out again. She did not understand why the certificate proclaimed a date of birth so much later than it should have been, but Tess found that she did not want Albert or the two boys to see it, and begin to ask questions. So she took the certificate over to the Welsh dresser and slid it under the knives and forks, where it had been before. Then she picked up the wallet, tucked it under her arm and prepared to leave the flat. Before doing so, however, she glanced around her, to make sure that all was as it should be, and noticed for the first time a musty sort of smell. Sighing, she decided that the next day she would give the flat a good clean. Jonty would doubtless lend a hand, but she did not mean to encourage Snowy to join them. It was all very well his pretending that he had forgotten their old quarrel, but she had a sneaking suspicion that he had done no such thing. She knew he no longer went out with Marilyn and that he had had any number of girlfriends in the years which had passed since the quarrel, but she knew too that he had no particular girlfriend at present. She thought he was clearing the decks for university and was subsequently at a loose end, but she did not intend to become embroiled with him again. If he meant to join her and Jonty the following day he would find himself handed a scrubbing brush and an apron, and she guessed that he would take exception to both.

Smiling to herself, she set off for the tobacconist's shop, letting herself in with Albert's spare key and running up the stairs two at a time. The mystery of the birth certificate would have to wait, and when she reached Albert's kitchen and was told that they felt it was unfair to examine the contents of the wallet she agreed eagerly, picked up her mug of cocoa and drained it. 'I only glanced at the contents, but I'm pretty sure there are insurance documents,' she said. She turned to Albert. 'Sorry I was so long, but there were two folders and I wasn't sure which one was important. In fact I had quite a search for this one.'

'So you didn't really examine the contents?' Albert asked, and Tess thought his glance was uncomfortably searching. 'Well, no one is going to go through it until we've had Edie's permission, and she won't be fit enough to decide for a week or two. So in the meantime, Tess my dear, I'd be happier if I kept the folder under lock and key in the little safe set into the wall of the stockroom. Is that all right by you?'

Tess was puzzled. Why should Albert assume that Gran had secrets which had to be locked up in a safe? Did he know something she did not? The drawer of the Welsh dresser had been good enough for Gran. But when she asked, Albert only replied that the landlord had keys to the flat and would doubtless be taking the prospective tenant around. 'I know you sleep in the flat, but you aren't there all day, queen,' he explained. 'But my shop is rarely unoccupied, which means no one is likely to go rifling through your gran's papers.'

Tess saw the sense of this, but when she went to bed that night she lay for some time staring up at the ceiling and wondering, wondering, wondering. Was it possible to alter a birth certificate? But why on earth should anyone do so? It seemed downright ridiculous to her.

However, she slept at last and woke sluggishly when the street noises became too insistent to be ignored. Her first thought was that this was probably Jonty's last day in the city. He had explained that though he could have stayed a couple of days longer, he thought it would be unfair on his parents. They would be harvesting their wheat and other cereals any time now – the weather had been hot and sunny for the whole of Jonty's stay – and now that her grandmother was out of danger the moral support he had offered, though eagerly accepted at the time, was no longer necessary. Tess got out of bed and wandered over to her washstand. Presently she would go into the kitchen, make herself some porridge, brew the tea and then go round to ask Jonty how he would like to spend his last day. She rather thought he might like to take a river trip, though he would doubtless compare the Mersey unfavourably with his beloved Broads; she knew he missed the countryside and complained that the air of the city made him sleepy and lethargic, so a trip on the water would blow away the cobwebs.

She was standing in front of her washstand vigorously splashing, for already the day was hot and the cold water was a positive blessing, when she remembered her grandmother's birth certificate, and as though her mind had been busy thinking it out whilst she slept the solution popped into her mind even as she began to apply soap to her flannel. Gran was not her gran, but her mother! That would explain the age anomaly. But no sooner was the thought born than Tess had to kill it. If Gran had been her mother she would have acknowledged the fact joyfully, if only to Tess herself, knowing how Tess had longed and longed for a family of her own. She had even asked Gran to tell her everything she knew about her mother, whom she could barely remember, and now that she looked back she could see how little Gran had actually known. If my mother had really been Gran's daughter, or if Gran herself had been my mother, then Gran would have told me a great deal, if only to keep me quiet, Tess said to herself. 'Perhaps Gran is my aunt, or perhaps we're just cousins, cousins who have a big age difference. But now that I've seen the birth certificate I won't rest until Gran is well enough to answer a few questions.'

Edie Williams lay in her hospital bed and fretted. Although neither Tess nor Albert had voiced aloud the problem which must have been nagging away at them, as it nagged away at Edie herself, it was a problem which would have to be faced.

Edie knew, none better, that a baker needs both hands. Even for cake decorating she would need both hands. And whilst it was possible that she might learn to manage to do certain tasks which involved her right hand and not her left, she realised that Deering's could not possibly wait on her convenience. They now employed two people to do the work which she had undertaken alone, and Mr Deering, a delightfully easy-going employer, had already visited her twice on the ward.

'I've warned the fellers I've took on that their jobs will finish the day you come back,' he had told her, his tone earnest. 'But I've spoke to Sister and she tells me you'll not be baking, nor rolling pastry, nor decorating wonderful birthday cakes for many a month. You'll get paid in full for some time yet because you've been with us a tidy while, but then you'll go on to something called sickness benefit and I thought we might ask you to do the books for us. I know you used to be an accounts clerk for Roberts and Smythe. I guess that'd mean a couple of hours a week, but if I ask around others will likely be glad to give you similar work.' He had looked at her, his eyes full of sympathy. 'Mrs Williams, if I could do more for you I would, honest to God I would. But the fact is, what with coupons, forms and running out of ingredients half the time, Deering's is in a parlous state. I don't deny there are weeks when we take a pretty sum, but there are other times when I have hard work to pay the staff. But if you have any ideas of how we might help . . .'

Edie had been sitting up in bed in her pretty pink bedjacket, her hair tied back with lavender ribbons and her person smelling very sweetly of lavender water. She read not only sympathy but also admiration in her old boss's eyes, but had to shake her head at the suggestion of work. 'Thank you, Mr Deering, it's very good of you,' she had said gratefully. 'But once I'm on sickness benefit I'm not allowed to earn, you know, not so much as a shilling. Yet I don't believe the money they pay me will cover the rent of a flat, let alone our living expenses. But I'm hoping that there are jobs which someone with only one useful hand can do, and if I'm right you may be sure I shall be first in the queue at the employment exchange.'

Mr Deering had looked enormously relieved. 'You're a courageous woman, Mrs Williams,' he said. 'I might have known you'd take it as a challenge and not give up. But don't forget, if I can do anything to help . . .'

He had left her, and Edie waited for Albert and Tess, who had taken to coming on the dot of visiting hour in the evenings since they had so much to discuss. Albert had actually begun to do something about the proposed ice cream parlour. He had visited the bank, and though the manager's enthusiasm for the scheme had been somewhat lukewarm, at least, Albert said, he had not shot it down in flames. In fact he had promised to look into it, but had added that before he did so he would like to see Albert's business plan.

'Which must include your setting-up costs,' he had reminded Albert, twinkling at him over the top of his spectacles. 'And you should remember, Mr Payne, that Change of Use can sometimes take many months to obtain, especially if the authorities decide to be difficult.'

'But if you approve my business plan and say that you think the scheme is not only feasible but likely to prove a winner, then I'm told the planning people are far likelier to grant Change of Use status,' Albert had said eagerly. 'My partner and I will begin to work out our business plan this very evening.'

That had been several days ago, and the business plan had not, if one were honest, progressed very far. Edie could not remember without an inward chuckle Albert's horror at the price of a coffee machine, a fizzy drinks dispenser and a great many tall glasses. Poor man, he knew to the last farthing how to cost tobacco products, but take him outside his own sphere of reference and he was as innocent – or ignorant – as a child of two. Edie was just thinking that they had a long way to go before they would manage to produce the sort of business plan which a bank manager would consider workable when she heard the tramp of many feet and knew that visiting time had arrived. She had been leaning back against her pillows, but now she sat up straight. The hospital rule that one should be in bed during visiting hours meant that there was a scramble from patients who had been in the dayroom, listening to the wireless, gossiping and, she gathered, smoking like chimneys. They would be hurrying back to the ward, to leap hastily into rumpled beds and try to look as though they had been there for hours.

The doctor under whose charge she was thought she would be able to get around on crutches once an X-ray had shown that the broken bone was mending nicely, but this would almost certainly take twelve full weeks, of which she had only served two. Every time the doctor visited the ward she demanded to be allowed to get out of bed and practise moving around. But the limb was hoisted up on a pulley so even had she decided to ignore medical advice and try to walk, it was impossible. She could only obey instructions and hope that, by so doing, healing would come more quickly.

Edie had explained to the doctor about the ice cream parlour and the business plan, and had said over and over that once their small business was up and running she would spend most of the day sitting in a chair, with her leg raised on another. The doctor had nodded, smiled, admired her courage and merely reiterated his conviction that impatience would get her nowhere. 'You must serve your time, my dear lady, just like everyone else,' he had said kindly. 'Believe me, we are as anxious to see the back of you as you are to see the back of us, but the old adage *more haste, less speed* applies to anyone with a badly fractured tibia. Patience is a virtue which I fear has been left out of your make-up, but it's a virtue I'm afraid you have to learn.'

So now Edie awaited her visitors with no good news to impart, though she always greeted them with a bright smile and asked eagerly how things were progressing. On this particular evening she saw that Albert was alone and greeted him anxiously. 'Where's Tess, Albert? I thought she was working a day shift at this nursery place until school starts again.'

'So she is,' Albert agreed, sitting down on the bench beside the bed. 'But she has booked an appointment with the headmaster this evening so I've agreed that tomorrow night she can come and see you by herself whilst I get on with my stock-take.' He looked anxiously at Edie. 'To tell you the truth, my dear, I have an uneasy feeling that Tess wants a word with you alone.'

'An uneasy feeling? What on earth should give you that impression? Oh, I know you told me she'd brought my business folder to you so that you might put it away for safe keeping whilst the landlord is taking prospective tenants round the flat, but you said she hadn't opened it, and anyway I've gone through it in my mind and there's nothing in it I wouldn't want Tess

227

to see. It's just insurance policies, wage returns, contracts and so on. Nothing which relates to Tess herself, so far as I can remember.'

Albert gave a sigh of relief. 'That's all right then,' he said thankfully. 'I know I've never been good at secrets – keeping them, I mean – so I'm probably just imagining that Tess has given me one or two strange looks lately. But I wanted to talk to you seriously anyway. I've got a whole heap of information from the people who advise small businesses, and we were quite right when we thought the milliner's shop wouldn't be suitable. It isn't just that it's too small, it's the wrong shape, if you understand me. The average ice cream parlour needs to have kitchen premises . . . oh, I can't explain . . .' He hooked out the briefcase which he had pushed under the bench, clicked it open and produced a pile of papers, handing them to Edie. 'There are plans for several different milk bars, ice cream parlours and small cafés, and try though I might I can't make the milliner's shop fit into any of these categories. As you know, it's wider than it's long, and the ideal ice cream parlour should be longer than it's wide. Oh, dear, that isn't a very good explanation, but you'll see what I mean when you've studied the examples our business adviser has found up.'

Edie looked up from her perusal of the first plan. 'Our business adviser?' she said. 'Who's he when he's at home?' She was amused to see Albert bridle slightly.

'I rather think he's a volunteer from the Chamber of Trade, of which I'm already a member,' Albert said. 'They're a great organisation and they'll help us in any way they can. They don't make mistakes, either. If they

228

say an ice cream parlour in Miss Foulks's shop is a non-starter, I'm afraid they're right, but Mr Clegg – that's his name – is going to keep an eye open for suitable property, hopefully within our budget, and will guide us through the shoals and hidden snags which we're bound to come across.'

'Well that's grand,' Edie said absently, and hoped Albert did not pick up on her lack of enthusiasm. The truth was she was worried over Tess's apparent desire to speak to her alone. Ever since Albert had told her that Tess had found the wallet which she had kept under the old crockery in the Welsh dresser she had had an uneasy feeling. Only Albert knew that she had been living a lie ever since she had taken Tess on, and now she feared that the moment of truth had arrived. She could not imagine how anything in the manila wallet could have caused Tess to suspect that she had not told her the whole truth, so perhaps it was something totally unconnected with the papers. Perhaps it was something someone had said; she had pretended to be delighted that the ancient quarrel between Snowy and Tess had been resolved, that they were now friends once more, but perhaps it was not such a good thing. She had sometimes wondered whether Marilyn Thomas's dislike of Tess came from some knowledge which Edie herself did not have. Perhaps Marilyn had passed this knowledge on to Snowy and now, with Gran out of the way, Snowy had told Tess something which Edie would much rather he had kept to himself.

But Albert was looking at her anxiously. 'Something's not right, Edie,' he said. 'Would you like me to come with Tess tomorrow evening, when she visits? I'll willingly do so, only I'm afraid she'll think it rather strange . . .'

Edie summoned up a bright and cheerful smile. 'Nonsense, Albert!' she said bracingly. She waved one of the plans. 'And now just explain to me all the jargon on this sheet of paper . . .'

Chapter Nine

Tess had had her interview with the headmaster, who had been very sympathetic. 'Naturally you'd like to get your Higher and go on to university, but like several of my pupils you feel that the financial strain on your parents would be unfair,' he said. 'Is that it, Miss Williams?'

'Yes, that's it exactly; only in my case I only have my gran,' Tess explained. 'At present she's in hospital and won't be able to leave the ward for another ten weeks. There are various complications too, such as the fact that our landlord is trying to let our flat as one unit with the shop beneath. Gran is in no condition to go searching for somewhere else for us to live, and since her injuries mean she won't be able to take up her old job again even when she's well, I can't even consider leaving her alone.'

'But if you get a job, any job, you'll still have to leave her,' the headmaster pointed out. 'However, I think I can guess what you're going to say. If you can earn sufficient money to pay someone to keep an eye on your grand-mother while you're at work you would be able to keep body and soul together, which wouldn't be possible if you stayed with us, since I never heard of any school paying a pupil to study. How about evenings? I've heard you mention a Mr Payne . . .'

'Oh, yes, Mr Payne's wonderful, but he's got his own

business to run, and can't neglect it,' Tess said. 'He'll give all the help he possibly can, but he can't be in two places at once. I don't imagine we shall find a flat or even a couple of rooms to rent in the centre of the city, near Mr Payne's shop. We'll have to move out to the suburbs where rents are cheaper.'

The headmaster looked thoughtful. 'Have you considered evening classes? Or even a correspondence course? It's perfectly possible to gain the results you would need for university entrance by either of these methods, though of course it would take longer.'

Tess smiled at him. 'I wouldn't go to university and leave my gran completely alone unless she was very much better and more capable,' she said quietly. 'But thank you for the suggestion; I really will think seriously about it. In the meantime though, I'm afraid I shan't be able to come back to school next month.'

The headmaster sighed. 'A pity, a great pity,' he murmured, 'but I feel sure you will make a success of whatever you decide to do, Miss Williams.' He held out a lean, well-manicured hand. 'Goodbye, and good luck.'

The following evening Tess made her way to the hospital alone. She should have felt disappointed, even cheated, but as she had walked away from the interview with the headmaster the previous evening she had been aware only of an overwhelming sensation of relief. She knew, none better, that she had had to study harder than ever in her life before just to get her School Cert. Maths had always been her weakest subject, and the thought of having to tackle Latin as well gave her nightmares. When she had taken Jonty to the station the previous week they had missed the train he had intended to catch, with the result that they had had an hour to kill and had spent it in the refreshment room where they had seriously discussed Tess's future.

She had admitted to Jonty what she would have told no one else, that she had only gone in for the scholarship in the first place in order to make Snowy eat his words, because he had told people that she was just a brainless little nobody who wasn't bright enough to get it. Also, Gran had told her that no one else in her family had gone to university, and she knew how proud it would make Gran if she succeeded. 'But I'm not academic, not really,' she had confessed to Jonty as they sat at a corner table in the refreshment room, sipping coffee and eating rather unappetising station buns. 'So if I'm honest, I shan't be a bit sorry to find myself a proper job. I might take evening classes in something useful – business management, for example – but I shan't even think about university because I'm absolutely certain that even if I did get all the exams and things I'd be completely out of my depth.'

Jonty had leaned across the table and patted her cheek. 'You don't need exams to be a farmer's wife, nor a course in business studies,' he had said. 'In fact all you need is a suitable farmer, preferably one called Jonty Bell. And us Bells would take good care of your gran, you know that, don't you? She'd be looked after like a queen, with no worries about rent or ice cream parlours or Mr Payne not being the pushy sort. I know I can't give you much right now, but one of these days I'll be offering to share all my worldly goods with you, so don't go doing anything foolish. Promise?'

'I'll promise not to do anything foolish, but I don't

233

mean to be anyone's wife until I've had a career of my own and a lot of fun,' Tess had said. 'And besides, what about this Melissa girl? Haven't you offered her your hand and your heart? As well as the rest of your gorgeous body, of course.'

Jonty had laughed. 'She's just a friend,' he had said airily, just as his train steamed into the platform.

Tess had jumped to her feet and grabbed the lightest of Jonty's bags. 'No more tomfoolery or you'll miss another train,' she had said briskly. 'Come along, Jonty, let's see if we can get you a corner seat; not that it matters much because Crewe is your first change, and that's only thirty minutes away.' They had reached the train, Tess handing over her penny platform ticket to be clipped, and had managed to get Jonty a corner seat despite the train's being crowded. Jonty had put his haversack on the worn upholstery, then hopped down on to the platform again and pecked her cheek.

'Don't forget that my offer was serious,' he'd said huskily. 'You're a grand girl.'

'I know I am; I'm worth two of you,' Tess had joked breathlessly. 'If I go down to the box on the corner at eight o'clock this evening will you telephone, just to let me know you've arrived safely and everything's all right at the farm?'

'Of course I will,' Jonty had said, and was beginning to remind Tess to thank Albert once again for his hospitality when a porter had come along the platform slamming doors and Jonty had had to leap back into his carriage. Almost at once the train had begun to move and Tess, waving until it was out of sight, had felt suddenly bereft. She was really fond of Jonty; he would probably always be her best friend, and it had been very good of him to leave the farm and come home with her, but she could scarcely expect him to stay on once he knew Gran to be out of danger. And there was, after all, little he could do to help her with her most pressing problem, which was finding accommodation, for when the landlord repossessed the flat in a couple of weeks she would have to live in cheap lodgings until she found somewhere they could afford.

But right now she knew she must concentrate on the coming interview with Gran, in which she intended to tell the older woman that she had, admittedly accidentally, seen Edie's birth certificate. She was still wondering how to approach such a ticklish subject when she reached the ward, and after their initial greeting and the handing over, on Tess's part, of a small bunch of hothouse grapes Gran looked up into Tess's eyes, indicated that she should sit down on the visitor's bench, and opened the subject herself.

'You know, don't you?' she said quietly. 'Albert said yesterday that you had been giving him strange looks ever since you took him my document wallet. It doesn't take a genius to work out that you saw something in it to make you suspect that you've been told an untruth.' She smiled at the younger girl. 'I've been wondering what on earth it could be, but that really doesn't matter now. What matters is that I must come clean. *Please* don't be cross with me, darling Tess; whatever I did I did for the best.'

Tess leaned over and took Edie's hand. 'We'll both stick to the truth from now on,' she said gently. 'And I'll start by telling you that I didn't look inside the wallet on

235

purpose. I didn't close the clasp properly and when I picked it up several papers fell out. Oh, Gran, I saw your birth certificate! You were born in 1905, weren't you? And since I was born in '33 that would make you an awfully young grandmother, isn't that so?'

Gran sighed. 'Yes, you're quite right, but that's not the case because, dearest Tess, I'm not your grandmother at all. I never had children; my husband, darling Fred, and I wanted a family, but he died after we'd only been married for two years. Your real grandmother and I were friends, though she was twenty years older than me, and I knew she'd had a daughter who'd died and a grand-daughter who'd been evacuated. So when she died just before the end of the war it seemed to me that you looked like ending up in a children's home. When you evacuees came home in September '45, I went to the dispersal point to see who would claim you, and there you were, looking so lost and bewildered that my heart went out to you. When the social services officer called out your name – Theresa Jane Williams – and asked if there was an Edith Williams present I stepped forward, and from the look on your face it was as though the sun had suddenly come out. You said "Gran!" and I said "Tess!" and that set the seal on it. I had intended to tell the officer the truth, of course, but I didn't because with that one hug I knew I had what I most wanted: a little girl I could love and guide, a companion who was also my dead friend's grand-child. After that it was plain sailing. I *was* Edith Williams, the same as your real gran, and you were Tess Williams.' She pulled a rueful face. 'And now I suppose you're going to desert me and go off in search of proof that your mother really is dead, or even to try to find your father, although

I'm not sure that even your real grandmother knew who he was, because I'm told that that's what adopted children usually do, and I suppose, in a way, you could be considered my adopted granddaughter.'

Tess had been holding Gran's hand, but now she transferred herself with great care to the edge of the bed and gave Edie a hug. 'Now that I know the true story I shall love you more than ever!' she declared. 'I've always known you saved me from a children's home, but I thought you had little choice because of our relationship. People would have thought badly of you if you'd left your real granddaughter to be brought up by strangers, but what you've shown is real love, the sort of love that Ruth shows to Naomi in the Bible.'

'Then you'll stay with me, queen?' Gran said, her voice breaking. 'Of course, as you grow older you'll want to leave the nest as all little birds do, but right now—'

'Right now I wouldn't leave you for a thousand pounds,' Tess assured the older woman, 'but if you ask me the boot is going to be on the other foot. I wouldn't be surprised if Albert were to ask you—'

'He already has asked me, and I've told him that I'm happy with our friendship but you and I don't need anyone else,' Edie said. 'Dear me, I feel as though a physical burden has been lifted off my back. And now that we both know everything, I want to talk about something else entirely. Albert told me you went to see your headmaster yesterday, and I can guess what you said to him. You're not going back to school, are you?' When Tess shook her head she went on, 'Oh, I'd give anything not to have been on that wretched bus. If I wasn't stuck here like this you'd be getting ready to start working

237

towards your Higher any day now, and as it is . . .' She sighed and patted Tess's hand. 'I feel so guilty, because as you know I promised myself that I would support you right up to and including university. I knew it would be a struggle but I thought I could manage it somehow, especially if you got holiday work. And to tell you the truth, Albert has very decently offered to give us some financial support which, if you insisted, you could pay back once you're earning real money.'

Tess had felt a pang of apprehension when Gran had referred to marriage and Albert in the same breath, and now she felt another pang. If she accepted help from Albert it would be an admission that she and Gran were not a self-sufficient little family, and she had no desire to have to share, perhaps especially after the revelation that Edie Williams was not related to her in any way. So she shook her head. 'It's awfully kind of Albert – he's a very kind man – but I don't mean to take money from anyone, and now that I'm not continuing with my schooling I very much hope it won't be necessary, because I mean to get full-time work. Any more questions?'

'Yes: any luck on the house-hunting front?' Gran asked. 'Time is not on our side. Albert has actually offered to move into a hostel so that we can take over his flat if we find ourselves on the street. But I know you wouldn't like that, and neither would I. So, any ideas?'

Tess sat back on the bench, shaking her head. 'No, I'm afraid not. Did I tell you that the person who was going to take on the milliner's shop and the flat has dropped out? The landlord, Mr Egbert, was quite nice about it really. He said he felt mean asking us to vacate the prem-ises whilst you were still recovering in hospital. So now we've got a breathing space, because he'll have to re-advertise and so on.'

'What about Miss Foulks, though?' Gran asked. 'She was going to leave at the end of last week. She'd made all her arrangements to move in with her sister.'

'Oh, she's already gone. There was no point in her hanging on since she had virtually no stock left to sell anyway,' Tess explained. 'It's rather annoying in a way because I told everyone that we'd let them know our change of address as soon as we know it ourselves, but in the meantime would they send all letters, invoices, bills et cetera to Mr Albert Payne, the tobacconist.' She laughed. 'Poor Albert, he'll be getting a bumper post for a while, but he says he doesn't mind. Oh, Gran, you've no idea how lonely it is in the flat without you! It wasn't so bad when Jonty was staying at Albert's because they either came round to our place or I went round to theirs in the evenings. But now when I'm not at work I'm on my own most of the time except when I'm here at the hospital.'

'What about Snowy?' Gran asked. She beamed. 'I like Snowy. He brings me presents.'

Tess sniggered. 'A bag of acid drops and you're anyone's,' she declared. 'But you're right, I do see quite a bit of him. But of course that will all stop when he goes off to university in October.'

Gran raised her eyebrows. 'Goes away? What's wrong with Liverpool, may I ask? He has a cousin working on this ward, so he's been able to get permission to pop in and see me in the afternoons, and he told me he'd almost decided to go to our very own place of learning, in other words Liverpool University. Hasn't he told you that? I only wish you were heading in the same direction, and it's all my fault that you're not. Snowy will go on to greater things whilst you, my darling, will lose the chance I've always wanted for you: to go to university and get a degree.'

Tess shook her head. 'I'm not clever enough really, Gran; the work was already beginning to get me down. And you know Snowy, or must do by this time. He waffles airily on about choosing between Oxford and Cambridge, but I believe most of their intake is from Eton and Harrow and places like that. And anyway, don't they have their own entrance requirements? I think settling for red brick is probably a good idea, since it will mean he can live at home and save his money. I think he's going to do a maths degree, or maybe physics and chemistry, but anyway something which would bore the rest of us rigid. Still, it's nice of him to visit you, Gran.'

'*And* to bring me little presents,' Gran said smugly. 'Last time he came he brought a bag of luscious William pears, which we shared.' She looked through her lashes at the younger girl. 'He likes you, Tess, honest to God he does. He likes to talk about you and he'll be really disappointed when you tell him you aren't bound for university after all.'

Tess sniffed. 'My life is my own and none of his business,' she said grandly. 'I wonder how he'll feel . . . but I won't say any more. I'll save it for when it's a fact.'

When she returned from the hospital she decided to nip up to Albert's, since she wanted to discuss her flat-hunting plans with him. As it happened, Albert was still in his shop and he welcomed her with a broad smile when he saw her peering at him through the glass panel in his door.

'Gran all right?' he asked as he unlocked the door and ushered her inside. 'How did she take the news that she's had a reprieve? On the flat front, I mean. It must have relieved her mind.'

'Oh, it did,' Tess assured him. 'I told her Mr Egbert was awfully nice about it, more or less said he wouldn't make too much of an effort to re-let the property while she was still in hospital. I say, Albert, you're working awfully late. Have you had your supper yet?'

Albert had sat down on his stool again whilst they talked, but now he stretched and yawned and Tess could see the lines of tiredness around his eyes, and guessed that he had been working on his books ever since closing the shop at six. 'No, not yet,' he admitted. 'But I think I've done enough for today. I'll go up and have a cup of tea and a piece of toast. Care to join me?'

Tess's conscience smote her. Albert had provided her with food on several occasions. He had put himself out not just for Gran but for Tess herself, and she had never thought to repay him. But now was her chance. Earlier in the day she had bought a meat and potato pie from Deering's – they always charged her staff rates – and she had stewed a quantity of apples and intended to make a custard to go with them as a pudding. So now she smiled at Albert and shook her head. 'Thanks, Albert, but you can jolly well save your toast for tomorrow because I've got one of Deering's meat and potato pies which is far too big for one, so I hereby invite you to share my supper. We can talk while we eat, because I want to ask you about looking for property in the suburbs.'

241

Albert sighed. 'I know it's the sensible thing to do really, because now that Edie won't be returning to Deering's there's nothing to stop you moving out of the centre, except that I'll miss you both dreadfully,' he said. 'And I accept your kind invitation. I'll just nip up to the flat and make sure I've not left a pan on the stove.'

He and Tess parted and Tess hurried along to the flat above the milliner's shop. As always, the minute she climbed the stair and unlocked the door she was aware of how much she missed Gran. Even the flat misses her, she thought ruefully, going over to the oven, lighting it and popping the pie inside to warm. Not so long ago, Gran would have been there, boiling the kettle for tea, slicing and buttering bread and asking Tess all about her day. But how different it was now! The kitchen was cold and still smelt faintly musty, and Tess, looking guiltily round the room, told herself that she'd have to pull her socks up before Gran came out of hospital. The draining board was cluttered with her porridge dishes for the past week, the sink was full of pots and pans, and a loaf of bread, a small block of margarine and various other items were scattered across the kitchen table, the Welsh dresser and the draining board. I'm becoming a slut, Tess told herself guiltily. When Jonty was here I kept the place reasonably tidy, but because no one sees it but me I've let things slide. I'll have to make it a habit to ask Albert in for a meal two or three times a week, she told herself. After all, he's as much my friend as Gran's. I might even ask Snowy to come up for a game of cards, or just for a natter. Gran's quite right, it's been kind of him to visit her; it relieves her boredom. Yes, from now on I'll be a changed person.

She began the preparations for the evening meal which had once been Gran's prerogative, and turning on the wireless set she realised that she had missed *Dick Barton, Special Agent* and would have to make do with light music, if she could find a channel which was not intent upon improving her mind by broadcasting the latest news. Rushing round the kitchen she tidied frantically, attacked the washing-up and unearthed a tin of peas to go with the meat and potato pie. Fortunately, Albert was a methodical man and she knew he would take at least twenty minutes over his own preparations before he arrived at her front door.

She was right. She heard Albert's knock and ran down the stairs, realising as she opened the door how she was looking forward to telling him all that had transpired between herself and Gran.

Beaming, she ushered him inside, poured two mugs of tea and turned the radio down. Then she produced the pie from the oven and opened the can of peas. Very soon the two of them were eating, and between mouthfuls Tess told Albert that she now knew Gran was not, after all, her grandmother, and in fact was no relation.

'. . . and Gran told me you already knew, so now there will be no more secrets,' she was saying, when Albert held up a finger.

'I'm truly glad that Edie's come clean at last,' he told her. 'But I think there's something wrong with your wireless set, dear. It's making the most peculiar whining noise.'

Tess cocked her head on one side and listened hard. She could hear nothing, except the sound of one of her favourite tunes, 'How High The Moon', and when Albert persisted in saying that the wireless had a squeak she frowned. Surely he was not criticising the melody? But when he went on frowning and staring at the set she got up and turned it off. Immediately, as though on cue, she too heard the noise. It was almost a howl, and for a moment she stared at the set, unable to believe that it could still make a racket when switched off. She turned to Albert. 'What on earth . . . ?' she began.

'It's not coming from your wireless set; I think it's outside,' Albert said. 'Dear me, it sounds like an animal in distress. Had we better go down? If it's a dog or cat that's been hit by a car . . .'

Tess was already at the door and the pair of them thundered down the stairs. Oddly, as the two of them erupted on to the pavement the noise immediately stopped. Tess stared all around her. Darkness had fallen and the street lamps flared, lighting up pavement, roadway and shops. Had there been an injured animal it too would have been illuminated, but both road and pavement were empty.

Tess looked at Albert and they both shrugged, and Tess, remembering how delicious the meat and potato pie had tasted, turned back towards the stairs which led to the flat. 'Whatever it was, it's gone,' she said. 'Come on, Albert. We don't want our grub to get cold.'

They were back in the kitchen when they both heard the noise again. It was almost a wail, and seemed to be coming from the cupboard in which the Williamses kept their food. Tess flew across the room, snatched the door open, and scanned every shelf with keen attention. Nothing lurked in the bread bin, or behind the jars of jam, or amongst the tinned goods neatly arranged. Tess

244

emerged from the cupboard and shut the door with some force. 'This is absurd,' she said angrily. 'The sound must be travelling from somewhere else. We had better ignore it and get on with our meal.'

But once they had both acknowledged that the sound was not the radio, nor their imaginations, it became increasingly difficult to ignore. They finished their meal in rather uncomfortable silence, and then Albert banged his hand down on the table and pointed downwards. 'We want our heads examined!' he exclaimed. 'Miss Foulks has been gone two or three days, during which time her place has been empty and no one has so much as peered inside. That noise is coming from her shop . . . coming up through the floorboards into your kitchen, plain as plain. Some animal has got itself trapped in there and of course during the day no one would hear its yowls because Heyworth Street is both busy and noisy. And in the evenings you are either visiting your gran, playing your gramophone or listening to the wireless, and anyway, it probably didn't realise it couldn't get out at first. It would only have been as it got hungrier that it realised it was trapped, and began to shout for help. Do you have the keys?'

Tess clapped a hand to her mouth, then lowered her fingers. 'No, I don't. Oh, Albert, whatever shall we do?'

But Albert was already across the kitchen and beginning to descend the stairs. 'We'll see if there's any possible means of entry,' he called over his shoulder. 'Miss Foulks must have had a back door for stock deliveries, and so she could use the communal lavatory. I wouldn't go breaking the new window or the door in the front of the property, but if there's a window round the back . . .'

245

'There is,' Tess said, pointing as they approached the wall. Immediately the yowling stopped. It was dark in the yard, the only light coming from the Williamses' flat above their heads, but when Tess asked Albert if he thought the animal might have escaped of its own accord he shook his head. 'It's listening,' he told her. 'It knows there are good people and bad, and it wants to be quite certain that we're the good sort before it reveals its hiding place by crying for help again.' He pointed to another door. 'Does that lead into the shop?'

'It must do, but I can't see any way of getting in,' Tess said. 'I wonder if we should get in touch with the police? I remember being told once that scuffers have the names of all key holders – people who can be contacted at night if the owner of the premises is not available. Do you think we ought to . . .'

But Albert was staring at the small window which was probably the only means by which daylight entered the millinery shop's stockroom. Then he looked at Tess, a look so calculating that she guessed he was about to suggest something uncomfortable. 'I believe this window isn't latched,' he said. 'If I gave you a bunk up do you think you could open it? And then wriggle through? Once you're inside you can unlock the door, because I'd put money on the fact that the key will be hanging beside the lock.'

'Right,' Tess said. 'Up we go!'

Five minutes later she had managed to open the window and was wriggling through it, commenting to Albert that she just wished she knew what she was going to land on, when a voice spoke behind them. 'What have we here? Midnight goings-on? Don't you know the shop's

246

empty? You ain't likely to find anything but a coupla musty old hats which Miss Foulks couldn't sell.'

The beam of the torch directed straight into his eyes made Albert blink, and caused the torch-holder to say in a surprised tone: 'Well, if it ain't Mr Payne! Wharron earth are you doin', Mr Payne, sir? And don't tell me you've took to house-breaking, because I shan't believe you.' The torch beam shifted to Tess's nether regions, for she was still half in and half out of the window. 'And who's your young friend?' His voice changed. 'Nice knickers house-breakers wear these days!'

Tess tried to turn round in the narrow space and nearly stabbed herself on the window ledge, but she had recognised the voice. 'It's me, Tess Williams, Constable Agnew,' she said breathlessly. 'There's a cat or something shut in here and yowling fit to bust. Mr Payne thought that if I could get through the window I might be able to unlock the back door and let us both out, me and the cat, and he was quite right about one thing: the key is in the lock.'

Constable Agnew sighed. 'I can't hear no animal, not cat, nor dog, nor guinea pig,' he muttered. 'And likely, when you get the door open, whatever it is will leg it so fast we'll never know if it were fish, fowl or good red herring. But carry on. It'll save me goin' back to the station and knockin' up Mr Egbert, what's the landlord, then bringin' him down here and stayin' with him while he checks his property . . .' He stopped speaking as Tess, wriggling frantically, suddenly disappeared from view, landing on the floor of the stockroom with a thump and a yelp. Albert, standing on tiptoe, could see nothing, but before he could so much as enquire if she was still alive, the key grated in the lock and the back door creaked open.

Tess grinned from Albert's face to the round and ruddy one of the police constable. 'There's a not very nice smell coming from somewhere . . . and the creature, whatever it is, can't get into the shop because the door between is closed. But it's very frightened, too frightened to make a bolt for the yard, so if you wouldn't mind, Constable Agnew, I'd like to borrow your torch and we'll shut the back door until we find out just what has spent the last three days trapped in this room. Are there skunks in England? Phew, what a pong!' She took the torch from the constable and began to sweep the beam methodically around the walls. 'Aha! Oh, look, Albert. Look, Mr Agnew. Isn't that a pretty sight?'

The 'pretty sight' was a smoke-coloured cat whose big golden eyes stared up into the torch beam unblinkingly. She lay on her side with four kittens tugging at her probably empty teats.

Albert sucked in his breath. 'Poor little blighter, no wonder she was so desperate and created such a din,' he murmured. 'Of course, even if she could have got out by some means she wouldn't have left her kittens. And the old felt material Miss Foulks used for making her hats makes an excellent bed.' He turned to the policeman. 'If I go to my shop and bring back a cardboard box, could we transfer her and the kittens into it?' The constable agreed and Albert went off, to return moments later with a roomy cardboard box which he stood on the floor of the stockroom. 'I'm sure Miss Foulks will want the cat, if not her babies. I suppose this cat did belong to Miss Foulks?' he said as he re-joined them.

The constable shrugged, but Tess shook her head. 'No, Miss Foulks didn't like animals at all. If a stray cat wandered in she'd get really frightened and ask anybody handy to chase it out of our yard. She'll be horrified when she hears of tonight's work, because the cat must have come in to have the kittens whilst the shop was still open. But before you try to move her, I'll fetch a bribe so she won't object when she and her kittens are put into the box.'

The constable laughed. 'Have you got a couple of mice up there?' he asked jovially. 'She'd get into the box for one of them, I reckon.'

Tess gave him an indulgent glance in the torchlight. 'Not a mouse; milk,' she said briefly, and disappeared, to reappear moments later carefully carrying a deep saucer full of milk, which she placed in the cardboard box. The little cat stretched its neck and sniffed the air hopefully, then jumped voluntarily into the box and began to lap. Tess lifted the babies with great care and put them into the box beside their mother, then took a length of the felt which had been the little cat's nursery and placed it across the top of the box. She and Albert watched as the constable closed the small window, ushered them into the yard, relocked the door, and put the key into his tunic pocket. Then they parted, Tess and Albert to return to the flat, Albert carrying the cats in their box and Tess going first to unlock and lock the doors. Constable Agnew had undertaken to return the key to Mr Egbert and tell him of the night's doings and Tess, bubbling over with excitement, remembered her first visit to the farm after the war when Jonty had taken her to see Tibbs's progeny, and thought that the next time she spoke to him she must tell him that she was now the proud owner of a mother cat and four beautiful kittens. She was saying as much to Albert when they reached her kitchen.

Albert smiled down at her but his kind brown eyes were worried. 'I agree cats are pretty independent, but surely the same can't be said of kittens,' he pointed out. 'Can you find good homes for them over the weekend? Because once you're in work again, who's to look after them? The smell in that stockroom was something awful; you wouldn't want your gran to come home to a flat stinking of cat do-dos, would you?'

Tess was watching the little mother cat eagerly disposing of the milk, into which she had just crumbled half a round of bread, but she turned a look of astonishment on Albert. 'Find homes for them over the weekend?' she asked incredulously. 'Albert, they're only two or three days old; their eyes won't open until ten to fourteen days after they're born. And they can't leave their mother until they're six or eight weeks old. But they're awfully pretty kittens, so I'm sure there'll be no difficulty in finding them homes then. In fact, I think I'll sell them, because folk value something for which they have paid good money.'

'You know much more about such things than I do,' Albert said ruefully. 'Have you ever thought of opening a pet shop?'

There was a moment of stunned silence whilst Tess's eyes got rounder and rounder and her mouth dropped open. For a moment she and Albert stared at each other, both bereft of words, but then Tess spoke. 'Albert Payne, you're a perishin' bloody genius,' she breathed. 'Why on earth didn't I think of that? Oh, Albert, the last time I spoke to Jonty on the telephone he was quite cross because he said all I talked about was an ice cream parlour, about which I knew nothing. He said there must be something I was interested in, but all we could think of was that I had learned to type, though not terribly well. He suggested I might look for a job as office junior, and make my way up until I was good enough to apply for secretarial positions. Neither of us thought about the one thing I really do know about, and that's what they call "animal husbandry". Oh, Albert, Miss Foulks's shop would be absolutely ideal, because at the moment if someone wants to buy day-old chicks and rear them in their back yard they have to either go into the country and try to buy stock direct from a farmer or go to the market, and you may be sure that buying that way, with no knowledge of poultry, you'll be sold rubbish. But if you went to a local pet shop owned by someone with a great deal of experience, who knew exactly what she was doing, not only would you get good birds, but if something went wrong, if they died or sickened, you could take them back, because a pet shop can't up and off the way a market trader can.'

Albert stared at her, a flush creeping up his neck. 'I believe you've hit on the only idea which really might work,' he said. 'But what about setting-up money? I can't see a bank shelling out to a girl of your age, even with Gran to add respectability.'

Tess began to say that maybe he was right, maybe it was not such a good idea after all, but then she stopped. 'I won't be put off,' she said fiercely. 'The rent is cheap because the shop isn't very big, so the cost of setting up would be tiny. I'll find some lad who'll knock me up cages from old orange boxes and chicken wire. Gran's got savings and I'm sure there are other people, folk who are fond of her, like her fellow workers at Deering's, who'd put up a few bob to get us started. Deering's could be enormously helpful because of the crumbs. If you'd seen the quantity of crumbs they chuck out for the pigeons every night, you'd know what I mean.' She glanced rather defiantly at Albert and saw he was regarding her admiringly.

'You've set your heart on it, haven't you?' he said in a wondering tone. 'The minute I mentioned a pet shop you realised it was what you wanted to do more than anything else. As for setting-up costs, you can discuss that with our financial adviser, but for myself I think you'll find backers. In fact, I'll talk to my fellow members of the Chamber of Trade . . .'

But Tess was no longer listening. 'I shall need bales of straw for bedding, hay and grain for feeding, poultry meal, and a great many other things,' she was murmuring. 'I'll talk to Jonty tomorrow evening, because I'm sure he would put a couple of bales of hay and a couple of straw and probably a sack of poultry meal on to the train so that I could pick it up at this end. I know that things are moved about the country by train, so why not animal feed? Unless, of course, I found I could buy it more cheaply locally. Then there are goldfish; I've yet to meet a kid who doesn't yearn to have a goldfish after a visit to the fair. There's a Christmas fair here every year; I'm sure the fair people would tell me where they get their goldfish if I ask politely. Of course all pet shops sell rabbits, guinea pigs, hamsters and the like, and until we're established and can breed our own . . .'

But Albert was laughing, clapping his hands, trying

252

to break into her monologue. 'All right, all right, I'm convinced,' he said. 'First things first, however! Before you can start doing anything, you must get Edie's consent to the scheme. After all, it's not everyone who would fancy living over a pet shop full of live animals and birds. And if you intend to ask her to use her savings . . .'

'. . . and kittens and puppies, of course; everyone loves kittens and puppies,' Tess went on, oblivious. 'Why, these dear little kittens could be our first attraction, because a box of kittens playing together would have every child for miles with its nose pressed against the windowpane. Parents might baulk at the price we would have to ask for a puppy, but kittens are not only cheap to buy, they're cheap to keep. Oh, and I can go round the slaughter-houses, down by the ferry port, and buy meat which isn't fit for human consumption, and sell it for dog and cat food . . .'

Albert was still laughing, holding up his hand like a policeman stopping traffic. 'All right, all right, I get the idea,' he said. 'It's time I left you, and you went to bed. Think it over, and tomorrow we'll both go to the hospital and see how Edie feels about her granddaughter starting up in business as a pet shop owner.'

Next day Tess went to the nursery wondering how she would get through the day until work finished and she could go to the hospital and tell Gran all about her exciting new scheme. But she enjoyed her work and somehow the time passed until she found herself at last making her way across the hospital foyer, heading for Gran's ward. When she pushed her way in through the doors, along with a crowd of others, Albert was already there and for a moment Tess felt the old familiar flame of jealousy flare up. He would have told Gran the news, said it was his own casual remark which had given her the idea, taken the credit for it. Not for the first time, she felt she hated Albert. But as she walked towards the bed and saw Gran smiling at her she chided herself. How could she have had such an ungenerous thought? She knew very well, really, that Albert would not have said a word. So she returned Gran's smile, and when Albert moved up she slid on to the bench beside him.

'Have you told Gran about the cat?' Tess began rather breathlessly, for she had run all the way from the bus stop. 'Before I went to bed last night I filled the big baking tray with earth because I didn't want any accidents, and believe it or not the little darling had used the earth during the night, and scraped it up into a sort of mountain so I could see she had performed.'

'Cat?' Gran said. She sounded bewildered. 'What cat? Tess, you're talking in riddles; let me have the story in plain English, if you please.'

Nothing loath, Tess began with great verve to recount the happenings of the previous evening from the very beginning – in fact from when Albert had believed that the yowling sounds were coming from her wireless set – right through to the moment when he had suggested that she should open a pet shop. Gran was about to say that she could scarcely do so with only four kittens to sell when Tess interrupted. 'You think he was joking, don't you, Gran? Well, he might have been, but the idea was a good one; still is a good one. The landlord isn't asking much rent and the premises are ideal; what's more, it means we could stay in the flat and wouldn't have to keep on searching for somewhere else to live. And Gran, if there's one thing I do know about, it's animals. I've not jumped the gun and gone to the authorities, or to Mr Egbert for that matter, because I wanted to make sure you approved. You could do the books, Gran, order up supplies on the telephone, including our stock, which would be small animals – lots of rabbits, guinea pigs, hamsters . . . that sort of thing – goldfish, those little tiny water tortoises – I can't think what they're called . . .'

'You mean terrapins,' Albert put in. 'But it might not be a good idea to start off with them because I imagine they're quite expensive. Begin with the more conventional pet shop animals . . .'

'Oh yes, of course, and I forgot chickens,' Tess said. 'They're really important because before the war everyone kept a few hens in their back yard, and most folk would like to do so again. But there are snags . . .'

She went on to explain to her grandmother how folk would buy day-old chicks and then, lacking the necessary knowledge, would feed them inappropriately, or expect them to live outside in a freezing winter. 'A simple light bulb, if you're on the electric, and a woollen tea cosy would be enough to save their little lives,' she said, 'and the right food is terribly important when animals and birds are tiny. But that's all in the future, once we've got our shop. Oh, Gran, you haven't said much. What do you really think? I can go to the authorities first thing on Monday morning and ask what sort of permission we shall need for Change of Use . . . What's the matter, Gran?' For Edie was slowly shaking her head.

'My dear Tess, you really must think; more haste less speed, you know,' Gran said. 'I understand why you

255

want to get things moving, but no landlord worth his salt is going to let a girl of your age rent his property. Everything will have to be done in my name, and until I'm out of hospital and able to visit the planning authorities I'm afraid we shall have to play a waiting game.'

Tess knew that her face had fallen, but she also knew that Gran was talking sense, so she smiled when Albert patted her shoulder. 'I'll do anything I can to help the pair of you, you know that,' he said. 'But Edie's right, as always. However, I will talk to the landlord and sort out the rent for the flat and the shop together, because it would be too bad if someone else turned up and took over the property. What's more, Mr Egbert is a sensible man, and knows probably better than most the importance of choosing a gap in the market for any new venture.' He saw Tess raise her eyebrows, and explained: 'There isn't another pet shop for miles around, which means you won't have aggressive competition trying to get rid of you by underpricing – meaning that if you have a rabbit for sale at five bob the competition would offer theirs for three and six. Do you understand?'

'Yes, I do,' Tess said thankfully. 'What a lucky thing for us that you know all the tricks of the trade, Albert.' She turned to Gran. 'What do you think, Gran? Aside from having to wait, do you feel we could succeed with a pet shop? Farm dogs and cats are always having puppies and kittens, rabbits breed like billyo, and goldfish are ten a penny; look at the number they hand out as prizes on the hoopla stalls, and most of the poor little things die because the kids who win them don't understand their needs. I mean to get hold of an old typewriter so I can type out lists of how to look after the animals, birds and fish we sell in our shop. Then I'll Roneo the lists and put them in a pile on the counter.'

Albert laughed. 'Miss Williams, you think of everything,' he said. He turned to Gran. 'Isn't she an example to us all, Edie? Yesterday morning the words "pet shop" weren't in her vocabulary. Today she could run one unaided and make her fortune.'

257

Chapter Ten

It took time, as both Gran and Albert had said it would. Christmas passed and the New Year was well advanced before at last they were able to start preparing their new premises. Gran's leg was still weak and she could only manage the stairs up to the flat provided someone walked behind her to steady her from step to step, but despite this Tess, impatient as always, wanted to start buying in her stock, for though the kittens were now young cats and had gone off to good homes, there were as yet no other creatures residing in what they had decided to call Tess's Pets.

But once again, wiser heads prevailed. Albert had had an excellent Christmas and willingly put money into the pet shop venture as well as doing a great deal of work on their business plan, but he pointed out that this was only possible because he closed his shop at two o'clock, since trade was always slow at this time of year.

'And if you open now, with the weather so miserable and folk having overspent at Christmas, you'll find you've got animals on your hands and no money to buy the necessary food,' he said gently. He had been sanding down the long counter and now he stopped and leaned over to squeeze Tess's shoulder. 'Look out of the window, queen! That'll tell you more than I can.'

Tess looked and saw that, bundled up in warm clothing

and bent double against the mixture of rain and sleet which was blowing into their faces, the few people on the pavement showed no inclination to linger, let alone window-shop.

She sighed. 'You're right as always, Albert,' she said resignedly. 'What do you think about opening just before Easter? We could do a special offer on day-old chicks; give away a packet of chick food with every half dozen birds sold. And then there's the Easter bunny . . . now what could we do to bring people flocking in to see the Easter bunny?'

Gran had been sitting behind the counter in an old rocking chair which Albert had bought cheap at an auction, and now she laid her knitting down in her lap. She was doing it continental fashion with one needle tucked under her left arm, leaving her right hand to do all the work since her left was almost useless. She smiled at Tess.

'A pet shop is wasted on you, or rather you are wasted on a pet shop; you should be running the country!' she said. 'Are you going to advertise? You could get a reporter from the *Liverpool Echo* to come and look at your stock and perhaps write a little article. If you open before Easter – just a few days before, mind – then they might give you space, because April is often what they call a slow news time.'

'I'll try that,' Tess agreed. 'But for now we'll stock the shop with animal food, fish food and stuff for poultry. Then when Easter arrives all we'll need will be the animals themselves.' She grinned at Albert. 'And thanks to your foresight, Albert, everything will be ready for the arrival of our pets.'

*

259

The Friday before the shop was due to open Tess was hurrying home from her latest part-time job as a waitress in a small tea room on Church Street when Snowy galloped up beside her, a grin spreading over his face as he skidded to a halt. 'Phew! You don't half walk fast,' he complained. 'I saw you as I passed that big jeweller's shop on the corner. Are you heading for a tram stop or shall I offer to carry your bag? Any news?'

Tess laughed. Snowy had finally settled on Liverpool University – or rather, Tess suspected, he had intended to take up a place there all along – and contrived to spend a good deal of time in the city with his friends. To Tess's surprise he was fascinated by the pet shop, and when she and Gran had been searching for backers who might lend them money to start up he had contributed quite a respectable sum. Tess had been delighted at the time but could not help secretly wondering now whether she would be as pleased once the shop opened, for Snowy was full of ideas, some of them very wild, and when she had laughed him to scorn he had reminded her that he was a shareholder and ought to be treated with respect. But now she considered his question seriously. 'Any news? What sort of news were you thinking of?' she asked. 'This is my last day working as a waitress because the first of the animals will be arriving on Monday and I'll have my work cut out to get them all caged, penned or boxed by the time we open. From then on I'll be rushed off my feet even if we don't have a single customer, because animals aren't like packets of cigarettes or bottles of beer; they need feeding and cleaning, giving fresh water . . . oh, no end of things. Albert will be back in his shop full time, and though

Gran will take the money and give change she can't do much else because the hospital have told her she must take it easy for another couple of months.' She did not add, as she might have done, that Gran's consultant had warned Tess that her grandmother might never have the full use of her left hand again.

'She's a very gallant lady, and I know she'll do the exercises I have given her, but that will merely keep the limb supple. Already, though she never complains to you, she's suffering from arthritis in her wrist and shoulder, so don't let her push herself.' He was a tall man, grey-haired and humorous, and he had smiled down at Tess. 'Give her little jobs which she can do one-handed. She won't be able to peel potatoes for a long time, but there are other tasks which will be well within her capabilities . . . oh, you will know much better than I what she can and can't do after she's been home for a few days.'

But now Snowy took her hand and smiled affectionately down at her. 'Well, I can see that once the animals arrive your life won't be your own, so how about coming to the Grafton for a spot of the light fantastic tomorrow? I expect there'll be a special dance over Easter, but by then you'll be too exhausted to quickstep or foxtrot and will want to loll in a seat at the cinema watching some rubbishy picture, whereas I've been sitting in a lecture theatre all week and am simply longing to dance the night away.'

'Oh, you!' Tess said, poking him in the ribs. 'When have you ever known me too tired to dance? Don't you wish you could be in the shop when the animals and birds and things start to arrive though? Gran is worried that I've overstretched myself and too many will be

261

coming in over the course of the next few days, but Miss Foulks's stockroom is enormous and we can keep what you might call reserve animals in there until there's space in the shop itself.'

'Then you'll come dancing? Jolly good,' Snowy said. 'Dancing helps one to relax, they say, and I do like my girlfriends to be relaxed. And as for missing out on your opening day, what nonsense! I shall be there with friends from university, all of whom are anxious to own a goldfish, or possibly a couple of day-old chicks. I've promised them special rates so one or two of them might even stretch to a rabbit . . .'

Tess was beginning to say, repressively, that she did not think his fellow students were the right sort of people to own pets when she heard the tap-tap of high-heeled shoes on the paving stones and a breathless voice crying: 'Wait for me, you two.'

Tess and Snowy stopped in their tracks as an elegantly dressed blonde came to a halt beside them, her eyes fixed on Snowy. 'Snowy White, I thought it were you!' she said triumphantly. 'Even from the back I knew you! Do you reckernise me? It's been years.'

Snowy had been staring hard, but suddenly he let go of Tess and shot his hand forward to take the other girl's. 'Well, I'm damned, if it isn't Marilyn Thomas,' he said. 'What are you doing in this neck of the woods? The last time I was in your mam's shop she told me you'd got work in the gowns department of a big London store . . . Harrods, was it?' He grinned brilliantly at Marilyn. 'Have they given you the big E already?'

Marilyn sniffed and tossed her head. 'I've gorra weekend off,' she said. 'Did my mam tell you I were a mannequin? I work in gowns, like she said, but I show clothes from eleven to twelve in the mornings and three to four in the afternoons. I get paid extra, 'cos they think a deal of me in gowns.'

Tess shifted from foot to foot. Not once in this whole conversation had Marilyn so much as looked at her; how rude the older girl was, Tess thought, but even as she was considering strolling over to the nearest window and pretending to look inside, Snowy took her hand again. 'Sorry, Tess, how rude of me,' he said. 'But of course you know Marilyn as well as I do, so there's no need for introductions.'

Marilyn sniggered. 'Oh, so it's you,' she said offhandedly, glancing at Tess. She turned back to Snowy. 'Where are you off to? Any chance of takin' me dancin' tomorrow? Or I wouldn't mind goin' to the flicks; there's a good one on at the Plaza.'

Snowy glanced quickly at Tess, then away again. 'Tomorrow,' he said thoughtfully. 'I suppose . . . Tess, would you be a real sport and let me put off our date until after Easter? It seems an awful cheek to ask, but you and I can meet any time, whereas Marilyn here . . .'

Tess felt outraged, but did not intend to show it. She said easily: 'Yes, that's fine by me. I'm awfully busy at the moment.'

Marilyn tossed her head. 'Oh, don't worry! If you're taking this – this person out then I suppose I can look up one of the guys.' She smirked, glancing quickly at Tess, then away again. 'They're all dead keen on me, it's just that I didn't know I was going to be home this weekend so I couldn't get in touch to tell them . . .'

'. . . of the treat in store,' Snowy said. He half turned

263

to Tess, and she thought she saw his left eyelid flutter. And was there a touch of sarcasm in his tone? But if so Marilyn did not notice it and he turned back to her, smiling. 'Right, then it's all arranged,' he said briskly. 'I'll pick you up at half-seven; be sure you are looking your best.'

Marilyn gave him what she no doubt considered to be a brilliant smile, Tess thought cattily. 'I always look my best,' she said. 'TTFN.'

Snowy and Tess watched her clicking away, then Tess turned rather coldly to her companion. 'TTFN,' she said scornfully. 'Have a nice evening, Snowy. See you around.'

She was turning away when Snowy caught her arm. 'Hang on a minute, where are you off to? What time shall we meet tomorrow? And we've not decided yet which ballroom to grace with our presence.'

'If you think I'm making up a threesome . . .' Tess said angrily. Snowy was shaking with silent laughter, but he sobered up when he read the annoyance in her face.

'Oh dear, oh dear, oh dear, what a little twerp you are, Miss Theresa Williams,' he said, pulling her into the circle of his arm. 'I wouldn't do an ungentlemanly thing like cancelling our date just to pander to Marilyn's perfectly enormous ego. I'm going to stand her up!'

Tess's eyes rounded. 'Stand her up?' she echoed. 'But why on earth would you do a thing like that?'

'Why not? It was what she did to me once, if you remember,' Snowy said easily. 'It'll just be getting a bit of my own back. What's wrong with that?'

'But Snowy, that was years ago,' Tess protested. 'It's a pretty mean thing to do, don't you think?'

Snowy grinned maliciously. 'Marilyn is a conceited,

selfish little bitch,' he said. 'She never thought of how you must feel, having your date snatched away from you. In fact she was pleased . . . No, don't shake your head, you must have been able to read her expression as well as I could. For once in her life, Marilyn Thomas will be the one hanging around, all dressed up with nowhere to go.' He grinned down at Tess and gave her a squeeze. 'Honest to God, queen, she bloody well deserves a bit of a set-down, if only for what she put you through all those years ago.'

Tess sighed, but in a way she could see Snowy's point. Marilyn had tried to do a mean thing, and would be served out for it. For a moment though she contemplated going round to the Thomases' corner shop and warning Marilyn that her escort had other plans, but Snowy must have read something of this intention in her expression because he shook an admonitory finger. 'No you don't; just you mind your own perishin' business, Tess Williams,' he said, and Tess could hear the laughter in his voice. 'It'll do bloody Marilyn good to be taken down a peg. If it hurts your delicate conscience, forget I told you. And if you're afraid of meeting Marilyn at the Grafton – I should rather enjoy it – we can go to one of the other ballrooms; heaven knows there are plenty to choose from.'

He and Tess parted outside the flat, agreeing what time Snowy would pick her up the following day. 'And I mean to come round on Sunday as well to whisk you off for a final treat,' he said. 'And not a word to Marilyn or her mother, or you will earn my severe displeasure.'

Tess agreed reluctantly to say nothing to the Thomases, but once back in the flat's kitchen, where Gran was dishing up the shepherd's pie they had made earlier, she told her Snowy's plan and asked what she thought she should do about it.

Gran laughed, then considered. 'Do? Why, nothing, because for all you know Snowy might have repented and already got in touch with Marilyn with some excuse for not taking her out. Of course it was very wrong of him to want to get revenge for something which happened years ago, but all he will be doing is denting Marilyn's self-esteem, which in my opinion isn't a bad thing. And now forget about it, which is what Snowy told you to do. Girls like Marilyn are like corks: you can put them in the water and hold them down but they'll bob to the surface again no matter what.'

Snowy came whistling down Heyworth Street the morning after he had failed to meet Marilyn. It was a beautiful April day, the breeze smelling of both the river and the countryside, and the sunshine fell warmly on his uncovered head. He was nearing the church to which most of the other pedestrians were heading when he spotted Marilyn. He guessed she was also bound for church and wondered for a brief moment whether to dive down a side street before she saw him or to approach her cheerily, as though he had no reason to avoid her. He decided on the second option when he saw she was alone, her mother having presumably gone on ahead with her cronies.

Marilyn was dressed demurely, as befitted a church-goer, and Snowy thought that her dark green coat with its swirling skirt almost touching her ankles and the little green hat perched on her gleaming gold head were a great deal more attractive than the gaudy clothes she had worn on their previous encounter. He crossed the road and saluted her lazily, a hand raised. 'Morning, Marilyn. On your way to church?' he enquired breezily. 'You're looking very smart.'

Marilyn turned to face him, eyes flashing, mouth tightening, and Snowy thought irreverently that one of these days she was going to look the image of her mother; not an attractive thought. Mrs Thomas ran her small shop with an iron hand, and Snowy had frequently thought that, when annoyed or overstretched, her mouth tightened into a positive rat trap, but now he smiled down at Marilyn as though he could not imagine why she was looking so annoyed.

Marilyn, however, enlightened him. 'You bastard!' she hissed. 'You bloody stood me up, you – you . . .' There followed a string of swear words which had Snowy blinking in disbelief. Everyone can swear, but Marilyn, it seemed, had taken a course in foul language, and had passed with flying colours.

But Snowy pretended puzzlement. 'What's the matter?' he asked. 'Have I done something to annoy you?'

Marilyn gasped, choked, and then started to giggle. 'You bloody stood me up, you bastard,' she repeated, but the fury had gone out of her voice. 'It were a mean trick, 'cos I were lookin' forward to catchin' up with all the latest gossip. And you an' me were good pals once, until that little snake in the grass—'

'Are you referring to the woman I love?' Snowy said flippantly. 'Because if you are, you're way out. And anyway, I've not heard yet why you're so annoyed with me. What can I have done to get up your nose?'

267

But this, it seemed, was too much. Marilyn clapped a hand to her mouth, but the giggles escaped and it was several moments before she could remind him again of his conduct. 'You stood me up,' she repeated. 'I were walkin' up and down the pavement outside Mam's house, a perishin' laughin' stock, until I give up at about eight o'clock. So where were you, Mr Desmond bloody White?'

Snowy spread his hands. 'I don't understand,' he said untruthfully. 'I made it quite clear that I was taking Tess out last night. Surely you couldn't have misunderstood what I was saying? But look, we can't stand here nattering, or you'll miss the church service. Though how you dare go into church with the awful language you've been using still hot on your lips I don't know.'

'You liar. It wasn't that way at all,' Marilyn said, but she no longer sounded angry or amused, merely sulky. 'You're rotten through and through, Snowy White, and I'm glad I found out in time.' Rather spoiling the effect, she looked at him hopefully. 'Why don't we meet after church? The weather's fine enough; we could go out to Princes Park, have a row on the lake . . .'

Snowy pretended to consider, then shook his head regretfully. 'Impossible, I'm afraid. Me and my girlfriend are taking a river trip; I'm on my way down to the Pier Head now.'

Marilyn used an ugly word, but they were now opposite the church, so Snowy seized her hand and shook it vigorously, making sure that he squeezed tightly enough to hurt. 'Nice to see you, Miss Thomas,' he said, retaining her fingers in a cruel grip whilst she tried in vain to pull away. 'No doubt we'll meet again one of these days.'

He let go of her right hand and watched her massaging it with her left, cheeks still flushed. But she did not answer, merely crossing the road and joining the other churchgoers whilst Snowy, his face lit by a satisfied smile, continued on his way. He told himself that Marilyn need no longer bother him, that he had already begun to tire of her all those years ago, and that he need have no regrets, because for all her careful upbringing and undoubted beauty the language she had used proved she was as common as muck and would never have been a suitable girlfriend for someone such as himself, a university student who would one day earn a salary, not a wage, and would hold an important position in the community. In fact, he was well rid of her.

Snowy smiled to himself. Tess Williams was bright and intelligent, though in his opinion not at all beautiful. Her soft fawn-coloured hair framed elfin features, but her large hazel eyes regarded the world steadily, and he had no doubt that she too would one day become a pillar of the community. And when that day dawns, he told himself, I shall want to be a part of Tess's life.

The thought made him smile more broadly than ever. Funny little Tess, who faded into insignificance when compared with beautiful, golden-haired Marilyn, how strange to think that one of these days she might become a force to be reckoned with. But he had watched with increasing interest as the pet shop became a reality and not just a dream. Tess, despite never having had any experience in business matters, was learning by leaps and bounds.

As he got nearer the Pier Head Snowy saw Tess ahead of him, making for the pleasure boat at the quayside. She

269

had tied her hair back from her face with a piece of ribbon and was wearing a blue gingham dress which he recognised as part of her school uniform. It was not at all glamorous, but Snowy knew it was far more suitable for a river trip than the clothing which had adorned Marilyn Thomas. He reached Tess's side and put an arm round her. 'All right?' He jerked a thumb at the large basket she was holding. 'Is that our picnic? We can buy a drink aboard, but food's bound to be expensive, and anyway the ship lets us off for an hour around lunchtime so we can eat our picnic then. Guess who I saw on my way here?'

Tess pulled a face. 'I don't have to guess, I know. Marilyn, of course.' Snowy saw that she was trying to repress a giggle and thought how pretty she looked when the dimple beside her mouth came and went. 'Did you speak to her?'

'Of course,' Snowy said, doing his best to sound surprised. 'After all, we're old friends, wouldn't you say?'

'Old friends, but new enemies,' Tess said. 'Or didn't she realise she'd been stood up? You might have told her she'd got the wrong day or the wrong time; didn't she ask where you were?'

Snowy pretended to consider, then spoke slowly. 'Ask me where I was? Well, I suppose she did, in a way.' He grinned down at Tess, his blue eyes dancing, his mouth curving into a smile. 'She called you a snake in the grass, my dear! What about that, eh?'

'Really? And what, pray, did she call you?'

Snowy chuckled. 'If I were to repeat what she called me you wouldn't understand half the words she used and your ears would burn for a fortnight. I was quite

270

shocked; she was on her way to attend the eleven o'clock service too. Ah, look, they've opened the gangway, which means we can board. Come along, because this is probably the nearest you'll get to a holiday until the shop is able to do without you for the odd day.' He took her basket, pretended to stagger beneath its weight, and then began to ascend the gangway.

Tess turned to stare at him. 'But I shall get every Sunday off, and the river trips go on a Sunday. In fact once June arrives we can catch the ferry to Woodside and have a lovely day in the country and a cream tea with strawberries,' she pointed out. 'And some of the farmhouses give you a Sunday roast for a few bob.'

Snowy looked down at her, slowly shaking his head and thinking how cute she looked when her pearly little teeth gripped her lower lip and her eyes looked so trustingly up into his. 'No, little goose, I'd bet money on the fact that you won't be able to have Sundays off. You'll be cleaning cages, refilling water pots, and mixing poultry meal for chickens. You'll be chopping and cooking dog meat so you have something to sell on Monday, exercising the puppies, cleaning the window glass . . .'

'I won't, I won't!' Tess squeaked, clearly horrified. 'I'll – I'll get up very early and do all the important work and then I'll pay a responsible schoolboy or -girl to do things like filling water pots. Gran will supervise and Albert will come in and check if I ask him – oh, you're having me on! I hate you, Snowy White. I think Marilyn's had a jolly narrow escape. I take it she has escaped?'

They had reached the head of the gangway and Snowy jerked his thumb towards the bows. 'Go and grab a seat

271

in the front,' he advised her. 'As for escaping, you make me sound like the Loch Ness monster.'

'So you are, just like it,' Tess said merrily. 'But stop fooling and tell me just what Marilyn said.'

'Oh, nothing much. She said only a rotter would have agreed to cancel an existing date in order to go out with an old flame . . .'

'And I quite agree that you are a rotter.' Tess said, plonking herself down on a white-painted seat in the bows and indicating that Snowy should take the place next to her. 'Well, if this is to be my last treat for ages I mean to make the most of it. Pass me the basket; there's a bag of mint humbugs right at the top which we can suck as we go along, admiring the beauties of the countryside.' She fished the sweets out of the basket, popped one into Snowy's mouth and took one herself. 'And now let's forget Marilyn and all other unpleasant things and enjoy ourselves,' she said thankfully. 'Ah, they're casting off! Isn't it exciting? When Gran was young she used to get the ferry to Dublin and spend a week with relatives; I'd like to do that one day, but first Gran and I must get the business properly established.' She wrapped her arms round herself and beamed at Snowy. 'I'm going to be a pet shop millionaire,' she announced. 'So hang on to your hat, Snowy White, if you're going to share our success!'

Tess, Gran and Albert stood on the pavement outside the pet shop staring at the window, which was all set now for the opening the next day. Tess had spent a great deal of time and thought on how the window was to look, and after half a dozen tries had finally settled on the display the three of them were now examining. In the middle was a large aquarium decorated with water plants, clean sand and a couple of branches of coral as well as forty or so tiny goldfish. The price of the coral had made Tess gasp, but Gran had pointed out that this was a commodity she would only have to buy once and there was no doubt that it improved the look of the aquarium as well as giving the fish something to swim round. To one side of the aquarium was a box of kittens, one ginger, one tabby and one black and white. Normally they would have been playing with each other or with one of the woolly balls which dangled from the top of the box, but now, with only the streetlights to illuminate them, they were snoozing.

On the other side was another box, containing two puppies. A canary in a cage hung from the ceiling and to the rear of the window, where once Miss Foulks had put her most expensive hats, stood a large cage with half a dozen rabbits in it.

Tess turned from her examination of the window. 'What do you think?' she asked huskily. 'Will it attract customers? I've taken your advice, Albert, and not put any prices in the window so that if folk are serious they have to come inside and enquire.' After Albert had nodded his approval she turned to Gran. 'I took your advice as well, and stopped trying to get virtually everything I sell into the window, and I must say it looks all the better for it. But now I'm going to lower my lovely new blind so that we can all get some sleep, including the pets. So we'd best say good night, Albert.'

The door to their staircase was still open, but Albert shook his head. 'I'm coming up with you; I've bought a bottle of fizzy Spanish wine to drink to the success of your venture, and I mean to broach it right away,' he said. He positioned himself closely behind Edie. 'Carefully as you go,' he advised her. 'If you were to fall down now, everyone would assume you'd drunk more than your fair share of the wine, and we can't have that, can we?'

The shop had been busy all day, for December was well advanced, but the crowds were thinning now as dusk approached. Tess was considering swinging the open sign on the door round to read: *Sorry, we are closed* when somebody came into the shop. For a moment, Tess thought it must just have been the wind, for she could see nobody, but then she looked again and realised that the intruder was a very small and very grubby boy, whose head scarcely came above the counter. Inwardly, Tess sighed. This customer was a sixpenny goldfish if ever she saw one; probably he was already holding, beneath the counter top, a glass jar into which she would decant the goldfish of his choice. And then he would bring out a collection of pennies and ha'pennies which might have taken him weeks to collect and would tell her that the goldfish was a present for his mam, and she would feel mean at taking money so hard earned.

Despite both her hopes and her hard work, the shop had not proved an instant success. Albert had said it was partly due to the fact that they were underfunded and of course also unknown to most of their suppliers. Understandably, she now realised, these had wanted paying as soon as they delivered rabbits, poultry, white mice and guinea pigs, and she simply had not had the money. She had tried explaining that she would pay up

274

as soon as customers bought, but this cut little ice with people who were in much the same position.

However, Tess had never been afraid of hard work and had slaved away, doing all her own cleaning, feeding and exercising, leaving only ordering and doing the books to Gran, until Snowy's prediction that she would have no time to herself had proved all too horribly true, and for several dark months she had actually wondered whether she would have to confess herself beaten and put the shop up for sale. But she had struggled on, never allowing her standards to drop, and gradually the business had begun to thrive. Now, at last, she was simply longing to find someone trustworthy who could, for a small wage, take some of the work off her hands and had interviewed several hopefuls, but none had come up to her expectations.

'Miss? Excuse me, miss . . .' The small boy grinned ingratiatingly up at her. 'Can I have a look around while you're quiet, like? Only pet shops is what I done me presentation on at the end of term. I gorra gold star. Mr Bleckinsop said it were the best out of the whole class.'

'Of course you can look around,' Tess said wearily. An idea occurred to her. 'Tell you what, you name the different species in the cages and aquarium and I'll tell you if I agree with your teacher.'

She had made the suggestion knowing it would please the kid to prowl amongst the cages, but she had not realised how thoroughly this scruffy urchin had researched his subject. At the end of ten minutes she was regarding her customer with awe. He not only knew the names of every animal, bird or fish in the shop, he knew their countries of origin, the food upon which they thrived,

275

the amount of exercise they needed and their lavatory habits.

At the end of the tour Tess stared at him with admiration. 'What's your name?' she asked. 'You know more about my animals and birds than any of the people who've come here asking for a job. Your Mr Bleckinsop knew what he was doing when he gave you that gold star.'

'Me name's Mitch and I'm ten years old, though I'm a bit small for me age,' the boy assured her. 'I come in for a goldfish, 'cos that's all I can afford. Do you sell 'em by size? Only there's one what's a sort of pinky-silver colour . . . I got sixpence.'

Tess thought of presents unbought, cards unsent, even mince pies unbaked, and smiled down hopefully into the grubby little face only just above the counter. 'You can have any goldfish you want, and how would you like a Saturday job, Mitch?' she said. 'I can't pay you much, but . . .'

The face beyond the counter was one enormous grin. 'A Saturday job!' Mitch breathed. 'Oh, miss, there ain't nothin' I'd like more. I'd do it for no money, so I would.' His small face clouded. 'The only thing is, me mam's got a job cleanin' offices on Saturdays so I've promised to look after me sister Elsie. She's three, but she's ever so good. If I tell her to sit in a chair and not move until she's told, she'd be good as gold, honest to God she would.'

At this point the door opened and Snowy appeared. He came over to the counter, leaned across it and kissed Tess on the tip of her nose.

'Hello, beautiful,' he said caressingly. 'Time to shut up

shop and accompany me to the flicks. Remember saying you wanted to see *All About Eve*? Well now's your chance. Have you had a good day?'

'Very good, but I can't come yet, Snowy, because I've got to clear up first, though I've just employed Mitch here as a helper.'

Snowy turned and stared at the small boy, then grinned. 'Hello, young Mitch! How are you?'

The boy grinned back. 'Hello, Snowy,' he said cheerfully. 'I've been lookin' at the animals and birds and that. If you like, miss, I can give you a hand right now; that way you'll get to the flicks quicker.'

'Thanks very much, Mitch, and now you're on the team you'd better call me Tess,' Tess said. 'And you can start your job by cleaning and feeding. Snowy will keep an eye on you whilst I nip up to the flat with today's takings so that my gran can make up the books.'

The boy stopped short. 'Wharrabout my goldfish?' he asked urgently. 'It's for my sister Elsie; it's the only thing I could afford and she's always wanted one.'

Tess laughed. 'Don't worry – I'll fish out the one you want just as soon as I come down again. See you presently.'

Half an hour later, as Tess and Snowy emerged on to the pavement, Snowy glanced up at the windows of the flat. 'I take it your gran's out? No lights showing, at any rate.'

'Well done, Sherlock Holmes,' Tess said approvingly. 'Gran and Albert have gone to the flicks, but not the one we're going to. And afterwards they're having a meal in the cinema café; Albert's treat.'

'And we shall do the same; *my* treat,' Snowy said

with a lordly air. 'I want to have a bit of a talk, sweetheart.'

'Talk away,' Tess said as Snowy took her arm and they began to hurry towards the cinema. 'But I must tell you that we had a very good day; I was on the go from half past nine until you came in, so I just hope I don't fall asleep and miss half the film.'

'I'll wake you if you do; can't have you snoring fit to drown the dialogue,' Snowy said. 'But we'll talk later when we're comfortably settled in the café. I've got enough sweet coupons left to buy you either a tiny box of chocolates or a quarter of a pound of mint humbugs; which shall it be?'

Laughing, Tess said that she would settle for the humbugs, and they joined the queue at the box office.

Despite the fact that the war had been over for more than seven years, menus were still not exciting. But it is always nice to have a meal cooked by someone else and served in pleasant surroundings, so Tess and Snowy ate fish and chips with marrowfat peas, followed by steamed ginger pudding and custard, and it was not until they were sitting back and sipping their tea that Snowy told Tess his news. 'You know I deferred my National Service until I got my degree? Well, I know you must remember *that*, since it was such a momentous happening,' he said, quizzing her with his eyes. 'But the dread moment has come at last. I'm to report to Catterick on the third of January, and from that moment on I am no longer a free spirit, but the property of His Majesty King George the Sixth, to send where he wills.'

'Oh, Snowy, I'm so sorry. But we knew you'd get your

call-up papers sometime soon,' Tess said. 'Don't you envy Jonty? Now if, like him, you were a farmer . . .'

Snowy pulled a face. 'I envy him one thing, and one thing only, and that's his friendship with you,' he said. 'Not that you've seen much of each other lately. Despite all his promises to come up and see the shop he's come neither near nor by, so I s'pose I needn't envy him . . . need I?'

Tess was conscious of a familiar pang of annoyance. Why did Snowy have to be so jealous of Jonty? He kept nagging on about that wartime friendship – damn it, we were nothing but a couple of kids, Tess thought crossly – every time the other was mentioned. She thought now that Snowy might be using that old friendship as an excuse to get her to become engaged, but fond though she was of Snowy she did not wish to be tied down yet. However, he was staring at her across the table, his gaze intent. 'Look, the army could send me anywhere; lots of the fellers go abroad, and even if it's only to Ireland, taking one's leave at home is difficult if not impossible. So you might as well say we shall be apart for the next two years. Please, Tess, say we can get engaged.'

Tess frowned and shook her head. 'It isn't on, Snowy, honestly it isn't. My friend Lucy got engaged to her boyfriend – yes, you're right, he was sent abroad – and spent two lonely miserable years not going to the flicks or to dances, not even to office parties, and when he came home he told her quite calmly that he was going to marry a girl he'd met in Malaya. Poor Lucy started to live normally again and met another national serviceman and agreed to go steady with him. Then he met someone else . . . Oh, Snowy, can't you understand? When you come home, if you still feel the same we won't just get engaged, we'll get married if you like, but I won't be like the owl and the pussycat . . .' she giggled, *'with a ring at the end of his nose, his nose, his nose, with a ring at the end of his nose.'*

Snowy laughed too but Tess reflected that his laugh did not hold much amusement. 'Tell you what, if you'll swear on your mother's life – no, on your gran's life – that you'll not go down to Bell Farm, nor let that tedious ploughboy come up here, then I won't ask you to get engaged,' he said. 'Oh, don't fire up at me and start shouting, because if there was nothing in it you wouldn't mind promising. Isn't that so?'

Tess opened her mouth to refute the remark but then thought better of it. During all the time that she and Gran had had the shop, Snowy had been a tower of strength. He had taught her how to balance the books, explained about tax and expenses, contacted suppliers and argued about discounts and prices. Jonty had done his best, but the distance had defeated him, though they had exchanged frequent letters at first. Unfortunately these had got shorter and shorter. Now they wrote probably every other month, and in the course of these letters the name Pamela Davies cropped up quite often enough to satisfy Snowy, or would have done had Tess allowed him to read her letters. But now, seeing the angry flush on his cheekbones, she decided that she was being rather unfair. Secretly, she thought there was little chance of Jonty's coming up to Liverpool and even less of her going to Bell Farm, so why not give Snowy what he wanted? Alternatively, she could show him the letters, the ones where Jonty mentioned going dancing with Pamela, taking Pamela to the flicks or getting out the Ford to fetch Pamela down to help with the harvest.

All might have been well had she made the offer at once, but she hesitated. 'If you aren't willing to commit then we might as well call it a day,' Snowy said sulkily. And then, apparently on impulse, he leaned across the table, cupped her face in his hands and kissed her.

Tess gave a startled squeak and pulled back. 'What on earth do you think you're doing?' she whispered angrily. 'Honestly, Snowy, in front of a whole café full of people!' She cast a quick glance around them, but no one seemed to be taking any notice. 'If that's the way you mean to behave . . .'

Snowy sighed. 'I thought one of my delicious kisses might make you change your mind,' he mumbled. 'Look, I suppose you've got a point when you say you don't want to get engaged until I'm home again. If we both promise to be faithful to the other one then that will have to do for now. Agreed?'

But by now Tess had got tired of the whole conversation. She felt that Snowy had backed her into a corner by choosing such a public place to tell her that his call-up papers had arrived. And his recurring urge to get engaged, though flattering, did not somehow ring true. If she fell in love with someone else during Snowy's absence, she was unlikely to let promises, or an engagement ring for that matter, get in her way. And as for kisses, well they were all very fine, but they didn't change anything. She jumped to her feet, snatched her coat off the back of her chair and her handbag from beneath it, and stalked towards the door. She would have liked to sweep out, but could not, in all fairness, do so. Snowy had taken her to see the film of her choice and bought her a meal, and all she had done was refuse to get engaged and tell him off. So she waited whilst he paid the bill, her temper cooling, and when he arrived beside her and did not attempt to take her hand or touch her in any way she was sorry she had upset him. After all, soon he would be off to training camp, or whatever they called it, and she might not see him again for two years. So she tucked her hand into the crook of his elbow as they began to descend the long flight of stairs. 'I'm sorry, Snowy, because you've been a good friend to me and a tremendous help. Jonty and I were close as kids but we're neither of us kids any more. Jonty's got a girlfriend – Pamela Davies – and I've got you, so why should either of us worry? When we get back to the flat, I'll get one of Jonty's letters so that you can read it.' She squeezed his arm. 'Agreed?'

'Agreed,' Snowy said rather sullenly. 'And now let's change the subject. That chap Mitch Roberts; they're a decent little family. If you ever want a cleaner, you couldn't do better than to employ his mam. I haven't had much to do with the father but I believe he's perfectly respectable unless drunk, and that goes for a lot of seamen, I understand.' He scowled at her. 'And don't try and tell me that you and Jonty aren't still pretty close, because you've just proved it. You keep his letters!'

Tess groaned. 'Oh, for God's sake grow up, Snowy White,' she said wearily. 'It just so happens that I keep one letter or possibly two until I've answered them . . .' she crossed her fingers behind her back, 'then I chuck them in the rubbish bin. Satisfied?'

'I will be when I've seen the letter,' Snowy said after

rather a long pause. 'Oh, Tess, why have I had the misfortune to fall in love with a pig-headed little person with a weakness for hicks?'

Tess laughed, though she was secretly annoyed with Snowy's constant attempts to diminish Jonty, and as they reached the pavement she gave him a punch in the ribs, hard enough to make him gasp. 'Serve you right,' she said merrily. 'I say, that was a super meal, but knowing Gran there'll be hot cocoa and shortbread when we reach the flat. Aren't you glad you didn't march off in a huff? I know you came pretty near it – I could read it in your face.'

Snowy shrugged. 'Sometimes I wonder why I love you,' he said, but his tone was teasing once more. 'Race you to the pet shop, Miss Theresa Williams.'

Tess had been right, Snowy thought as, having said good night, he set off in the direction of home. As he and Tess had entered the kitchen they had seen Gran and Albert sitting over their mugs of cocoa, looking so like a long-married couple that Snowy had remarked: 'Darby and Joan, I do declare! Gosh, those biscuits look good.'

'Told you so,' Tess had said, heading across the kitchen. 'Shan't be a tick.' True to her word she returned almost immediately and handed Snowy a sheet of notepaper. 'Read that,' she had commanded, 'and say you're sorry.'

'What's all this?' Albert had said curiously as Snowy took the sheet and began to read. 'Secrets?'

'No, not secrets; just settling a bet,' Snowy had said untruthfully. He read the line which Tess was indicating: *Took Pamela to see* Winchester '73; *she's mad on Westerns, can't get enough of them. But as I was saying . . .*

'Told you so!' Tess had said triumphantly for the

283

second time, snatching the sheet from his hand before he could read another word. 'And now, having . . . er, settled the bet, how about some cocoa before you leave?'

Snowy had agreed rather stiffly to have a mug of cocoa, though he had given her a very cold look when she handed him his cup. He could not wait to get her alone so that he could object to the way she had taken the letter back, and come to think of it it wasn't a whole letter anyway, just one miserable page. If she was going to be frank and honest, if there was really nothing between her and the ploughboy, then she should have handed over the whole letter for him to read at his leisure.

But Albert and Edie, clearly unaware of a slight frostiness in the atmosphere, had chattered gaily on about the film they had seen, and the meal they had eaten afterwards in the cinema café, so Snowy had drunk his cocoa too hot and burned his tongue, turned down the offer of biscuits and got to his feet. 'Thank you very much, Mrs Williams,' he had said formally. He had not taken off his overcoat when he entered the flat, and now he simply fastened the buttons, then turned to Tess. 'Going to see me off the premises, love? Make sure I shut the door properly and click the Yale down?'

Tess had begun to say that she would do so when Albert too got to his feet and reached for his overcoat. 'Well, it's time I was off as well,' he had said. 'Thanks very much, Edie. See you tomorrow.'

Snowy could have screamed with frustration. How could Albert be so stupid? He was determined to have a word with Tess about the letter, since he thought her behaviour had been downright suspicious. But Edie, also getting to her feet, went over to the sink, giving Albert a warning look as she did so. 'You can dry the crocks for me, Albert,' she said. 'I dare say these young people will want to say good night without an audience.'

'Oh, rubbish, Gran,' Tess had said breezily. 'We sat in the back row at the cinema, you know!'

Gran and Albert both laughed and Snowy had done his best to smile. 'I do want a word with Tess,' he had admitted. He grinned self-consciously at Edie, already clattering dishes in the sink. 'After all, I may be off to foreign parts very soon, so every moment is precious.'

'And you may not; you may find yourself stationed at Seaforth Barracks and able to come home every night,' Tess had pointed out unkindly. 'Why must you always imagine the worst?'

Snowy had begun to protest that he was doing no such thing but merely putting into words what they both knew to be true; that the army, once you were in, ruled your life; but Tess had snatched the door open and was gesturing him to precede her down the stairs. There was another exchange of good nights, but when they had emerged on to the pavement, and Tess would have gone back into the flat, he had grabbed her and pulled her over to stand against the pet shop door. 'If there's nothing between you and the ploughboy, why didn't you let me read the whole letter?' he had demanded harshly. 'Or at least the entire page?'

It was a cold and frosty night and Tess's face in the light of the full moon looked pale, the gentle lips pulled into a hard line. She had stared up at him, her eyes dark with surprise. 'Look, Snowy, that letter was written to me, not for general publication. I showed you the bit about Pamela because it seemed you didn't trust my word but wanted proof. As far as I'm concerned, that's the end of the matter. I'm afraid I can't think of any other way to convince you that Jonty and I are just good friends. So perhaps the best thing for us to do was what you suggested earlier; perhaps we should call it a day. Apart from anything else, I really resent you calling him a ploughboy. It's rude and unfair and thoroughly nasty.'

All this time they had been standing against the door of the pet shop, but now Snowy shook his head violently and pulled her roughly into his arms. 'I'll wash my mouth out with lye soap, and swear never to be rude about Mr Jonathan Bell again!' he had said, trying to sound humorous and not outraged, which was how he felt. 'As for not trusting your word, I didn't mean to imply you would lie to me. Oh, darling Tess, can't you see that I'm jealous and can't bear to think of you with another bloke? Let's just put the whole thing behind us and never mention it again.'

Tess had agreed. 'Kiss and make up,' she declared, suiting action to words, and then she had turned quickly back towards the stair which led up to the flat, leaving Snowy to set off home, wondering whether he had done the right thing in not insisting that he should read the entire letter, which had been his initial impulse.

Turning up his coat collar – for once out of the shelter of the doorway he was conscious of a nippy little wind – he thought back over his evening. He was still not sure why he felt as he did about Tess, because she was neither strikingly pretty nor brilliantly clever, though she ran an exceedingly successful little business. Because he helped Gran with the books he knew just how successful that business was, and admired her for that. But you didn't suggest marriage to a girl because she had a pet shop, or because she was bright and intelligent. You suggested marriage, or he thought you did, when someone lit a fire of wanting within you, a fire so hot that it could not be ignored. He had known that feeling years ago, when he had first taken Marilyn out, and even now, whenever she happened to cross his path, he was aware of what, to himself, he referred to as a 'slow burn'. But when he had discussed it with his friends at university, they had laughed the idea that this might be true love to scorn. 'It's lust, old feller, just plain wicked old lust,' his pal Marlowe had said. 'I've met your Tess; she's the sort of girl who gets under your skin, and not because of her looks. If I were you I'd grab her and stop thinking about busty blondes, fiery redheads or sultry brunettes.'

Snowy admired Marlowe, who had his pick of girls, and had decided to take his advice, telling himself that if there had been no ploughboy – there was nothing to stop him thinking *ploughboy* in his head, was there? – then he would never have doubted Tess's affection. And now he knew that Jonty had a girlfriend of his own he must stop worrying and start looking forward to the next two years, because though he had got his degree, and when he came out of the forces would be able to apply for maths teaching posts, such work seemed very dull when compared with Tess's life in the pet shop. She had plunged wholeheartedly into the business and now knew most of her suppliers personally, and all her regular customers. He had suggested that in a couple of years she might open another shop, but though she had considered the idea she had decided against it in the end.

'Because I'd not trust a manager to go to the lengths Gran and I do,' she had explained. 'I've heard that there are some pet shops where money and a quick turnover are all that matters. If I imagined someone was not treating my birds and animals right I wouldn't be able to sleep at night.'

Now, however, walking briskly along the icy pavement so that the sound of his footsteps echoed off the surrounding buildings, Snowy thought that one of these days he would persuade Tess to turn her undoubted business talents into something rather smarter than a pet shop. He was not sure yet exactly how, but in the fullness of time he and she together might set the town on fire . . . Perhaps a bar? Or that ice cream parlour she had once talked about?

Snowy reached the gate of his parents' house, opened it and put his key in the lock. At this time of night both his parents would be in bed, and the house was in darkness. Snowy sighed, pushed open the front door, closed it softly behind him, and headed for the stairs. As he undressed and got into bed he was telling himself that it had been a good evening. He and Tess had quarrelled, but they had made it up. He flattered himself that he had no need to fear competition from any but the ploughboy, and judging from the tiny bit of letter Tess had allowed him to read Jonty Bell now had other interests. Snowy remembered hearing someone say once that land married land, and if it was true, and he rather thought it was, then this Pamela, no doubt a farmer's daughter, would be a far more suitable match for young Bell than a girl living a couple of hundred miles away, whose only connection with the land lay in her ownership of a pet shop.

Satisfied, Snowy slid into bed. His fears had proved groundless, and if he dreamed of Marilyn Thomas he did not remember doing so when he woke next morning.

Chapter Eleven

More than four years had passed since Tess's Pets had been opened for the first time and Tess was just unlocking the door of the pet shop when she saw, through the glass, a large figure with what looked like a box in his arms approaching her door. She pulled it open before the man had a chance to knock, and ushered him inside. 'This'll be my day-old chicks,' she remarked cheerfully. 'Morning, Mr Haslett. Isn't it a grand day?'

'Aye. We'd better make the most of it – summer will be over before we know it,' Mr Haslett agreed. He eyed Tess's grey suit and white blouse with interest. 'Where's you off to? Or haven't you had time to put on your overall yet?'

'I'm off to Wales to interview a new supplier,' Tess told him. 'Mitch can cope, though if he does need help Gran's only a shout away.'

Mr Haslett put his burden down carefully on the counter. He delivered all manner of things, coming up from the country on most days with everything from foodstuffs to live animals, and Tess was a regular on his route. 'Who's your new supplier? Don't say someone's begun to do exotics, 'cos I know that's what you're after.'

Tess laughed. 'I shan't be doing exotics for a while yet, if I ever do; there's not much call for exotics in Everton. It's more the cheaper end of the market.'

The large man laughed too. 'Cheep, cheep, as them chicks would say,' he commented. 'Tell you what, miss, I supplies three or four pet shops now in the city and none of 'em shift their stock as fast as you do. Why is it, d'you think?'

Tess smiled. 'It's because I know how to treat the animals and birds I sell, and now that I've had over four years' experience of the trade I know better than to let day-olds go to people who won't look after 'em right. But I can't help feeling sorry for the poor cockerels, who are fed like princes until Christmas is just a few days off . . .'

'Aye, well, most folk like a bird for Christmas if they can afford it,' the man said, producing a bunch of rather mangled papers and beginning to sort them out on the countertop. 'Have you ever thought of selling piglets?'

Tess groaned. 'Imagine cleaning the cage out at the end of the day,' she said. 'Puppies are bad enough, not like kittens, who seem to be born with lavatory habits and always use the sand tray.' As she spoke she had been opening the till and extracting the money for the chicks, and now she handed it to Mr Haslett, watching as he scrawled *Paid* on the bottom of the invoice and added his signature. How wonderful it was to be solvent, she told herself. Four years ago, when the shop had first opened, even paying for a box of chicks would have been a headache. Then, she had juggled bills and invoices and the tiny amount of money in the account she had opened for Tess's Pets, grateful for every customer, and appreciating more than ever the generosity of those friends who had lent money to keep her head above water. Now, Tess's Pets was a viable business, paying everyone's wages and enabling her to repay loans and buy in stock knowing that it would be sold soon after it arrived. Mitch, who was now fourteen, was employed full time, and though Gran still did the books and cashed up she was no longer needed on a regular basis.

'There you are, miss, there's your copy,' Mr Haslett said, shoving the remaining papers back into his pocket. 'How old's the lad now? I see'd him a couple of weeks ago; it's astonishin' how he's shot up.'

'You're right there; he's a proper beanpole,' Tess agreed. 'He's only fourteen, but he's taller than I am, not that that's saying much.' She swung the door open. 'Ah, here he comes, with Elsie in tow. See you soon, Mr Haslett.'

Mitch entered the shop, closely followed by his small sister. She had started school the previous September and was making the most of the holidays, though since Mrs Roberts was now working full time at Tate and Lyle's this chiefly meant accompanying her brother to his place of work. Fortunately, Elsie was happy enough to help clean, feed and water the animals and birds, and speedily became fond of her charges; in fact she was forced to go into the stockroom when one of them was sold, in order to shed bitter tears.

There had been a never-to-be-forgotten occasion when Elsie had asked a customer, leaving the shop with a large buck rabbit, what he intended to call his new pet. 'I call him Fatty Arbuckle. What'll you call him?' she had asked.

The man had stared down at her for an uncomprehending moment before his face cleared. 'I'm gonna call him Sunday dinner,' he said airily, and was gone before the true horror of this statement had sunk in. Mitch had pretended it was just a joke, but with meat on ration and hard to come by they all knew that the man had spoken the simple truth.

Now, the two Robertses entered the shop cheerfully, Elsie dancing over to the medley of rabbits in the big cage which stretched along the back of the counter. 'Good morning, bunnies, how are you today?' she asked in her shrill little voice. 'Shall I start by cleaning the big cage, Tess? Only Mitch will have to take them out for me and carry them through to the stockroom 'cos of the kicks.'

Tess, remembering her small helper's effort to carry a fat grey rabbit, smiled. Elsie had done her best but the rabbit knew an amateur when it met one. A couple of wriggles, several hearty kicks, and the rabbit was belting towards the back door and freedom whilst poor Elsie ran in his wake, pleading tearfully, 'Come to Elsie like a good boy! Oh, please, Mr Bunny, come to Elsie!'

Mr Bunny, bewildered by the juvenile cries – and the height of the wall between it and the jigger – had bolted into the outside lavatory, and was easily captured by Mitch, but it had taught all concerned a lesson: small children and large rabbits do not go together. So now Elsie was allowed to sit quietly on her little stool holding a baby rabbit or kitten in her lap, but larger animals, though she might clean their cages, fill their water pots and provide them with their daily bread, were taboo as far as taking them out of their cages was concerned.

'I think the puppies could do with fresh sawdust. If your brother lifts them out into the playpen you can give an eye to them when you've finished the rabbits' cage,' Tess decided. 'Then when Mitch has done the puppies the pair of you can get started on the guinea pigs, hamsters and gerbils. We've plenty of clean sawdust and straw, and when their cages are clean you can feed them, only they mustn't have anything which Mitch hasn't given you. Remember what I told you?'

She watched with amusement as Elsie's cheeks grew pink and she hung her head. 'Hamsters is greedy pigs and will eat themselves inside out,' she recited. 'Like they did when I give 'em all that grain. It were 'cos they looked so hungry, poor little dears. And – and their tummies fell out of their bottoms, and Mr Vet had to put 'em back. So I won't ever do that again, Tess.'

'I know you won't, and I shouldn't have teased you,' Tess said remorsefully. 'You're a good girl, Elsie, and when you're grown up you shall have a proper job in the shop, and earn proper money, because I trust you with my animals. Indeed, I'm going to give you a choice for today. I'm going off into the country to meet a man who's breeding angora rabbits. They have wonderful long fur, soft as silk, so I want to see what his rabbits are like, and whether we would find a sale for them. You see, people don't just want them as pets. With angora rabbits they comb the fur out every few weeks and weave it into yarn. Then the yarn is made into lovely soft clothing . . .' She stopped talking, since it was plain that Elsie was no longer listening.

'Mitch told me,' she said excitedly. 'He said I could be his dep – dep – deputy, and have my dinner at Lyons Corner House . . . Ooh, Tess, I'd rather do that than anything in the world.'

Mitch, already starting to move the rabbits from their big cage into an even bigger one in the stockroom, grinned at Tess. 'So if you was hoping for company on your trip into the country, hard luck! You did say you'd pay for Elsie's dinner and your gran said she thought we might close for an hour so that she could come with us. If it's all right by you, of course,' he added hastily.

Tess was about to say that it would be fine by her when the door opened again and Sammy Higgins came into the shop. He was an old school friend of Snowy's and had always been a keen bird fancier, and now he bred budgerigars and canaries in a large aviary which took up most of his back yard. Because he was genuinely fond of his birds he declared he would only sell them through Tess, knowing that she would take great care of them while they were with her and would make sure buyers knew what they were taking on when they were sold.

'Mornin', Tess. How's me old pal Snowy gerrin' on?' he asked. 'I keep meanin' to write to him, but somehow I never get round to it.' He was carrying a large and well-appointed cage containing three bright-eyed little occupants which he now put carefully on the counter before turning his attention to Tess once more. 'Snowy were always interested in birds, so when he comes home mebbe he'll come into partnership wi' me. I could put up an aviary at the end of his garden, if Mr and Mrs White would agree, and we could share the profits.'

Tess pulled a doubtful face. Snowy's parents lived a good half-mile away and had a proper back garden. She could not imagine either of them taking kindly to an aviary on their spotlessly maintained lawn. Since Snowy had gone to Malaya she had visited his parents several times and liked them both. Mr White had congratulated her on her business acumen, whilst she and Mrs White had talked of make-up, clothes and other feminine matters, and Tess thought they approved of her. Naturally enough, when she visited they had compared notes about their son's letters, and Mr White had suggested jobs in the teaching profession which he thought might suit him.

The last time this had occurred Mrs White and Tess had exchanged quick, apprehensive glances, which proved to Tess that Snowy's mother, like herself, had reservations about Snowy's ever taking to such a post. Had he gone into one straight after leaving university it might have been different, but by the time he came home he would have lived in the real world, as he put it, for more than two years, and Tess thought that he might find academia both unexciting and tedious after life with the army.

Sammy cleared his throat. 'I axed you how me ol' pal Snowy was gerrin' along,' he reminded her rather reproachfully. 'I really will write him a line one of these days . . .'

'He's doing fine,' Tess said quickly. 'He's in Malaya, you know, doing what he describes as "clearing up". He loves Singapore, which is where they go when they're off patrol for a day or two, but of course he's only there for another six months.' She laughed. 'Poor Snowy. He wanted to go somewhere tropical all right, but he hadn't bargained for the flies and having to work in a temperature of a hundred degrees, and of course he'd not thought of putting up with the rainy season. Apparently the fellers were washed out of their tents in one particular downpour.'

'He'll be rare glad to get back to England, then,' Sammy

observed. 'Though in six months' time we'll be in the middle of winter and likely up to our knees in snow . . .'

'But not in steamy, hot, jungly rain,' Tess reminded him. 'The army makes Snowy take some sort of medication which turns his skin yellow and is supposed to save him from being bitten by a malarial mosquito. He went off all cock-a-hoop, looking forward to moonlit beaches and tropical maidens, and all he's got is mosquito bites, greasy food and a yellow face, poor old lad.'

Mitch and Elsie came through from the storeroom and began to admire the new arrivals. 'Do any of 'em talk yet, mister?' Mitch asked eagerly. Then he frowned. 'Ain't you the feller what's a mate of Snowy White's?' And when Sammy nodded he gave a satisfied smile. 'I thought you was; we're mates of his too, ain't we, Elsie? When he comes back he's goin' to be a teacher and marry our Tess here. Ain't that so, Tess?'

Tess leaned over and tried to put her hand across his mouth, but he resisted, giggling. 'It's true that he's my boyfriend, but marriage is a whole different kettle of fish, and don't you forget it,' she said. 'And don't put words into Elsie's mouth, because she couldn't possibly remember Snowy. She was three when he left and she'll be a proper little schoolgirl by the time he comes back.'

'That's right. And I does remember him. He's a tall feller,' Elsie said excitedly. 'Will you let me be bridesmaid, Tess? Oh, say I can, 'cos I've never been a bridesmaid.'

Tess and Sammy both laughed, though Tess shook her head reprovingly. 'Since I'm not considering marriage I'm not choosing my bridesmaids either,' she said. 'But if I was, you'd be first on the list. Now let's release these birds into the aviary. We'll deal with them properly later.'

She paid the asking price without hesitation, noting the amount and getting Sammy's signature on the receipt. Then she waved him off and returned to her work. Nice, she thought, to have something to tell Snowy in her next letter. She wrote once a week and often found it difficult to fill her pages. Snowy enlivened his with descriptions of the Malayan countryside and stories of the other men in his regiment, but she had to rely upon events which took place in the pet shop. Because of her promise she went to the cinema only with Lucy or with Gran, and though she had been to dances at the local ballrooms she never mentioned such outings to Snowy. It would not have seemed fair with him far away in a foreign land and apt to imagine her clasped in someone else's arms, even though the men she danced with were always just friends.

Checking once more that the aviary door was securely latched, she smiled at her two young helpers. 'And now I must catch a bus to Central station.'

In the country bus from Bidston to her destination, Tess glanced at her watch and sighed. If Snowy had been home, she reflected, this entire tedious journey could have been shortened by as much as a couple of hours. The army had taught him to drive and Snowy had said in one of his letters that he meant to buy himself wheels just as soon as he could shake the British army dust from his boots. A mental picture of him sprang into Tess's mind: tall and fair, his skin bronzed by the hot sun, his teeth looking whiter than ever against the tan. Dear Snowy! Letters arrived rarely, but when they came he always signed off *Your loving Snowy*, which, to Tess at least, indicated that he was as faithful to her as she was to him.

Gazing out of the window, Tess congratulated herself on the fact that there appeared to be few women in Malaya anxious to grab themselves a British soldier, even one as attractive as Snowy. Most of the women he mentioned were nurses or worked in the offices, and though there were occasional dances and presumably other social events it appeared from Snowy's letters that he did not indulge in such pastimes. In fact, in one letter he had written that the nurses all had faces like horses and the office workers were pale and pimply. Knowing Snowy as she did, furthermore, she discounted the local girls as competition. In the secret depths of her mind she had to acknowledge that she thought Snowy was a snob. She remembered a jeering remark he had once made regarding the slanting eyes of a friend, and also his references to Jonty as the 'ploughboy'. No, if she feared any competition, which she did not, it was unlikely to come from a beautiful coffee-coloured maiden, no matter how tempting her wiles. Besides, Snowy was fighting a war, albeit a strange one. It was referred to as 'the emergency' and she gathered, from Snowy's cautious comments, that his platoon patrolled the jungle, pushing the insurgents back whenever possible, and feeding and protecting the natives in the tiny, pathetically poor villages. They would do this for a matter of weeks and would then be recalled to Singapore for what they called R and R – rest and recreation – during which they might enjoy such entertainment as the showing of old British films, the odd dance at which men outnumbered women by ten to one, or a meal in a local restaurant.

Remembering how indignant Snowy had been upon discovering that she kept Jonty's letters, she had acquired a smart green folder for Snowy's correspondence. Some of his letters were short, stained with sweat and occasionally depressing, for two of Snowy's platoon had died, and though he had not given her any details she supposed it to have been from a tropical disease such as malaria. Tess's heart bled for him; a friend, badly wounded, had been in hospital for several weeks before he had been invalided home to Britain and Snowy had said, frankly, that he envied the bloke. *I'd give a good deal for a cold beer and a night's sleep undisturbed by the whining of mosquitoes,* he had written. *Still, I've served just over two-thirds of my sentence, so roll on the New Year. It can't be too cold or too blowy for this little soldier boy!*

The bus began to slow as it reached the outskirts of the village, and Tess dismissed thoughts of Snowy as she thanked the conductor and jumped down. It was a nice village, with half a dozen shops including a bakery and a blacksmith's forge, and it reminded her sharply of Jonty and the Bells. She decided that when she got home she would write to Jonty and tell him all about the angora rabbits. He would be interested, not in what sort of profit she might make from them, but in the animals themselves: what they ate, how they bred and how best to treat their long silky fur. Snowy, on the other hand, would only be interested in how much money she would get for each one. But she must not judge Snowy unfairly, because he was not a country boy and had no real interest in country matters.

Tess hefted her shoulder bag and headed for the small post office where she would get directions to the Sheraton farm, which she knew to be half a mile outside the village. She entered the shop and five minutes later was out again with the postmistress's precise instructions ringing in her ears. 'Miss it you cannot, cariad,' the wizened little woman behind the counter had said. 'Go straight along the road till you reach a muddy little lane. The Sheratons' place is amidst the trees on your left.' Her eyes had gleamed with curiosity. 'Goin' to see them fancy rabbits, is you? Eh, old Mr Sheraton would ha' laughed his son to scorn, but already young Aled is doin' all right with 'em.'

Tess, not wishing to spend half the morning gossiping, thanked the woman for the information and set off along the road at a brisk pace. But now her thoughts had turned from Snowy to Jonty and she found herself remembering her time at Bell Farm with real nostalgia. When she had first gone there she had been a miserable, awkward child whose bed-wetting habits had already caused three prospective foster-mothers to reject her. She had begged to be allowed to return to the city, promising good behaviour, dry beds, anything, if only she could go back to her own home, but her mother, summoned from Liverpool to remove her from the third household, had grown cross and Tess remembered wincing back as her shoulders were seized and she was given a spiteful shake. 'You'll do as you're told. I've applied to join the ATS and I don't intend to back out because you're a selfish little beast,' her mother had said. 'My war work will be with the army and yours will be to make a success of your next posting, so don't let me hear one word of complaint.'

No wonder I wasn't upset when I was told she'd been killed, Tess thought now. I was afraid of her; she was always quicker with a slap than a kiss. Then her mind returned to her first three foster-mothers. How were they different from Mrs Bell? It was a question she could not answer; she just knew that within forty-eight hours of arriving at Bell Farm and being accepted without ceremony or fuss by the family the hard knot of misery and rejection had melted and she had begun to feel, if not at home, at least not unwanted. It was not Mrs Bell's way to cuddle or caress, but Tess's vague memories of her mother were that she too had not been a particularly loving or demonstrative parent. And then, of course, there had been Jonty. Right from the moment she arrived at the farm he had made it plain that she was his pal. He was older than she, and when Mrs Bell had told him to take Tess to school and see that she was not what she termed 'put upon' the small Tess had expected to be dumped as soon as they reached the playground. But Jonty had taken her to meet her teacher, introduced her to the rest of her class, many of whom were evacuees, and without once raising his voice he had told her classmates that he would chop them into little pieces if they tried to bully her.

Tess had wanted to hide, or run away, until she heard the laughter and saw the friendly smiles, the desire not to beat her up but to get to know her. Yes, Jonty and the Bells had been her true friends, and as soon as she could arrange matters she would leave the shop for a few days and jolly well go down to Norfolk and spend time with the people who had been so good to her. She realised she had held back partly for Snowy's sake and partly because Jonty's girlfriend Pamela Davies might have resented a visitor from her boyfriend's past. But now she decided that Pamela must be a nice girl, or Jonty wouldn't have looked twice at her. Pamela would greet her as a friend.

As Tess reached the gate of Sheraton Farm and turned into the yard she was smiling to herself. When she got home she would write to Jonty suggesting that she might visit Bell Farm just as soon as she felt Mitch and Gran could cope for a few days without her.

She crossed the yard, which again reminded her pleasantly of Bell Farm, and knocked on the door.

Tess arrived home late and tired but feeling considerable satisfaction. She had bought four baby angora rabbits and meant to buy more if these sold easily. She went into the shop and saw the new acquisitions comfortably settled, and then ascended the stairs, though rather more slowly than usual, and beamed at Gran as she entered the kitchen.

'Get on all right without me?' she asked, slinging her coat on a hook, slumping into a chair and accepting the offered cup of tea. 'It's a lovely farm and the young chap, the farmer's son, is really nice and treats the rabbits just the way I would.'

'Well, that's grand,' Gran said vaguely. 'You've got some post; want to read it now, or save it till later? It looks like young Bell's writing to me.'

'Oh, I'll read it now,' Tess said, taking the envelope eagerly, slitting it open and producing a single sheet. She stared at it uncomprehendingly for a moment, then turned to Gran. 'It's – it's from Jonty all right,' she said. 'The Bells are having a little celebration for their ruby wedding and Jonty would like me to be there. He says it would be an ideal opportunity for me to meet Pamela. It's not for a while yet, but Jonty's let me know in plenty of time because he guessed I'd have to arrange for someone to keep an eye on the shop.'

'Well, isn't that lovely?' Gran said, but Tess thought her glance was far too searching. 'You'll go, of course?'

'Of course,' Tess echoed. She stood up and had the oddest feeling that the room was whirling around her. She went over to where her coat hung and fished in the pocket, producing a card of the angora wool which young Mr Sheraton had given her. She put it down on the table rather blindly. 'Take a look at this,' she invited, and then gave a loud and unconvincing yawn. 'I'm awful tired, Gran. If you don't mind, I think I'll go straight off to bed. You can tell me how you and Mitch managed in the morning.'

Feeling very guilty, Edie had let her eyes scan Tess's letter as the girl had held it rather helpelssly in one hand, and now she sat at the kitchen table, her mind buzzing quite as actively as she guessed Tess's must be. Poor girl, poor little Tess, Edie mourned, for she had read the despair in Tess's expression as the child had stared blindly in front of her. What a mess, what a muddle, and how many lives would be ruined if Tess refused to admit her own feelings and if Jonty, believing her to be unobtainable, actually married this Pamela girl.

But there's nothing I can do, because it truly is none of my business, Edie told herself miserably. All I can do is be there for Tess after she's seen Pamela and Jonty together. Oh dear, young love! How complicated and how sad; yet sometimes how happy and beautiful!

Edie stood up and carried her empty mug over to the sink, reflecting that she and Albert were lucky; their friendship was warm and close but, as she put it, without strings. They had none of the uncertainties which were part and parcel of young love, yet the warmth of their companionship was a real comfort, something to cling to when life's storms broke. Edie rinsed her mug, stood it on the draining board and checked that the fire was banked down, and the table laid for breakfast next day. Then she left the kitchen, closing the door softly behind her, and went into her own bedroom to prepare for bed. Albert had been in earlier and they had discussed the day's work in the pet shop and the tobacconist's and had decided that it was high time they booked another coach trip. Tess and Mr Clarke were more than capable of managing without them for a day.

If we were married, we could be talking about Tess and her young men now, Edie thought as she began to undress, and felt an entirely unexpected shiver of pleasure at the thought. You're nothing but a ridiculous old woman, Edie Williams, she told herself, climbing into bed. You and Albert are just good friends, which is the way it should be. I've had a happy marriage and so has Albert. You know what they say: never go back, because that way disappointment lies. We've had young love with all its trials and tribulations, all its highs and lows; now we've got friendship, respect, and . . . yes, I suppose a sort of love. We must be content with that – no, no, no, we *are* content with that. And now, Edie Williams, will you stop all this nonsense and go to sleep, because that's what beds are for.

Edie turned over and buried her face in the pillow. I will *not* worry about Tess, or Snowy, or Jonty, let alone this Pamela girl whom neither Tess nor I have even met, she resolved, and presently fell asleep, only to dream about a ravishing blonde who looked remarkably like Marilyn Thomas and came triumphantly into the pet shop to inform Edie that the rules were different in Malaya and she intended to marry both Jonty and Snowy, which she thought would be a nice Christmas present from herself to herself. Edie tried to smack her, saying that English rules were different, but in the way of such dreams this one faded away and Edie found herself on the beach, walking hand in hand with her beloved Fred, only when she turned to look at him and smile it was not Fred but Albert, and she was surprised and a little shocked to realise that she was not disappointed when Albert squeezed her hand . . .

Tess too was tired, but the letter had made her think, and think hard. She might tell herself that her affection for Jonty was merely that of an old friend, but she was beginning to wonder whether it was that simple. She had felt a pang of fierce jealousy at the thought of seeing Jonty and Pamela together; surely one would not feel like that over an old friend? But if she did love Jonty, it wasn't the sort of love the stars shared in the cinema, and anyway how could she possibly admit to making such a terrible mistake? There was poor Snowy for a start, enduring jungle warfare and all the miseries which went with it, whilst believing her to be his own true love and simply longing to come home and claim her. Then there was Jonty himself. He had accepted without argument that there was nothing between them except friendship and, having accepted it, had turned to Pamela Davies. How can I ruin her life – and possibly Jonty's – by admitting that I've changed my mind and want to steal her boyfriend? Oh, dear heaven, I can't possibly do any such thing. But I will go to the party and see for myself if Jonty really is in love with this girl, and she with him. What I'll do if Jonty really does love me and is just making do with Pamela remains to be seen, but I won't make the worst mistake of my life without trying to do something about it.

She had expected sleep to claim her within minutes, but midnight struck, then one, then two, and still her fretful thoughts forbade relaxation, let alone sleep. At five-thirty she fell into an uneasy doze and a bare hour later a paper boy, whistling down the street, awoke her. After that, she made no further attempt to sleep but must have dropped off anyway, because she slept through the alarm and didn't wake until Gran called from the kitchen that it was gone eight and the pet shop opened at nine. As she got up and began to wash, she told herself that at least her sleepless night had given her time to think, and those thoughts were no longer chaotic or frightening. She knew what she must do and told herself that she would consult Gran; Gran would know whether the decision she had come to in the night was right or wrong.

Satisfied, she rubbed herself dry on a rough towel and began to dress.

Gran was in the kitchen about to dish up the porridge when Tess entered the room.

307

'Morning,' Tess said cheerfully. 'Another nice one judging from what I saw when I drew back the curtains.'

'Good morning, my love,' Gran said. 'You had a long day yesterday, so no wonder you slept in.' She looked shrewdly at Tess, noting her heavy eyes and her pallor, but said nothing. She thought she could guess the reason for Tess's obvious inability to sleep, but knew it would not do to remark on it. She must wait until Tess chose to confide in her, if she ever did.

'I see you've stolen a march on me,' Tess said. 'Honestly, Gran, I meant to get the breakfast this morning because it is my turn, but I didn't have a very good night; it must have been after six before I actually fell asleep, and when you called it was all I could do to crawl out of bed and reach the washstand. But splashing lovely cold water on to my face woke me up just enough.' She crossed the kitchen, took the kettle off the stove and began to make the tea in the big brown pot. 'Gosh, that porridge looks delicious. I didn't have any supper last night, what with the angora bunnies having to be made comfortable . . .' She sat down at the table and drew her porridge bowl towards her, glancing up at the clock on the mantel as she did so. 'Oh, dear, I can see I shall be late opening, but there's never much trade first thing in the morning, and Mitch will be along dead on nine, with Elsie in tow as usual. They don't have a key, of course, but I can nip down and open up and then leave them to it until I've got myself together.'

Gran sat down opposite Tess and spooned honey over her porridge. 'I'll go down when Mitch arrives,' she volunteered. 'I'll start the feeding and filling the water pots, because I can manage that if I'm careful only to use my right hand. If I forget and try to use the other one my grip isn't reliable. And I'm really keen to see the rabbits you bought yesterday. What colour are they? The card of wool you gave me is bluey-grey, but I understand angoras come in a variety of shades.'

'The four I bought are all bluey-grey, and they've got golden eyes; they're really awfully pretty, but of course it isn't their looks, it's their wonderful wool which makes them expensive.' Tess laughed. 'They are the luxury end of the market, so to speak. I don't think many ordinary pet owners will want them, but we'll have to wait and see.'

Gran nodded wisely. 'Wait and see is often the name of the game,' she said. She began to eat her porridge, finished her helping and reached for her cup of tea. 'Will Mitch ring the bell when he arrives? Or ought I to go down right now and wait for him?'

'I don't know, 'cos I've never been late before,' Tess said ruefully. 'But knowing Mitch, I suspect he'll simply stand in the doorway and wait.' She glanced up at the clock. 'No need to rush down, Gran. It's not even a quarter to nine, so you're safe for a bit, and I want to ask you something.'

'I thought you might,' Gran said shrewdly. 'That letter, the one from Jonty, upset you, didn't it?' She watched as Tess finished her porridge and picked up her teacup, then put it down again.

'It didn't exactly upset me, but it made me think,' Tess said. 'You see, I believe I've taken my friendship with Jonty for granted. He was just a boy who had been kind to me when I was a kid, and then a workmate on his dad's farm. I never truly thought of him as a young man, even when he was grown up. But it was different with Snowy. When I first met him he was Marilyn's boyfriend, very much a grown-up. And when he took my side it was like a film star stepping down from the silver screen to champion a beggar maid . . .'

Gran laughed. 'Some beggar maid!' she observed. 'Even in those days you had a lot going for you, queen. But right now I can see you're in a difficult position. You were always far more at ease with Jonty than you are with Snowy. But you've not seen Snowy for the past couple of years and he's been fighting a war, a man amongst men, which will have changed him. When he comes home it'll be a different Snowy White from the one you waved off so merrily two years ago. And Jonty too will have changed, though not as radically as Snowy—'

'But I've changed as well, Gran,' Tess cut in quickly. 'Haven't I?'

Gran smiled. 'Two years changes everyone,' she observed. 'Particularly when you're young. Now, Tess, your trouble is that you've been forced to realise that Jonty has a life of his own, as indeed do you. I don't know whether Jonty is really in love with this Pamela or whether they're just good friends, but you're scared you've made a big mistake . . .'

Tess had been gazing into her empty porridge dish as though it were a crystal ball, but now she raised her eyes and met Gran's glance squarely. 'I think that Jonty is as muddled and unsure as I am, or that was what I thought until the letter arrived. That's changed things, put them on a different footing. When I go back to Bell Farm I'll be able to see at a glance if he really loves Pamela, and if he does then that just leaves Snowy, and I'll have to be content with him, because he never so much as mentions other women.'

Gran snorted. 'You conceited little beast,' she said. 'You *do* have a good opinion of yourself, Tess Williams! We've just been discussing how people change and what a spell in the army may have done to Snowy. Yet you calmly assume that he'll still want to marry you, regardless of the fact that in effect you are both different people.' She was laughing as she spoke and Tess, after a moment, laughed too.

'I'm being daft,' she said remorsefully. 'Meeting troubles more than halfway, eh, Gran? But first things first; I'll go to this party and meet Pamela and see how she and Jonty get along. And now let's go downstairs, open up the shop and introduce everyone to our new acquisitions.'

'Got a fag?'

Snowy plunged a hand into his pocket and produced a crumpled pack of Woodbines, which he regarded ruefully. 'Only two left; got a match?' he asked.

Already the two young men and the rest of their platoon were beginning to relax, and this, they knew, was dangerous. But ahead of them in the dark, entangling jungle they could see the gleam of metal as sunshine filtered through the canopy of the great trees hundreds of feet above and fell on the truck which would take them into Singapore for a period of R and R. Telling himself that the bandits – communist guerrillas – were unlikely to operate so near a road, Snowy put one of the cigarettes between Capper's lips, the other between his own, and took the box of matches, lighting up both cigarettes and reflecting with wry amusement that he felt a bit the way he had done as an eight-year-old, filching a cigarette from his father and sneaking off to the tool shed at the end of the garden for his first taste of forbidden fruit – or forbidden tobacco, rather.

When on patrol one hung on to matches and cigarettes, did not waste either, in case one had to ford a stream. The Malayan jungle was home to a thousand deadly creatures, but the ones which attacked every patrol when it got near water were the leeches. The men never removed their boots to cross any water, stagnant or running, yet it was standard procedure as soon as they were on the other side to shed boots and socks and roll up trousers in order to remove the great fat leeches, firmly attached and greedily sucking their blood. Here was where cigarettes and matches became an essential part of any soldier's equipment. If one simply pulled a leech off then the head and many-toothed mouth remained embedded, and if left could lead to a deadly blood infection. But if a glowing cigarette end was applied to the creature it would remove itself hastily, dropping to the floor of the jungle with a disgusting plop.

Snowy took a deep drag on his cigarette, then puffed the smoke out at the cloud of mosquitoes which surrounded the entire platoon. Thinking of leeches made him remember some of the other disadvantages of jungle warfare. There were enormous scorpions whose sting was death, huge pythons which could squeeze the life out of a national serviceman before he could shout for help and, when the rivers were in spate, saltwater crocodiles which had been known to exceed twenty feet in length. Then there were the countless malarial mosquitoes, so that the men were forced to take anti-malaria medication which turned their skin yellow and was much hated. And there were bushes whose thorns could cause nasty wounds, upon which myriad flies would feast. In fact, Snowy thought, as they broke cover and approached the lorry, their eyes wincing at the bright sunlight, it was no wonder that the British troops loathed and feared the jungle and consequently disliked not just the animal inhabitants but the human ones too.

Incredible though it seemed, Snowy told himself as he and Capper climbed aboard the lorry, there were actually tribes of Malays living in that jungle, yet the troops never got so much as a sniff of them. Silent as the other creatures which were all around them yet seldom seen, the natives of this incredibly hostile habitat did not seem to have any permanent abodes but moved invisibly from one place to the next.

But we know they're somewhere, somewhere quite near, Snowy reminded himself, because even in the impenetrable dangerous darkness the troops could feel eyes on them. They were not necessarily hostile eyes, because had they belonged to communist bandits the insurgents would have attacked already, wiping out the platoon whilst they slept. No, these eyes were curious, doubtful, and had as little desire to meet these heavy-footed intruders as the heavy-footed intruders had to meet them.

Now, Snowy and Capper were first aboard the truck and settled themselves on the narrow seats which ran along either side of the vehicle, where they were presently joined by the rest of the platoon. Cigarettes were

313

handed round, men began to grin, to anticipate what they would do with the week's leave that was coming to them. Snowy and Capper joined in.

When they reached the camp they dispersed to the rooms that had been allocated to them. Snowy and Capper went straight to the showers, had a meal and then went back to their room. They would sleep uninterrupted for twenty-four hours and then, having changed into civilian clothes, they meant to take their place on the truck heading for the bright lights. Despite their clothing, they knew they were immediately identifiable as soldiers, but that did not worry them. What was worrying were the prices; a soldier's weekly pay was small and, as Capper remarked, they could only window-shop, astonished by the variety of goods which had been unobtainable in Britain before they left, and here were being bought by rich Chinese in their flashy American cars. There were enormous cinemas showing the latest films as well as five-star hotels and classy nightclubs, the enjoyment of which was far beyond the means of any lowly member of the British army.

Because Snowy and Capper were both nearing the end of their time they had been saving up so that they might buy small gifts for those at home. Snowy had his eye on a delicate silver filigree necklace for Tess, some pau shell earrings for his mother and a half-bottle of gin for his father. Capper meant to splash out for his girlfriend on a bottle of perfume and some of the brightly coloured bangles which the local girls valued and bought in large quantities in what the men termed the bazaar, but was really Chinatown. Here were shops selling cheap merchandise, and a restaurant run by a Chinese who spoke excellent English – he had lived in London before the war – and catered almost exclusively for British soldiers, for the military presence was enormous.

As the truck drove along the narrow road the next day, Snowy caught glimpses of the jungle they had so recently left and felt a deep shudder within him at the thought of returning there, for despite the fact that there was not long left before he would go back home he knew he would have to do more patrols before that happy day dawned. That meant nights spent in his *basha*, the hut the army provided for jungle patrols, lying beneath his mosquito netting and trying to sleep, trying to tell himself that the horrible cacophony of sounds which made a jungle night hideous held no threat provided one lay still and quiet and waited for morning. But of course it was at night that the bandits were most active . . .

The truck, jerking to a stop just outside the Capitol Cinema in the heart of the city, brought Snowy back to the present. He and Capper descended on to the pavement and exchanged delighted grins. The street was lined with stalls, each one brightly lit and containing mouth-watering displays amongst which were affordable gifts for those back home. The two men plunged into the crowds already milling along the pavements and proceeded to wander, stopping every now and then for the sheer pleasure of not being in the jungle but back in civilisation. Snowy found the necklaces and Capper began to compare bangles. Snowy had actually picked up a necklace which he thought would suit Tess, paid for it, and slipped it into his shirt pocket, when he noticed a girl coming towards him. She was slim and straight-backed, with gleaming black hair and skin the colour of honey, and she came over to the stall, picking up a couple of bangles and eyeing them wistfully before replacing them, with finicky care, on the stall.

Snowy stared at her, a frown creasing his brow. She looked familiar; in fact he was sure he had seen her somewhere before. But she was a local girl, what the other men on his patrol would have called a 'bint', so unless she worked at base camp . . .

As though his glance had been intense enough to be felt she rearranged the bangles and turned towards him, her delicate brows rising. Snowy felt his face grow hot; she was a respectable girl, no matter that she was a Malay, and it was rude to stare, he remembered his mother telling him so as a small boy. She might think that because she was in the bazaar and looking at bangles he might assume her to be a bad girl. She might think he was 'pricing her up', as his fellow soldiers would say. But as she turned back to the array of jewellery on the stall, he realised why he had thought her familiar. There was something in the way she moved, straight-backed and slim, and in the way she bent her head over the display, which reminded him of Tess. He was so surprised that he was unable to stop himself from smiling; how could he possibly think this girl was like Tess Williams? But it was not her face, or her hair; it was the way she moved, even in the delicate way she touched the many-coloured bangles. And this decided him that he had been right. She was what his mother would describe as a 'real little lady' and it was this that had reminded him of Tess, not the golden skin or the gleaming, coal-black hair.

Snowy had never even considered approaching a local girl, but now he put out his hand towards the bangles and smiled. 'I was wondering which one to take home,' he said. 'I am going to buy one or two for my girl. Would you be very kind and help me to choose the most suitable?'

Even as the words left his lips he was shocked at himself. Here he was, a British soldier soon to be repatriated to his homeland, trying to pick up one of the local girls! She probably didn't speak a word of English, had not understood what he said. He began to apologise but she put a slender hand on his arm, nodding as she did so. 'Of course I will help you to choose,' she said in only slightly accented English. 'But you will have to tell me a little more about your young lady, if you please. Is her hair light or dark? Are her eyes blue or brown? Perhaps she likes bright colours, or would prefer gentler shades . . .'

'She's little, dark,' he began, and then realised that the bangles would not do for Tess. He was going to give her the necklace. But Marilyn had been his girlfriend once, and she would love the brilliant, gaudy trinkets. The girl was waiting. Snowy rushed into speech once more. 'Only the bangles are for my – my sister,' he said. 'I've already bought a necklace for my girl.'

The girl nodded understandingly. 'And your sister? She is like you – fair, blue-eyed?'

Snowy nodded. 'She's got a – a – curvy sort of figure, she's quite tall, taller than you, she likes bright colours, sparkly stuff – oh, I can't describe her . . .'

But the girl was rapidly selecting bangles, pushing them over her slender hand on to her wrist, and Snowy saw at once that, despite his fumbling attempts at description, this little Malay had chosen exactly what Marilyn would like.

'All right?' she asked, slipping the bangles off and handing them over to Snowy. 'They will please your sister?'

Snowy was beginning to say they were just right and pulling his wallet out of his shorts pocket when he saw that the girl was laughing. 'I think you have two girlfriends,' she said gaily. 'Two girlfriends and no sister!' And Snowy, whilst shaking his head and laughing too, knew that she was right. He had never got over his hunger for Marilyn . . . but when he saw Tess again . . .

A minute or two later Capper, who had wandered some way ahead, suddenly realised he was alone, and came back. He looked a little puzzled when Snowy introduced him to his companion. 'This is Lyana. She's helping me to choose bangles,' he said. He turned courteously to the girl. 'Lyana, this is my friend Capper.'

The two exchanged rather awkward smiles and shook hands and Capper said: 'But I thought you were going to buy your Tess that silver necklace?'

'Oh yes, I've bought that. But there's another girl I need a present for,' Snowy said quickly, scowling at his pal. 'The necklaces are pretty but they wouldn't be suitable for her.' He held out the bangles he and Lyana had chosen, paid for them, saw them popped into a brown paper bag and turned away from the stall to address the girl beside him. 'Care to come along with my pal and myself to the Shackles for a meal? They have a band and a dance floor . . .'

The girl looked up at him and Snowy could read her doubts. 'It's all right, honest to God it is,' he said quickly. 'We're dead respectable, Capper and me. We've both got girlfriends back home and it won't be all that long before we get sent back to the UK. So you see, all we want is your company . . .'

He was looking down into the girl's small, heart-shaped face and saw it suddenly lit by laughter. 'No strings,' she said. 'That's how you say it: no strings, no ropes, no shackles, just friendly company. Have I got it right?'

Snowy laughed with her. 'That's it exactly,' he assured her. 'No strings, no ties, no handcuffs, no nothing, just a nice meal and maybe a turn or two around the dance floor. Let's go!'

Chapter Twelve

It was the evening before Tess was due to leave for Bell Farm. She had bought her train ticket, packed her haversack, got out her working overalls and stuffed her best dress into her case. Then she poured lemonade into a bottle, made a packet of sandwiches in greaseproof paper and chose a couple of apples. She thanked everyone who was helping out, kissed Albert and Gran and went to bed early, for she would have to be at Lime Street station at seven o'clock in the morning to set out on the first leg of her long journey.

As she set the alarm for six and climbed between the sheets, she reflected that she would not be surprised if, when she returned, it was to find that Gran and Albert had come to an understanding, if not actually got engaged. The thought gave her a little stab of pain. Rejection – was it going to happen to her all over again? Memories of those first unsuccessful attempts to find a foster-home for her could never be entirely forgotten, nor her own mother's indifference to her plight. Yet there could be no doubt that marrying was the right thing for Gran and Albert. Gran managed beautifully now despite her injuries, but Albert would positively love spoiling her, seeing that she got the best of everything. And in her heart, Tess knew that it was she who was standing in the way of their happiness. Not deliberately, not out of selfishness, but because she was so afraid of being once more on the outside, looking in. It would all be different once Snowy was home, of course. She did not know whether he would ask her again to get engaged or whether they would simply marry, but she was pretty sure it would be one or the other. As the time for his release from the army drew near, Snowy's letters had become more and more affectionate. He talked freely of the life he was leading, the ten-man patrols which penetrated deep into the jungle seeking the enemy. From reports she read in the newspapers, Tess knew that this so-called 'emergency' was a very real war, and a bloody and beastly one at that. There had been a photograph in the *Daily Mail* of a grinning national serviceman holding up the severed head of a bandit, which had roused horror in everyone who saw it and had resulted in an order that the men must, in future, bring the whole body of a dead enemy back to base camp to prove a 'kill'.

Lying in bed now, waiting for sleep to claim her, Tess realised that she was no longer thinking of Jonty as a possible mate. Now he was simply her dearest and best friend, a young man for whom she would do anything in her power. Gran often said that she and Albert were just very, very good friends; well, that could apply equally to herself and Jonty, Tess thought; they were indeed very, very good friends. When the chips were down and storm clouds gathered it was to him that her thoughts turned, but that did not mean that they might become lovers. Satisfied that she had their relationship sorted out, Tess turned her face into her pillow and was drifting into that pleasant state between waking and sleeping when another thought occurred to her. Jonty had told her that Pamela Davies was a nurse, a sister in charge of a ward where her patients received intensive care, and that must mean that she was almost certainly older than Tess and indeed Jonty himself. Even in her sleepy state, Tess felt her mouth curve into a little smile. And it would do Jonty good to take orders now and then, instead of always being the one giving them. It will be grand to meet her at last, and forewarned is forearmed, Tess told herself just before she fell asleep. I wonder what she'll think of me? She'll be earning a proper salary, and she'll be used to responsibility. She may despise me as a mere pet-shop girl. Or we may become firm friends, which would be nice. And if there was a little stab of pain at the thought of being just Jonty's wife's friend and having no other claim on him it soon passed, and Tess fell asleep at last.

Two days later Albert decided to chance his arm with Edie as soon as the opportunity arose. He often mentioned how well they got on together, how he enjoyed the practice which had now evolved of taking it in turns to cook Sunday lunch, how pleasant it was to finish off most days with cocoa and biscuits and a great deal of talk, either in Edie's place or his own. When he had first hinted at marriage, however, Edie had slapped him down at once. Sitting behind the counter of the tobacconist shop now, Albert pulled a rueful face. Slapping him down was an unfair way of putting it because Edie was too kind to slap anyone down. She had merely said that whilst Tess was so dependent on her other relationships would always have to come second. She had explained, as though he did not already know it, that Tess desperately needed a family and that she, Gran, was all the family available.

'But if you were to marry then Tess's family would expand, wouldn't you say?' Albert had said hopefully, but Edie had shaken her head.

'No, because Tess would feel that she had been supplanted and that we had shut her out. Oh, I know you'll say her relationship with me would be quite separate from the relationship shared by us as a married couple, but that wouldn't be how Tess would see it. She would see it as yet another rejection. It will be different when she has a man of her own.'

Now, however, Albert glanced at his wristwatch. It was five-thirty, time to close for the day. He slid off his stool and went across to the door to hang up the closed sign. It was high time, he considered, to have another go. Tess had a thriving business, which was enabling her to save a good sum of money in her post office account. She was happy and fulfilled; she and Snowy were in love and meant to marry, which meant that as far as Albert could see there was no good reason for delaying his proposal any longer. This time, he thought hopefully, he would be able to counter any argument that Tess would be made unhappy by such a move. Why on earth should she? All young things leave the nest at some stage in their development, and it was about time Tess began to flutter her wings and let her gran do the same.

Every Friday Albert and the Williamses took it in turns to buy fish and chips. Tonight it was Albert's turn, so when he had satisfied himself that all was in order in the shop he put on his coat and set off for Pownall's, wondering whether this evening might be the right time to broach the subject nearest to his heart. However, when he presently joined Edie in the flat above the pet shop, two steaming parcels of haddock and chips in his hands, he saw at once that his proposal would have to wait. With Tess away, Edie had been working hard all day, and was clearly too tired to be confronted with yet another dilemma to resolve.

When the meal was over and they had talked companionably through the day's business, Albert returned to his own flat, where he put the kettle on and got out the tin of shortbread biscuits Edie had made for him. He had never told Edie how lonely he sometimes felt here, but now he decided he would do so. It would have to be quite soon, however, because when Tess came back from the farm he and Edie would not have many chances to be alone.

It was a shame, he thought, that Snowy would not be home for the New Year, but Tess had said that Mrs White intended to save their Christmas, turkey and all, as a surprise for their only child. There would be crackers, a tree laden with tinsel and small gifts, a pudding flaming with brandy, and of course presents, gaily wrapped, and all at the end of January.

Albert, with his own preparations well advanced, had asked apprehensively whether they too should put off Christmas, but to his relief both Tess and Edie had shaken their heads. 'Put off Christmas?' Tess had said, sounding downright shocked. 'No, indeed! Mitch and Elsie are coming round to us for a grand Christmas tea . . .'

'And since you are providing the bird for our Christmas

dinner, I trust you'll arrive at the crack of dawn,' Edie had reminded him. 'We'll have our presents immediately after breakfast – you'll come round for breakfast – so don't worry that we might change our minds and defer it, because we shan't.'

Albert had been relieved. He was old-fashioned enough to believe that the festivities should include attendance at both midnight mass and morning service, and would have felt cheated had Christmas been celebrated at any time other than 25 December.

Now, instead of going straight to bed, for it was still early, he lit the oven and opened the door so that the room speedily became comfortably warm. At this time of night it was never worth lighting the fire, which would scarcely have had time to get going before he had to let it go out, but the oven was a good substitute.

Reminding himself that he would have to be up betimes next day, for he and Edie had agreed to take turns to open the pet shop whilst Tess was away, he settled himself at the kitchen table and was reaching for a biscuit when the bell rang. Cursing beneath his breath he went over to the window and peered down, but could see no one. 'Bloody kids. If I could get downstairs quietly enough I'd open the door and give the little blighters a thick ear,' he muttered. 'But as it is . . .'

The bell sounded again and this time, when Albert went over to the window, he saw a dark figure, uniden-tifiable in the faint street light, whose face, a pale disc, was turned up towards him. An adult, anyway, though not one with whom he was familiar. A neighbour perhaps? It was unlikely to be a customer and he knew it wasn't Edie. But it was no use wondering; he would have to go down, since the man below – if it was a man – must have seen him peering out. Albert took one last look round his warm and welcoming kitchen and began reluctantly to descend the stairs. He crossed the stockroom, clicking the electric light on as he went, unlocked the door and pulled it open.

In the bright light his caller blinked and moved back a step, and Albert saw that it was a woman wearing a dark winter coat and a felt hat pulled down over her eyes. He began to ask her whether she had rung his bell in mistake for someone else's, but she cut across his words, her voice thin and reedy. 'Aren't you going to invite me in? It's bleedin' freezin' out here and I'm just about done in. I've been on the go for days and days . . .'

She started to step forward, but Albert moved in front of her. 'I'm very sorry, but I'm sure you've made a mistake,' he began, but the woman ignored his words and pushed passed him, snatching off her hat as she did so.

'Don't say you don't recognise me,' she said. She pushed her hair out of her eyes and tucked it behind her ears, then pointed an accusing finger at the shop door, which Albert was about to close. 'You've left me suitcase outside; wharrever are you thinking of? All me worldly goods, just about, is in that suitcase, so I'll have it in out of the street before someone makes off with it, if you don't mind. Come on, Dad, shake a leg!'

Albert was so astonished that he stepped backwards and collided with the counter. 'Janine!' he gasped. 'What on earth are you doing here?' Realising suddenly that this was no way to greet a long-lost daughter he tried to take her in his arms and give her a kiss, but Janine, though she submitted to the embrace, did not return it.

'Never mind that for now,' she said rather sulkily. 'It's pretty clear you aren't exactly over the moon to see me. And it's not as though you didn't expect me, because I sent you a telegram.'

Albert was about to say contritely that the telegram must have gone astray when he remembered something his dear Louisa had once said. 'Our Janine has a special voice she uses when she's telling fibs,' she had told him. 'You must have noticed, Albert; it's a syrupy sort of voice.' She had laughed. 'She doesn't mean any harm, it's just when she's trying to play down something she thinks we might disapprove of.'

Now, Albert heard that syrupy note in his daughter's voice and knew that the telegram had never been sent; was, in fact, a figment of Janine's imagination. So he bit back the words of apology, picked up her suitcase, which was extremely heavy, and gave her a little push towards the stockroom and the stairs which led up to the flat. 'We'll discuss the whole matter over a cup of cocoa. Luckily I've got into the habit of keeping the bed in the spare room – your old room – made up, so I'll pop a hot water bottle into it and then you can tell me just what's happened to bring you flying over here without a word of warning,' he said. As they entered the kitchen Janine began to reiterate that she had telegraphed, but Albert shook his head. 'Telegrams don't just go astray, my dear,' he said. 'Come and sit down and have a shortbread biscuit while I make the cocoa. Let me help you out of your coat.'

327

Whilst Albert boiled the kettle again Janine ate several biscuits, and presently she sipped eagerly at the hot cocoa. It was warm in the kitchen with the oven still alight, and without her coat Albert saw that his daughter had put on a fair amount of weight and that her hair had gone from light brown to a rather brassy gold. He had not seen her for nearly ten years, and his mental picture of her was of a slim, pretty creature with a mass of tumbled curls, rosy cheeks and sparkling light blue eyes. Now she was pale and pasty, seemingly reluctant to explain her arrival, and her mouth became sulky when he tried to press her for some sort of explanation.

'Ain't it enough that I'm home?' she said when he queried her sudden reappearance. She sniffed and her mouth turned down at the corners. 'I'm that tired, Dad, I scarcely know how to put one foot before the other. Can't we talk in the morning?'

Albert was about to agree when he realised something else. If Janine was given time to think up a convincing story, that was probably what he would get. Right now his poor child was at a low ebb, which meant that the truth would come tumbling out. So he shook his head firmly and when she tried to get to her feet he pushed her gently back into her chair.

'Janine, no matter what has happened to you, you are still my beloved daughter,' he said gently. 'But whilst you've been making a life for yourself in America, I have had no choice but to make a life for myself too. You haven't written often, but the letters I have received seemed to indicate that you were happy and fulfilled. So just you sit there and tell me the truth: why are you here?'

Janine began to say she was too tired, that her story was too long and too complex for telling after such an exhausting journey, but Albert had sat himself down opposite her and now he rested his chin on his folded hands and met her eyes squarely. 'My dear child, I love you, but I can remember all your little tricks. If I wait until tomorrow I'll get a sanitised version. You'll tell me what you want me to hear and that won't necessarily be the truth.' He smiled lovingly at her as she began to protest. 'No, I'm serious. You can begin by telling me whether there is trouble between you and your husband.'

Janine heaved an enormous sigh and put both hands round her mug of cocoa as though to warm them. Albert waited patiently whilst she sorted out her ideas, and when at last she began to speak he listened intently and did not interrupt.

'As you know, Dad, I followed Mario to America quite soon after the war ended. He had told me his parents were rich business people who owned a ranch just outside a small town. Before the war they had owned several properties there, including a soda fountain and what they call a diner, which is just another word for a café. He said if I went over we would marry and his father would hand the soda fountain over to me.' She sighed, and Albert saw her lower lip quiver. 'We married all right, but Mario continued to behave like a bachelor, which as you can imagine I found difficult to take. We had a small apartment over my workplace but Mario's work was mainly on the ranch. He seldom took me out there and but for a surprise visit some months ago I should never have known that he was being unfaithful. Oh, I had suspected it, but had no proof until he slipped up. Apparently he had met an old girlfriend, the daughter of a rancher whose spread bordered the Da Silva property, and planned to divorce me. By then, I'm not sure that I minded terribly, but when I received a tax demand from the authorities I discovered that Mr Da Silva had never given me the soda fountain as he and Mario had promised, but had claimed that I was just an employee. I might have demanded a lump sum so that I could move to another town and start up in business on my own account. It would have been hard, but not impossible. Only then a letter from you arrived saying how successful your ice cream parlour had become and how you were in partnership with some elderly woman – Edie, wasn't it? – and both your businesses were thriving. I told Mario about it and he advised me to come home. He said I should claim my inheritance before this old woman got her claws into it.'

Albert sighed. 'Oh dear, what a tangle,' he said sadly. 'But I'm afraid, dear Janine, that you have brought it on your own head. If you'd read my letters properly you would have known that we gave up the idea of an ice cream parlour a long while ago. We didn't have the knowledge, you see. And when the right sort of premises came along it was my friend Edie's grand-daughter who started up a business, neither Edie nor myself, though Edie did become a partner; a senior partner, in fact.'

Janine scowled. 'But I'm certain you said you had some sort of interest in an ice cream parlour,' she persisted. 'Don't try and lie to me, Dad, because I can see right through you. You and this Edie woman were just using the granddaughter to keep anyone else out, and that anyone else is me. I wouldn't have come home if I had thought I was coming home to nothing.'

Albert felt anger well up in him, but he reined in a desire to tell his daughter a few unpleasant truths. Instead, he spoke with measured calm. 'Janine, please listen to me. You failed to read my letters properly because the truth is, once the Atlantic was between us, you lost all interest in your "dear old dad". In fact you've only come home for what you can get . . .'

'Oh, Dad, how can you! To say such a thing to your own flesh and blood!' Janine wailed. 'When you said you had an ice cream parlour I guessed you'd be hard pressed to make it pay because you've not had experience of that sort of retail trade. I made Mario give me a bit more money, which I mean to use for any improvements needed to make the ice cream parlour support us both. I presume the tobacconist's is doing okay, though you hardly ever mention it now, but the ice cream parlour . . .'

Albert's careful hold on his temper began to waver. 'Be quiet and listen to me,' he said sharply. 'There is *no* ice cream parlour; do you hear me? *No* ice cream parlour! Mrs Williams and her granddaughter are running a very successful pet shop. They gave up the idea of an ice cream parlour because the premises they rent would not be suitable, and besides Tess knows a great deal about animal husbandry. It is true that when they started the business I put in a small amount of money to help with setting-up expenses, but that has long been repaid . . .' he crossed his fingers behind his back, since despite Tess's many offers he had never allowed her to refund that by no means negligible sum, 'so please forget the idea that either you or I can have anything to do with the pet shop.'

He expected an angry retort, remembering how the old Janine had hated being crossed, but to his dismay his daughter flung herself down on the table and began to weep.

Albert immediately felt deeply remorseful. How could he have said such cruel things to the child he and Louisa had so adored! It was not her fault that she had failed to notice when the ice cream parlour idea had become the pet shop scheme. And she had come all this way, travelling right across America and taking a berth aboard a ship bound for Liverpool, all under the mistaken impression that when she got to England she would find a nice little business which with the benefit of her undoubted expertise would become a nice big business. Janine had never liked animals, so the Payne family had never owned so much as a white mouse. She would be useless in the pet shop and in any event, as he had taken pains to point out, the shop had nothing to do with him. But when he went round to her side of the table and tried to stroke her hair, to tell her how sorry he was, she pushed him away.

'Well, I'm damned if I'm going back to the States,' she mumbled, knuckling her tear-wet eyes. She sniffed, produced a handkerchief from her skirt pocket and blew her nose resoundingly.

For a moment there was silence in the small kitchen. Janine was gazing into space. Albert returned to his own chair and took her cold hands in his warm ones.

'Did you seek legal advice regarding ownership of the soda fountain?' he asked gently. 'Surely you have some rights?'

'I tried, and got nowhere. There was no proof, you see, no contract, nothing. And when I wanted to go back in after my visit to the lawyer I was forbidden admittance, and when I tried to get into our apartment upstairs Father-in-law had changed the locks. I was pretty desperate, so when Mario advised me to come back to England and gave me the money for my fare it seemed the only thing left to do. I got one of the staff from the soda fountain to steal the keys from the manager they had put in my place and she, dear little girl, packed a suitcase with all my clothing and found out where to catch a train to New York.' She had been gazing into the middle distance but now her eyes focused on her father's face. 'Of course I tried to persuade various members of the Da Silva family to help me, but nobody would. Mr Da Silva is very much the big man of the neighbourhood; nobody would willingly go against him. Even Mario is afraid of him. So in the end I took Mario's advice and left. There were things in our apartment which belonged to me so Mario gave me what he thought was their value in cash, and saw me on to the train for New York. And that's all there was to it, Dad. Mario said the tobacconist shop was my inheritance as well as the ice cream parlour, but since there's no ice cream parlour I suppose I'll have to housekeep for you like my mam did. I might be able to find a little job, I suppose . . . but now you've got me back, Dad, you won't need that Edie woman. I know you say you're not in partnership with her, but judging

333

from your letters – which I *do* read – you spend a lot of time together.' She sniffed and pushed her handkerchief back into her pocket. 'What do you think Mam would say if she knew you were seeing another woman? It's not right, Dad! I suppose you've been spending time with this Edie because you're lonely. Well, you won't be lonely any more, because I mean to take up my old life where it left off. I've probably still got friends around here and I can learn the tobacconist trade so that when you retire I can take over. It's what Mam would like, after all, and this woman, this Mrs Williams, can concentrate on her pet shop.'

Albert looked long and hard into his daughter's face and saw the lines of strain and the way her mouth tightened with annoyance when things did not go her way. She was only just thirty but could have been forty, and he supposed that all the unhappiness she had gone through must be beginning to show on her face. But for whatever reason he must make it plain to her that she could not rule his life. Since she had left England they had gone their separate ways, and Albert realised that he was very happy with things as they were. To be sure, Janine was the daughter of his beloved Louisa, but he knew that his wife would have applauded his friendship with Edie, would have told Janine unequivocally to leave her father alone. Janine herself had made the decision to return to England, so she must start to build a new life for herself and not try to interfere with Albert's.

As Janine rose from the table he tried to say something of this, but she brushed him aside. 'Don't wake me tomorrow morning; I'll get up late,' she said. 'I shall need some time to recover from the journey before I can start to sort out what's best to do.' She turned away from him, began to open the door which led into the small hallway, then turned back. 'It's all your fault, Dad,' she said pettishly. 'If only you'd told me that you'd given up the idea of the ice cream parlour we wouldn't be in the mess we are now. I might not even have come home, because I could have got work in New York. Or there was a young fellow working in the candy store not two minutes' walk from the soda fountain . . .'

Albert recognised that Janine was just trying to blame others for a fiasco which had been, in truth, all of her own making. If she had only read his letters properly disaster might have been averted, though of course it wouldn't have helped what must have been an extremely rocky marriage, nor have reversed her non-existent ownership of the soda fountain. She had boasted of her business acumen, but if she had really possessed such a thing she would have made certain that the soda fountain had truly become her own property and not relied on the word of an unscrupulous man.

But Janine was yawning. 'Well, I'm here now, and I mean to make the best of it. Tell you what, I'll come down between ten and eleven tomorrow morning and you can shut up shop for an hour or so and take me round to meet this Mrs Williams and her granddaughter. What did you say her name was?'

Abruptly, Albert remembered all that had happened during the course of the previous week. 'Her name is Tess, but you won't be able to meet her for several days,' he informed his daughter. 'She's gone to a ruby wedding in Norfolk. As for shutting the shop, that won't be necessary since I've arranged for Mr Clarke to come here whilst Tess is away so that I can give Mrs Williams a hand.' He cast his daughter a quizzical look. 'If you'd read my letters you'd know that Mrs Williams was quite badly injured in a coach accident.'

'Oh, yes, I remember something of the sort,' Janine said indifferently. 'But that was ages ago; she shouldn't still be relying on you, Dad. After all, she's got her granddaughter and doubtless other friends . . .'

Albert felt irritation well up within him once more. He had filled his own hot water bottle and now he tucked it under his arm and headed for the hallway and his own room. 'This is a friendly neighbourhood; when the chips are down we all help one another,' he said stiffly. 'But you aren't the only one who's tired; I've been on the go since six o'clock this morning, so I think the rest of this conversation had better be deferred until tomorrow. Naturally, you're very welcome to lie in, but when my alarm goes off at seven o'clock I shall get up as usual and make breakfast. Mr Clarke will arrive here just before nine, and I shall then go to the pet shop to open up. I'm sure I'll be able to come back here at around eleven o'clock, however, and then we can talk.'

As Janine pushed open the spare room door as cautiously as though she expected it to be booby-trapped, he was reminded suddenly of the little girl whose room it had been long ago. When she had left, it had remained a young girl's room for quite a long time, since Albert was reluctant to believe that she would never return. But after a couple of years he had stripped the posters from the walls and the faded curtains from the window and had parcelled up the toys, books and games, putting them into the attic and telling himself that he would bring them down again when he had grandchildren who would appreciate them. But as though she had read his thoughts and to some extent shared them, Janine turned in the doorway and gave him a lopsided little smile.

'You've changed my room, but you've made it awful pretty; thanks, Dad,' she said. 'Sorry if I've been a bit tetchy, but I'm dead tired and longing for my bed.' As Albert passed her to reach his own room she caught hold of his arm and stood on tiptoe to kiss his cheek. 'See you in the mornin' then, Dad. Night night, sleep tight, make sure the bugs don't bite.'

The repetition of the little rhyme touched him as nothing else could, and all his doubts and fears disappeared. They would work something out. Janine didn't understand how dependent he had become on his friendship with Edie, but once she grew accustomed to the idea all would be well. Telling himself that Janine would be a pleasant addition to their little family, Albert made his way to bed and slept soundly until morning.

The train drew in to Norwich Thorpe and Tess, who had put on her haversack and hefted her suitcase, descended on to the platform. She had not been able to tell Jonty exactly what time her train would get in and in fact, she thought to herself, it was as well that she had not done so since she had missed a connection and was a good hour and a half later than she should have been. Not expecting to be met, therefore, she was startled when someone took the suitcase from her hand and slung an arm round her shoulders, giving her a quick squeeze. 'Hello-ello-ello,' Jonty's voice said in her ear. 'Not expecting me? You daft ha'p'orth, how did you mean to get to Bell Farm? Walking?'

Tess gasped, then reached up impulsively to kiss Jonty's cheek and promptly rubbed her mouth vigorously. 'When did you last shave, Jonty Bell?' she asked accusingly. 'Don't say you're trying to grow a beard!'

Jonty gave her another squeeze, then put his arm round her and guided her towards the concourse. 'I haven't had much time to attend to my personal beauty lately,' he said, grinning down at her. 'We've all been busy with the preparations for the party, as well as our everyday work. But now you're here I shall shave every morning and have a bath on Friday nights. I don't *think* I smell because Pamela, being a nurse, is awful fussy and she's not said I pong.'

'I think you smell nice,' Tess said dreamily, then pulled herself together. This was no way to behave with someone else's boyfriend. She had been within a cat's whisker of resting her head against his ancient tweed jacket, for the moment she had set eyes on him she had felt a rush of warmth and affection so strong that she thought he too must be aware of it. Now she pushed him away, half playful, half serious. 'Oh, Jonty, you smell of stables and cowsheds and hay and straw . . . even a little bit of the horses. Oh, you've got a new car; very sporty.'

Jonty, unlocking the passenger door of a low-slung bright red vehicle, gave the seat a proprietorial pat. 'That's it. We call her Ginger, after Ginger Rogers,' he said, and Tess, who knew him well, could hear the pride

338

he was trying to conceal. As she climbed into the passenger seat a rather disturbing thought occurred to her, but she waited until Jonty was driving out into the road before voicing it.

'Is Pamela on duty? She works at the Norfolk and Norwich, doesn't she?' she asked anxiously. 'Will I meet her? Only no one puts their best bib and tucker on when travelling by train and I got pretty smutty and dirty one way and another . . .'

'No, you won't meet her this evening,' Jonty said reassuringly. He drew up at the lights and cast a quick, comprehensive glance at her from top to toe; then grinned. 'What odd creatures women are! That's exactly what Pamela said: that she didn't want to meet you for the first time wearing her nurse's uniform.'

Tess leaned back in her seat with a relieved sigh. She told herself that of course she wanted to meet Pamela, but she knew she lied. From the moment that Jonty had put his arm round her she had known, without a shadow of a doubt, that he mattered more to her than anyone else on earth, even more than Gran, and definitely very much more than poor Snowy, though it was scarcely fair to think that since they had not seen one another for the past two years. For all she knew, as her feelings for Jonty had changed, so might her feelings for Snowy.

The lights changed and Ginger Rogers moved smoothly forward, and the rest of the short journey was punctuated by Tess's questions and Jonty's answers. It seemed that things had not changed very much on Bell Farm. Jonty told her that the dairy herd had doubled in size and that there were more store cattle

339

out on the marshes. But when she started to ask questions about the land they had bought from the Larkins next door Jonty said that she would see for herself in due time, and refused to answer any more questions.

Chapter Thirteen

As soon as Albert finished his breakfast next morning he tidied round the kitchen and wrote a note for Janine saying that he had left for the pet shop, but that she would find oats, milk and bread in the pantry and must get herself some breakfast. Then, as soon as he had settled Mr Clarke behind the counter, with the float in the till and a list of current prices, he set off for the pet shop, sheltering beneath his large black umbrella, for it was raining steadily. He expected to see Mitch and Elsie, soaked to the skin, waiting outside the door, but as soon as he entered he saw that Edie had come down early to open up. Smiling, he went into the stockroom to hang up his coat and hat and returned to find that Edie had made a pot of tea. She handed him a cup. 'The children will start the cleaning now you've arrived, so as soon as the cages have fresh sawdust we'll fill the water pots and food dishes,' she said, peering out through the windowpane. 'It's still raining like billyo, so I don't suppose we'll have many customers. I take it Mr Clarke has arrived?'

Albert nodded. 'He has indeed,' he admitted. 'And Mr Clarke isn't the only one. I had an unexpected visitor last night, and she stayed over. In fact at this very moment she's probably asleep in my spare room.'

Edie stared, a puzzled frown on her brow. 'A woman?' she said, and Albert heard without comprehension a little quiver in her voice. He also saw a pink flush blotch her neck and invade her cheeks. 'A woman?' she repeated. 'Oh, Albert, what do you mean?'

Whenever Albert had suggested that he and Edie might enjoy a closer relationship than one of mere friendship Edie had never shown any obvious enthusiasm for the idea, but now, for the first time, Albert could see she was dismayed at the thought of this unknown woman entering their lives. However, he did not mean to prevaricate. 'Yes, a woman. My daughter Janine,' he said bluntly. 'There have been ugly goings-on in America, from what I could gather. Her husband has met an old girlfriend and means to divorce Janine, and his father has thrown her out of the business which she thought was her own. It's a long and involved story and I've not got to the bottom of it yet. All I really know is she's come running back to her old dad and will expect me to support her until she finds herself a job.'

There was a stunned silence. Edie was staring at him, her mouth dropping open. Mitch, with the tray that went beneath the guinea pigs' cage clasped to his chest, was statue still, and Elsie, filling a water pot with the big enamel jug, continued to pour until the water overflowed on to her own small feet.

Mitch, seeing this, dropped the tray and dived across the shop to grab the jug. Elsie began to weep and Edie to laugh, whilst Albert picked up the tray, handed it to Mitch with a command to take it out the back, and lifted the tearful Elsie on to the counter so that he could remove her wet shoes and socks whilst explaining that his daughter's arrival had been as much of a surprise to him as it was to them.

'She turned up quite late yesterday evening, and to

tell you the truth she was in a bit of a state,' he said. 'But she calmed down before she went to bed.'

Edie leaned back, blew out her cheeks in a long whistle and pretended to fan herself. 'Albert Payne, what a dreadful shock you gave me!' she declared. 'I thought either you had gone mad or I had, but I'm sure she's done the right thing to come home. Is she like you, good with animals? Only if so—'

'No, she's never had a pet in her life; in fact she's frightened of animals, or was, at any rate. Louisa once bought her a white kitten; it was a most attractive little creature but Janine couldn't bear it, so Louisa gave it to Mr Shaw's daughter – the greengrocer, you know – and I believe it's still around somewhere.'

'Oh,' Edie said rather doubtfully, beginning to fill little dishes with bird seed for the canaries and budgerigars. 'Well, it doesn't really matter, because no doubt you'll find her useful in your shop.' She twinkled across at Albert. 'She could take care of the fancy goods, particularly the brasses. I know you loathe cleaning them, but you must have noticed that you sell twice as many when they're gleaming like gold.'

Albert grinned back. Edie had noticed that other tobacconists sold ornaments, particularly brass ones, and at her suggestion Albert had purchased several such items. He had not really expected them to sell, but they had done so and now brought in a tidy sum.

'That's a brilliant idea,' he said. 'Mr Clarke did offer to come in after Christmas and clean them, but he isn't terribly good at it. I'll suggest it to Janine when I see her next – I told her I'd pop back home at around eleven o'clock, so we'll talk about it then.'

343

At eleven o'clock precisely the door to the pet shop opened and Janine came in. Last night, Albert realised, his daughter had not looked her best, but now she had obviously put a good deal of effort into her appearance. She was wearing a dark blue sling-back overcoat which Albert took from her and carried through to the stockroom, noting as he did so that the coat had hidden a smart suit in heather tweed with a pale pink blouse beneath it, worn with a jaunty little matching hat. She carried an umbrella which Albert recognised as the one Mr Clarke had sheltered beneath earlier that morning, and her shoes were very high-heeled and made of black patent leather. Last night, Albert remembered with a wrench, her face had been pale and devoid of make-up, but now her lashes were mascaraed and her nose was powdered, her cheeks were touched with rouge and she wore a great deal of lipstick. In fact, Albert thought, she looked nothing like the young woman he had left outside the door of the spare room the previous night.

But Janine was looking from face to face, the beginning of a puzzled frown creasing her brow, and Albert remembered that he hadn't mentioned Mitch or Elsie when discussing the pet shop. Hastily, he took the dripping umbrella, shook it out and furled it, then took Janine's hand. I was just telling Mrs Williams here that you had come home,' he said. 'This is Mrs Edith Williams, Janine, an old friend of mine.' Edie, who had been sitting on the chair behind the counter, got to her feet, gave the newcomer the benefit of her friendliest smile and held out her hand.

'How do you do, Mrs Da Silva,' she began, but Janine interrupted at once.

'Please call me Janine. I don't want to hear the name Da Silva ever again,' she said. 'In fact I want to put the past few years behind me and return to my old life. I expect my father has told you that I worked in one of the big stores, modelling gowns. It was a well-paid position, so if I can find something similar . . .' she turned to smile at Albert, 'but for the time being I mean to housekeep for my dear old dad, and help out in the shop.'

Edie murmured something appropriate but Albert felt distinctly uncomfortable. He was aware that Edie must know as well as he did that his daughter had never modelled clothes for anyone, not whilst she was in England at any rate, and now she was expecting him to accept and indeed verify the story she had chosen to tell. Immediately, it occurred to him that if she was prepared to fib so blatantly over one thing she was probably equally prepared to fib over another. He thought back over the story she had told him about her life in America and realised that even at the time it had not altogether rung true. But Janine was being charming, accepting Elsie's offer to show her around the shop and tell her all about the animals and birds whilst Mitch and Mr Payne got on with the real work.

Albert watched as, hand in hand, the two bent over a cage in which three tabby kittens rolled and played. 'Oh, the darlings!' his daughter was saying. She poked a finger through the wire and withdrew it hastily as one of the kittens pounced. Then she straightened and took Elsie's hand once more, moving along to the next cage. 'Tortoises; and very nice ones too,' she said. 'Don't they go to sleep in the winter, though? I think it's called hibernation.'

345

'They only do that if you let them get cold,' Elsie said instructively. 'Would you like to give them a lettuce leaf?'

Janine took the proffered greenery, poked it through the wire and moved on to the next cage. 'Them's guinea pigs; we've already sold 'em to a very nice lady what wants them as presents for her grandchildren,' Elsie said. 'But we're keeping 'em until Christmas Eve, else the kids would find out what they'd got before the day itself.'

Janine chuckled, and it occurred to Albert that the chuckle had been the first genuine reaction his daughter had displayed since entering the shop. Possibly, he thought wryly, the first genuine reaction she had shown since returning to her own home. But Janine, turning away from the guinea pigs, was speaking directly to him. 'Isn't this all nice, though?' she said approvingly. 'Tell you what, Dad, if it would help I wouldn't mind giving a hand here. I've noticed when I'm in a confined space with folks smoking all around me I get to feel sickish. I even felt kinda squeamish when I were helpin' Mr Clarke with a batch of Gold Flake just now.'

Albert frowned. Where had he heard those words before? But Edie was suggesting that Janine might enjoy taking over the fancy goods side of her father's business, and Janine seemed to think this was a good idea. 'I saw Dad had gone in for brasses, but there's other things that would bring in customers,' she was saying enthusiastically. 'Would you let me do the orderin', Dad? It's a bit late for the Christmas market, I suppose, but how about a notice in the window saying you are now selling gifts? I'd make the notice – I'm real good at lettering – and if necessary I'd ring your suppliers and bully them into giving us a special pre-Christmas order.' Albert thought she must have read the doubt in his face, for she added hastily: 'But I'd only do that if we were running out of stock and were sure we could sell more.'

Albert agreed to all these plans, secure in the knowledge that they might come to nothing and would, for a time at least, keep his daughter happily occupied. He could see that she now no longer saw herself modelling gowns, but turning the fancy goods side of his business into a far more profitable concern. Edie, much taken by the idea, said that when Tess returned she would be all in favour, for she had long thought Albert did not make the most of the possibilities of his shop.

Realising that Janine was still uncomfortable with the animals and birds, Edie sat her down at the back of the shop and set her to measuring out small quantities of pet food, labelling and pricing the bags, and putting them on the shelf. Customers came and went, sales were made and the till rang merrily, but at one o'clock Albert decided that he and Janine should have a proper lunch break, for he noticed with a little concern that his daughter was looking pale beneath the rouge.

Edie reminded Albert that she had made sandwiches and brewed a pot of tea for everyone to share, but Albert, though he thanked her politely, said that he rather thought his daughter had done quite enough for one day, and helped her into her smart coat. 'I'll see you later,' he said to Edie, donning his own overcoat, for the rain had turned to sleet and the crowds which had thronged the pavements earlier in the morning had become a trickle. He picked up Mr Clarke's umbrella and smiled at his daughter. 'Come along, my dear. Do you fancy going to

Dorothy's Tearooms for a light luncheon? Or we can pop into the bakery and buy a pasty.'

Janine opted for the pasty, admitting that she was worn out and would do as her father suggested and have a nap when they'd eaten. Back in their kitchen Albert warmed the pie, buttered some bread and made a pot of tea, the words that his daughter had used repeating themselves in the back of his mind as he did so. *I even felt kinda squeamish when I were helpin' Mr Clarke with a batch of Gold Flake.*

They had finished their meal and Albert was rising to his feet, about to start the washing up and telling Janine that she must go and lie down on her bed, when he remembered where he had heard the words before. His dearest Louisa, the best helpmate a man could hope for, had used those very words, or something very like them, not long after the doctor at the clinic had confirmed her pregnancy. Without a moment's hesitation he sat down again opposite his daughter. 'You're in the family way,' he said. 'My dear child, why didn't you tell me? I do trust you aren't going to try to deny it, because I remember, when your mother was expecting you, she had to stop helping me in the shop because the smell of tobacco made her feel sick. Oh, not at once, but later on, when her time was near.'

Janine stared at him, opened her mouth, Albert thought, to repudiate the whole idea, and then changed her mind. She nodded. 'Yes, Dad, you've hit the nail on the head. I'm pregnant. Are you shocked?'

Albert raised his brows. 'Why on earth should I be shocked?' he asked fondly. 'But when you told Mario, didn't that soften his attitude? And you will be making

348

Mr Da Silva a grandfather; if I am delighted at the thought of – of grandfatherhood, then surely he must feel the same. When's the baby due?'

Janine shrugged. 'I'm not sure,' she said sulkily. 'It could be any time, I suppose.' She prodded a finger at her stomach. 'I seem to have been huge for at least a year already.'

'Then you must have known you were expecting in plenty of time to tell the Da Silvas the happy news,' Albert said. Janine raised her eyes from the contemplation of her drink and met her father's gaze squarely.

'Oh, Dad, they aren't like us . . .' she began, but Albert had heard the syrupy note enter her voice and knew at once that he would not get the truth from her without a struggle. She was beginning to say that Mr Da Silva had several grandchildren already when Albert brought his fist down hard on the kitchen table, stopping her in mid-sentence.

'Janine, I can always tell when you're lying, and you're lying now,' he said harshly. 'I'm willing to help you in any way I can – for the child's sake as well as your own – but I won't let you draw me into a life of lies. Why did you tell Edie that you had modelled gowns? It wasn't true and it got you nowhere. Why did you pretend you liked animals, when it rapidly became obvious that you were frightened of them? You behaved as if the kittens had claws like scimitars, or as though you thought the tortoises would seize the lettuce leaf you were offering and drag you into their cage with them! My dear child, your mother and I called it fibbing when you were young, but now that you're an adult we must both acknowledge that you've been telling lies. So make up your mind that unless I get the truth out of you I shall simply write to the Da Silvas to ask why they have treated my daughter so badly.'

Janine had been looking sulky, but now her expression changed to one of alarm. 'You can't . . . you mustn't . . . Mr Da Silva's a very important man . . .' she began, her voice rising to a wail. 'Oh, Dad, I've been such a fool! I never did get married, because when I reached Silverpeak I discovered that Mario had lied. He was married already; and though he had told me the truth in one respect – the Da Silvas do own a sizeable property, a cattle ranch just outside the town as well as the soda fountain and the diner – it was about the only true thing he had said. Oh, Dad, it was dreadful! I was so far from home and I was still more than half in love with Mario even though I knew he didn't love me. I should have left the area, gone somewhere far away where I could have licked my wounds and recovered my self-respect. But Mr Da Silva offered me the job of manageress of the soda fountain and said I could have the flat above it rent free. I should have turned him down but I still hoped that Mario would grow tired of his fat little wife and turn to me. I worked real hard, Dad, bringing the soda fountain into profitability, and Mr Da Silva really had made it plain that he would hand the business over to me . . .' She stopped speaking for a moment and shot Albert a quick, sly glance from under her lashes. '*Please* say you understand,' she said pleadingly. 'I expect you can guess what happened next . . .'

Albert looked at his daughter's pale, mascara-smeared face and his heart went out to her. Of course he could guess what must have happened, but he felt that it was essential to hear the truth from her own lips. If she and I are to remain friends there must be truth between us, he told himself. He fixed Janine with an unfaltering stare, and though he spoke kindly it was also firmly. 'No guessing; you must tell me the truth,' he said. 'What happened?'

Janine had begun to cry but now she hiccuped, blew her nose on her handkerchief and spoke more calmly. 'Mario's real wife, Madalena, became pregnant. It affected her strangely. She became bad-tempered, cried a lot and refused Mario his marital rights; at least that was what he said, though he put it a good deal more crudely. He turned to me for sympathy at first, and then for – for other things. I should have denied him, but I didn't. I was lonely, far from home . . .'

'Rubbish!' Albert said angrily. 'But it's no good repining now that the damage is done. Tell me, have I got this right? Madalena Da Silva had her baby and regained her sweet nature. You tried to persuade Mario to leave her and told him you were in the family way. He was not unnaturally horrified, as was Mr Da Silva, senior. They gave you money for your fare home and probably some extra for lying-in expenses, and back you came, having no alternative.'

Janine had been snuffling into her handkerchief but now she burst into floods of tears once more. 'How could I guess he wouldn't stand by me?' she wailed. 'You've only left out one thing, Dad, and that is that I truly love Mario, and always will. If only he'd not lied to me right at the beginning none of this would have happened. Oh, Dad, I'm so unhappy, tell me you understand and forgive me!'

351

Despite himself, Albert could not resist such an appeal. 'Of course I do,' he said soothingly. 'And we'll stick to your story, since no one in America is likely to hear how you've been blackening the Da Silva name. So now we must decide what is best to do. It's a great pity that the smell of tobacco affects you, but if it reaches the flat and becomes too much we'll see about renting you a couple of rooms . . .'

This led to the loudest wail so far. 'Oh, Dad, don't turn me out, don't reject me,' Janine said between sobs. 'The smell isn't likely to reach the flat and I've learned to keep house, cook and manage on a small budget. We can be very happy, you and I, only I don't see any need for you to spend time in the pet shop, or with that Mrs Williams. I dare say she's very nice, but now you've got me you won't need anyone else.'

Albert opened his mouth to disabuse her, then changed his mind. She was upset enough already and now that he knew the truth he thought that further explanations could be put off until she had calmed down. Then there would be all the other things which expectant mothers had to do. He imagined she would need to visit Brougham Terrace to explain her predicament and become a patient on a doctor's panel, and he rather thought she might be eligible to apply for some sort of financial help whilst she was unable to work. He knew there were clinics and classes which prepared young women for the birth, but all that was for the future. Right now he did not even mean to tell her that nothing would persuade him to give up his friendship with the Williamses. Perhaps it was natural that she should resent the closeness which had grown up between himself and Edie, but natural or

352

not she would simply have to accept that she could not possibly take the place of his dearest friend.

But she was staring at him across the table, her lip trembling, her eyes filling with tears once more, so Albert hastened to reassure her. 'All right, that's enough talking for one day! I'll make you a hot water bottle while you trot along to your room and get into your nightgown. Tomorrow will be quite soon enough to decide what other action we need to take.' He got to his feet, went over to the stove and filled the kettle, then held open the kitchen door. 'Off you go! You'll feel all the better for a good night's sleep.'

'Tess? Where on earth . . . ? Ah, there you are!'

At the sound of Jonty's voice Tess backed out of the pantry, carrying a large loaf of home-made bread and a full butter dish. She gave a squeak as a blast of icy air blew into the kitchen, and was begging him to shut the door and not let in the snow which had begun to fall when she saw that he was not alone. A slim girl muffled up to the eyebrows in a hooded coat with a scarf wound round her throat was entering behind him.

'Sorry,' the girl said, pushing the door closed. 'That's mortal cold out there.' She began to unwind the scarf from round her neck and then to unbutton her coat. 'I say, it's lovely and warm in here.' She smiled brightly at Tess, who could now see that she was fair-haired and blue-eyed and very slim in her navy blue dress. Not a nurse's uniform, but something perilously close to it, Tess thought.

Smiling, she held out her hand. 'How do you do? I don't need anyone to tell me that you must be Pamela Davies, and I expect you can guess that I'm Tess Williams.'

353

They shook hands. 'Nice to meet you,' Pamela Davies said. She turned to Jonty and put a proprietorial hand on his shoulder. 'I do trust you warned Tess that I've been invited to tea. I'm afraid I'm not much use when it comes to cooking a meal, because my mother has always spoiled me and I've never learned to cook. But I'll give you any help I can. I can lay the table, or cut bread and butter it, or do any other menial task which occurs to you . . .'

'Thanks. It would be nice if you laid the table, but apart from that everything is more or less finished,' Tess said politely. 'And whilst we wait for Mr Bell and the farmworkers we can get to know one another.'

Jonty looked across at Tess; it was a wistful look, Tess decided. But whether he was feeling wistful because he could not stay in the warm kitchen or because he wished he could ask her to go out into the cold with him, she could not tell. Then Jonty saw Tess glancing at him and the wistful look vanished. 'There are cows out there waiting to be milked, but I suppose I'd better do it since you girls will want to chat,' he said. He opened the back door again, letting in a blast of cold air which made both girls shriek a protest, and went out, slamming the door behind him. Tess stood the kettle over the flame, made the tea, and handed a cup to her companion. The two of them settled themselves comfortably on either side of the fire.

'I believe your young man, Snowy White, Jonty calls him, is serving with the army in Malaya. I understand it's a dangerous place for our national servicemen,' Pamela said. She shuddered expressively. 'I thank God that my man is in a reserved occupation; I'd die if they sent him away.'

354

After that the talk became more general, and when Jonty and his father came in Tess was able to examine Pamela more closely. She saw a woman not a lot older than she was herself, with soft fair hair pulled back from her face, steady blue eyes, and an air of self-confidence which, Tess assumed, nursing the sick had given her. She wore no make-up and her skin was clear, her nose commandingly high-bridged and her lips firmly set. Tess simply could not envisage her as the ideal mate for easy-going, fun-loving Jonty. She herself had been at the farm now for two whole days and had begun to believe that she would be very happy as a farmer's wife, particularly if that farmer was Jonty. But though he was friendly and charming towards her, there was nothing lover-like in the way he behaved. And very soon, when the meal was over and they went through into the parlour with a tray of tea, she was able to see that he showed no ardency in his dealings with Pamela either. Nor did Pamela herself evince any of the signs of young love, which gave Tess hope, for she had found to her dismay that she rather liked Pamela, admired her absorption in her work and her good sense, and did not think she could bring herself to compete with her for Jonty's affections. Indeed, had either of them shown any deeper emotion she would have dismissed the idea of competing with Pamela in any way, but as it was she was pretty sure Jonty had no stronger feeling for Pamela than he did for herself, so she would be entitled to lure him back to her in any way she could.

But at the thought of luring Jonty she had to fight a desire to laugh. How ridiculous she was being! The only sort of lure Jonty would recognise would be the one falconers used to bring their birds back to the glove. Jonty's not in love with anyone; if and when he does decide to marry it may well be to someone he's not even met yet, she concluded. But thank goodness I'm not jealous of Pamela; in fact I really like her. So, when I get the opportunity, I shall buttonhole her to talk about her relationship with Jonty, a thing I could never do if either of them was in love with the other. But do it I shall, and before I return to Liverpool.

Albert was making breakfast as his daughter came, or rather slouched, into the kitchen, still in her nightie and dressing gown. The reason she was slouching was probably because she was wearing a pair of his old slippers, but even so she managed to produce a smile before slumping into a chair.

'Good morning, queen. You didn't have to get up so early, you know,' Albert said rather reproachfully. He had grown accustomed to a solitary breakfast and enjoyed propping the newspaper up on the marmalade pot whilst eating his porridge or cereal. But now there was Janine, sitting in the creaking old chair which had been Louisa's and asking rather pettishly whether he had any cornflakes since she supposed he had eaten all the porridge.

Albert raised his brows. 'You said you were going to lie in this morning,' he said mildly. 'But since you're here I can always make more porridge; or you could have Weetabix or Shredded Wheat, I've got both.'

'Shredded Wheat is lovely; I'll have some of that,' Janine said, summoning up a smile. 'Ooh, hot toast! I wouldn't mind a couple of rounds, even if you've only got margarine to spread on it.'

356

'I've got plenty of marmalade,' Albert said. 'I gave Mrs Williams my extra sugar ration and bought several oranges, a couple of lemons and a grapefruit. She made me six jars of the most delicious marmalade; you must try it.'

'I will,' Janine assured him. She began to eat her cereal, remarking as she did so that housekeeping must be difficult with so many things still on ration and the rest, so far as she could gather, unobtainable.

Albert struck his head with the palm of his hand. 'I *knew* there was something I wanted to discuss with you,' he said. 'Ration books! I don't suppose you've got one. If you attend the clinic for expectant mothers you'll be given all sorts of stuff – well, perhaps not given, but if you have to pay for it it'll be very cheap. You'd better get along to Brougham Terrace as soon as you can, and whilst you're there you could ask where you should apply for a ration book. You'll probably need identification – your passport and your birth certificate should be enough.' He eyed her critically, though in her large, loose-fitting dressing gown it was difficult to see her shape. 'You aren't showing much yet, but by Christmas there'll be no hiding your condition. Not that we want to hide it,' he added hastily.

As he spoke he was taking his coat off the hook and the interested expression on Janine's face turned suddenly to annoyance. 'Don't you go running off to that bleedin' pet shop to gab about me and my secrets,' she said, her voice sharpening with every word. 'I *told* you, Dad, I'll keep house for you – and I'm a real good cook. I'm a good manager too, so why do you need to go chasin' after that Mrs Williams?'

357

Albert put his coat on, wound a muffler round his neck, jammed his hat upon his head and picked up his umbrella. 'It's a proper blizzard out there,' he said. 'Since an addition – you, Janine – to our circle will affect each and every one of us, right down to Mitch and little Elsie, I intend to tell them that not only do we have one new member but very soon it will be two. What fault can you find with that, queen?'

'I don't want folk to know too soon,' Janine mumbled. 'And when we talked yesterday I thought I made it plain that you and I didn't need anyone else, didn't want the perishin' Williamses in fact. We'll manage better alone, honest to God we will.'

Albert buttoned his coat and reached for the door, handle. 'If you want to muck in with the rest of us and become one of our extended family, as Edie calls it, then we'll start as we mean to go on. No more lies or evasions, just the plain unvarnished truth.' He opened the door, and despite the fact that the staircase led into the store-room and not into the open street the cold wind swirled in, making him catch his breath. But he turned back for a moment nevertheless. 'You silly child! Very soon now you won't be able to button that smart coat, or fasten the zip at the side of your tweed skirt. So why lie, when the truth will out? Come to the pet shop when you're ready to go up to Brougham Terrace, and I'll show you the way. After all, Liverpool has changed considerably since you went away.' He opened the door whilst Janine was still muttering, shut it on her complaining voice and clattered down the stairs. At supper the previous evening he had returned to the subject of finding a couple of rooms or even a small flat for his daughter, meaning it

358

as an enticement, a way of giving her some independence. But it was soon clear that she had seen it as a threat, and now Albert decided that if she tried to make trouble or interfere in any way between himself and Edie then he would use that threat to good effect. Smiling grimly to himself, he crossed the stockroom, turned on the lights, for it was indeed a nasty snowy day, and began to open up. He unlocked just in time for Mr Clarke, who looked like a mere bundle of clothes as he entered the shop almost at a run and began to unwind his layers.

'Phew!' he said. 'Horrible day, Mr Payne, sir. You're lucky you don't have to go out to get to work . . .' He eyed his employer thoughtfully. 'Or do you? I see you're togged up for the weather. I take it you're off somewhere?'

Albert nodded and thought of the warm pet shop, where the heating would have been on all night. 'Blow the expense, it's a necessity, not a luxury,' Tess had said. And, Elsie had added, it would also prevent the tortoises from hibernating.

But Mr Clarke had shaken and furled his umbrella and was staring at Albert, plainly waiting for a reply to a question which Albert could not even remember.

'Are you off out?' Mr Clarke repeated. 'It ain't a day for customers, not even them who've not yet bought all their Christmas cheer, so I doubt we'll be very busy, even if the snow eases up.'

'I am,' Albert confirmed. 'Oh, you've met my daughter; she'll be down later and will probably go straight to the pet shop. All right? The float's in the till and there's money in the drawer under the counter in case you have a delivery, though most of our suppliers are paid by cheque.' He headed across the shop towards the outside door. 'I'll be back around one o'clock so's you can have a bite of lunch,' he finished, letting himself out into the street.

He hurried along the pavement, rehearsing in his mind what he would presently say to Edie. He would have to explain his daughter's condition in front of Mitch and Elsie, but why should that matter? They would have to know in the end, and anyway, he thought they were unlikely to be much interested. Girls grew up and became young women, and young women had babies; both Mitch and Elsie would be well aware of the facts of life even if working in the pet shop had not taught them all about the birds and the bees.

As usual, the children were on the doorstep waiting to be let in when Albert arrived and greeted him cheerfully as they all entered the shop together and began to shed their outer clothing. When Edie joined them, her first question concerned Janine.

'How's your girl getting on?' She lowered her voice, though the two youngsters were already cleaning cages and chattering away to one another. 'She's expecting, isn't she? I imagine that's why she's come home . . . There's nowhere like home when things go wrong.'

Relief flooded Albert; he might have known that Edie would have read the situation after a few minutes in Janine's company, let alone a couple of hours! 'Yes, that's it,' he said. 'She didn't want folk to know too soon, but I told her she was being daft so she agreed to go along to Brougham Terrace, to the clinic for expectant mothers, and then to wherever one goes to apply for a ration book.'

'I dare say she'll be busy all morning, if not all day,'

Edie said ruefully. 'Has she left yet? Only I thought I might offer to go with her; it's not much fun being hassled and pushed around by officials when you know you're not looking your best, nor feeling it for that matter.'

'She was still in her nightie when I'd finished my breakfast, but she's coming here before she goes off because, as I told her, the Liverpool she used to know has changed considerably.' He beamed at his friend, noticing that her beautiful wavy white hair was not strained back by a rubber band today but was loose on her shoulders, and she was wearing a touch of lipstick, possibly even a little powder. 'It's really good of you. If I offered to accompany her, which I meant to do, I'd stand out like a sore thumb and the last thing Janine wants is to be different.' He hesitated, glancing towards the two youngsters, but they were still cleaning cages. Nevertheless, Albert lowered his voice. 'But I do have a worry, Edie. I'm afraid Janine isn't always truthful, and if she starts telling lies, pretending the father of her baby is a rich American or saying she's the owner of a successful ice cream parlour in the States, then she could be in all sorts of trouble. I'll warn her to stick to the truth, but if I'm not with her . . . Oh, dear, Edie, what a fix we shall both be in if she lies to make herself seem more interesting, and not just a silly little girl who's got into trouble and fled from the results.'

Edie nodded. 'You'd better tell me all the truth then,' she said quietly. 'At a guess I'd say she never married the Da Silva boy or, if she did, he didn't father the child. Not that she'll need to say that exactly . . .'

'She didn't marry anyone, because Mario was married already, but she had a fling with him some time ago which resulted in her condition,' Albert said delicately. 'She shouldn't mention him by name, of course, because once the authorities can put a name to the father they will pursue him for maintenance. It's best if she says she had a holiday romance and doesn't know anything about the man, save that he's an American.'

'If she sticks to that story we should be all right,' Edie said, giving Albert an inquisitive look. 'It's essentially true, isn't it? Except of course that she knows Mario's name and address. But she wouldn't want to ruin his marriage by letting his wife know he had been unfaithful.'

'If I'm honest, my dear, I think Janine would like nothing better than to make trouble for him. He seems to have lied to her right from the start,' Albert said, just as the door opened and Janine slipped quietly into the shop.

'Good morning, everyone,' she said in a very subdued voice. 'I'm ready, Dad. I'm dreading the whole business, but I've brought my passport and my birth certificate like you said . . . Oh, dear, if only I had a pal who'd be willing to come with me!' She looked up at her father and he saw that once more she wore no make-up and was pale and wan, with dark circles under her eyes.

'I don't think I'd be much good, queen,' Albert said gently. 'But Edie here knows how to deal with officialdom and has offered to go with you. It's up to you, of course . . .'

Albert had had his doubts about how Edie's offer would be received, but he need not have worried. His daughter might be – indeed was – jealous of the other woman, she might dislike or even mistrust her, but as Albert repeated Edie's offer he saw the brittle smile on

Janine's face become full of delight and relief and was not surprised when Janine almost fell into the older woman's arms. 'Oh, thank you, Mrs Williams, you are good,' she gabbled. 'It'll make all the difference to have another woman sticking up for me. Can we go at once, please? I'd really like to get it over with, and then I mean to rest on my bed for an hour or so . . .'

'That's right, you take care of yourself and my little grandchild,' Albert said expansively as Edie took off her shop overall and put on her coat. 'I'll hold the fort here with Mitch and Elsie, but I doubt there'll be many customers, or not until the snow eases up at any rate.'

He went behind the counter and glanced into the stockroom. Elsie and Mitch, armed with scissors, paste, and several jars of poster paint were now busily creating paper chains out of old copies of the *Echo*. As the two women let themselves out of the shop Albert went into the stockroom. 'Have you two finished cleaning the cages?' he asked suspiciously. 'I know you want to make the shop look festive but you mustn't forget we're here to work.'

Mitch looked up and grinned. He had a smear of paste running across one cheek and a blob of bright blue paint on the end of his nose. But he assured Albert that they had finished the cages some time before. 'Though you're quite right, Mr Payne; we ought to check the food and water,' he admitted. 'Tomorrer Elsie and me is going to cut holly in the country; enough for the flat and the shop, Mrs Williams said. She's goin' to give us a bottle of tea and a load of mince pies as well as some sangwidges, it bein' so cold.' He glanced around the shop, which was empty, as though there were a dozen listening ears.

363

'We've not told Mrs Williams, but we're hopin' to root up one of them Christmas trees what grows in the woods. We've already started making decorations for it whenever Mrs Williams ain't around so it's to be our present to her and Tess. Tess'll be back before Christmas, won't she?'

'I expect so,' Albert said. 'So don't you go ruining everyone's Christmas by being caught nicking a tree and being hauled before a magistrate. Tell you what, I'll give you five bob to buy one from the stalls on St John's market. That'll be my present to you, and your present to the Williamses can be the decorations. What do you say?'

Mitch was agreeing that this would be grand when Elsie raised her head from her work. 'Trees is everyone's; you can't steal a tree,' she said matter of factly. 'I don't see why we're any different from other people. I 'member a scuffer chasin' us when we were nickin' holly from the big houses round Princes Park, and our dad said holly belonged to everyone 'cos it was only a tree. But the scuffer said we'd made a big hole in the feller's hedge . . .'

'What happened?' Albert asked curiously. He could just imagine Elsie, even tinier than she was today, defying a dozen scuffers to take her holly from her. But this, apparently, had not been the case.

'Happened? Nothin', 'cos I headed him in the belly and runned like the perishin' wind an' got home afore he had a chance to grab me,' Elsie said indifferently. 'We sold the holly, me an' Mitch, an' bought oranges wi' the money.'

Albert grinned; trust Elsie to get away with murder! And even had she been caught he suspected that she

364

would have charmed her way out of trouble somehow. But right now he had work to do. He returned to his counter and began to check on the amounts of various foodstuffs they would need to order before Christmas. Outside the shop the wind continued to whirl the snow into the faces of passers-by and Albert began to feel uncomfortably chilly. He glanced at his watch and saw that it was almost eleven o'clock; how time flew when one was busy! He looked across at the stockroom where the paper chain, lavishly painted, had grown by ten feet since he saw it last. Albert got to his feet and set the kettle, which Edie had filled, on the Primus stove. 'Elevenses in ten minutes, kids,' he called. 'Get out the shortbread!'

Chapter Fourteen

It was market day and Mrs Bell had joined other farmers' wives at the WI stall where they sold their excess produce. Consequently, Tess had made the breakfast and was eating toast when Jonty slung the post down on the kitchen table. She reached for Gran's letter – always full of news – and began to read, her eyebrows rising almost to her hair as she digested the contents.

'Tess? What's up? Not bad news, I hope?'

Tess gulped. Oddly enough, her first reaction to the news that Albert's daughter had returned was jealousy, and this feeling did not dissipate when she read that Janine was pregnant. In fact, it became worse. Tess was no stranger to jealousy, she realised with shame. She had been jealous of the growing affection between Gran and Albert for a long while, though she knew it was ridiculous; over and over, Gran had said that she and the tobacconist were just good friends, and Gran would never lie to her. So why on earth should she feel jealous because Janine had come home? Surely it would mean that Albert and Janine would be like herself and Gran, a nice little family of two, needing only each other? As for the baby, it would simply strengthen their family ties when it came, she supposed. Jealousy of Janine must be banished, because it was an ignoble emotion; Tess banished it and realised, suddenly, that father and son

366

were staring at her, and she had not answered Jonty's questions.

'Sorry, I was a thousand miles away. I'll read you Gran's letter, then you'll know why I'm somewhat surprised,' she said. 'It's good news, but – but unexpected.'

She read the letter aloud and Jonty's reaction was immediate. 'Gosh. I never even knew Mr Payne had a daughter,' he exclaimed. 'Wait till Ma hears! She's been saying for a while now that she doesn't understand why he and your gran haven't plighted their troth, but I suppose they're both too old to think about marriage.'

Mr Bell had been eating toast and marmalade and had not yet commented, but his shrewd blue eyes dwelt thoughtfully on Tess's face before he spoke. 'I always did reckon you didn't much fancy having that chap around the place,' he said. 'Ah well, the young are always selfish.'

'Do you mean me when you say that?' Tess said, astonished at Mr Bell's words. 'I love my gran dearly, and while we've got each other . . .'

Mr Bell picked up his mug of tea and took a swig. 'One of these days you and that Snowy White lad, or some other feller, will doubtless want to get wed,' he observed. 'What'll happen to Mrs Williams then, eh?'

'Oh! Well, I suppose we'll move out, get a place of our own . . . No, I suppose we'll stay in the flat above the pet shop and Gran will move out . . .' Tess said uncertainly. 'But that won't be for ages and ages, perhaps not for years . . .'

'There you are, you see,' Mr Bell said kindly. 'You're selfish, like all young things. But there, mebbe I'm wrong and Mrs Williams and Mr Payne have no thought of marrying.' He took a last long drink of his tea, set the mug down and scraped his chair back. 'Well, tomorrow's the great day, so I've warned the men that they'll need to get ahead with their work and they've promised to do so, which means Jonty and myself have got to get a move on as well.'

But all day Mr Bell's words kept repeating themselves inside Tess's head. *Was* she being selfish? She knew very well that Albert was fond of Gran – more than fond – and she believed he had suggested marriage, albeit tentatively. As she helped around the farm she pondered on her own behaviour and came to the sad conclusion that she had indeed thought only of herself and never of Gran. Oh, she had grown accustomed to Gran and Albert's going to the theatre or cinema together, taking coach trips down to the coast, even attending occasional tea dances, but she had always behaved, she realised now, as though she and Gran should need no company other than their own. She had not exactly excluded Albert from the pet shop – she could scarcely do so since he had put a fair amount of money into the venture – but she had always made it plain that he was there more or less on sufferance.

This thought came to her whilst she was collecting eggs and she was astonished to feel her cheeks grow hot. How could she have behaved so badly? It had simply never occurred to her that one day *she* might be the little bird who flew the nest, leaving Gran to grow old alone. As soon as she got home she must put her arms round Gran and give her a big hug, admit that she had been both selfish and thoughtless and tell her that she must make Albert Payne the happiest man on earth by agreeing to marry him.

368

Not unnaturally, this made Tess think of her own situation. Snowy had had one of the many horrible fevers to which the men were prone when on jungle patrol, and as a result was being repatriated a month or so earlier than he had expected. Before he left England he had given her a locket in the shape of a heart with a small photograph of himself inside. Subsequently he had sent her photographs of himself in his tropical kit, sometimes with other soldiers, sometimes alone, but always looking so different from the little photograph in the locket that she thought she would scarcely have known him. When she had commented on this one day to Albert, he had said that Snowy had gone out to Malaya a boy and would be coming home a man, and now, faced with the truth about her own behaviour, Tess realised that Snowy was not the only one. She too had changed, from a girl to a young woman, and a young woman who was still uncertain of her own feelings – except that she was not in love with Snowy, had never been, would never be. Her feelings about Jonty, however, were muddled. Snowy had been very physical, embarrassingly so to the young Tess, but Jonty had never kissed her, save in the most brotherly fashion. She supposed that he must love Pamela Davies, though she had never seen them exchange more than the most casual of greetings or farewells. But who could fail to love Pamela, with her glowing skin, glorious gleaming hair and neat figure?

So it's no use imagining that Jonty will ever look at you twice, Tess Williams, she told herself. You made your bed long ago when Jonty asked you to come to the farm in your school holidays. If you'd encouraged him then . . . but you didn't. You thought Snowy was the be-all and end-all, and by the time you realised you did have feelings for Jonty it was too late. Pamela had snared him.

By this time, Tess had finished collecting eggs from the nesting boxes and was about to comb the hedgerows and ditches for the hens which stubbornly insisted on laying astray. As she searched, she reflected ruefully that her time here was now very limited. The next day everyone would be engaged on matters pertaining to the ruby wedding party and the day after that would be the last of what would probably, almost certainly, be her final visit to the farm.

There had been no mention of a wedding between Pamela and Jonty, which was a little strange since farmers, Tess knew, liked to marry in the winter when there was little doing on the land. She had been careful never to intrude when the pair were talking, so had no idea what plans might have been made, but now she hurried back to the farmhouse. Jonty was sitting at the table peeling potatoes, so she washed her hands over the sink and outlined her plans as she did so. 'There's an early train I can catch the day after tomorrow, or the next day, which would get me into Liverpool before dark,' she told him, smiling brightly. 'Will you be able to drive me to the station? Your mum says I'm to take a dozen eggs, a pound of butter and a bacon joint for Gran, so if you could help me to get everything on to the train that would be grand.' She turned from the sink, reaching for the roller towel on the back of the door and saw Jonty's eyes widen.

'Help you to get on to the train?' he said. 'I'm coming with you, girl! I've already phoned your gran asking her to get me a bed just for a couple of nights, but all the hotels are full because of Christmas, so she says I can have a shakedown on your living-room floor. There are presents which I hope to buy in Liverpool since I've been unable to find them in Norwich.' He pulled a comical face. 'Don't say you can't be doing with a visitor so close to the holiday. After all, us Bells put up with you for a lot longer than that!'

Tess stared. 'But . . . but . . .' she stammered. 'But Jonty, you're needed here! I'd love you to come back with me, of course, but . . .'

'But me no buts,' Jonty said breezily, pushing past her to run water into the pan of peeled potatoes. 'I've made it all right with everyone so you needn't worry. Any more objections? Anything left undone that I could help you with?'

'Well, I was going to decorate the kitchen and parlour with those paper chains we made when we were kids. They're up in the attic along with the sparkly things and the tinsel you always put on the tree . . .' she cast him a twinkling glance, 'when you've pinched one from the plantation t'other side o' fen,' she concluded in her best Norfolk accent.

'We'll decorate the place the day after tomorrow, then,' Jonty said. 'Don't be such a perishin' fusspot! Leave everything to me the same as you always do.'

Tess tipped the potato peelings into the big black pot already half full of chopped cabbage leaves, apple peel and other waste. It would be cooked until it was just a mush, then thickened with poultry meal and fed to the hens which clucked constantly around the yard.

'Well?' Jonty said. 'Haven't I been efficient? All you'll have left to do is pack your case, say your goodbyes, and get into the car . . .'

'And explain to Pamela how it comes about that I'm stealing her beloved and ruining her Christmas,' Tess pointed out. 'She'll be mad as fire, and probably want to stick a knife in my ribs.'

'Her beloved? Whatever makes you think that?' Jonty asked. He sounded disproportionately astonished. 'She's a damned good friend, my girl, but that's all there is to it.'

Tess goggled. 'But – but you wrote that you'd got a new girlfriend! And she comes here so often . . . She's going to give your mother a helping hand to clear up after the party . . .'

Jonty grinned. 'Oh, that. We changed our minds,' he said.

'Changed your minds? But . . .' Tess said stubbornly, though her heart was singing. She was pretty sure Jonty did not love her, but it was like a bright light on a dark day to know that he did not love Pamela either.

Jonty heaved a sigh. 'To be honest, we said it to make one of the doctors at the hospital jealous,' he said. 'He'd been dating Pamela for some while but then he met another girl and began to go out with her. He was only here on some sort of specialist course and has now gone back to his hospital in London, but Pamela means to follow him there in the New Year and hopes that their affair – if you could call it that – will rekindle. I don't think it will myself, but maybe I'm wrong.'

'Ye-es, but that doesn't explain your part in it,' Tess said doubtfully. 'Why did Pamela choose you to be her – her pretend boyfriend?'

Jonty shrugged. 'I dunno; it just seemed like a good idea at the time,' he said. 'Pam and I have always been

372

friends, and of course when you stopped coming to the farm I suppose I was at a bit of a loose end. So when Pamela asked me to help her out the obvious thing to do was to pretend that she was planning to marry me.'

Tess giggled. She felt quite faint with relief. 'Just keep your fingers crossed she doesn't expect you to go through with it,' she observed. 'The feller – the doctor, I mean – might get nasty.'

'I don't imagine he will, since Pamela's been writing to him and it seems he's written back.'

'And you aren't involved in any way, except as some sort of stalking horse?' Tess asked incredulously.

Jonty stood up. 'Oh, go on with you! That's right, and now let's change the subject, because I'm tired of it. Will you come up to the attic and help me get the decorations down?'

On the day following the ruby wedding celebrations Tess and Jonty got up early, meaning to decorate the kitchen and parlour as well as the sizeable tree which one of the farm hands had brought in the previous day. As they ate their breakfast they discussed the party, which had been a great success. There had been dancing in the big barn, and a wonderful supper, to which most of the guests had contributed, had been served in the farm's enormous kitchen. It had been after midnight before the last guests left and now Jonty and Tess eyed each other blearily across their breakfast porridge. 'Last day before you go home,' Jonty said miserably, then brightened. 'But since I'm coming with you – just to do some extra special Christmas shopping, you know – we don't need to say cheerio just yet. What do you want to do today?'

Tess began to reply that they ought to start putting the Christmas decorations up, but Mrs Bell cut across her words. She had been eating a round of toast, but now she shook a reproving head at her son. 'Putting up them paper chains you made when you was kids won't take more'n half an hour or so, 'cos we leave the drawing pins in the picture rails year after year,' she said. 'I reckon Tess deserves a day off . . .' she beamed at Tess, 'because I don't know how we could have managed the party without her.'

'Oh, Tess enjoys farm work . . .' Jonty was beginning when he caught his mother's disapproving eye and hastily changed what he had been about to say. 'But on the other hand, there's the big Christmas market at King's Lynn; why don't we go along to that? There's every sort of stall you can imagine, including lots of folk selling hot food, and if we wait until the market's beginning to close prices will drop and we can get real bargains.' He grinned at Tess. 'Would you like that, queen?' he said in a very passable imitation of the Scouse accent.

'I'd love it,' Tess said eagerly. She could think of nothing she would like more than to spend her last day at the farm in Jonty's company. She did not think he loved her, was not at all sure that what she felt for him was love, but now that he had admitted Pamela Davies was just a friend you never knew. He might suddenly realise that Tess was the only girl for him . . . Tess's toes curled at the mere thought. Across the table, their eyes met, but instead of lighting with love Jonty's merely looked questioning.

'You're sure? You really would enjoy a drive over to King's Lynn? We could have a meal at the Duke's Head, if you don't fancy eating the stuff from the stalls.'

374

'I *do* fancy it,' Tess said. 'Oh, Jonty, there's nothing I'd like more. Do you know, in all the time I've spent in Norfolk no one's ever suggested a visit to the market in King's Lynn. I've been to the Norwich one countless times, and very good it is too, but they say King's Lynn is even better.' She finished the last of her porridge, drained her tea and jumped up. 'Good thing we didn't lie in, despite getting to bed so late. Let's start hanging the paper chains at once; we'll decorate the tree when we get home this evening.' She turned anxiously to Mrs Bell. 'Are you sure you can manage without us?'

Mrs Bell tutted. 'Think I'm made of icing sugar, my woman?' she asked derisively. 'You go off and enjoy yourselves, the pair of you.' She smiled understandingly at Tess. 'You *both* deserve a day off, Jonty an' all.'

Tess and Jonty arrived back in Heyworth Street to discover that all the plans which Gran and Albert had made for the holiday were about to come to nought. When they reached the pet shop at three in the afternoon they found it was shut, a most unusual state of affairs when only three days remained before Christmas Day. Frowning, Tess peered through the large glass window, but though the lights were on the closed sign was up, and when she tried the door it was firmly locked. She swung round and stared at Jonty. 'I don't understand it; we never close this early and it's not as though we didn't have plenty of help,' she said. 'Gran said that although Janine is nervous of the animals she's quite happy to take the money and so on, provided she doesn't have to deal with the stock. Apparently she's a really good salesperson . . . but you know all that. Goodness, I hope Gran's in the flat . . .'

375

Jonty grinned. 'I hope she's not,' he said. 'It would be nice to have you all to myself for a change.'

Tess felt her cheeks warm. 'You've had me all to yourself for ages,' she pointed out. 'Both at the farm and in the train . . .'

'Pooh! You know very well there's always someone around at the farm, and the carriage was so packed that folk were standing all along the corridor. And you refused to sit on my knee, though I thought it might be rather fun.'

Tess glared at him, but knew her lips were twitching. 'As if I would sit on your knee in front of dozens of people,' she said. 'But let's get up to the flat and see if Gran can tell us what's happening.'

Tess tried the door and found it locked, so she produced her own key and let them in. They climbed the stairs briskly, but when they reached the top the flat was cold; the fire had either not been lit or had gone out, and of course there was no sign of Gran. Jonty looked round rather disparagingly, then dumped both the suitcases he was hefting down and turned to his companion. 'Should I carry my baggage through to the living room? And then I think we ought to go round to Mr Payne's place, see if he can throw any light on the mystery.'

'I wouldn't call it a mystery, exactly—' Tess was beginning, but was interrupted.

'Not a mystery? When Mrs Williams and Mr Payne both knew which train we'd be catching? It's a good job I had a few bob in my pocket – apart from my money for presents, I mean – because I bet you couldn't have forked out for a taxi, and the stuff my mum packed for us to give Mrs Williams weighs a perishin' ton.'

'Well, yes, I suppose it is a bit of a mystery,' Tess admitted. 'But before we go rushing off to Albert's place I think we ought to light the fire and see if there's a note anywhere.'

'Right; I'll do the fire whilst you look for a note,' Jonty said, and presently, with the fire banked down, the suit-cases stowed away and no note discovered, they set off for the tobacconist's shop. They reached it only to find Albert missing and Mr Clarke sitting on the tall stool behind the counter reading a copy of the *Echo*. He looked up as the two burst in.

'Hello, Tess. Any news?' he asked. Tess was beginning to say that this was the very question she was about to ask him when Jonty spoke over her.

'We've only just arrived back from Norfolk and of course we went straight to the pet shop only to find it locked and barred, so to speak,' he said. 'So I guess Janine's wait is over. Is everyone at the hospital?'

'The baby!' Tess shrieked. 'Oh, how could I have forgotten? But it's not due until January; the end of January they thought at the clinic. Does this mean something's gone wrong?'

'I don't think so,' Mr Clarke said, but Tess thought he sounded rather uneasy. 'Albert told me that the pains – I mean the contractions – started late last night.' He looked from one face to the other. 'It's been a while since me and the missus had our family, but babies is always contrary things; they come when they're ready, not when they're expected. You go off to the maternity hospital; they'll tell you what's what there.'

When they reached the hospital it was to find it decked with holly, paper chains and small Christmas trees. 'As

377

though the babies cared,' Jonty whispered, but Tess gave him a reproving glance as a nurse took them along to a waiting room and said that no doubt Mrs Williams and Mr Payne, upon hearing of the arrival of their guests, would hurry along to tell them how things stood, and she was soon proved right. Tess was idly leafing through a magazine and Jonty was sitting, head tilted back, watching through a tiny window the slow descent of snowflakes, grey against the white-clouded sky, when the door of the waiting room opened and Edie rushed in. Tess ran across the room and gave her a hug. 'The baby's come, hasn't it?' she said excitedly. 'Oh, Gran, you're like the Cheshire cat, you're one enormous smile from ear to ear. What did she have? Can we see it? Where's Albert . . . the proud grandfather, I mean?'

'It's a dear little boy. He's very tiny, because he's premature I suppose, and Sister says we can visit him in the nursery as long as one of the nurses comes with us, but we can't take him out for a couple of days. Albert's there now, positively bursting with pride. He and Janine had already discussed names and if it was a boy Janine wanted to call him Philip, because she says she's always liked that name. Only this being Liverpool he'll get called Philly, I expect.'

'And very nice too,' Jonty said approvingly, and Gran blinked and held out her hands to him. 'Jonty! My dear boy, I had no idea you were here; you must have thought me dreadfully rude, but I'm afraid in all the excitement I quite forgot that you were coming to stay for a couple of days. But now it's time we all went home. Albert's going to buy celebratory fish and chips for everyone and I've baked enough mince pies to supply an army, so if I make a custard we can have them as a pudding.'

'Lovely,' Tess said. 'Jonty's mum has sent a big bag full of goodies, so we look like having an excellent Christmas . . .' The door shot open again at this point and Albert, beaming, came into the room. Tess was surprised when he gave her a kiss before grabbing Jonty's hand and giving it a hearty shake.

'Nice to see you again, young man,' he said. 'How long are you staying? I take it it won't be over Christmas – we'd love to have you, of course, but I expect your mam would have a thing or two to say if you announced you weren't going home.'

'You're right there; she'd be terribly hurt and upset,' Jonty said regretfully. 'I'd love to stay, of course, but it's impossible.' He shot a quick glance at Tess. 'Besides, I know Tess has plans of her own. I gather Snowy will be home any day, and the saying *two's company, three's a crowd* is very true. Still, I reckon I'll hang on until Christmas Eve, and go back then. I've some presents to buy, so if you can put up with me for a couple of days I'd be grateful.'

'Of course we can,' Edie and Albert said in chorus, then broke into laughter. 'Sorry, sorry,' Albert said. 'I expect you've guessed that you can have Janine's room whilst she's in hospital, so no need for a shakedown on Edie's floor.'

Jonty and Tess, hand in hand, were wandering through Paddy's Market, looking for some stocking fillers for Elsie and Mitch, when Jonty grabbed Tess's arm. 'Who's the fillum star?' he hissed. 'Eh, she's a looker and no mistake.'

He pointed, and Tess stared at the young woman coming towards them. Her gleaming gold hair was cut and curled into a fashionable poodle style and she wore high-heeled shoes and a scarlet sling-back coat with enormous mother-of-pearl buttons, whilst around her neck was a blue chiffon scarf which exactly matched her eyes.

Tess recognised her at once, but having no desire for a confrontation she said airily: 'I dunno. Do you think Elsie would like a monkey on a stick? Or a cardigan? Only when I was small I hated getting clothes, and Gran's already bought her the prettiest dress, so—'

She was interrupted. 'Well, if it isn't little Tess Williams! Abandoned them animals to fend for themselves, have you? I'm home for Christmas, I am. And who's this?'

'Oh, hello,' Tess said reluctantly. She thought privately that Marilyn looked like a high-class call girl with so many bright colours upon her person, but she certainly drew the eye. Whilst the other girl was busily staring Tess up and down, Tess, in her turn, was staring at Marilyn's bright blue patent leather shoes, long pointed nails dripping with scarlet varnish, and a week's wages' worth of make-up. But fortunately she remembered it was rude to stare, dragged her eyes away from the glittering image before her and answered the question she had been asked. 'Sorry, Marilyn; I forgot you didn't know Jonty. This is Jonathan Bell, who's staying with us for a few days.'

'How do you do?' Marilyn said, but she spoke perfunctorily. She turned back to Tess. 'I've heard a rumour that Snowy's about due home. Well, it was more than a rumour; he wrote that he'd been in hospital so might be back in time for Christmas after all.'

Tess felt a flush of annoyance rise in her cheeks. 'He *wrote* to you?'

'Yes; anything wrong with that?' Marilyn said belligerently. 'You aren't the only person Snowy writes to, you know!'

'Then if you've been corresponding you'll know as much as I do,' Tess said. 'Look, Jonty and I have a lot of shopping to do . . .'

'It don't matter then, don't trouble yourself,' Marilyn said rudely. 'I'll go round and see if his mam knows a date . . .'

'Oh? Then why ask me what Snowy's up to when you can ask his mam?' Tess said rather waspishly.

Marilyn pouted. 'Oh, I dunno; I remember when I lived in Everton he was quite kind to you.'

'Quite kind!' Tess felt her cheeks grow hot, but did her best to keep her voice steady. 'He was my boyfriend, you mean,' she said. 'Still is, for that matter.' She turned a falsely sweet smile on the older girl. 'Perhaps you didn't know that Snowy and I came to an understanding before he left?'

Marilyn gave an affected little laugh. 'Poor old Snowy! So does that mean you've still got your eye on him?'

Tess ground her teeth. It was useless to hope that Marilyn might have changed. She was just the same spiteful, selfish, single-minded girl she had been in the old days, but nevertheless Tess gave her her sweetest smile. 'I've not seen Snowy for two years, but we write every week,' she said calmly. 'If he's been writing to you, I'm sure when he does come home he'll look you up . . . only by then, of course, you'll be back in London. It was London you went to all those years ago, wasn't it?'

381

'That's right . . .' Marilyn was beginning when a hand dropped on her shoulder. It belonged to a tall, grey-haired man with a neat little Hitler moustache and what appeared to be a very heavy basket in the other hand. 'Whatever are you doin', Marilyn Thomas? I've been huntin' for you all over,' he said in a sharp cockney accent. He glanced at Tess and Jonty, then gave an apologetic smile. 'Ah, old pals, I see! I might have guessed me best girl would forget all about me. But we've gotta train to catch . . .'

He was taking Marilyn's hand and tucking it into his arm as he spoke, but Marilyn pulled free and turned back to Tess. 'I'll be in Liverpool for a week; tell Snowy,' she hissed. 'I'd – I'd like to see him again.' Suddenly the big blue eyes were pleading. 'You'll tell him? We're still at the corner shop . . . you won't forget?'

Tess opened her mouth to reply but she had scarcely got two words out when Marilyn's escort gave an exclamation of annoyance and towed Marilyn away from them. 'Sorry to break up the party,' he called over his shoulder, 'but we're off to visit Marilyn's family on the Wirral. Nice to have met . . .' The rest of the sentence was lost as the pair dived across the road, heading for Central station.

Jonty glanced curiously at Tess. 'Who *is* she?' he demanded rather petulantly. 'Oh, I know her name's Marilyn Thomas, but who is she?'

Tess smiled. 'She was Snowy's girlfriend when we were kids in school,' she explained. 'But she dropped him because she thought he was two-timing her with me.' She giggled. 'Imagine, Jonty! I was a scruffy kid, no more than thirteen or so, and Miss Perfect was jealous!

She didn't like me anyway, because I was a lot younger and smarter than she was, and she held it against me for years. And now let's forget all about her and get on with our shopping.'

Snowy sat in the train on Christmas Eve and gazed out through the rain-flecked window. He thought he had never seen country so green and beautiful, though he guessed that probably there were few on the train who felt as he did. He had travelled by troop ship and army lorry to the depot where he had been given a rail warrant and become a civilian once more, and now he was on his way home, not just home to good old Blighty, but home to the particular part of it where he had been born and brought up. The man next to him was also a returning soldier and presently he dug an elbow into Snowy's ribs. 'Ain't it just grand to see rain drippin' off the trees?' he said as the train emerged from a tunnel and began to pick up speed through densely wooded country. 'I reckon you've been in Malaya, same as me. Am I right?'

Snowy nodded ruefully. 'The tan's a dead giveaway,' he remarked. 'And I still can't get used to long trousers after years of jungle fatigues.' He ran a finger around the rather too tight collar which had fitted him at twenty-one, but was not so good at twenty-three. 'And this perishin' shirt is a deal too small round the neck.'

'Aye, but it's free,' the man observed. Snowy grinned at him and the other grinned back, a gleam of white teeth in his deeply tanned face. 'You goin' all the way to Lime Street?'

'That's right,' Snowy said. 'I've not told a soul when I'll be back because I wanted it to be a surprise.' He glanced up at his kitbag lying on the string rack above his head. 'I've got presents for everyone in there – the sort of thing you get in the bazaar – but right now I'd swap the lot for a drink. Is there a buffet car on the train? If so we might go along and get ourselves a beer.'

The other man shook his head. 'No buffet car. I walked along the platform checking before I got aboard,' he said. 'But this perishin' train stops at every little station; next time one of us can nip down and buy a bevvy while the other keeps our seats.' He grinned again, a trifle self-consciously. 'Only it'll have to be you what gets the beer because of me leg.' He pointed, and for the first time Snowy realised that his new friend's left leg was encased in plaster to the knee.

'Suits me,' Snowy said just as the engine announced its approach with a shrill whistle and the train drew up alongside a small country platform. He stood up, then pointed at the plaster cast. 'Where did you get that lot then?'

'I'd like to say I got it on jungle patrol – I probably shall say that when I get back to me girlfriend's anxious embrace – but in fact I were hospitalised with a bout of jungle fever, and on my way to the canteen one day I slipped at the head of a flight of stairs, took 'em in one graceful swoop and ended up wi' this.' He tapped the cast just as the train ground to a stop, a porter began shouting the name of the station, and Snowy departed on his mission.

During the rest of the journey, Snowy and his new friend, Tappy Arbuthnot, told each other their life histories. Tappy described his girl in glowing terms and then asked, 'Well, what's your girl like? Bet she's a corker!'

384

Snowy smiled and nodded. 'Blonde, curvy . . .' He stopped short, shocked at himself, but fortunately Tappy simply nodded understandingly.

Having finished the beer and sympathised with Tappy over his fears that his glamorous girlfriend might have given him the go-by in his absence, Snowy leaned back in his seat and began to think seriously of his home-coming. His parents would be over the moon, his friends would greet him raucously and drag him over to the nearest pub for a celebratory drink, and Tess, he supposed, would start talking about engagement rings and marriage plans. That would please his parents, who thought her a real little lady, intelligent, bright and humorous. But hard though he might try to dismiss Marilyn from his mind she would keep pushing in, all blonde curls, enticing bosom and pink and white complexion. Not a bit like Tess, who was skinny, sallow and far too ladylike to leap into his arms and take him home to bed, he thought, horrified, but also thrilled. In his mind his hand plunged down the front of Marilyn's showy white blouse and felt the satisfying weight of her rounded, pink-tipped breast in his palm. The slow burn in his stomach made him gasp with remembered pleasure – and pleasure anticipated. He realised, ruefully, that he was haunted by a deep inner conviction that he and Marilyn were somehow linked, as a couple. It was madness, of course. She had written to him, and though the letters were not illiterate, exactly, they did not compare with Tess's lively epistles. Yet he kept each one, and threw Tess's missives away once they were answered. His mother referred to Marilyn as 'that little blonde shop girl' and made no secret of the fact that she was glad Snowy's fancy for her had not stood the test of time, that their schoolday friendship had been just that, something unfortunate which he had 'got over', as though it had been a bad head cold or an attack of measles.

The train jerked to a stop once more and Tappy got to his feet and let down the window. The rain had become first sleet and now snow, and the unheated train felt freezing to men newly returned from the tropics. Snowy jerked Tappy's elbow. 'Where are we?' he said. 'This isn't a station, judging by what I can see of it. Shove over, Tappy, and let the dog see the rabbit.'

He had barely stopped speaking when a porter came along the corridor, announcing that due to unforeseen circumstances the train would have to pause for a while and would therefore be late in arriving at its ultimate destination, Liverpool Lime Street.

Tappy and Snowy groaned in unison, put up the window and returned to their seats. 'I thought it were unusually slow and awful jerky when we stopped at the last station,' Tappy said, staring out miserably at the whirling snow. 'Oh, Gawd, I wish I'd not told Angie that I'd be on this train. She'll be mad as fire, blame me for what I couldn't possibly help and very likely storm off home, leavin' me to foller like a pet dog.'

Snowy chuckled. 'You just described her as being sweet, willing and good-natured,' he said reprovingly. 'If she's all of those things then she's unlikely to throw a fit just because you're ten or fifteen minutes late.'

Tappy snorted. 'Ten or fifteen minutes late?' he said scornfully. 'More like a couple of hours. If there's something seriously wrong with the engine they'll have to send for another and that can take hours, as I know. It's all very well for you, you didn't tell anyone you were coming. Must be the wisdom of the ancient . . . So why *are* you older than me?'

'Deferred,' Snowy said briefly. He had learned not to say 'deferred whilst taking my degree', because if he did so the fellers were apt to think him conceited.

But Tappy merely nodded. 'Oh well, at least I gorrit over early,' he observed. 'I guess the pair of us will be searchin' for a job, but I'm not too worried. When I joined I was pretty wet behind the lug'oles. I couldn't drive, hadn't read a book since I left school and didn't know a spark plug from a dipstick, but now I'm a fully trained motor mechanic, and I reckon there'll always be a place for one of them, don't you think?'

Snowy agreed, and the rest of the journey was enlivened by a discussion of the various jobs which might or might not be on offer to a motor mechanic who could also drive any vehicle from the largest to the smallest. But as they neared their destination they both fell silent and Snowy realised, with a stab of dismay, that when he thought about Tess, a teaching post, marriage and, later, children, the picture of Tess had become so faint that it was almost unrecognisable. The fact that he had thought Lyana was like her was a case in point. At the very beginning of their friendship, he recalled now, he had been attracted by her resemblance to Tess; but was she *really* like Tess or was it just his imagination? He knew their characters were totally dissimilar . . . but then he realised he could not even say that. He had been seeing Lyana for a few weeks and he had not seen Tess for two years. Why should he assume that she had not changed when he was well aware of the changes in himself? He told himself that he was looking forward to seeing Tess again and was just trying to remember which of the presents carefully packed away in his kit bag were for her when his companion spoke. 'Tell you what, mate, I'm not sure I want to get hitched to young Angie after all. Wish I were as certain she were the only girl for me as you are about your Tess. But Angie's been writing to me ever since I was sent out to Malaya. She's not been with another feller . . .'

'How do you know? You've only got her word for it,' Snowy said, but Tappy shook his head.

'That horse won't run,' he said half regretfully. 'She's been ever so good to my old mam, has Angie. Visiting once a week, sometimes more, givin' the old gal some nice fruit or a few chocolates every so often, takin' her shoppin' or to the flicks . . .' He grinned ruefully. 'Me mam thinks a great deal of Angie; she'd go mad if I told her I'd changed my mind.'

Snowy had a brief vision of his own mother's face if he presented her with Marilyn as a prospective daughter-in-law. To be sure the girl was a beauty, but Snowy could not imagine either of his parents regarding his liaison with a shop girl, no matter how beautiful, with complaisance. He opened his mouth to share his thoughts with Tappy, then closed it again. Whatever was he thinking of? He had no intention of changing his plans, of substituting Marilyn for Tess. Snowy sighed, then got to his feet as the train drew in at a brightly lit station and a porter hurried along the train, opening doors. They were at Lime Street station at last. The two young men gathered their possessions and climbed down on to the platform. They fought their way across the platform, which was

388

crowded with would-be passengers as well as those descending from the train, handed their tickets in at the barrier, then stood their kit bags down and shook hands. 'Well, it looks like we made it . . .' Snowy said.

'Of course, if you really beg me, I suppose I could put off returning to Norfolk until after Christmas,' Jonty had said thoughtfully earlier that afternoon, eyeing the preparations for high tea which Edie and Tess had just completed. 'Still, as I said, two's company and three's a crowd, so I'd best say goodbye, Mrs Williams, and thanks for your generous hospitality over the past couple of days.'

'Thank you – and your parents – for all the good things which have made my Christmas catering so much easier,' Edie had said. She had pinched Jonty's cheek. 'People change; you've grown up a lot in the last few years, young man. Let's not say goodbye, however, but *au revoir*.' She had glanced shrewdly from Tess's determined smile to Jonty's bland expression. 'Something tells me we'll be seeing more of you in the New Year, and very welcome you'll be. After all, you've scarcely seen Janine or the baby, and since Janine says she wants you and Tess to be godparents you'll have to come back for the christening, if nothing else.'

'I say, that's a real honour. I've never been a godparent before,' Jonty said. He turned to Tess. 'Did you hear that, my woman? We're going to be godparents.'

Tess heaved a sigh, 'Yes, I know; Gran told me earlier,' she said. 'Look, we've already missed two trains and if you're to catch the next one we need to get a move on. Have you got everything? Right, then off we go.'

'I really ought to go round to Mr Payne's and thank him again . . .' Jonty began, but at this Tess's patience snapped.

'You've said you're grateful a dozen times to my knowledge,' she said crossly. 'Do get a move on, Jonty. If you miss this train you won't be home till midnight. And I shan't wait with you, so there.'

Heyworth Street was crowded, for there were always people who left everything until the last minute – apparently Jonty was one of them – and at three o'clock on Christmas Eve prices tended to drop, so shoppers were many. Tess was carrying Jonty's lightest bag whilst he struggled along with his suitcase, and she reflected sourly that though she was now certain she loved Jonty she was more and more sure that he did not love her. Earlier, she had led him by stalls sporting bunches of mistletoe; she had turned up her face hopefully when he went off to sleep at the tobacconist's, thinking he was sure to give her a goodnight kiss; she had snuggled up to him in the cinema, but apart from looking a little red around the gills he had not seemed to notice such overtures.

They reached the station. A train was just pulling in and the porter was shouting. 'That'll be yours, Jonty,' Tess said, 'so we'd best say our goodbyes now. She moved closer to him, whereupon Jonty took a step backwards.

'Tess, I – I've been meaning to ask you . . .' he began, but Tess had had enough of shilly-shallying. She snatched his big case away from him and slammed it down on the platform. Then she flung both her arms round him and cuddled her cheek into the hollow of his neck. Jonty made an inarticulate sound and suddenly he was

390

clutching and kissing her, mumbling into her ear that he loved her more than anyone else he had known in all of his life. Then he pulled back from her a little. 'I've longed and longed to do that, oh, for weeks . . . months . . . *years*!' he said. 'But I'm an awkward sort of chap, wouldn't know a fancy speech if it bit me on the nose. And that Snowy, he's smooth as ice and handsome as a film star. Oh, Tess, can you possibly love me as much as you love him?'

Tess threw her arms about him again, but just then the engine's whistle sounded and she bundled Jonty's various possessions on to the train. 'As much? I love you far more; I don't believe I ever did love Snowy,' she assured him just as the porter came along the train, slamming the doors and warning the passengers to stand clear. Tess held on to the nearest door handle and pushed Jonty aboard. The porter waved his green flag, the engine whistled . . . and Jonty grabbed Tess round the waist and pulled her into the carriage just as the train began to move, whilst the porter yelled at them and other passengers stared.

Inside the train, Jonty plonked her down in a vacant seat, took the one beside her and gripped her hands tightly. 'I'm not letting you go back to Liverpool until you're wearing my ring on your finger,' he announced, much to the interest of the other people in the compartment. 'Oh, Tess, my love, will you – can you bear to marry a farmer, and leave your pet shop, and your gran, and all your friends behind?'

'Oh, hush, everyone's listening,' Tess whispered. 'And I shall love being a farmer's wife, provided you're the farmer in question.'

Jonty leaned back in his seat and blew out his cheeks

in a relieved whistle. 'Phew! Then that's settled,' he said. But Tess had jumped to her feet and was staring out at the passing scene.

'Jonty, the train's moving and no one knows where I am, not Gran or Albert, not even Mitch. Whatever will they think? Oh, God, and what about Snowy? He thinks we're still together. How on earth can I explain, admit that it was all a horrible misunderstanding?'

'Don't care; don't matter,' said Jonty, his face wreathed in a blissful smile. 'If they don't guess then we'll ring them the first time we have to change. Oh, darling Tess, you're going to spend Christmas with me after all, and I promise you it will be a Christmas to remember!'

Snowy looked up at the clock, then hefted his kitbag. 'Well, it looks like we made it in good time for our families to buy a few extra spuds and so on, since it's only three in the afternoon,' he said. 'Have a grand day tomorrow and don't grab all the turkey for yourself. Times are pretty hard, I'm told, but I reckon just being home will make up for all this austerity we've heard about. Don't forget, you're going to come round to the pet shop on Heyworth Street and ask for me as soon as the festivities are over. We'll have a good jangle and a bevvy.'

'I shan't forget,' Tappy said. Festooned with bags and bundles they stood for a moment, watching a train come in, seeing the disembarking passengers, mostly uniformed men, all smiling, all heading for home. They were still watching, suddenly reluctant to move away, when the crowd of arrivals began to thin and would-be leavers surged towards the barrier. Tickets were clipped and folk began to climb aboard, mostly well wrapped up and armed with parcels and packages. Snowy frowned; one of the chaps looked familiar. He watched, puzzled. Had the fellow been at school with him? But he wasn't in uniform: he wore a fawn mackintosh and a cap on the back of his head; and even as he watched, Snowy realised that the man was not alone. He was with a small girl wearing a navy overcoat and carrying an umbrella, which she suddenly cast down on the platform in order to wrap both arms round the bloke's neck and kiss him passionately, indifferent to those around her.

Tess! It was Tess Williams, the girl who had waited for him for the past two years, had written to him every week, had talked of marriage! Yet here she was, wrapped in the arms of some feller . . . and then, abruptly, he recognised the other man. It was that ploughboy, Jonty or whatever his name was, and Jonty was making love to Snowy's girl right under his very nose!

'Snowy?' Tappy's voice seemed to come from a long way off. 'What's up? Ain't you comin'? I thought we could share a taxi, 'cos of all our luggage . . .'

Snowy could not wrench his eyes away from what was happening on the platform, but even as he watched, Tess – if it really was Tess – picked up the suitcase that Jonty – if it really was Jonty – had been carrying, and threw it into the train. The porter was waving his green flag, there was a great slamming of doors . . . Fascinated, Snowy continued to stare. Tess – if it was Tess – pushed Jonty – it was definitely Jonty – aboard the train, and just as the engine was about to move off, having announced its intention with a shrill whistle, Jonty appeared again, hauled Tess aboard and slammed the door. The porter shouted and began to remonstrate, but he was too late. The train was on its way with the sandy-haired young man and the dark-haired girl aboard.

'Snowy? Wharrever are you thinkin' of? Ain't you comin' out to join the taxi queue? Only if we doesn't get a move on . . .'

Snowy pulled himself together. He knew, now, that the couple embracing on the platform had indeed been Tess and Jonty, and with the knowledge came, astonishingly, wave after wave of relief. It was all right! He knew now that he had never really loved Tess, knew also that had he not seen for himself that Tess and Jonty were in love he would have been most uncomfortably situated. Tess had been true to him for two whole years and to turn round now and repudiate her love, admit to everyone that he had made a terrible mistake, would have been so difficult that his mind shied away from the very thought of it. But darling Tess and darling Jonty had made him a present of guiltlessness. Why, Tess had gone away with Jonty regardless of the fact that he, Snowy, was due to come home within the next two or three days. Nothing mattered to her but Jonty, and nothing mattered to Jonty but Tess.

'Snowy! For Gawd's sake stop staring at that train and let's gerrout of here and join the queue, else it'll be Christmas Day and you'll still be standin' here starin' into space. Don't you want to surprise your Tess? When will you give her the ring? Christmas mornin' would be nice – a sort of extra special present – but of course you'll know when's best.'

Snowy began to pick up the items he had dropped at his feet upon seeing Tess and Jonty. He shouldered his kitbag, grabbed his other packages and set off across the concourse with Tappy close beside him. 'I shan't be giving that ring to Tess,' he said, grinning at his new friend. 'I shall be giving it to my very first girlfriend, and boy won't she be surprised!'

'Hang on a minute,' Tappy said. Snowy glanced at him and saw that his eyes were rounding with astonishment. 'You've been tellin' me how you meant to marry that Tess, how you'd bought an engagement ring – a ruby surrounded by diamonds – you talked about a wedding in the spring and a honeymoon in Ireland . . . have you gone mad?'

'Nope; come to my senses, more like,' Snowy said. 'That couple on the platform, hugging and kissing and that, was Tess and an old flame of hers, Jonty Bell. Did you see 'em?'

'If you mean the gal what got on the train just as it started to move . . .' Tappy began.

'That's them. Phew, what a bit of luck my seeing them. It'll save a deal of explaining, 'cos once Tess is out of the picture no one will think me a cad if I start seeing Marilyn again.'

'You're mad,' Tappy said with conviction. 'Who is this Marilyn anyway? A local bint?'

Once, Snowy would have taken offence at this description of his love, but now he was too delighted to object. He nodded. 'That's right. Dear God, what a fool I've been, trying to convince myself that once I clapped eyes on Tess again I would forget all about Marilyn. But it was just the opposite. As soon as I saw Tess I knew that we could never be anything more than friends because I'm in love with someone else.'

They reached the end of the taxi queue and Tappy looked at his new friend with pity. 'Well, you're in for a hard ride, mate,' he said. 'I wish you joy of it. You know what women are like . . .'

Snowy grinned. 'It won't be nearly as bad as having to tell Tess what a fool I've been,' he observed, as a cab drew up beside them. 'You'll like Marilyn; she's a bit like your Angie. Wish me luck, old feller!'

It was not until they reached the point on the lane at which the farmhouse could be clearly seen that Tess hesitated, suddenly unsure. She turned to Jonty, her eyes widening at the thought of what was to come. Jonty would have stepped out up the drive without a second thought, but she caught his arm, drawing him to a halt. 'Oh, Jonty, what will your mum and dad say when they see me?' she asked anxiously. 'The last thing they expect will be an uninvited guest for Christmas, and when we have to tell them that we plan to marry they'll think we've both gone mad!'

Jonty laughed and put an arm round her shoulders. 'They won't even be a little bit surprised,' he said comfortingly. 'They've both been nudging me on to make our relationship permanent for weeks and weeks. Come on, best foot forward.'

'Oh, but . . .' Tess began, and had still not completed the sentence when Jonty threw open the back door, allowing brilliant lamplight to spill, golden as syrup, across the cobbles.

'In you go,' he said cheerfully, giving her a push when she tried to turn tail. He raised his voice. 'We're home, both of us. Since we're going to get married I thought it was only right to bring Tess back for Christmas. Is that okay?' Tess blinked in the sudden bright light, for the journey had not been a speedy one and darkness had fallen long since. She opened her mouth to explain, but wasn't allowed to begin.

'Well, what sort of time is this? We've been expecting the pair of you this past three hours,' Mrs Bell said. 'Being as tomorrow's Christmas Day there's a scrap sort of supper, but no doubt you'll be glad of a bite before you go up the wooden stair to Bedfordshire.' She crossed the room and gave Tess a kiss. 'Welcome home, my woman,' she said. 'And about time too!'

Chapter Fifteen

Edie awoke and for a moment she lay in her warm and cosy bed, wondering why she kept glancing towards the door as though expecting someone to enter. Then she remembered and sat up on her elbow to stare at the face of the alarm clock. It was Christmas Day, and though Tess would normally have come in at any moment, bearing a tray of tea and a couple of small presents, she could scarcely do so today, since she was in Norfolk at Bell Farm.

Edie lay back on her pillows, remembering. Yesterday afternoon, as dusk fell, she and Albert had sat in the kitchen of the flat above the pet shop, waiting for Tess to return from seeing Jonty off. But when the phone rang at a little past four o'clock, neither of them had been really surprised. Tess had apologised, explained, burst into tears and then had to leave the station telephone booth because the train they were about to catch was making the sort of sounds which presaged its departure. Edie had done her best to assure Tess that everything would carry on according to plan, that her absence was not entirely unexpected, and that she would await another telephone call from her when she reached Bell Farm.

She had put the phone down and begun to explain to Albert, but he had shaken his head. 'It's all right, I could hear every word, and it's what I know we've both been expecting,' he assured her. 'That child has been in love with Jonty Bell since she was just a forlorn little kid whom nobody wanted. It's taken time for her to admit her feelings and Jonty didn't help by being such a gentleman and never pressing her, but now everything will go swimmingly, just you see if it doesn't.'

And when Tess had rung from the farm, Edie had assured her that they could manage beautifully. She, Albert and Mitch would go to the pet shop as soon as it got light to clean and feed the occupants. Then they would have the quiet sort of Christmas Day they had envisaged and would do the same on Boxing Day. In the unlikely event of Snowy's turning up they would obviously have to tell him that Tess had mistaken her heart, but Edie did not think that Snowy would be much surprised. Two years was a long time, and both parties must have known that their relationship would have changed. Snowy, being older than Tess, would take it in his stride, and Edie thought he was far too attractive to be alone for long.

So now she got out of bed, grabbed her dressing gown and hurried across to the kitchen. She riddled the ash, put fresh fuel on the fire, filled the kettle and put together the makings of a tea tray. She intended to take Albert a cup of tea, for he had accepted the use of Tess's room since they would both be working at the pet shop first thing, but now, before the kettle had even boiled, the kitchen door opened and Albert wandered in, clad in dressing gown and slippers. He grinned at Edie and sat down at the table. 'You've spoiled my surprise,' he said reproachfully. 'I meant to take you a cup of tea.'

'Snap!' Edie said with a giggle. 'Oh well, at least I managed to get the kettle on before you arrived. It won't be two ticks. Do we exchange presents now, or is that for later?'

'Now,' Albert said promptly, producing a small gaily wrapped box from his dressing gown pocket. Then he looked at Edie and grinned. 'Hair uncombed, teeth unbrushed, still in your nightie and dressing gown, to say nothing of those terrible old slippers,' he remarked, pushing the box back into his pocket. 'I think we'll put off exchanging presents after all.' A thought seemed to occur to him. 'Can you imagine what Janine would say if she could see us now? There's no way on earth she would accept that we spent the night in our own beds! I don't claim to be a Lothario but I do like to do things in their proper order. I'm old-fashioned enough to believe that marriage comes before bed, and—'

'All right, all right,' Edie said, giggling. 'If I say we're just good friends and we don't mention you spending the night in my granddaughter's bed then perhaps we'll be forgiven for our forward behaviour. Ah, the kettle's boiled. I'll make the tea.'

On Christmas Day Tess and Jonty had a long talk regarding the future of the pet shop. Mitch was still young, but Tess was sure that he and Gran between them, with Albert hovering and Janine apparently keen to find work, could keep the shop running smoothly without Tess herself. She meant to return to Liverpool for a confab about staffing levels, but was pretty sure that she would not need to employ anyone other than family and Mitch. Gran could deal with ordering and keeping the books, and would telephone Tess if any snags occurred.

Tess felt a twinge of sadness at the thought of cutting her connnection with the shop, but knew that she could not be in two places at once, and every part of her longed to be with Jonty. Going to university, expanding the pet shop, watching over Mitch and Elsie, even being with Gran, all faded into insignificance beside the love she felt for her 'ploughboy'.

Edie and Albert had a quiet Christmas Day, a day as near perfect as any Edie could remember. They drank their tea, then parted to get dressed and ready for the day ahead. They had a light breakfast because they intended to have a large dinner, and as soon as the last slice of toast was eaten they went down to the pet shop, where Mitch, who had been given his own key when the arrival of Janine's baby had thrown everything into disarray, was already cleaning cages.

By ten o'clock they were back in the flat preparing their Christmas dinner, and at three in the afternoon, well fed and content, they listened to the King's speech before going to the hospital to visit Janine and her little boy. Janine seemed in an oddly softened mood, was far more polite to Edie than usual, but saw them off with the reminder that she would be home in three or four days. 'I suppose you've kept Dad from feeling lonely,' she said to Edie, when Albert had gone to visit a friend in another ward. 'When's Tess coming back? Did she say?'

Edie shook her head. 'No, she didn't mention it, but we can manage very well without her, you know. The place runs like clockwork and in fact we've very little stock in since we had an excellent Christmas.' She looked quizzically at the younger woman. 'In the old days, January, February and March were always called the hungry months, when belts were tightened and people stayed in their houses and waited for spring. But you'll have your little boy to keep you busy.'

'And Dad, of course,' Janine cut in. 'He and I are learning to build a life for ourselves. I want a little job once we're settled, but for now I shall just be like every other housewife, cooking, cleaning and making do.'

Edie read this as a *keep off the grass* message, but simply smiled and said that she hoped Janine's aversion to the smell of tobacco would have vanished along with her pregnancy. 'You'll want to give your dad a hand, no doubt,' she said. 'And as for making a new life . . .'

But here Albert arrived back, gave his daughter a kiss on the brow and stroked his grandson's cheek gently, then spoke to Edie. 'It's time we were off,' he said briskly. He turned back to Janine. 'Do you know, we've not even opened our Christmas presents yet? And I've got quite a surprise for Edie here.'

He would have turned away from the bed but Janine clutched his arm. 'Don't go doin' anythin' I wouldn't like, Dad,' she said urgently. 'Remember, I don't know nothin' about babies; I'm goin' to need all the help I can get. Lookin' after babies is a two-man job . . .'

'One man and one woman, you mean,' Albert said airily. 'And *not* one mother and one grandfather. And now we must be going, because we're having Mitch and Elsie round for tea.'

Mitch and Elsie, scrubbed and brushed and in their

best clothes, helped in the preparation of a huge high tea and showed off their presents. Albert and Edie saw them home at eight o'clock and reminded them that they were all to go to the pantomime the following day. Then they returned to the flat and slumped in the creaking old basket chairs on either side of the hearth. 'Phew!' Albert said. 'What a day it's been, my love. I dare say you've guessed what's in this little box.' He fished it out of his pocket and handed it to her. 'I'm not trying to tie you down, it's just the prettiest thing . . . Oh, open it, for God's sake.'

'And my gift is so mundane,' Edie said, opening the small box and revealing a pretty ring. 'Oh, Albert, it's lovely. Thank you so much! And now do open yours.'

Albert opened the tinsel wrapped parcel to reveal a thick sweater in navy blue wool. 'I made it myself, which is why I had to keep hiding my knitting whenever you came into the kitchen unexpectedly,' Edie said, but Albert was not looking at the jumper but at her.

'Edie?' he said softly. 'That little ring is because I wanted a new way of asking you to marry me. If you slip that ring on your wedding finger it will save you having to say "yes, Albert", because you seem rather shy of doing that. But I'm sick and tired of your dithering. This, may I remind you, is not the first time I've asked. I want an answer and I want it now. And it had better be . . .'

Edie began to say that she could not possibly give him an answer when her mind was so full of other things, but then she raised her eyes to his and she saw his face as though for the first time, eyes alight with hope, mouth already curling into a smile. And Edie admitted at last what she had always known: that he was a good man, kind, supportive and totally honest; and in that moment she also knew that only a fool would turn away from him, turn him down. She opened her mouth to speak but Albert was smiling, his arms held out. He had read her answer, she realised, in her expression, and as she slipped the ring on her finger she gave a tremulous smile.

'Oh, what will Janine say?' she asked. 'She won't be very pleased, you know.'

Albert's smile was wall to wall sunshine. 'Blow Janine!' he said. 'This is *our* life, and I can't wait to start living it!'

Christmas Wishes

Katie Flynn

It is the autumn of 1945 and identical twins Joy and Gillian Lawrence are on their way home to Liverpool, having been evacuated to Devonshire five years earlier. Their mother has been killed in the blitz but the girls hope that with their beloved father's help they will be able to manage without assistance.

All goes well until there is a terrible accident and Joy loses her sight. At first she is bitter and resentful whilst Gillian is racked with guilt. However, as time passes Joy gains confidence, hopeful that her sight will return since life is not easy when you can't see the face of the boy you think you love.

Then there is a chance meeting on a train and once more the girls lives are in turmoil . . .

arrow books

A Sixpenny Christmas

Katie Flynn

As the worst storm of the century sweeps through the mountains of Snowdonia and across the Mersey, two women, Molly and Ellen, give birth to girls in a Liverpool maternity hospital.

Molly and Rhys Roberts farm sheep in Snowdonia and Ellen is married to a docker, Sam O'Mara, but despite their different backgrounds the two young women become firm friends, though Molly has a secret she can share with no one.

But despite promises Ellen's husband continues to be violent, so she throws him out and years later, when Molly is taken to hospital after an accident, Ellen and her daughter Lana are free to help out. They approach this new life with enthusiasm, unaware that they are being watched, but on the very day of Molly's release from hospital there is another terrible thunderstorm and the hidden watcher makes his move at last . . .

arrow books

ALSO AVAILABLE BY KATIE FLYNN

The Forget-Me-Not Summer

Katie Flynn

Liverpool 1936

Miranda and her mother, Arabella, live comfortably in a nice area. But when her mother tells her she can no longer afford their present lifestyle, they have a blazing row, and Miranda goes to bed angry and upset. When she wakes the next morning, however, her mother has disappeared.

She raises the alarm but everyone is baffled, and when searches fail to discover Arabella's whereabouts, Miranda is forced to live with her Aunt Vi and cousin Beth, who resent her presence and treat her badly

Miranda is miserable, but when she meets a neighbour, Steve, things begin to look up and Steve promises to help his new friend in her search, and does so until war intervenes . . .

arrow books

THE POWER OF READING

**Visit the Random House website and get connected with
information on all our books and authors**

EXTRACTS from our recently
published books and selected
backlist titles

**COMPETITIONS AND PRIZE
DRAWS** Win signed books,
audiobooks and more

AUTHOR EVENTS Find out which
of our authors are on tour and
where you can meet them

LATEST NEWS on bestsellers,
awards and new publications

MINISITES with exclusive
special features dedicated to our
authors and their titles

READING GROUPS Reading
guides, special features and all
the information you need for
your reading group

LISTEN to extracts from the
latest audiobook publications

WATCH video clips of
interviews and readings with
our authors

RANDOM HOUSE INFORMATION
including advice for writers,
job vacancies and all your
general queries answered

Come home to Random House

www.randomhouse.co.uk